Angela Thirkell

Angela Thirkell, granddaughter of Edward Burne-Jones, was born in London in 1890. At the age of twenty-eight she moved to Melbourne, Australia where she became involved in broadcasting and was a frequent contributor to the British periodicals. Mrs. Thirkell did not begin writing novels until her return to Britain in 1930; then, for the rest of her life, she produced a new book almost every year. Her stylish prose and deft portrayal of the human comedy in the imaginary county of Barsetshire have amused readers for decades. She died in 1961, just before her seventy-first birthday.

The substance of the book is pure fun, that glancing humor of situations somehow expressed in apparently irrelevent phrases which is Mrs. Thirkell's special art.

—*Weekly Book Review*

[Angela Thirkell's] world manages to be charming without being precious. Her secret, I think, is the drop of vinegar she stirs into her fictional societal soup.

—Maureen Corrigan, National Public Radio's *Fresh Air*

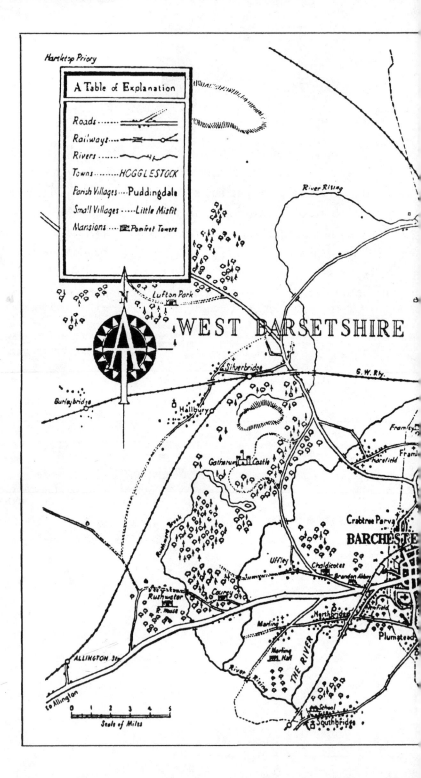

A Table of Explanation

Roads	
Railways	
Rivers	
Towns	HOGGLESTOCK
Parish Villages	Puddingdale
Small Villages	Little Misfit
Mansions	Pomfret Towers

Hartletop Priory

River Rising

WEST BARSETSHIRE

Lufton Park

N

Silverbridge

G. W. Rly.

Burleybridge

Hallbury

Framley

Framl

Barefield

Gatherum Castle

Crabtree Parva

BARCHESTE

Uffley

Chaldicotes

Brandon Abbey

Rudd's Brook

Rushwater

H. House

Courcy

Marling

Northbridge

Plumstead

Allington St.

Marling Hall

to Allington

River Rising

THE RIVER

School

Southbridge

0 1 2 3 4 5

Scale of Miles

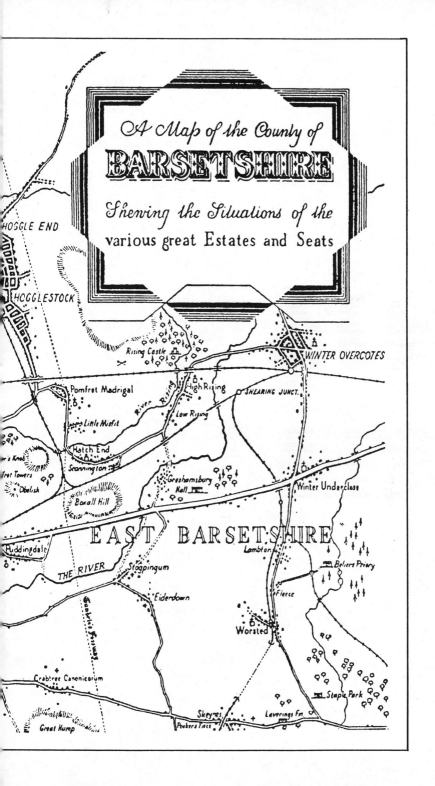

Other books by Angela Thirkell

MISS BUNTING

A Novel by

Angela Thirkell

MOYER BELL
Wakefield, Rhode Island & London

Published by Moyer Bell
This Edition 1996

Copyright © 1945 by Angela Thirkell
Published by arrangement with Hamish Hamilton, Ltd.

**LIBRARY OF CONGRESS
CATALOGING-IN-PUBLICATION DATA**

Thirkell, Angela Mackail   Miss Bunting

1.
2.

PR6039.H43A82   1996   96-46714
823'.912—dc20   CIP

ISBN 1-55921-174-1

Cover illustration: *Young Girl in Red Jacket* by James Tissot
Chapter illustrations from *William Morris: Designs and Motifs* by Norah Gillow

Printed in the United States of America
Distributed in North America by Publishers Group West, P.O. Box 8843,
Emeryville CA 94662, 800-788-3123 (in California 510-658-3453).

To
My Father and Mother
from
their loving Angela

MISS BUNTING

CHAPTER I

The great Duke of Omnium, as is well known, not only disliked railways but refused to acknowledge their existence. After the death of the old Duke's successor, formerly Mr. Plantagenet Palliser, the next Duke found it necessary to come into line with the times and even to sell land, but by this time the network of railway that connects the outlying parts of the far-flung county of Barset was finished, the contractors had made their fortunes, been knighted and died of drink, the Irish navvies had gone back to Ireland to die of drink themselves till their wages were spent, and Parliament was not interested in more railway bills. This state of things lasted into the new century, when a branch line was constructed which leaves the main line just outside High Rising, links the parts of Barsetshire that lie outside the Omnium estate and runs within five miles of the Castle. With Gatherum Castle itself we shall not be concerned and we are happy to say that the Duke and Duchess can still afford to live there and that although all three sons are in the Army they are so far safe and there are several grandsons, while Lady Glencora and Lady Arabella, who both married well, have flourishing nurseries, besides doing valiant work in the Red Cross and W.V.S.

Among the villages or small towns on this line is Hallbury. It is on the Omnium property, but as the estate is now for the most part a limited company, it does not have with the Castle the

friendly feudal relations of former days. Until the coming of the
railway it had remained almost untouched by progress; a street
of little dignified stone houses and equally dignified red brick,
living its own life, viewing from the gentle eminence on which it
stands mile upon mile of pasture land, a certain amount of arable
and the downs in the distance. It was the rising land that saved
it from the degrading suburbs that so often accompany the
march of progress. The railway, with one angry look at the town,
kept on its course across the level, avoiding the River Rising,
here no more than a stream, and pursued its way to Silverbridge
and so into foreign parts. In course of time some marshy land
was drained and the local speculators began to build. Tradesmen and small business people from Barchester began to settle
there, followed by people from London, who wanted to walk or
fish at the weekend and were well served by the excellent trains
before the war. The roads were prettily laid out and planted with
flowering trees and shrubs, the architecture was just what we
might expect, for Pattern and Son, the builder and estate agent,
had what he called Ideas, which included every style of building
from half-timbered and pebble-dash to Mixo-Totalitarian with
semicircular ends and windows that rushed round corners. So
far the foundations (not that there were any because Old Pattern, now succeeded by Son, said it stood to reason where you'd
got a space under a house you got rats) had endured, and the
present Mr. Pattern was always ready to rehang a door that a
warped jamb was causing to stick, or push a window-frame
gradually extruded by the pressure of sagging brickwork back
into place, or even to poke at a blocked waste-pipe with a
mysterious upward bend.

As may be imagined, the town on the hill did not mix with the
town beyond the railway, and society fell tacitly into two groups:
the Old Town, consisting of the original inhabitants of the
stone houses and the aboriginal cottagers and work-people, and
the New Town, the status of whose citizens was almost inde-
finable, but may be expressed in the words of Engineer-Admiral

Palliser at Hallbury House who, inarticulately conscious of a house at least five hundred years old in parts, held by his family since the Commodore Palliser who did so well in the matter of prize-money under Lord Howe, remarked that those houses on the railway line were always changing hands, and so dismissed the whole affair.

Admiral Palliser, a distant connection of the Duke of Omnium, was a widower. Deeply attached to the wife from whom the sea had separated him so often and so long, he sincerely mourned her and as sincerely believed that the best he could do for her, as she was now probably able to see from wherever she was exactly what he was doing and even know what he was thinking, was to carry on; to think as well of his neighbors as human nature would allow; to do all for them that a certain amount of money and a certain local influence could ensure. Both his sons were in the Navy, both daughters married to naval men. The elder daughter lived in Sussex and could rarely leave her young family. Lieutenant Francis Gresham, the husband of the younger daughter, had been missing since the loss of our battleships in the Far East, so Jane Gresham with her little boy Frank had come to live with her father. She would have liked to drown her sorrows in a factory or in the Wrens, but her father needed care, her little boy needed a mother, and she probably felt, as inarticulately as her father, that her mother, being rather unfairly in a position to know all that was being done or thought, would like to see that Admiral Palliser was being properly looked after and the old servants kept up to the mark.

It was not an amusing life for her. She loved her father and Hallbury, but all was changed. Her father was as often as not in Barchester where he was on the board of a large engineering works, or in London on business connected with it. Nearly all her contemporaries were away on various war jobs. The girls came home on leave from time to time, the young men more and more rarely as their duties called them overseas. The houses formerly of friendly leisure in the Old Town, were mostly servantless and packed with relatives or paying guests, there was no point in going to Barchester as there was nothing in the shops and it was impossible to get lunch anywhere unless before 11:30 or after 2:30, she did not like to go to London and leave her little Frank, and to take him with her would have been foolish. So she stayed in her father's home, glad of its shelter, always waiting to get away, and blaming herself for feeling depressed. And deeper than all these griefs was the knowledge, for she did not willingly deceive even herself, that the longer Francis Gresham was missing the less she minded. It was not that she didn't love him, or that the dull ache at the heart, the dreary waking from dream to real life every morning grew any less; but the whole thing seemed so infinitely far away, and the longer he was absent the more difficult it would be, she feared, to begin their life again—if ever he came back. Sometimes she almost prayed to hear that he was dead. Then she blamed herself bitterly and knew she would die of joy if the door suddenly opened and he were there. But of course none of these things happened, and she sank into an almost painless monotony of life and always thanked charmingly the people who asked if there was any news of her husband.

"There's something you could do for me, Jane," said her father at breakfast one morning. "You know Adams."

Jane Gresham had often heard of Mr. Adams, founder and proprietor of the big rolling mills and engineering shops at Hogglestock. Her father took a great interest in his work on the board and usually told her what he was doing, for she liked to hear about what she called "real things" and had even made one or two very intelligent suggestions, but she had never met the director.

"It seems he wants a house outside Barchester for the summer holidays," said the Admiral, "not for himself, but his girl is going up to Cambridge in the autumn, and he wants a place where she can get some extra coaching. Apparently he has found a woman coach for her, but he says if she stays in Barchester she will be in and out of the works all day. He asked my advice so I said I would speak to you. He is a good enough fellow," said the Admiral, by which his daughter perfectly understood that Mr. Adams was, not to put too fine a point upon it, by no means a gentleman, "and I've a great respect for his business methods. What do you think?"

Jane Gresham thought and gave it as her opinion that there was not a house to be had in Hallbury, and probably not even room for any more paying guests, but that she would go to Pattern and inquire.

"He will pay anything so long as he gets value for his money," said the Admiral, getting up and taking the *Times* with him to read in the train, which always irritated his daughter, because more often than not he forgot to bring it back with him. And then he kissed her and went down to the station.

It was an unpleasant morning in July, though no more unpleasant than most, for Providence in its inscrutable incompetency had altogether given up the question of summer for the duration of the war. A winter of much wind and no rain had been succeeded by a windy and arid spring, followed in its turn by a chill summer of gray skies and drought, with the weary sound of wind still flapping aimlessly about. The rivers were low, many springs were dry; overworked and understaffed farms were having to water the cows and horses and sheep. At Grumper's End over near Pomfret Madrigal water was being carted, and Sir Edmund Pridham, the local magnate, had had violent passages at arms with the Barsetshire County Council and the Water Company. No prayers had been offered for rain, for most people felt it was really safer not to interfere with Powers who had obviously let everything get out of their control. So gardens and fields lay cold and untidy, and everyone's temper was daily exacerbated.

But not the temper of Master Frank Gresham, aged eight and a half, who had a snub nose, a wide grin and the best opinion of himself and the world, so that whenever his mother looked at him she felt that things weren't so bad after all, and what a good thing it was that he didn't remember his father well enough to miss him; for four years is a long gap out of eight and a half. In the autumn he was to go to the preparatory school at South-bridge, and at present attended a small class at the Rectory every day, coming home for lunch.

When she had done her share of the housework and talked with the elderly cook and parlormaid, Jane Gresham took her shopping-basket and went out to do the shopping. No sooner had she closed the front door behind her and gone down the garden path into the street than a buffet of wind drove down on her, whirled her hair into confusion, tossed a few bits of paper and straw into her face and blustered itself away, thus setting the key for what she felt sure would be a difficult morning. Her one comfort was that she had admitted defeat at the very beginning of the day and put on a woolen skirt and cardigan instead of a washed-out summer frock that most of the other shoppers were wearing, so she would at least be warm.

The fish was visited, also the grocer, the little linen-draper and all-sorts shop, and the stationer. The fish after some fifteen minutes' wait produced an anonymous piece of stiff whitish slipperiness called fillets, the grocer at last had in stock a little washing soda for which she had been waiting three weeks, the linen-draper's had just got in its quota of non-elastic elastic and was able to let her have a yard, the stationer had one copy of the month's local bus and train guide.

Her luck being for the moment in, she decided to begin her search for lodgings and went straight to the office of Pattern and Son.

The late Mr. Pattern, founder of the firm, had always been, or so he said, one for practicing what he preached. As no one knew what he preached, the accuracy of his practice was a matter for speculation, but he undoubtedly built as he would be built by. His office, for which he had been designer and contractor, was erected on a corner where some very picturesque cottages had stood. The cottages, it is true, were below ground level, unsanitary, a home for rats and bugs, the thatch a mass of decaying vegetation, and it was high time they went. But while the gentry were beginning to talk of doing something, Mr. Pattern, who though not exactly on the Council had a good many friends there, had got in first, bought the cottages and erected a stately pleasure dome to his own heart's desire. And when we say pleasure dome it is not poetical license, for the crowning feature of his resurrection-pie architecture was a pepper-box turret, precariously attached to the corner of the building, with a small wooden dome which he caused to be painted to look like verdigris'd copper.

Though the late Mr. Pattern had built a great many houses in the New Town and owned many of them, he had never left the Old Town, preferring to live over the shop, thus earning the reputation of being one of the old school, though of what school no one quite knew. Young Mr. Pattern, having married slightly above him into a bank manager's family, preferred to live in the New Town and had let the upper part of the house at an excessive rent to various mid-European refugees who mysteriously always had plenty of money and got very good jobs, replacing local men and women who had been called up. Young Mr. Pattern's ambition was to build what are known to the trade as California bungalows on the banks of the Rising, and to make what is almost universally called a Lye-do, and it was only by the special intervention of the German Chancellor that his plan came to nothing. For in 1937, scenting trouble ahead, the Duke of Omnium's agent Mr. Fothergill had persuaded his employer to make over two miles of the River Rising with a wide strip of land on each side to the National Trust, and it was said that old Mr. Pattern's death was hastened by this deliberate waste of building land.

Often had young Mr. Pattern cast a longing eye upon Admiral Palliser's property, comprising a large garden, a small paddock for horses, and a field beyond, usually let for grazing to a farmer. But the Admiral was pretty well off, had no occasion to sell and would probably have been very short with anyone who had suggested it. So Mr. Pattern continued to regard him with admiration as an old buffer who knew his own mind and with contempt as one who kept good money locked up in land. He would also dearly have liked Mrs. Francis Gresham to become acquainted with his wife, but though the war had mingled all races and creeds, it had not as yet mingled Old Town and New. Why the Old Town butcher's wife, Mrs. Wandle, should attend working parties and committees at Hallbury House and the Rectory, while Mrs. Pattern (as he called his wife) was never invited, he could not understand. Nor will he ever understand. We perhaps may.

After exchanging a few genteel commonplaces, Jane Gresham asked Mr. Pattern if he knew of any house of a moderate size to let in Old Town, New Town or the neighborhood, from the end of July for two or three months. After making a great show of running through the pages of a large book, during which Jane felt sure she heard him say: "Mrs. Aggs, Mrs. Baggs, Mrs. Caggs, Mrs. Daggs, Mrs. Faggs, Mrs. Gaggs *and* Mrs. Gresham," he looked up with a fevered brow and said there was simply not a house to be had.

"I know there isn't," said Jane. "There never is now. But what I want to know is if there *is* one."

This request Mr. Pattern appeared to find quite in order.

"Well, there *is* The Cote," said Mr. Pattern, "and I dare say The Cedars might consider a let."

"I don't think they would for a moment," said Jane. "They've got three ex-Land Girls each with a baby and her husband abroad, so things are quite comfortable. And The Cote is far too large. The friend who wants a house only wants it for his daughter and a governess, and he might come down at weekends himself."

"Well, there *is* Mrs. Foster's house, Mrs. Gresham," said Mr. Pattern, warming to the game, as he always did. "Quite a small nest but cozy. She might be thinking of going to her sister at Torquay for the summer."

"That wouldn't do a bit," said Jane. "You know there are only two bedrooms and an attic where no servant would sleep even if you had one. Well, I'll have to try Barchester."

"Just one moment, Mrs. Gresham," said Mr. Pattern. "Slow and sure wins the day as they say. I suppose your friend wouldn't care to try the New Town, or further afield?"

As Jane had already mentioned both Old and New Towns, not to speak of the neighborhood, she only said she thought he would. Mr. Pattern, with damped forefinger, then made an excursion through various large books and loose-leaf holders, while Jane wondered if a woman would do it better, and came to the conclusion that she would probably do it far more quickly and efficiently, but would also wreck herself in the process, and this Mr. Pattern was quite obviously, and perhaps rightly, determined not to do. So, being quite used to waiting for nothing to happen, she waited.

"Ah!" said Mr. Pattern, shutting a large book with a lordly gesture, but keeping his finger in the place he wanted "*here* we are, Number 28 De Courcy Crescent, three bed, one large sit. with alcove dining, kitchen, and usual offices. Bath is in kitchen, Mrs. Gresham, but it's a luxury bath, with a splendid cover that your friend could use for an ironing-table or for the sewing-machine."

Jane said she didn't think her friend would want to iron or use the sewing-machine as he was in Barchester all day, and she was sorry Mr. Pattern had nothing suitable. Besides, she added, De Courcy Crescent had the railway on one side and the gasometer on the other, and everyone knew the smuts were dreadful, especially when the washing was out.

"Of course, if I'd known the gentleman wished to wash at *home*," said Mr. Pattern, sibilantly and pityingly.

"Well, thank you so much, and you'll let me know if you hear of anything," said Jane, getting up.

"Now, just one moment, Mrs. Gresham," said Mr. Pattern, who was enjoying to the full the age-old conventions of bartering. "There's a house just come in this morning in Riverside Close."

Abstracting her mind from an unbidden vision of a peripatetic house—perhaps on chicken's legs like Baba Yaga's—Jane said she would look in another time.

"Three bed., two sit., lounge hall, lock-up garage, constant hot water, fridge, tiled bath and ekcetera," said Mr. Pattern with a resolute display of his fine uppers.

"I can't wait now," said Jane. "But if you'll give me the address again I might look at it. Is there anyone there or shall I take the key?"

"Well, Mrs. Gresham, there is someone there," said Mr. Pattern. "I don't think I made it quite clear that it's not to let, Mrs. Gresham, at least, not *as* a house if you see what I mean. The owner, Mrs. Merivale, takes paying guests. She is a widow and she always makes everyone very comfortable. Canon Banister's mother was with her for some months before she died, and I know some of Mrs. Crawley's daughters have been there with their children during the war."

The mention of Canon Banister and the Dean's wife, both old Barchester friends, made the whole affair seem much more possible. Jane took the address, thanked Mr. Pattern and, for much time had gone in shops and at the house agent's, had to hurry to the Rectory to fetch Frank home to lunch. This was not really necessary, for Frank had taken himself to and from school unaccompanied since he was quite small, but it was a pleasant diversion for her before lunch, and as Frank had not yet reached the stage of being ashamed of her, she profited by his tolerance.

Hallbury Rectory was a modern building by Hallbury standards, certainly not earlier than 1688. The original Rectory, which stood on the north side of the church and almost against it, naturally got no sun from the south. Owing to a thick screen of clerical vegetation such as dark conifers, ilex, a kind of cypress and high laurel hedges, it got little or no light from the east or west, and on the north looked across a wall on to a large barn. As there was also a well in the cellar, fed mostly by the town drainage, the incumbents and their wives and families had died off like flies until a lucky fire one Guy Fawkes Day had reduced it to a blackened shell. The Rectory was then moved to a commodious brick and stone house and produced quantities of valuable children, among whom was the Augustus Palliser who had served under Lord Howe and bought Hallbury House. As a thank-offering for this mercy the special prayers for Guy Fawkes Day were regularly read on the Sunday nearest to November the Fifth, and though, owing to a deplorable access of broadmindedness, the Rev. the Hon. Reginald de Courcy had suppressed them in the eighteen-thirties, many of the old prayer books still had them, and Admiral Palliser always made a point of reading them to himself with some ostentation during the sermon on the appointed day.

The church, one of the many beautiful and unpretentious stone churches of these parts, with a tower and battlements, was called St. Hall Friars. The origin of this name was rather obscure. Early local antiquarians with simple enthusiasm had decided that Saint here stood for Holy or Blessed, and referred to a supposititious hall or lodging house for monks from the great abbey at Brandon, now utterly lost. As there was known to have been a church on that spot in one form or another since the conversion of Wessex, and no indication of the monks from Brandon Abbey having ever lodged there or anywhere but in their own house and in any case monks are not friars, this theory was held up to ridicule in the *Barchester Mercury* (one of England's oldest provincial papers, now incorporated with the *Barchester Chronicle*) in about 1793 by a notorious freethinker, Horatio Porter, Esq., who subsequently died of a stroke while having a debauch in his kitchen with his cook. Such was Mr. Porter's profligacy, and such the weakness of the owner of the *Mercury* who was heavily in his debt over cards, that his letter was printed entire, with an ingenious suggestion that for Hall Friars, Hell-Fire should be read. Mr. Porter's death (accompanied by a violent thunderstorm and the birth of a calf with six legs at Brandon Abbas) so shocked the public that the whole matter dropped until a disciple of John Keble, digging among old papers in the Bishop's library at Barchester, found that a certain rude Saxon swineherd named Ælla had been slain by the bailiff of the monastery to which he was attached for refusing to drive the pigs afield during Lent, owing to which saintly action, most of the pigs (six weeks being a long period) had died of hunger and thirst, while the swineherd was in due time canonized. As there was no corroboration of any kind for this story it obtained great credence and even caused a weak-minded young gentleman of good family to draw back from Rome. Under the influence of Bishop Stubbs a variety of further research was made, leading nowhere at all, and there the matter rests. It is true that the Hallbury branch of the Barsetshire Mothers' Union has a banner heavily embroidered in gold representing St. Ælla in mauve and green robes with a shepherd's crook, but the present Rector, Dr. Dale, is rather ashamed of it and keeps it reverently in tissue paper in case the gold should tarnish.

When Jane Gresham got to the Rectory she passed the front door and went through a gate in the wall into the old stable yard. Here what used to be a stable with grooms' quarters above had been converted into a light and airy two-story building with a furnace to heat it, and from it came a chirping of young voices, high above which Jane, with mingled love and irritation, could hear that of her son. She looked cautiously through an end window, but her caution was not necessary, for the whole school of seven or eight little boys was tightly clustered around a young man who was showing them something. She sat down on a stone mounting-block and looked about her. A deceptive gleam of sunshine lit the stable yard, though with no warmth in it; the smell of horses and leather still lingered in the air, she could almost hear the rustle of straw, the pleasant jingle of harness, the steady champing of oats, almost hear the clank and splash of buckets being filled at a pump and the hissing of the grooms at work. Then the half-hour after noon sounded from St. Hall's tower. The babel inside was suddenly stilled, a little boy ran out and began to pull the wrought-iron handle of the yard bell and out came the whole class, nearly tripping up their master.

"Hullo, Robin," said Jane Gresham.

"Hullo, Jane," said the young man, and sat down on the horse-block beside her.

"What was all the noise?" said Jane.

"I promised I'd show the boys how my foot fastens on," said the young man, "and now I can't get the foul thing fixed again. Do you mind?"

Without ostentation he pulled up his right trouser leg and busied himself with his artificial foot. Having accomplished the job at last to his satisfaction, he smoothed the crease in his trousers.

"Ass," she said. "One day you'll do it once too often. Anyway, they've all seen your foot about a hundred times."

"I know," said the younger man. "I expect it's showing off. It isn't everyone who has a foot like mine. I remember when I was little I had a book called *Otto of the Silver Hand*, with illustrations, woodcuts I think, rather grim and frightening, and always wished I had one. I didn't think of a foot. But a silver one would be a bit heavy."

Jane Gresham looked at him. Robin Dale whom she had known all her life, the Rector's only son by a late marriage, had been a junior classical master at Southbridge School just before the war. Then he had gone into the Barsetshire Yeomanry, got a commission, fought all through Africa and Sicily, and finally had his right foot so badly shattered in Anzio landing that it had to be amputated, and he had been discharged. Southbridge School would willingly have taken him back, but he still felt too crippled and self-conscious to face the school life. His father, a widower for many years, living alone, wanted Robin to stay at home for a time. Robin had done his best to be valiant, but he moped sadly till Admiral Palliser, who did not like to see people mope and found work a cure for most evils, suggested that he should give little Frank some tutoring before he went to South-bridge. The tutoring was a success, other little boys in the Old Town joined the class. The Rector, who had private means, managed to get the stables altered and the furnace installed, and Frank Gresham was the first pupil. When we say that the horses' racks and the original narrow box staircase to the grooms' quarters had been left untouched, as had the rather terrifying kind of gallows over which sacks of oats and bales of straw were hauled up to the loft, the reader will realize what an unusual and delightful school Frank and his fellow scholars had.

"I think a silver foot would be horrid," said Jane. "You'd have to keep it clean and if there's anything I loathe it's the feeling of plate polish on my hands."

"There was Götz with the Iron Hand," said Robin, entering enthusiastically into the subject, "but I daresay it got rusty and anyway it wasn't a foot. And Nez-de-cuir; but that was his nose, so it's different. I never heard of a Leather Foot."

"No," said Jane, thoughtfully. "There was Leather Stocking, but he had a leg inside. And there are leather-jackets in the garden, beastly things. Oh, Robin, I do wish it hadn't hap-pened."

"However much you wish it, I wish it more," said Robin. "Any news of Francis?"

Very few people asked Jane this question now. Partly they thought it might wake painful thoughts ("thinking of the old 'un," she said sardonically to herself), partly they had honestly forgotten about it, for the whirligig of time has so bruised and stunned us all that yesterday is swallowed in oblivion almost before today has dawned. Jane did not want inquiries, nor did she resent them. Her surface self responded pleasantly to the kindly and sympathetic and was unmoved by the forgetters. As for her inner self she did not quite know what it thought, and sometimes wondered if it knew itself. A sense of duty made her say to Frank from time to time that they would do this and that when father came home: and what this meant to him she did not know and had no means of knowing. And as he was very cheerful and ate enormously and slept like a dormouse, she saw no reason to delve deeper.

"No, no news," she said. "But I don't expect any. It will come some day. Or else it won't."

At this moment Master Gresham came up, bursting with suppressed giggles.

"I say, Mother," he began, "do you know this poem?

> 'It was the miller's daughter,
>   Her father kept a mill,
> There were otters in the water,
>   But she was 'otter still.'

Tom Watson told it me. There are a lot more verses. Shall I tell them you?"

Horrified at the resurgence of this hoary and vapid echo of early Edwardian humor, Jane said they must hurry up or they would be late for lunch.

"But, Mother, isn't it *funny*," said Frank, dancing from one foot to another.

"I know a much better one," said his mother, "in Latin."

"You don't know Latin, do you, Mother?" said Master Gresham, obviously incredulous.

"Not as well as Robin, but much better than you," said Jane, manfully. "Can you read this?"

She took a pencil out of her bag and wrote something on the back of an envelope.

"*Caesar adsum jam forte*," Frank read. "That's not Latin, Mother. I mean it doesn't mean anything. Sir," he added, appealing to his master, "it doesn't mean anything, does it?"

"If your mother says it does, it does," said Robin not wishing to commit himself.

"Mother, it's nonsense, isn't it?" said Frank. "It *is* nonsense, isn't it, Mother?"

"What you tell me two times is true," said his mother enigmatically to her son. "I'll say it to you. 'Caesar had some jam for tea!'"

It touched and amused her to see her son's round face, temporarily serious, his soft brow puckered, his eyes remote, till the light of reason began to dawn and he broke into a joyful smile with a toothless gap at one side of it.

"Oh, *Mother*," he shrieked. "I'll tell Tom in afternoon school. I'll bet him I know Latin better than he does. Oh Mother! Is there any more, mother?"

"Quite a lot," said Jane, "but I don't remember it all. "I expect Robin knows it, because he knows Latin properly."

"I'm ashamed to say I'd forgotten that one," said Robin. "But there's another awfully good one that I can't quite remember too; something about 'here's a go, forty buses in a row'—how does it go, Jane?"

"Lord! I had quite forgotten it too," said Jane. "The boys used to teach me odd bits in the holidays. Didn't it go on something about *trux, As quot sinem: pes an dux?*"

Frank looked perplexed.

"But that's English," he said.

"Well, come along now," said his mother, feeling herself out of depth, "or we'll be later for lunch than ever. And it's fried fish with lots of fried parsley."

Robin went back to the Rectory while Jane and her son walked home. And when we say walked, Master Gresham's mode of progression was rather in the nature of a hop, skip and a jump, hanging on his mother's arm the while, highly fatiguing to the hung-upon.

Lunch which was also new potatoes and early peas from the garden and a summer pudding having been dispatched, Frank went back to afternoon school, and Jane, having no particular job that afternoon, thought she might as well pursue her inquiries about a house for Mr. Adams, so that she might have something to tell her father when he came back that evening. So she rang up Mrs. Merivale and asked if she might come and see her, being authorized thereto by Mr. Pattern, and a pleasant voice said yes, adding that the house was three houses down Riverside Close from where it branched off from Rising Crescent and the name was on the gate, Valimere, and anyone would tell her.

Accordingly Jane, after picking some strawberries for supper and doing some ironing and mending some places where the laundry had wrenched or hacked holes in sheets and pillowcases, went down the hill, crossed the railway by the footbridge and entered the New Town. Rising Crescent was about ten minutes' walk from the station and near its farther end she found Riverside Close, so called for no reason at all as it was neither. Owing to the ravages of war many of the names on the garden gates were almost effaced and she thought she must have heard the instructions wrongly, but on retracing her steps she found the name, Valimere, almost invisible, on a gate which had sagged away from its gatepost and could never be shut again. As she walked up the little path she noticed that the garden, though bright with flowers, was also quite out of hand and the hedges running riot. The house was just like a hundred other New Town houses of so many styles that it had no character at all.

She rang the bell. The door was opened by a plumpish woman of about fifty who must have been very pretty and still looked very agreeable, with a kind expression, rather anxious eyes, and gray hair which curled becomingly around her face.

"Mrs. Merivale?" said Jane. "I am Mrs. Gresham. It was very kind of you to let me come."

"Oh, how do you do?" said Mrs. Merivale, and shook hands. "Please do come in. We can talk more cozily in the lounge."

Owing to Mrs. Merivale's great politeness, Jane found it quite difficult to squeeze past her in the narrow hall, but by dint of a kind of sidling high and disposedly the difficult passage to what Mrs. Merivale had called the lounge was effected. This was a good-sized room at the side of her house, full of sun and looking into the tangled garden. It was furnished with two hideous elephantine chairs covered with sham leather, a hideous cupboard with some ugly silver on it, two more hideous bulky chairs with a kind of plush covering, a tottering little bookcase of two shelves with some magazines on them, and a couple of what Jane could only think of as occasional tables. There were a few water-colors obviously of "abroad" hung very high on the walls, and over the fireplace was a flight of wild ducks in china, being as it were Elle-ducks with a bulgy side for the public and a flat side which only the wall could see. They were of various sizes and Jane felt that they were of great value to their owner.

As Mrs. Merivale, though obviously friendly, was twisting her hands together in a demented way and quite speechless, Jane thought she had better break the ice and said she had heard that some of Mrs. Crawley's married daughters had been with her.

Mrs. Merivale said, "Yes."

"And Canon Banister's mother," said Jane.

Mrs. Merivale, wrenching her fingers nearly out of their sockets, said "Yes."

A friend of her father, Admiral Palliser, said Jane, had asked if they would find some lodgings for his daughter and governess during the summer holidays, and would like to be able to come down himself at week-ends. Could Mrs. Merivale consider that kind of let?

"Well, I suppose you'd like to see the rooms," said Mrs. Merivale after a choked silence and looking desperately about her.

"Please, if I may," said Jane. "And may I say how much I was struck by those flying ducks. I have never seen anything quite like them before."

Mrs. Merivale twisted one foot around the other in agony but appeared gratified.

"This is the lounge," said Mrs. Merivale as if she were saying a lesson.

"And what a lovely view of the garden," said Jane, feeling herself getting sillier and sillier.

"It *is* pretty," said Mrs. Merivale, and untwisting her feet she stood up. "And if you look through the glass door you'll see we've a nice lodger."

Jane also got up and looking through the glass door at the far end saw that there was a little veranda where one could sit enjoying the view, but the lodger was not visible.

"This makes a nice room for a gentleman, or a party," said Mrs. Merivale in desperation.

Jane said yes, of course it was and how nice, especially the little green china hearts let into the back of the sideboard.

"And this," Mrs. Merivale continued, opening another door, "is the dining-room, it's all fumed oak, you see; and this would be the sitting-room, with a nice view."

"And what a lovely vase of flowers," said Jane gazing awe-struck upon another Elle-figure, this time the face of a rather depraved girl, its flat back glued and hooked to the wall, a bunch of floppy yellow roses in an opening in the top of its head.

Mrs. Merivale said it always made her think of the Lady of Shalott and Jane, to her horror, found herself saying that it was quite out of the common.

After another minute of politeness, the ladies got to the first floor where Jane was shown three light, airy bedrooms each with fixed basin and gas-fires; also a good bathroom. Mrs. Merivale insisted on her looking at the mattresses, which Jane's expert hand and eye admitted to be excellent.

"There's another room, the one we just call the Other Room," said Mrs. Merivale, showing Jane a slip of a room with a bed in it and otherwise occupied by a table and sewing-machine. "If your friend wanted a spare room at any time he could have this.

It's really Annie's room, that's my girl in the A.T.S., but she's abroad now."

Jane thanked her, and so genuine had she been in her praise of the obvious good points of the rooms that Mrs. Merivale further unbent and asked if she would like to see the top floor. So they went up a very steep stair.

"This," said Mrs. Merivale, opening the door of a kind of superior attic, "is Elsie's room, that's my girl in the Waafs, but she's overseas now. And this little room next to hers," she continued, showing Jane a smaller attic, "is Peggie's, that's my girl that's in the Wrens, but she's at Gibraltar. If they bring a friend home we can put a mattress on the floor and they talk all night. We've had as many as seven sleeping here, Mrs. Gresham, not counting myself. That was the time Evie was at home, that's my girl in the Foreign Office, but she's in Washington now."

"Where did Evie sleep?" Jane asked, deeply interested in this life of doubling up, unknown to her.

"Oh, she came in with me," said Mrs. Merivale. "We've got a little camp bed. The girls laughed all the time and we all thoroughly enjoyed it. We've got our own bathroom up here."

She opened the last door and disclosed to the visitor a room evidently scooped out of one of the gables that were a feature of most New Town houses. A large cistern occupied most of it and a very small bath was squashed into a corner. On the sloping wall beside it was a notice saying, "MIND YOUR HEAD," below which was a rough drawing of a head banging a beam with stars and exclamation marks radiating from it.

"Evie did that," said Mrs. Merivale. "She's the artistic one. Peggie's the musical one, she's got some lovely records."

"Are the others artistic, too?" said Jane.

"I suppose you would say so," said Mrs. Merivale. "Elsie was studying dancing in Barchester with Miss Milner before the war and Annie isn't exactly artistic, but she crochets shawls and doilies and things quite beautifully and used to make quite a lot of pocket-money."

As she spoke she was leading the way downstairs again, and in the most friendly way offered to show Jane the kitchen, which was quite the nicest room in the house, spotlessly clean, with gay yellow paint, bright curtains, a dresser with pretty china, a long old-fashioned sofa under the window, and a cooker with an open-fire front, before which a large cat was dozing. Jane expressed her admiration and Mrs. Merivale beamed.

"I quite agree with you, Mrs. Gresham," she said. "It is so cozy here and if I'm tired after getting the supper I just put my feet up on the couch and turn on the wireless and write a letter to one of the girls. And when any of them are at home we have such fun in the evenings that I have to say: 'Hush, girls, or you'll disturb the guests!'"

Rather humbled before such capacity for cheerful gratitude under such cramped and hardworking conditions, yet extremely thankful that she was not called upon to show gratitude for that particular form of enjoyment, Jane felt she really must inquire about terms and so bring her talk to an end. Thanking Mrs. Merivale for letting her see the house she said she thought her friends would be very glad to hear of it and what would they pay for the rooms.

Mrs. Merivale became dumb and began to twist her hands again in a most distressing way.

"I'm so frightfully sorry," she said, in a tearful voice, "but when people ask me how much I charge I could *kill* them."

Jane looked at her with some alarm.

"I know I'm *horrid*," said Mrs. Merivale, "but it's so *awful* talking about money. I'd rather let the rooms for nothing if I could afford it."

This, though highly creditable to human nature, was hardly helpful and indeed rather silly. Jane, who really did not know what to suggest, stood silent.

"Would three guineas be too much, do you think?" said Mrs. Merivale, nervously.

Jane at once said it would be far too little, especially if the boarders were to have a dining room and sitting room to themselves, not to speak of the lounge, and begged Mrs. Merivale to name a higher figure. But as that lady would do nothing but repeat that she knew she was horrid but it seemed so unkind to ask people for money, Jane had to say that she would tell Mr. Adams how nice the rooms were, and probably he would come and settle everything himself, to which Mrs. Merivale agreed. As they went towards the front door Jane paused to look through the glass door of the lounge into the garden.

"It *is* nice to have a lodger," said Mrs. Merivale. "Especially on a summer evening."

It seemed a curious preference, but there is no accounting for tastes. At the front gate Jane said good-bye.

"It was very good of you to let me take up so much of your time," she said. "I'm sorry I was late, but I missed your house and went right to the end of the road. What a pretty name Valimere is," she added, untruthfully.

"Thereby hangs a tale, Mrs. Gresham," said Mrs. Merivale.

Seeing that she wished to be encouraged, Jane encouraged her.

"When Mr. Merivale bought this house, Mrs. Gresham," said Mrs. Merivale, earnestly, "we didn't like the name. It was called Lindisfarne."

She paused. Jane said it was certainly a horrid name for a house, and was ashamed of herself for time-serving.

"That's what Mr. Merivale felt," said his relict. "So we talked it over thoroughly, till we were quite at our wits' end. But Mr. Merivale said not to worry and I went to stay with Mother for a few days for her eightieth birthday, poor old soul, and when I came back the name was on the gate."

"How *very* nice," said Jane, feeling this a distinct anti-climax.

"You see it's Merivale, only the letters all mixed like the crosswords," said Mrs. Merivale. "It seemed so original. The girls love it and Elsie, she's my baby, the one that's in the Waafs, sometimes calls me Mrs. Valimere, just in fun, and we all thoroughly enjoy it."

Jane then managed to get away. As she walked home, she pondered on the niceness of Mrs. Merivale; also upon her exhaustingness. What her father's Mr. Adams would think of it she could not guess, but she knew he was rich and wanted accommodation, and hoped that Mrs. Merivale and her daughters might benefit. All she could do was to give a good report of the rooms and hope for the best.

When she got back she found Master Gresham and his friend Tom Watson having their tea in the garden. Beside them was a large iron dipper containing a quantity of snails frothing themselves to death in salt and water.

"How disgusting," she said, unsympathetically.

"Well, Mother, you don't want the snails to eat the vegetables," said Frank, reproachfully. "Oh, Mother, I told Tom about *Caesar adsum jam forte*, but he's only just begun Latin so he didn't laugh."

"I don't think it's kerzackerly funny," said Master Watson, who had perhaps inherited from his father, the Hallbury solicitor, a habit of thinking before he spoke and speaking with rather ponderous authority.

"Never mind, Tom, when you know Latin properly you'll laugh like anything," said Master Gresham, with a kindly patronizing manner which his mother found intolerable, but which Master Watson appeared to take gratefully. "Oh, Mother, Mrs. Morland rang you up. She's going to ring you up again. She says Uncle Tony is fighting in a canal. Mother, Tom got twenty-eight snails and I got thirty-three. Oh, Mother, can we pick lettuces?"

"I don't think we want any today," said his mother, answering his last remark first.

"I don't mean *us*; I mean for Tom's rabbits, Mother. Tom's cook told him the gardener had sold all the lettuces so Tom said he'd get some of ours. Can we, Mother?"

Jane found this vicarious generosity rather embarrassing. The lettuces were not Frank's, they were not hers. They belonged in theory to Admiral Palliser, in usage to the cook and the gardener. There had already been words about them, the cook accusing the gardener of neglecting to bring any in, so that she had to take a basket and go down the garden just as she was if the Admiral was to get his dinner that night, the gardener maintaining that in the gardens *he'd* been in the cook never set foot in the garden and he'd rather not bring the vegetables up to the house if it was going to make unpleasantness. To which the cook had replied, if kitchen garden *meant* kitchen garden, it was for growing kitchen stuff and she'd put the gardener's elevenses in the wash-house. All this Jane, unfortunately for her own peace of mind, had heard from the bathroom window, as she was washing Frank's vest and stockings.

"I think they are Grandpapa's lettuces, Frank," she said, trying to sound as if she knew her own mind. "But if Tom's rabbits really need some, we'll go to the kitchen garden after Chaffinch has gone home, and see if there are some very tall ones. Cook won't want them."

On hearing this joyful news the little boys fought each other with bears' hugs and the snail-pot was upset.

"Come on, Tom," said Frank to his friend, "we'll pretend the snails are Japs and put them on a stone and scrunch them."

"I don't like Japs," said Tom stolidly.

"All right. Yours can be Germans and mine can be Japs," said Frank. "Come on. I bet I'll scrunch more than you."

Leaving the little boys to their wartime avocations, Jane went back to the house, wondering if children ought to be allowed to hate enemies. Being pretty truthful with herself, she came to the conclusion that if enemies were not only unspeakably horrible, but highly dangerous, it was just as well for everyone to hate them. And if hating them meant being un-Christian, she was jolly well going to be un-Christian. And if she saw a real Japanese she hoped she would be brave enough to hit him with the first sharp and heavy object she could find, or throw him down the bricked-up well in the churchyard. Full of these reasonable thoughts she telephoned to several people about the camouflage netting work-party, and was answering some letters when Mrs. Morland rang up.

That well-known but quite unillusioned novelist was an old friend of the Pallisers and though she was really old enough to be Jane's mother, the two had always been very intimate and Mrs. Morland's youngest boy, Tony, had adopted himself as an uncle to the small Frank, who thought him the cleverest and most delightful person in the world and copied faithfully all mannerisms least suitable for a boy of eight. What Mrs. Morland wanted to say, in her usual circumlocutory manner, was that the Fieldings has asked her to dinner and spend the night next Wednesday, and would Jane and her father be there. Jane said they would.

"I'll tell you everything at dinner," said Mrs. Morland, "or at least after dinner, unless it's the kind of war dinner party where we sit next to a woman because of not enough men, which is very restful but not exactly what a dinner party is for. Not that there's anything to tell. There never is. At least not here."

"Sadly true," said Jane. "Nor here either."

"I'm sorry," said Mrs. Morland, who understood by this that Jane had no news of her husband, just as well as Jane had understood that Mrs. Morland was asking if she had heard of Francis. "Oh, Jane, do you know anything about a Mr. Adams? Mrs. Tebben's son Richard has been turned out of the army, I don't mean for cowardice or drink or anything, but some tropical disease I think, though nothing that *shows*," she added, in case Jane envisaged a hideous leper or an acute case of elephantiasis, "and I saw her in Barchester, and she says he has been offered a job at this man Adams's works who is immensely rich and Richard has had very good experience before the war in some kind of business and can talk Argentine, or whatever they talk in Argentina which seems to me a most *disloyal* place, and

Mr. Adams is going to have a branch there and it sounds very suitable, but Mrs. Tebben wondered if it was all right."

When Jane was quite certain that Mrs. Morland had said all she had to say for the time being, she was able to reply that she had never met Mr. Adams, though her father was on his board, but that she believed he was coming to Hallbury for part of the summer and she would tell her what he was like.

"Oh, if your father is on the board it is *quite* all right," said Mrs. Morland, "and I'll tell Mrs. Tebben. I'll see you on Wednesday then."

Jane would have liked to ask after Mrs. Morland's boys, but as this would have meant at least ten minutes' monologue she said good-bye.

Then she took the little boys to the kitchen garden where she gave Master Watson four lettuces that had run to seed and sent him home. The evening was as cold and blustery as the day. As she gave Frank his bath she thought with unpatriotic dislike of Double Summer Time. All very well in peace when summer *was* summer, she thought crossly. But in wartime when the weather was always beastly and we had hours of gray north daylight after dinner and it was too cold to garden or sit out, it was a horrid infliction and what was more it kept Frank awake and while he was awake he talked and sometimes if he talked once more she thought she would burst. But when she saw him clean and pink in his pajamas, she knew she wouldn't really mind if he talked from now till Doomsday, as indeed he showed every sign of doing.

It was Admiral Palliser's habit after doing his business in Barchester to go to the County Club and then take the 6:20 to Hallbury. Before the war he had got home well before seven, but now the train did not get to Hallbury till 7:10, an unconscionably long journey, so that by the time the train had been held up en route and the Admiral had walked up the hill, often with Sir Robert Fielding, it was dinner time. Frank, being eight years old and going to real boarding school after Christmas, and the evenings being so light, was allowed to sit at the table in his dressing gown and eat his supper with the grown-ups, with the proviso that he must go to bed at eight exactly or never come down again. It is probable that if left to himself his doting grandfather would have given in to his pleadings for another five minutes, but his mother had determined that she would have the leavings of the day to herself, and steadfastly resisted all attempts on grandfather's and grandson's part to modify her rule.

Supper was enlivened by a classical discussion between grandfather and grandson, Frank, who had been learning Latin under Robin Dale since the preceding autumn, for Robin believed in catching them young, was rather uppish about his knowledge, and certainly Robin had found him, with his quick mind and retentive memory, a very promising pupil. Which was just as well, for Southbridge School under old Mr. Lorimer and later under Philip Winter, now a colonel in the Barsetshires, had attained a very high level of scholarship, Percy Hacker, M.A., senior classical tutor at Lazarus, winner in his time of the Hertford and the Craven, being their high-water mark. So Master Gresham, finding it necessary to be a snob about something, as indeed we all do and perhaps bird snobs are the worst, did boast quite odiously about deponent verbs and gerunds, finding an appreciative audience in the kitchen, where the old cook, Mrs. Tory, said to hear Master Frank (for to the effete and capittleist title of Master she grovellingly clung) say all his dictation and stuff (which was, we think, a portmanteau word for conjugation and declension) was as good as chapel; though the Reverend (by courtesy) Enoch Arden, Mrs. Tory's pastor, who believed in direct inspiration and that Greek and Latin were works of the devil, would have denounced this belief with fervor.

Frank, who had spent half an hour in the kitchen treating Mrs. Tory and the old parlormaid Freeman to the first line of *Caesar adsum jam*, with a promise of the rest when his schoolmaster could remember it, was bursting to try it upon a more widely educated audience. So as soon as the Admiral had begun his dinner Frank, pushing a large mouthful of biscuit into one cheek with his tongue, said, rather thickly:

"Grandpapa, did you do Caesar at school?"

"I did," said the Admiral. "And if I didn't do my work properly I was caned."

"Mr. Dale doesn't cane people much," said Frank apologetically, "but when one of the boys threw the ink at Tom and it went on the wall instead, he gave him three good ones."

"I'm glad to hear it," said the Admiral. "Have you been caned yet, young man?"

"Not quite," said Frank, feeling that he was wanting in the manlier qualities. "But Mr. Dale said if I gave him the vocative of filius as filie again he'd kill me."

He looked hopefully at his grandfather.

"And are *you* doing Caesar?" said the Admiral.

"Not quite, Grandpapa," said Frank. "But Mother told me a poem about him. Oh, Grandpapa, do you know the poem about Caesar had some jam?"

"Caesar had some——? Oh, yes, of course I do," said the Admiral, and gravely repeated that short but admirable lyric. "And what's more both your uncles know it."

"The boys taught it to me one holiday," said Jane, going back to her childhood. "And I told Frank the first line, but I couldn't remember the rest."

"Do you suppose, Grandpapa, that Caesar *did* have jam for tea?" said Frank, anxiously. "I mean did Romans have jam?"

"I couldn't say for certain," said the Admiral, "but they did have honey. When you get to Southbridge you'll learn Vergil, and he will tell you all about bees and honey."

"Will it be funny?" asked Frank.

"No," said his grandfather, decidedly. "Even better than funny. But if you like funny Latin," he continued, noticing that it was nearly eight o'clock, "I can tell you a good poem. It begins:

Patres conscripti
Took a boat and went to Philippi. . . ."

Frank listened gravely to the end.

"I don't think it's funny, Grandpapa," he said, "it's more what I'd call schoolboyish. I think Tom would like it when he knows Latin better."

"Touché," said the Admiral to his daughter; and the clock melodiously struck eight and the bells of St. Hall Friars sounded from the battlemented tower through the chill July evening.

"Grandpapa," said Frank, quickly. "Mr. Dale said the Romans had water clocks. Have you ever seen a water clock, Grandpapa?"

"Bed, Frank," said his mother.

"Oh, Mother, can't I just wait? Grandpapa hasn't had time to say if he saw a water clock. Did you ever see one, Grandpapa? I should think it would make rather a mess. Tom's mother has a sand-glass, Grandpapa, that tells you how long it takes to preach a sermon. Did you ever go to church where the clergyman had a sand-glass, grandpapa. Tom preached a sermon when Mrs. Watson was out, but the sand-glass took much too long and he couldn't think of anything more to say. He said——"

"Bed, Frank," said his grandfather.

"Yes, Grandpapa," said Frank. "And Tom said: 'Oh, people be good and you will go to heaven, but if you are not good you go to a far worse place.' Do you think that was——"

"*Bed*," said his mother and grandfather in one breath, and this time Frank recognized the voice of doom. Getting down from his chair he pressed his face with careless violence against his grandfather's naval beard and his mother's cheek, left the dining room door ajar, came back in answer to his mother's call, shut it just as Freeman was going in with the coffee, and went upstairs clinging to the outer side of the banisters, as he had frequently been forbidden to do.

Left to themselves Admiral Palliser and his daughter drank

their coffee in peace. Jane told her father about her visit to Mrs. Merivale; the Admiral engaged to speak to Mr. Adams on the following day. Then they did a little chilly gardening and so the evening passed.

CHAPTER 2

S ir Robert Fielding, Chancellor to the Diocese of Barchester, had a very handsome house in the Cathedral Close next to the Deanery, and before the war only made use of Hall's End, his charming little stone house in Hallbury, as a villegiatura, or as a convenient residence for his only child Anne who had perpetual chests and coughs and colds in Barchester; for the houses on the Deanery side of the close are very little above river level and for the greater part of the year have a tendency to damp, while a winter rarely passes without the river coming into the cellars. Indeed in the winter of 1939–40, as our readers will not remember (and we have had the greatest difficulty in running the reference to earth ourselves), rumor had it that the flood carried the Bishop's second-best gaiters as far as old Canon Thorne's front doorstep; and as the Bishop had accused the Canon, who was extremely popular, of Mariolatry, everyone hoped it was true.

In spite of all that care and money could do, Anne Fielding was still an anxiety to her parents. Dr. Ford, who had known her all her life, still maintained that two or three winters in a warm dry climate would do the trick, but this was out of the question, so Anne continued to lead a contented but rather remote life, going to Barchester High School when she was well enough. About a year before this unpretentious narrative begins, being then sixteen, she had had to register under the Registration of

Boys and Girls Act which frightened her parents a good deal, but Dr. Ford, who knew the Labor Exchange people very well, and had been of considerable assistance to them in one way and another by refusing to give medical certificates to various would-be exempteds (notably in the case of the Communist hairdresser with fine physique and no dependents, in the winter of 1940–1), told them that no Labor Exchange would even look at Anne. This was doubtful comfort, but her parents took it in the best spirit and retained a firm faith that as soon as the war was over they would take her to the Riviera, or even to Arizona if necessary, and see her make a complete recovery.

The question of Anne's further education also occupied their minds. As the war went on it was evident that she could no longer go to the High School, which was crowded to bursting point and though an excellent school, no place for a semi-invalid. Her parents, both extremely busy people, enmeshed in really valuable war work as well as their ordinary work, were at their wit's end. If it was a case of dire necessity Lady Fielding could give up everything and live at Hallbury: but she knew it would not be a success. She would be too anxious about Anne and Anne not quite at her ease with her. Then, by a great piece of luck, Lady Fielding happened to mention her difficulties to Mrs. Marling of Marling Hall after a W.V.S. meeting in Barchester. Mrs. Marling had sympathized and looked thoughtful. As they stood talking outside the Town Hall a car stopped beside them, driven by a commanding young woman in Red Cross uniform.

"You know my girl Lucy, I think," said Mrs. Marling. "She is going abroad with her Red Cross next month. Lucy, Lady Fielding doesn't know what to do about Anne. She gets too tired at the High School and Dr. Ford says she must stay at Hallbury. It's all very awkward."

"I'll tell you what," said Lucy Marling, who was obviously going to stand no nonsense from anyone. "Why can't Bunny go to Lady Fielding for a bit? Now Lettice and the children are in Yorkshire she can't even pretend she's governessing."

Now Bunny was Miss Bunting, an elderly ex-governess of high reputation, who had taught Mrs. Marling and her brothers in their schoolroom days, and had come as an honored and very useful refugee to Marling Hall soon after the outbreak of war. Mrs. Marling, a very practical woman of swift decisions, was struck by her daughter Lucy's suggestion and asked Lady Fielding to meet Miss Bunting.

The upshot was that Miss Bunting consented, with her own peculiar mixture of gratitude and independence, to come to Hallbury for an unspecified length of time to keep an eye on Anne's health and wellbeing, and to assist her in her studies; the whole for a very generous stipend.

We doubt if even Miss Bunting, for all her practical sense and power of organizing, could have run a house in Hallbury in war-time, but that Lady Fielding had already found and installed a Mixo-Lydian refugee recommended by Mrs. Perry, the doctor's wife at Harefield. She was an unusually plain and unattractive young woman of dwarfish and lumpish stature, with manners that struck an odious note between cringing and arrogance, named Gradka. As for her surname, it had so often been rehearsed and so often found impossible to say or to memorize that no one bothered about it. Gradka was studying with all her might to pass the Society for the Propagation of English examination by correspondence course, and had already successfully tackled several subjects. When Lady Fielding discovered this she was anxious, feeling that the housework and food might suffer, but to the credit of Mixo-Lydia it must at once be said that Gradka did the housework and cooking excellently and never wanted holidays, because she barely tolerated the English and actively disliked all her fellow Mixo-Lydian refugees.

Miss Bunting came to Hallbury with Lady Fielding to inspect her new domain, and in one interview reduced Gradka to a state of subservience which roused Lady Fielding's admiration and curiosity.

"How did you do it?" she asked Miss Bunting subsequently, awestruck.

"I was in Russia before the last war with a daughter of one of the Grand Dukes," said Miss Bunting. "The Russian aristocracy knew how to treat their inferiors. I observed their methods and have practiced them with some success."

"But you can't exactly call Gradka inferior," said Lady Fielding, nervously wondering whether she was listening outside the door. "Her father is a university professor and very well known."

"I think," said Miss Bunting, "that you will find the facts much overstated. The young woman, who is probably listening outside the door at the moment, is an inferior. No well-born Mixo-Lydian would dream of being connected with a university. Until this war they kept up the habits of a real aristocracy: to hunt and get drunk all autumn and winter, and to go to the Riviera and get drunk in the spring and early summer. For the rest of the year they visited their palaces in Lydianopolis where they entertained ballet girls and got drunk."

Whether Gradka overheard this or not, we cannot say, but from that moment she recognized Miss Bunting as a princess and the household went very well, with excellent cooking, and Anne, in her governess's firm and competent hands, looked better and felt happier. That her charge was grossly uneducated was at once evident to Miss Bunting, who had no opinion at all of Barchester High School and its headmistress Miss Pettinger (now by a just judgment of heaven an O.B.E.), and a very poor opinion of the whole system of women's education and the School Certificate examination in particular. It was too late to go back to the beginning, as she would have liked to do, so she contented herself with encouraging her pupil to read. Anne, like so many young people of her age, even with a cultivated background, had somehow never acquired the habit of reading, but Miss Bunting, by reading aloud to her in the evenings from the works of Dickens, Thackeray, Miss Austen and other English classics, besides a good deal of poetry, had lighted such a candle as caused that excellent instructress to wonder if she had done wisely. For Anne, a very intelligent girl who had never used her intelligence, fell head over ears into English literature and history, and made excursions into many other fields. Never had Miss Bunting in her long career had a pupil who had tasted honeydew with such vehemence, or drunk the milk of Paradise with such deep breaths and loud gulps; but it didn't appear to do Anne's health any harm, so the two of them had a very agreeable time in spite of the war, the weather and their rather lonely life; for though the Fieldings were liked in Hallbury, they were not natives, as were the Pallisers and the Dales; and were still treated with caution by most of the old inhabitants.

Pleasant exceptions to this were Admiral Palliser who had known Lady Fielding's family well, and Dr. Dale, the Rector, who after paying a parochial call upon Miss Bunting had conceived the greatest admiration for her peculiar qualities, and talked books and families with her by the hour, which was a good education for Anne; for say what you will, to know who is whose mother-in-law or cousin among what we shall continue to call the right people is as fascinating as relativity and much more useful, besides being a small part of English, or at any rate county history. His son Robin too, back from the wars with his shattered foot, found in Anne another human being who was handicapped physically, and though neither of them complained, each recognized in the other, inarticulately, a disability which had to be fought and as far as possible overcome. With Dr. Dale Anne also began to read some Latin as a living language, and when her father approached with nervous determination the question of pay for his instruction (for Dr. Dale was a good scholar and his articles in the Journal of Classical Studies were models of precise thought), Dr. Dale accepted his wages and put them aside for Robin's benefit.

As may be imagined, Miss Anne Fielding, now nearly seven-

teen years old, had not seen much of life in the way of parties, so
the thought of Admiral Palliser and Mrs. Gresham and Dr.
Dale and Robin Dale, all of whom she saw quite often, coming
to dine was so exciting as to make her feel rather sick. To add to
the excitement her father and mother, who usually only got
down from Saturday to Monday, were going to stay at Hall's
End for a whole week and Mrs. Morland was coming, and Anne
wondered if it would be rude to ask her to write her name in her
latest novel which Anne had bought with her own money, or
rather with a book token given to her by a dull aunt. Gradka was
also excited, for she was going to make a Mixo-Lydian national
dish for dinner which needed sour milk; and what with milk
rationing and the difficulties of keeping what milk could be
spared till it was exactly of the right degree of sourness, she got
a good deal behindhand with her work, which was to write an
essay about the influence of Hudibras upon English comic
rhyming, as exemplified in Byron, the Ingoldsby Legends and
the lyrics of W. S. Gilbert. And how Mixo-Lydians could be
expected to write such an essay we do not know, but write it she
did, and got very good marks, probably because the examiner
had just about as little real sense of humor as the examinee.

The great Wednesday dawned as gray and blustery as all other
days, but the east had gone out of the wind, which was veering,
with many capricious rushings back to find something it had
forgotten, through north into northwest. By noon it was a mild
summer breeze and great loose clouds were billowing away to
the southeast, leaving a blue and not unkind sky. By one o'clock
it was almost warm, and on the south side of the house really
warm. Gradka was in a frenzy of preparation which included
decorating the dinner table with trails of leaves from the outdoor
vine. This vine, popularly supposed to be coeval with "the
monks" (a date embracing practically everything between St.
Augustine's conversion of Kent and the Reformation), grew
against the south wall of the house and brought forth in most
years rather lopsided bunches of little hard green grapes which

occasionally under the influence of an exceptional summer turned purplish, but were none the less sour and unwelcoming, while this year, the weather having been uniformly not only cold but very dry, the miserable grapelets had withered and fallen almost as soon as they formed.

Here, to leave the field clearer for their staff's activities, Miss Bunting and Anne ate a frugal but sufficient lunch of a nice bit of cold fat bacon, salad from the garden, baked potatoes with marge (an underbred word, but it has come to stay) and some very good cold pudding left over from the night before. While they ate they talked of the party, and Miss Bunting watched complacently her pupil's happy anticipation of what a year ago would have made her so nervous that she would probably have run a temperature.

Owing largely to her poor health, Anne was still immature compared with most of her contemporaries. At present her nose was a little too aquiline for her young face, her hands and feet though well-shaped too apt to dangle like a marionette's and her body seemed to consist largely of shoulder blades. But Miss Bunting's Eye, in its great experience and wisdom, knew that if things went well her pupil would, at nineteen or twenty, be a very much improved creature; that her face would fill out and her nose appear in scale, her hands and feet would be brought into obedience and coordination, and her figure be very elegant. In fact, she would be a handsome young woman, very like her father, though Sir Robert's leonine head was rather large for his body; and *that* Anne's head would *not* be, said Miss Bunting to herself, defying any unseen power to contradict her.

"Miss Bunting," said Anne after a silence, during which the governess had been thinking the thoughts we have just described. "Do you know who I think you are like?"

Miss Bunting ran rapidly through, in her mind, a few famous governesses: Madame de Maintenon, Madame de Genlis, Madame de la Rougierre, Miss Weston, the Good French Governess, Jane Eyre: but to none of these characters could she flatter herself that she had the least resemblance. So she said she could not guess.

"I think," said Anne, her large gray eyes lighting as she spoke, "that you are like the Abbé Faria."

Even Miss Bunting, the imperturbable, the omniscient, was taken aback. For the life of her she could not place the Abbé. Meredith's Farina dashed wildly across her mind, but she dismissed it coldly. No, think as she would, the right echo could not sound.

"Because," continued Anne, pursuing her own train of thought, "I really was a kind of prisoner and getting so stupid and you did rescue me in a sort of way. I mean telling me about books and about how to write to Lady Pomfret or the Dean if I had to—oh and heaps of things. I don't mean making a tunnel *really* of course."

Light dawned upon Miss Bunting. Finding that Anne's book French was pretty good she had turned her loose on the immortal works of Dumas *père*: that is to say, on about ten percent of his inexhaustible and uneven output. And this was the result of Monte Cristo.

"What would you do if you were *really* in a dungeon, Miss Bunting?" said Anne, who was evidently examining the whole subject seriously.

"I should use my intelligence," said Miss Bunting, and there is no doubt that she meant this.

"I expect you'd unravel your stockings and make a rope and strangle the jailer and dress up in his clothes," said Anne, gazing with reverent confidence at her governess.

Miss Bunting did not in the least regret having led her young charge into the enchanted world of fiction, but she certainly had not bargained for this very personal application of the life story of Edmond Dantes and found herself—a thing which had very rarely occurred in her life—quite at a loss. So she said Anne had better finish her lunch so that Gradka could get on with her work.

The beginning of Anne's exciting party was to go down to the station to meet her parents who were coming by the one good afternoon train which runs from Barchester to Silverbridge on Wednesdays only, getting to Hallbury in time for tea. As Wednesday is early closing in Barchester, it is useless for shoppers besides being too early for business people. We can only account for this by guessing it to be the remains of the system by which the railway companies had got their own back on such parts of England as had stood out against their coming.

This expedition she was to undertake alone, as Miss Bunting always disappeared from two to four, when according to the belief of all her friends, though they had no ocular proof of it, she took out her teeth, removed her false front and reposed upon her bed with a hot-water bottle to her respected toes. Anne also was supposed to rest after lunch, but Miss Bunting in her wisdom had relaxed this rule as the year advanced, and her charge's health had improved. Accordingly Anne, too excited to try to rest, betook herself to the kitchen where she was allowed to help Gradka by reading the Ingoldsby Legends aloud to her while she got the vegetables ready, Gradka interrupting from time to time with questions of an intelligent stupidity which Anne found rather difficult to answer.

"There is overheadly," said Gradka, "something that I should like to understand, which is namely the lines,

> In vain did St. Dunstan exclaim, '*Vade retro*
> *Smallbeerum! discede a layfratre Petro,*'

which to me is incorrect. Or perhaps it is doggish-Latin, yes?"

Anne, who was laughing so much that she had hardly been able to communicate the words of St. Dunstan, said she thought it was meant to be funny: a kind of parody of the kind of Latin the monks spoke, she supposed.

"Aha! parody!" said Gradka. "Then do I understand perfectly. The author wishes to make a laughable imitation of the monkish Latin, and smallbeerum is the accusative of a jocular form of small beer. That is highly amusing. Please go on, Prodshkina Anna," for, as our readers have quite forgotten, Prodshk and Prodshka are the Mixo-Lydian names for Mr. and Mrs. (or possibly Count and Countess, for nobody knows or cares), and thus Prodshkina is probably equivalent to Mademoiselle; or so Mrs. Perry said, whether anyone was listening or not.

So Anne, impeded by giggles, read to the end of that moral work and then went down to the station. In her anxiety to miss nothing of the treat she arrived a quarter of an hour too early, so she went up the stairs onto the footbridge and had a good look up and down the line, which here runs in a dead straight line through a cutting for two miles in the Silverbridge direction, finally vanishing into a tunnel, and is often used for testing engines. In the far distance a puff of dirty smoke appeared, followed at a short interval by a distant rumble, and a very long goods train came out of the tunnel and clanked towards her. There is to all ages a fearful fascination in standing on a bridge while a train goes under it. The poor quality of wartime coal has considerably lessened this attraction for those of riper years, but to Anne the sulfurous stench, the choking thick smoke were still romantic. Just as the engine was nearly under her, a voice remarked:

"Rum, how those Yank engines keep all their machinery outside, like Puffing Billy."

Anne looked round and saw Robin Dale.

"Hullo, Robin," she said. "I didn't know it was American."

Robin began to explain that our allies were lending us railway engines, but the noise of engine, trucks and ear-splitting whistle made it impossible to hear, so Anne shook her head violently. When the train had got through the station she turned to Robin and said: "I love watching trains come under the bridge. It makes me feel like Lady Godiva."

"And might one ask why," said Robin, "especially in view of an almost total vacancy of the kind of hair needed for the part?"

Anne's gray eyes gleamed in appreciation of Robin's Dickens phraseology and she said, seriously, "I mean the beginning:

'I waited for the train at Coventry.'"

"Well, I always thought that half my intellect had gone with my foot," said Robin, "and now I know it."

"It's Tennyson," said Anne, with an anxious look at him, fearing that she had said something silly.

"Then I must read him," said Robin.

"Haven't you ever?" said Anne, incredulous. "Oh, Robin, you *must*."

"Well, I have and I haven't," said Robin. "When you are as old as I am you will despise him; and when I am twenty years older I shall read him again like anything and love a lot of him as much as you do. I promise you that. I've got a nasty bit of ground to get over—disillusionment and so on—but I'll meet you again on the other side."

Robin was talking half to himself, finding Anne as he often had in the past years a help to self-examination. Sometimes he told himself that he was a selfish beast to use that Fielding child (for as such his lofty twenty-six years looked on her) as a safety valve. But having thus made confession to himself he considered the account squared and again made her the occasional awe-struck recipient of his reflections on life.

"Well, I must go and see about a parcel from Barchester that hasn't turned up," said Robin. "Are you coming down?"

"Not your side," said Anne. "I'm meeting Mummy and Daddy's train."

"Goodbye then till this evening," said Robin and went down-stairs again towards the parcels office.

Shortly after this the Silverbridge train was signalled, and after what seemed to Anne an endless wait, came puffing round the curve and into the station. Whenever Anne met a train she wondered if the people she was meeting would really come by it. So far they always had and today was no exception for out of it came her father and mother, delighted to see her, ready to hug and be hugged. In happy pre-war days the footbridge at Hall-bury had been within the platform railings, though open to all, but so much cheating had there been that the authorities had been obliged to put a new railing and gate to make it impossible for people to get into a train without a ticket. At the gate a little crowd was waiting for Godwin the porter, who was always doing something on the up platform when the down train came in, to come and let them loose. Anne noticed a large, heavily-built man in a suit which looked too new and too expensive, who was steadily squeezing his way to the front. The man saw her parents, sketched a kind of greeting, gave up his ticket and got into a waiting taxi. The Fieldings then gave Godwin their tickets and went out of the gate and over the bridge.

"Who was that man that knew you, Daddy?" said Anne, as they walked up the hill. "That rather enormous one."

"A man called Adams," said Sir Robert. "He owns those big engineering works at Hogglestock. I came across him last year when he insisted on being a benefactor to the Cathedral."

"But you like benefactors, don't you?" said Anne.

"Within measure, within measure," said Sir Robert. "But he gave so large a sum that even the Dean was a little embarrassed. He fears that Adams will want to put up a window to his wife and that would not do at all."

Anne asked why.

"It is rather difficult to explain these things," said Sir Robert, who though he thoroughly believed in class distinctions to a certain extent, felt he ought not to influence his daughter.

"I suppose it might be rather an awful window," said Anne thoughtfully. "Oh, Mummy! Gradka is making a perfectly lovely pudding with sour milk, and Miss Bunting and I had our lunch under the vine today, and Miss Bunting had a letter from one of her old pupils called David Leslie and he says it is very wet where he is."

Sir Robert and his wife heaved a silent sigh of relief. That any window given by Mr. Adams would be quite out of place in the Cathedral they had no doubt, even as they had no doubt that his benefactions were his protest against E.P.T.; but chiefly did they wish not to become socially embroiled with that gentleman who, finding that they had an only daughter, had talked a good deal of his own, now in her last term at the Hosiers' Girls' Foundation School, temporarily housed at Harefield Park.

"I'll carry your suitcase, Mummy," said Anne, gently but forcibly wresting it from her mother's grasp. It was only a small affair, for the Fieldings kept at Hall's End such clothes as would be useful and only brought a few extras with them when they came.

"Carefully then," said Lady Fielding. "There's something in it for you," which made Anne flush with pleasure.

When they got to Hall's End they found Miss Bunting in the drawing room and tea spread.

"Anne, dear," said Miss Bunting, "will you get the teapot from the kitchen and the hot-water jug. Gradka," she explained to her employers, "does not wish to be seen till after dinner, when she says she will come in and receive the compliments of your guests before she begins her evening studies. It is, I understand, a Mixo-Lydian custom."

"I can't say that I'll miss her," said Sir Robert, who liked those about him to be pleasant to the eye. "I've never been in Mixo-Lydia, and if they are all like that I hope never to go."

"Robert!" said his wife anxiously, for she had an amiable though often embarrassing weakness for oppressed nationalities and was afraid that Gradka, busy in the kitchen at the other end of the house, might hear her husband's words and give notice. Then Anne came back with the teapot and hot-water jug on a tray and they talked comfortably. Presently Lady Fielding went up to her room with Anne and there unpacked her little suitcase and showed her daughter a charming flowery silk dress exquisitely folded in pre-war tissue paper.

"Oh, *Mummy!*" said Anne, "for me? Oh, how *did* you do it?"

"I found this silk in the cupboard in the sewing room," said Lady Fielding. "I had quite forgotten it. So I took it to Madame Tomkins and asked her if she had your measurements and she looked at me with great contempt and said, 'Je connais par cœur le corps de Mademoiselle Anne,' which frightened me so much that I went away."

"She wouldn't have taken any notice of you if you'd stayed, Mummy," said Anne. "Mummy, do you think that Madame Tomkins is really French? It doesn't *sound* French."

But Lady Fielding said she knew she was, because she remembered how Tomkins, the boot and knife man at the Palace, had brought back his French wife after the last war and had shortly afterwards disappeared.

"Had she murdered him, Mummy?" said Anne, hopefully.

Lady Fielding said: Oh no, but she had a frightful temper and Tomkins had gone to New Zealand and was doing very well there and sent Madame Tomkins a card with a kiwi on it every Christmas.

"And now I think you had better rest before dinner, darling," said Lady Fielding, with solicitous care for her daughter.

"Oh, Mummy, I hardly ever rest now except after lunch," said Anne, and she looked so well and seemed so happy, her mother agreed.

The next two excitements of the day for Anne were rather badly timed, for if she went to the station to meet Mrs. Morland, which she had very daringly thought of doing, she would have to hurry to put her new frock on afterwards; and if she put her new frock on first she could not go and meet Mrs. Morland. From this dilemma, which had made her quite pale with agitation, she was rescued by her father calling her to walk round the garden with him. So they walked, and then sat in the evening sun, while Anne prattled about her work and her reading, and was altogether such an alive and eager creature that her father felt very grateful to Miss Bunting, the author of the improvement. So pleasant in fact a time did they have, that when Sir Robert looked at his watch and said it was seven o'clock, both were surprised. Anne fled upstairs to put on her new dress, and so much enjoyed herself peacocking before her mother's long mirror that when at last she went downstairs, Mrs. Morland had already arrived and was having a gentlemanly glass of pre-war sherry with Sir Robert and Lady Fielding.

What Anne expected a well-known female novelist to look like, we cannot say. Nor could she have said; for any preconceived notion that may have been in her head was forever wiped out by the sight of the novelist herself, her unfashionably long hair as usual on the verge of coming down, dressed in a deep red frock which bore unmistakable traces of having been badly packed.

"You haven't seen Anne since she was quite small, I think, Laura," said Lady Fielding to her distinguished guest.

"No, I don't think I have," said Mrs. Morland, shaking hands with Anne very kindly. "At least one never knows, because you do see people in church or at concerts or all sorts of places without much thinking about them, and if you aren't thinking about people you don't really see them, at least not in a recognizing kind of way. And I'm getting so blind," said Mrs. Morland, proudly, "that I shall soon recognize nobody at all."

Had any of Mrs. Morland's four sons been there, and more especially her youngest son Tony, now in the Low Countries with the artillery of the Barsetshire Yeomanry, any one of them would unhesitatingly and correctly have accused his mother of being a spectacle snob. For Mrs. Morland, who had never taken herself or her successful novels seriously, had, in her middle fifties, suddenly made the interesting discovery that she was really grown-up. This day comes to us all, at different times, in different ways. It may be the death of one of our parents which puts us at once into the front line; it may be the death or removal of a husband; it may be some responsibility thrust on us; in the case of Mrs. Turner at Northbridge orphan nieces; in the case of the present Earl and Countess of Pomfret the succession to wealth and estates. But Mrs. Morland's parents and also her husband had died before she was, as she herself expressed it, ripe for grown-upness, and with her four boys she had felt increasingly and very affectionately incompetent and silly, which indeed they, with equal affection, would have admitted, so she had found no real reason to be grown-up.

This fact she had lamented, though with her usual detachment, till two or three years before the date of this story, when she became for the first time in her life conscious of her eyes. Oliver Marling, whose mother had supplied Miss Bunting, had strongly recommended his dear Mr. Pilman, lately released from the R.A.M.C., to look after the neglected civilian population. Mrs. Morland had visited Mr. Pilman, read as far as TUSLPZ quite easily, boggled over XEFQRM and failed hopelessly at FRGSBA. She had then been quite unable to make up her mind whether the left or right arm of a St. Andrew's cross looked darker or lighter, furthermore insisting that even an X cross couldn't have a left or right because each arm went right through, if Mr. Pilman could understand, and what he really meant was the northwest to southeast arm, or the northeast to southwest, and he oughtn't to say: "The right arm is darker than the left, isn't it?" because that was a leading question. A busy oculist might have been excused for losing his temper at this point, but Mr. Pilman not only had great patience, partly natural, partly acquired, but was a devoted reader of Mrs. Morland's books. So disentangling with great skill what she said from what she meant, he had finished the examination and written her a prescription for spectacles.

"I believe," said Mrs. Morland, after pinning up a good deal of her hair which the putting on and off of spectacles had considerably loosened, "that when it is a specialist one puts it in an envelope on the mantelpiece. But as I don't know how much, I can't. Besides, it might fall into the fire. But I did bring a checkbook and if my fountain pen is working, or you would lend me yours, I could write it now. Unless, of course, you'd rather have pound notes because of avoiding the income tax, though I'm afraid I haven't quite enough if it is five guineas which Oliver said."

"Will you let me say, Mrs. Morland," said Mr. Pilman, "that I have had such pleasure from your books that I could not think of charging you for this consultation?"

Upon which Mrs. Morland, who never thought of herself as being a real author, let alone a pretty well-known one by now, was so much surprised that she sat goggling at her oculist while her face got pinker and pinker and a hairpin fell to the floor.

"But that doesn't seem fair," said Mrs. Morland at last.

Mr. Pilman, both gratified and embarrassed by the effect of his words, picked up her tortoiseshell pin and handed it to her.

"I shall be more than satisfied," said Mr. Pilman. "Especially," he added, "if you will give me one of your books with your autograph in it."

"Of *course* I will," said Mrs. Morland. "Only I'm afraid they are all exactly alike. You see I wrote my first book by mistake, I mean I didn't know how to write a book so I just wrote it, and then all the others seemed to come out the same. But if I gave you the last one, would it do? My publisher, who is really very nice and not a bit like what you would expect a publisher to be," said Mrs. Morland, "I mean he is an ordinary person, not like a publisher I once met who simply sat in a room and depressed one, says I could afford to write a few bad books by now, but I think this would be a bad thing because someone who hadn't read any of my books might think they were all bad, and not read any more. Not," Mrs. Morland continued, standing up and clutching various pieces of portable property to her in preparation for her departure, "that I would really *mind*, only I do earn my living by them."

At this point Mr. Pilman who, much as he enjoyed his new patient's spiral conversation, had his own living to earn, managed by a species of stage management perfected by him over a number of years, to waft her out of the room and into the arms of his secretary and so into the street. Her latest book was duly sent to him and since then she had revisited him once or twice, always on the same very friendly footing.

Now writing is a rum trade and eyes are rum things, and what is all right one day is all wrong the next. Mrs. Morland's sight was affected as most people's is by health, weather, heat, cold, lighting, added years, and by the sapping strain of some six years' totalitarian war. She was impatient with her eyes as most people are who have always had very good sight and nearly went mad with rage while accustoming herself to the bifocal glasses Mr. Pilman had ordered on her second visit. Finally she had collected four pairs of spectacles of varying power, from a rather dashing little semicircular lens for reading only, through the hated bifocals to which use had more or less reconciled her and an owl-like plain pair for cards (which she never played) and music (which she had almost entirely dropped), to a much stronger pair now really necessary for close work. To these she had added what she quite correctly called her face-à-main, feeling a pleasant inward disdain for her friends who said lorgnon or lorgnette. And what with mislaying all four pairs in every possible permutation and combination and catching the ribbon of her face-à-main in her clothes and the furniture, or bending it double by stooping suddenly, she hardly ever had the pair she needed. But the gods are just and of our pleasant vices do occasionally make something quite amusing, and we must say that Mrs. Morland got an infinite amount of innocent pleasure out of her armory of glasses, and as she never expected people to listen to her she maundered on about them with considerable satisfaction to herself.

What Mrs. Morland would have liked to do was to raise her face-à-main to her eyes, examine Anne with the air of a grande dame (to which phrase she attached really no meaning at all) and then dropping it greet her warmly and say how exactly like one of her parents she was. But the red dress she was wearing had red buttons down its front, and the red ribbon (to match, for this also gave her much innocent pleasure) had got entangled in the buttons, so she had to give it up as a bad job, and being really a simple creature at heart she embraced Anne very affectionately.

"Tony always says that I fly at people and kiss them in a kind of higher carelessness," she said. "But I do assure you I never kiss people I don't like. If I did begin to kiss the Bishop's wife, even by mistake, something would stop me."

"I only met her once," said Anne, finding it, to her own great surprise, quite easy to talk to someone as celebrated as Mrs. Morland, "at a prize-giving at the Barchester High School and she said prizes really meant nothing, so all the girls who got prizes hated her. If I'd had a prize I'd have hated her too. But I hated her anyway because she had a horrid hat."

Mrs. Morland looked approvingly at a girl who had such sound instincts, and then Miss Bunting came in, preceding Admiral Palliser, Jane Gresham and the Dales, who had all walked up together, enjoying what afterwards turned out to be the one warm evening of a very nasty summer. The newcomers were all acquainted with Mrs. Morland, so there were no introductions to be made. Sherry was offered, talk was general. The sound of a gong was heard.

"Oh, Mummy," said Anne, "that's to say dinner is ready because Gradka doesn't want anyone to see her yet, so will you come in, and Robin and I will do the clearing away."

Accordingly the party went across the stone hall into the dining room. Here Gradka had draped vine leaves and tendrils most elegantly if a trifle embarrassingly on the shining mahogany round table, among the shining glasses and silver. Steaming soup was already on the table in Chinese bowls. Mrs. Morland was loud in her admiration of the exquisite way in which everything was kept, much to the pleasure of her host who had inherited beautiful things and added to his possessions with great taste.

A slight poke on her left shoulder made Mrs. Morland look

up. Robin was standing beside her holding a bowl of tiny cubes of bread fried to a perfect, even, golden brown.

"Excuse my manners," he said, "I'm only here on liking."

"One moment," said Mrs. Morland putting up her glasses. "Oh, croûtons! Heavenly. But I must find my spectacles. I can't hold these things up and help myself at the same time."

She routed about in her bag, found a red spectacle case and put the spectacles on.

"It is so *stupid* not to see," she said in a voice of great satisfaction as she helped herself. "Thank you Robin. What is so boring," she continued, turning to Dr. Dale on her right, "is that though I can see my soup—what divine soup it is—with these glasses, I can't see faces across the table. Mrs. Gresham and Anne look almost the same. To see them I need this pair."

She grabbed about in her bag again and drew out a blue spectacle case, exchanged the glasses and announced with pride that she could see both ladies quite well and how nice they looked.

"But for my soup, I must return to the first pair," she said, taking the second pair off and putting it away.

"Do you know that you put the spectacles you have just taken off into the red case?" said Dr. Dale. "I don't want to interfere, but I think you took them out of the blue case."

"Oh, thank you, I am *always* doing that," said Mrs. Morland. "And sometimes I get so mixed that I don't know which pair is which until I suddenly can't see."

"Why not have different-colored frames?" said Dr. Dale.

Mrs. Morland laid down her spoon, took off the spectacles she was wearing and looked with deep admiration at her neighbor.

"That," she said, "comes of having a good classical education. Now a person that only knew economics or things of that sort would never think of a really sensible thing like that."

Dr. Dale looked flattered, though more on behalf of the

classics than himself, for he was a modest man as well as a good scholar.

"Next time I break the legs of one of them, which I'm always doing," said Mrs. Morland, "I'll have a new frame the same color as the case and then I'll know."

"But suppose you break the glass and not the frame," said Dr. Dale.

"I expect I shall," said Mrs. Morland resignedly. "And that is a great nuisance, because it takes at least three or four months now to get new lenses and by the time you've got them you may be squinting in quite another direction. I did ask my oculist if he couldn't give me a prescription for the kind of glasses I'd probably be wanting six months later, but he thought not. I don't see why not myself, because my eyes just go on gently going bad, so surely he would know how bad they ought to be by October."

Dr. Dale said his sympathies were on both sides and then, the conversation now being well sustained all round the table, Mrs. Morland asked him about Robin, which she had not liked to do before in case he felt he was being discussed. Dr. Dale, who realized her sympathy, was able to give her a good account of Robin's progress and said the difficulty now was to decide whether he should go back to Southbridge where they wanted him for classics or keep on his pre-preparatory class for little boys and make it his profession. Mrs. Morland, who had known Robin since his own schooldays at Southbridge, where he was a couple of years senior to her youngest boy Tony, was very much interested in these plans and forgetting her spectacles managed to eat a large helping of an excellent chicken pilaf with a wreath of young vegetables of all kinds surrounding it.

Meanwhile Lady Fielding was having much the same conversation with Admiral Palliser, inquiring about Jane and whether she still hoped for news of her husband, to which the Admiral replied that the whole position was very trying and they had stopped discussing it.

"We are used to losing our men in naval families," he said.

"Jane knew what the chances were when she married Francis, just as my sons' wives did—one is a brother Admiral's daughter you know, and the other the granddaughter of the captain of my father's first ship. But it's different now. Killed in action is bad; but you do know. This Japanese business is as black as midnight," said the Admiral, his face darkening. "She behaves excellently, but what kind of life is it? It may be months and years of uncertainty. She may never know. And she is young."

His face softened again and Lady Fielding guessed what he was thinking.

"Young and very charming," she said. "And all among older people. It is going to be very hard for these young wives, half widows."

"One may as well say, straight out," said the Admiral quietly, after glancing at his daughter who was deep in the kind of middle-aged flirtation that Sir Robert enjoyed, "that if any of them fall in love with a man on the spot, one won't feel able to blame them. My Jane is a good girl and it's going to be far more difficult for the good girls than the easy-going ones. But no good looking for trouble. Your Polish girl is a wonderful cook."

"She would probably run a knife into you for that," said Lady Fielding. "She's a Mixo-Lydian."

The Admiral began to laugh.

"I met the Admiral of the Mixo-Lydian fleet once," he said. "The fleet is an old Margate paddle-steamer that patrols the River Patsch where it forms the eastern boundary of Mixo-Lydia. She came round by the Mediterranean and up the Danube under her own power, I believe, about 1856 when Mixo-Lydia broke away from Slavo-Lydia. He was a smuggler and gave me some very good brandy."

A good deal of noise now stopped their talk. The noise was Robin and Anne taking away the pilaf with its accompaniments and bringing in the sour-milk pudding, Gradka's masterpiece. A piece of exquisitely flaky pastry, about the size and shape of a huge omelette, lay on a large china dish. It was encrusted with some kind of delicious nutty-sugary confection, and when cut was found to contain a species of ambrosial cheese cake. With it was served a bowl of hot sauce of which we can only say that if everyone will think of the supreme sweet sauce and add to it an unknown and ravishing flavor, it will but feebly explain its silken ecstasy. Conversation was stilled while sheer greed took its place.

"Well," said Robin reverently, "I never thought much of Hitler, but as he made the Mixo-Lydians be refugees, I suppose we must give the devil his due."

Anne industriously scraped the last flakes from the dish and handed him the spoon.

"God bless you for that kind act," said Robin. "One more mouthful of that pudding and I feel my foot would grow again."

His father looked at him, half in distress, half in pride.

"And two more mouthfuls and I'd be sick," he added thoughtfully.

"Oh, please, everybody," said Anne's light voice.

The table was silent, everyone looking at her.

"Oh, it's only," said Anne, blushing furiously and pleating her table napkin with agitated fingers, "that Gradka will come in now. Please, Daddy, say something nice to her. She will bring the coffee in. Come on, Robin, and get the table ready."

While she and Robin tidied the table and put fruit from the garden and glasshouse upon it and took the pudding dish away, Sir Robert went to the sideboard.

"Only Empire port, I fear," he said. "But we must drink to Gradka's health. I wonder if it would be etiquette in Mixo-Lydia to offer her a glass."

As he spoke he was walking round the table, filling glasses.

"Put an extra glass beside me, Fielding," said the Admiral. "I think I know what Gradka likes."

Surprised, but willing, Sir Robert did as the Admiral asked and returned to his seat. Robin and Anne came back, shutting the door behind them and sat down.

"It's all right, Daddy," said Anne. "She has to knock at the door, and you must say—"

But before she could finish, there was a loud single knock or rather bang on the door. Everyone felt nervous, for the capability for taking offense among Mixo-Lydian refugees is well known to have no bounds, and it was probable that whatever they did would be wrong.

"Oh, Daddy!" said Anne in an agonized whisper, "say—"

But the Admiral, who had been looking on with some amusement, uttered a loud and barbarous monosyllable, the door was opened and Gradka came in. Seldom had she looked less attractive than at this moment, her large face and the plaits encircling her head damp with the heat of cooking, her lumpish figure enveloped in a checked apron.

The Admiral handed the spare glass to her, raised his own, and uttering some more barbarous words, drank the contents. Gradka replied in her native tongue, drank her wine and raised the empty glass shoulder high. The Admiral, with a peculiar expression which Mrs. Morland, sitting directly opposite him with her right spectacles on for once, thought unaccountably amused, spoke once more. Gradka shrugged her shoulders, put the glass on the table, said a few words to the Admiral and left the room, shutting the door quietly behind her.

"It's all right," said the Admiral to the gaping party. "The proper thing is to break the glass, and I thought you had rather not. She says I am her grandfather now: but it doesn't mean anything. My smuggler-friend was her uncle."

"I have always said," said Miss Bunting, who according to her own peculiar habit had sat almost silent through dinner, observing and making her own reflections, "that we should thank God for the British Navy."

Everyone except Miss Bunting felt slightly uncomfortable, and when a second loud knock was heard Lady Fielding almost jumped. But it was only a warning that the coffee was there, and Robin fetched the dinner wagon from outside with the coffee equipage on it and the talk fell into more familiar channels again as Miss Bunting asked Dr. Dale about the next meeting of the Barsetshire Archaeological Society, of which he was a vice president.

"I saw in the *Barchester Chronicle*," said she, "that it was to be held here. If there is any part of the proceedings to which the general public is admitted I should very much like to be there, and bring Anne."

Dr. Dale said there would be, if the weather permitted, a visit to the churchyard to inspect the ruins of the earlier Rectory and the disused well, over which a controversy had been raging: some saying that there were traces of Roman brickwork in the well, others again that there were not.

"That," said Miss Bunting, "would be very nice for Anne. Any educational excursion of that kind is good for her and she responds to it."

"May I say, Miss Bunting, how much your pupil has improved under your care," said Dr. Dale. "It is rare to find a girl who can enjoy her work so intelligently. And she looks so much better."

"That is partly Gradka's excellent food," said Miss Bunting. "As for Anne's education, I was lucky in finding almost virgin soil to work upon."

Dr. Dale said he thought Anne had been at Barchester High School.

"That," said Miss Bunting, "is precisely what I mean. School Certificate and Honor of the School. All very well for the daughters of Barchester tradesmen, but most unsuitable for Anne. When she came into my care she was in a pitiable state of nerves over this examination which any girl of average intelligence can pass. You only have to look at them to realize how little real education it means."

Dr. Dale was delighted by these reactionary sentiments and Sir Robert moved to a chair near them the better to take part in the discussion, Mrs. Morland and Jane Gresham who had been talking across him about the boys for some time hardly noticing his absence.

"Tell us, Miss Bunting," said Sir Robert, "what your idea of a really good education for a girl would be."

"In the first place, " said Miss Bunting kindly but firmly, "it is much better, I might say almost essential, to have a large family."

Both gentlemen felt there was nothing for it but an apology. Each had an only child and it was far too late to do anything about it. And neither had felt so convicted of guilt since the crimes of boyhood.

"But I recognize," said Miss Bunting, straightening the little black velvet bow she wore at her neck, "that there are small families as well as large."

Both gentlemen breathed again.

In spite of an uneasy feeling that they were in Eton suits with inky collars and dirty fingernails, the gentlemen much enjoyed their talk with Miss Bunting. Both believed in standards now almost submerged and both would uphold them to the end though their faith was often sorely tried. In Miss Bunting they recognized an unwavering faith and a habit of looking facts in the face unflinchingly and very often staring them down, which they found comforting and refreshing.

The party then drifted to the drawing room, still lit by the sunset. Robin and Anne cleared the dining room table and washed up the glass and silver in the pantry (Gradka being now locked into the kitchen grappling with the Ingoldsby Legends) and Robin told Anne a good deal about what a fool he felt when one thought one's foot was there and it really wasn't; to which Anne listened as usual with sympathetic interest, saying little, but in her mind drawing not unfavorable comparisons between Robin and such mutilated heroes as Benbow directing the sea battle with his shattered leg in a cradle, or Witherington with both legs shot away fighting upon his stumps, or even Long John Silver. But this last comparison she recognized to be a poor one and resolutely ignored it.

Jane Gresham would have liked to be in the pantry too; nor, we must say, would Robin or Anne have minded a third person in the least, and if it were Jane they would have welcomed her. But she had gradually slipped into a quite unnecessary feeling that she was not much wanted by what she rather conceitedly called young people. The foolish creature was only four years older than Robin, and even if thirteen years lay between her and Anne, those years were bridged by so many things: by Anne's rather invalid life which had in some ways marked her, by their common friends and interests in Hallbury, by Anne's very friendly nature when once the barrier of her timidity was down. But Jane, otherwise a sensible young woman, had invented for herself a theory that people who didn't know if their husbands were alive or dead and sometimes forgot about them for hours and even days at a stretch, who had to plan everyday life as if their husbands would forever be wanderers in Stygian shades, their words unheard, their thoughts unshared; that such people were on the whole not wanted. In which she was undoubtedly silly, for she was both wanted and needed by a quantity of people, beginning with her father and her son and including quite a number of people in Hallbury and the neighborhood of Barchester. But the heart does not always quite know its own folly, especially when it lets an overwrought mind interfere.

So Jane, looking elegant and unruffled, drifted to the drawing room with the rest, and continued her conversation with Mrs. Morland about little boys, on whom that gifted authoress was something of an authority, having had four whom she liked very much and never pretended to understand. To do her justice she rarely spoke of them unasked and never made a nuisance of herself by motherly pride, but if encouraged in a friendly way was quite ready to talk.

The least egoistic of us like occasionally to dramatize ourselves. Mrs. Morland's trump card in this direction was the grandchildren she had never seen, as her two eldest boys had married shortly before the war, one in Canada, one in South Africa, and had never been able to bring their families home.

"You see," she said to Jane, "things are never so bad as you might hope, and I do really get the *greatest* pleasure out of my grandchildren, because it is lovely not to have them all living with me as I probably would have to if they were in England, and I can be as sentimental about them as I like without any fear of having to honor my bill, if that is what I mean. And when I think I have three grandchildren I feel so splendidly snobbish. And I sometimes hope that people will be surprised, for though I know I look quite fifty-four, which is what I am," said Mrs. Morland, pushing her hair off one side of her face with her face-à-main, "I don't think people expect a person who writes books to be a grandmother. Oh dear, I am all entangled."

Jane, skillfully extricating the face-à-main from the Rapunzel net in which it had become involved, asked why writers shouldn't be grandmothers.

"I can't imagine," said Mrs. Morland with an air of great candor, "for if they have grandchildren it stands to reason they must be grandmothers. But people will write to me as Miss Morland, a thing I never was, and probably if they know I have grandchildren they think they are illegitimate. But there is one very good thing," she added, earnestly, putting on the spectacles from the red case as she spoke, "which is that Henry, my husband you know, died such a long time ago, because I do not think he would have understood my grandchildren in the *least*. He did not really understand his own boys—not that I do either, but that is so different—and I used to think it would really have been far better if he had died before the boys were born instead of after, because it would have simplified everything."

Jane said that if Mr. Morland had died before his boys were born, he might not have had any.

Mrs. Morland took off her spectacles, closed them and put them into their case, the whole with one hand.

"I know one ought to take them off with alternate hands," she said, "just to keep the balance and prevent their warping, but whenever I think of it it is too late. Yes, I expect you are right about Henry. The fact is that though I have not and never have had anything against him at all, I never think of him. And I must say when he was alive I didn't think much about him either."

So rare was it for Mrs. Morland to allude to the husband whom old Mrs. Knox had described as *excessivement nul*, that Jane was taken aback. In common with most of Mrs. Morland's friends she had come to look upon the young Morlands as somehow the peculiar and unaided product of their mother. So much surprised that she took courage and said:

"Didn't you feel wicked when you didn't think about your husband, Mrs. Morland?"

"Never," said Mrs. Morland firmly. "And if you don't always think about Francis, my dear," she added, toying with the blue spectacle case as she spoke and looking earnestly at the middle distance, "it isn't wicked in the least. People *cannot* help being what they are like, and if it is a choice between being miserable and anxious all the time, or being fairly happy and having such a very nice happy little boy, and not depressing people, your attitude is very reasonable. And natural," said Mrs. Morland putting on her spectacles. "And right. Now which pair *have* I got on? If I look at something about as far off as playing a game of patience I shall know if they are the ones I can see with. I mean that I can see that distance with."

She looked wildly round and not seeing any card game at hand became depressed, but as quickly brightened. "For," she explained, "if I can see your face clearly where you are sitting, then they are the ones I can see people's faces in a railway carriage with. Yes, they are the ones," she continued. "But don't look so unhappy, Jane."

"One might be unhappy if one thought less and less about someone one did love very much," said Jane looking straight in front of her.

And then, luckily for Mrs. Morland who had no further help

to offer from her own experiences and hated to see Jane so distressed, Robin and Anne came in from the pantry. Anne was carrying Mrs. Morland's last novel and as she approached her parents' famous guest, began to show such signs of confusion as kicking her own feet, going pink in the face and opening and shutting her mouth without producing any sound.

Mrs. Morland, who was used to this behavior among her younger admirers, asked if that was a book she had.

Anne, not finding the question at all peculiar, said it was. Then summoning her courage she said pushing the book desperately towards its author:

"Oh, Mrs. Morland, would you *please* mind very much writing your name in this? I bought it with my own money because I *adore* your books, and think Madame Koska is the most *wonderful* person. I called a dog I had that died Koska."

Mrs. Morland who, in spite of a large circulation on both sides of the Atlantic was not in the least blasé about appreciation of her books, to which we may say, she attached no great literary value herself, said of course she would love to. A small table was handy, Robin produced a fountain pen and Mrs. Morland made a suitable inscription. Anne, pinker than ever with pleasure, was about to clutch the book to her bosom when Robin interrupted.

"Hi, Anne!" he exclaimed. "You'll blot it. Wait a minute."

He took the book to a writing table, blotted it and returned.

"Good gracious!" said Mrs. Morland. "I wrote that without either of my spectacles! I must be going blind."

At this Robin, for all his endeavors, burst into a fit of laughter, followed by Anne, though she did not quite understand the joke. Jane smiled and went to talk to Lady Fielding.

"I suppose I am silly," said Mrs. Morland laughing herself. "But Robin, and Anne, I want to have a conspiracy with you," she added, leading her young friends out onto the stone path above which the highest tendrils of the vine caught the sun's dying glow. "Jane seems very unhappy because she can't worry about her husband as much as she ought to. What can be done?"

"It's a rotten position," said Robin. "She might hear he was dead, or he might walk in tomorrow. No, that's a bit too dramatic for this regimented war. But she might hear he was in a Swedish ship being repatriated and that he would be at a delousing camp in Stornaway till further notice and no questions to be asked. I beg your pardon, Miss Bunting," he added as that lady stepped out of the french window.

"If you mean for the use of the word delousing, I was familiar with it in the last war," said Miss Bunting.

She did not add "before you were born," but the effect was equally crushing.

"We were talking about Jane Gresham, Miss Bunting," said Mrs. Morland, feeling that in this elderly spinster with the little black velvet bow at her neck lay a far better and wiser knowledge of the world than she would ever have. "It seems so dreadfully unhappy to have this long uncertainty."

They were all silent for a moment, oppressed by the thought of a grief that no one could cure.

Anne was the first to speak.

> "'Said heart of neither maid nor wife
> To heart of neither wife nor maid,'"

she remarked with a kind of sad pride in having found the mot juste.

If Miss Bunting felt a shock at her literature-besotted pupil's highly inapt quotation, she was not the woman to show it.

"There is nothing that you can do," she said, looking round at a promising class. "You are doing all you can. The rest she will have to do for herself. I have seen it again and again in two wars. Come in now, Anne, it is getting chilly."

The one warm day of that summer was over. They all went back to the drawing room, where Jane was describing with kind malice her visit to Mrs. Merivale at Valimere.

"Have you seen Mr. Adams about it yet, Father?" she said to the Admiral.

The Admiral said he had spoken to Adams at the club, and he was coming out to see the lodgings.

"Oh, it was you who put Adams on to those rooms, Palliser," said Sir Robert. "He is like a clam—loves to make secrets about things. He was on the Silverbridge train with Dora and myself this afternoon, but he didn't say what he was up to. Mrs. Merivale's husband was in our office. Quite a good clerk, but would never have gone very far, even if he had lived. The sort of man who doesn't want responsibility."

"Adams? Adams? Now where have I heard that name?" said Dr. Dale.

No one offered an opinion.

"I have it!" said Dr. Dale. "He is a member of the Barsetshire Archæological Society, though why I cannot think, for he has no tincture of learning or any kind of letters. But he sent a handsome donation to our President Lord Pomfret's appeal for the excavations in that field on Lord Stoke's property where Vikings are supposed to be buried—Bloody Meadow. I believe Tebben, the Icelandic man over at Worsted, thought highly of some bones they found."

"Tebben," said Jane. "That's the man you said was offered a job at Adams's works, wasn't it, Laura?"

"Not the Icelandic one," said Mrs. Morland. "That's the father. It's the son, Richard, that Mrs. Tebben was talking about."

"Dr. Madeleine Sparling, the headmistress of the Hosiers' Girls' Foundation School," said Miss Bunting, while a reverent hush fell on the room, "with whom I have the pleasure of being slightly acquainted, told me, when we met at Lady Graham's one day, that she had under her charge a girl called Heather Adams, whose father was self-made and owned a large engineering works. This girl, she said, though with no particular background, had what amounted to a distinct talent for the higher form of mathematics, and was sitting for a scholarship at Newton College."

Miss Bunting's rolling periods, while received with the respect that was her due, rather flattened general conversation.

"I remember Miss Sparling," said Anne suddenly.

"Doctor now," said Miss Bunting. "She was given an honorary D.Litt. at Oxbridge last year. One should remember these things, both for politeness and for accuracy."

"Doctor, then," said Anne, taking the correction in good part, much to her parents' admiration. "She was living with Miss Pettinger at the High School for a bit, and the boarders said how ghastly the Pettinger was and how Miss, I mean Dr. Sparling's secretary had to make her cups of tea and find bits of food for her, because the Pettinger was so stingy. The secretary was called Miss Holly. She was rather like a plum pudding—only very quick."

Anne was indeed coming out with a vengeance, thought her parents again. A few months ago she would have sat silent all evening, let alone talking in a quite interesting way.

> "'Plum pudding Flea,
> Plum pudding Flea,
> Wherever you be,
> O come to our Tree,
> And listen, O listen, O
> listen to me,'"

said Robin.

"It sounds like a charm to call fools into a circle," said Sir Robert, more versed in the works of Shakespeare than those of Mr. Lear.

Then Jane said they must be going and the Dales said they would walk with them.

"By the way, Laura," said Jane Gresham. "If you are staying

on tomorrow would you like to come and see us doing camouflage netting? It's quite amusing."

"And if you'd care to come and look at my little school
afterwards," said Robin, "I'd be proud. I am also," he added,
"speaking for my father, who is sure to want to show you his
study. It is a ground-floor room with a lot of books in it and
a good many photographs of school and college teams and
societies—altogether remarkably like a study."

Mrs. Morland said if it suited the Fieldings she would love to.
The Fieldings said then do stay to lunch and go by the good
afternoon train. Mrs. Morland thanked them and her bag fell on
the floor. Before the chivalry of Hallbury could rally she had
stooped and picked it up herself. She then uttered a plaintive cry.

"Have you ricked yourself?" asked Jane, sympathetically.

"No, thank you," said Mrs. Morland. "It's only this. It's
always happening."

She held up her unlucky face-à-main, the glass bent at an
angle to the handle, so that it looked rather like the Quangle-
Wangle when he sat with his head in his slipper.

"It is useless like this," said its owner, tragically. "And if I try
to straighten it, it usually snaps or else the spring breaks."

She pushed the hairpins further into her head in a despairing
way.

A perfect babel of advice arose. Some said have a longer
ribbon, some a shorter. Others again said stick it down your
front and chance it, while yet a further opinion was that it would
be much safer to have one of those little ones that fold up and
become a clip, only then it would cost about a hundred pounds
with the purchase tax.

Robin stepped lightly to Mrs. Morland, took the corpse,
straightened it carefully and returned it to her.

"Oh, *thank* you," said Mrs. Morland. "How you do it with
your false foot I cannot think."

CHAPTER 3

In nearly every village or little town there is one middle-aged woman who has a passion for committees, and runs or wishes to run every local activity. If it is the great lady of the neighborhood, all the better, for she is still accepted where another might be questioned. But in Hallbury, in spite of its considerable antiquity, there had never been the equivalent of a squire's lady. Possibly it lay too much under the shadow of Gatherum Castle for any local magnate to rear his head, and it is a fact that there were no large landowners near the Omnium estate. A few of the old established families had shared the leadership in a republican way. The Rectory, Hall's End, Hallbury House, the doctor, the solicitor, had at different times provided the unofficial ruler. Mrs. Dale had led the town very ably from the Rectory until her early death when Robin was five or six, inheriting the office from Admiral Palliser's autocratic old mother who had kept everything going through the last war. Then the doctor's wife had come to the front and managed very well till her husband died, and she went back to her old home in Ayrshire. This was at the beginning of the present war and for the time being no candidate offered. People wandered if Jane Gresham would step into her grandmother's place, but though intelligent and practical, she was better as a worker than an organizer, and knew it. The Fieldings, as we have already said, were still slightly suspect as newcomers, besides which Lady Fielding was far too busy on county matters in Barchester to give proper attention to local affairs. So by degrees, no other leader being available, Mrs. Watson, the solicitor's wife, had slipped into the part. Not by any desire to push, but as being by nature and circumstances the best fitted. Her little boy Tom was attending Robin Dale's classes; she had a good elderly maid; her husband's family had been known and respected in Hallbury for several generations; and she was herself of good sub-county stock accustomed for generations to take responsibility and get things done. With such qualifications there was no opposition to her sway, especially as there was an unspoken feeling that her husband, who was extremely sensible, would be behind her and keep things in order.

By great good luck there was at the end of the Watsons' garden a large wooden building with a corrugated iron roof, which had been erected during the South African War by the present owner's grandfather, to serve as a Drill Hall and recreation room. Though the use of the hall was freely given to Hallbury, old Mr. Watson had never let any rights over it go out of his possession, nor had his successors. So when this war began, Mrs. Watson with great foresight had the heating plant overhauled and bought quantities of thick blackout material, and whether used as one large room for meetings or working parties, or as two rooms partitioned by folding doors, it was invaluable to the town. Two or three years previously the Hallbury W.V.S., at a request from their Barchester head office, had taken on the making of camouflage and to this one end of the hall had been entirely given up; the end which had a separate entrance from the Watsons' garden as well as the entrance from the lane beyond. A band of workers, skilled and unskilled, W.V.S. and non-union, regular and not very regular, had been collected by Mrs. Watson and had on the whole done remarkably well. Jane Gresham had been one of her first helpers and her most faithful, coming four mornings a week, whatever the season or the weather, from nine-thirty to twelve-thirty and two afternoons from two to five, except when she took Frank away for the holidays; and this happened less and less as traveling became more difficult and darkness seemed to encroach more and more. Upon her and three or four others Mrs. Watson could rely. The rest appeared to look upon it as an agreeable and movable feast, their attendance at which was in the nature of a concession and need not be taken seriously. More than once Mrs. Watson had been tempted to dismiss her least reliable helpers with honeyed lies, but life in a small town is difficult enough at any time and more difficult when each settlement is as it were marooned, and to give offense is even easier than it looks. So she contented herself with despising the slack members inwardly and treating them with great courtesy outwardly.

It is possible that by so doing she had builded better than she knew, for Mrs. Freeman, wife of the verger and sister-in-law to Admiral Palliser's parlor maid, otherwise a valuable worker, was far too apt to ring Mrs. Watson up at lunch and say would it frightfully matter if she didn't come that afternoon as her sister wanted her to go to the pictures in Barchester, or to approach her at the end of a tiring afternoon's work with what she obviously considered to be a winning smile, and say she did hope she wouldn't be upsetting anyone if she didn't come next morning as Jennifer would be so upset if she didn't take her to the Bring-and-Buy Sale for Comforts for Gum-Boilers at High Rising. To which Mrs. Watson, valuing good feeling in a small community even above war work (and also knowing that her faithful helpers would always work overtime without a murmur if necessary), would reply with the utmost appearance of un-ruffled approval that of *course* Mrs. Freeman must go and she was *sure* they could manage without her, though her help was always missed and anyway she deserved a holiday. But one day a year or so previously when Mrs. Freeman had just backed out of next day's work owing to having to take the cat to the vet and had been assured that it didn't matter in the least, she had heard Mrs. Watson say to Mrs. Gresham who had suddenly managed to get someone else's canceled appointment with her dentist: "All right, Jane, we'll manage somehow, but you know Wednesday is always hell. You are a nuisance." To which Mrs. Gresham had replied that if that tooth of hers hadn't prevented her from eating and sleeping for two days she wouldn't have taken the appointment and she would be back by four and put in an hour's work. Upon this both ladies had parted in a perfectly friendly manner.

Now Mrs. Freeman, though rather silly, was not a fool and considering this matter while Mr. Freeman was out with the Home Guard that evening, she came to the conclusion that it was perhaps a sign of higher social status to be scolded for not keeping one's engagements than to have the slackness condoned. She was a good wife. She knew that her husband had ambitions, reporting items of local news for the *Barchester Chronicle*, and busying himself in Hallbury affairs; and being of good Barsetshire stock she realized that it still pays to be in with the gentry. So without saying anything she turned over a new leaf. She kept her word to Jennifer about the Bring- and-Buy for a promise is a promise, but we are glad to say that she sent that rather spoiled only child, whose first teeth stuck out horridly, as a weekly boarder to Barchester High School next term. Here Jennifer was very happy, believed in the honor of the school and was a substitute in the junior lacrosse team almost at once, besides making what her parents considered some nice friends: and the school doctor so frightened her mother about her front teeth that she was sent to Mrs. Gresham's dentist and had them straightened. And Mrs. Freeman, with real perseverance, stuck to her three days a week and became a valuable helper. All of which will be of considerable assistance to Mr. Freeman on his upward path.

On the morning after the Fieldings' dinner party, Mrs. Morland, as had been arranged on the previous evening, walked from Hall's End to the Watsons' house a little further down the hill, through the side gate up the long garden which looked very depressing after the year's winds and drought, to the Drill Hall. Here, being a diffident creature and quite unable to realize that she had a certain value as a writer quite apart from her own personality of which, living at close quarters with it as she did, she had the lowest opinion, she began to wonder if Jane really wanted her to come, if Mrs. Watson would want someone who wasn't going to work coming bothering in, if it was really rather secret and she oughtn't to know about it, and if it wouldn't be better to go away again. She then with great courage gave a half-hearted knock on the door and waited. There was no answer. By this time she had so muddled herself that she did not dare to go in (thus possibly profaning some mystery and being cast out again with scorn), or go back (with the chance of being seen going down the garden and being thought mad or rude). So awful was this dilemma that she might have stayed there till lunch time, had not Jane, who had seen her come up the garden, guessed that her knock had been too gentle to be heard among the talk and movement, and opened the door.

Mrs. Morland followed her guide into the hall, where she was introduced to Mrs. Watson, a jolly, rather fat person with a loud voice, who expressed her great pleasure that Mrs. Morland was favoring them with her company.

"I hope you won't think it rude," she said, "if I tell you what a help your books have been to me. Often when I have been so tired and worried that I couldn't rest I have taken one of your books to bed with me and forgotten *everything*. You will find a lot of your admirers here."

"I can't tell you how pleased I am," said Mrs. Morland, anxiously tucking a bit of hair away under her hat as she caught sight of herself in a small mirror on the wall. "I can't tell you how nice it is to meet *real* people who have liked a book, because though if it weren't for the libraries I wouldn't be able to afford to live in my house and give presents to all my boys and my grandchildren, it is quite different to meet a real *person*."

"Well, I do buy your books," said Mrs. Watson. "At least I make my husband give me the new one every year. Now I expect you would like to see what we are doing. We are very proud of our work, because headquarters say we are the best team in the country."

Mrs. Morland looked around. Two great forms, rather like giant beds set up on edge, stood across the hall, decorated apparently with green and brown rags. At a table several women were cutting lengths of brown and green, others were drawing. Everyone seemed very busy and Mrs. Morland felt a drone among bees, and was just going to ask if she hadn't better go away and leave them to go on with their work when Mrs. Watson said:

"Now, we all know that Mrs. Morland is a very busy person with many calls on her time, so we must not waste it," which so took that lady aback that she felt inclined to say lawk-a-mercy on me, this is none of I.

Mrs. Watson then showed her the patterns they had to work by, the way the frames were strung, the material cut in long strips, the strips woven into the netting and every detail of the work, with a quick, clear way of explaining which Mrs. Morland much admired.

"Jane and Mrs. Freeman—this is Mrs. Freeman; Mrs. Free-man, I want to introduce you to Mrs. Morland whose books we all enjoy so much—are our best workers on the frames," said Mrs. Watson and stood back, proudly watching the effect.

"I think it is *wonderful*," said Mrs. Morland, more nervous than ever at the sight of so much competency and anxious to give satisfaction without having in the least grasped what they were doing. "Don't you get very tired?"

"Well, we do," said Mrs. Freeman, "but it is all in the good cause, Mrs. Morland, and when we think of Our Boys out there, we can't do enough for them."

"Oh, have you boys in the forces?" said Mrs. Morland, catch-ing at a familiar straw. "All mine are fighting somewhere though of course with the naval ones one never quite knows where. But my youngest boy, who is in the Artillery with the Barsetshire Yeomanry, writes a great deal when he is out of action, and wonderfully clearly considering the Germans. Are yours in Holland?"

Mrs. Freeman said she had only the one girl, but one couldn't help thinking of Our Boys, and she hoped it wasn't anything serious with Mrs. Morland's son being out of action like that, though his mother must be quite pleased he wasn't in that dreadful fighting.

Pulling her wits together, Mrs. Morland said Oh no, Tony wasn't out of action like that: it was only that he wrote when he wasn't *in* action, and it was so kind of Mrs. Freeman, but Tony would be quite furious if he weren't fighting.

"And so should I," she said, ferociously. But anyone who knew her would have known that she meant it, and Tony, while deprecating his mamma's way of making herself a motley to the view with all fresh acquaintances, would have strongly supported her attitude.

"Stringing the frames is hard on the hands," said Jane. "We've tried gloves and we've tried wrapping rags around our fingers like French soldiers' feet, but nothing except human skin stands up to the work."

"Gilding fades fast
But pigskin will last,"

said Mrs. Morland, sympathetically. "Not that it's true, because if you have ever had a pigskin bag you will know how crumbly all the corners of it go until they come to pieces; but an old frame with gilding on it and images in churches seem to last for hundreds of years."

Realizing that her distinguished visitor might go on like this forever, Mrs. Watson led her to the other workers, who were all admirers of her books. Mrs. Morland in her turn humbly and

sincerely admired their industry and neat fingers and everyone
was on the very best of terms. Mrs. Freeman asked her to write
her name on a piece of paper for Jennifer, which she willingly
did. Warmed by this piece of fame, she recovered her poise,
expressed the greatest interest in all she had seen, complimented
them on being the only team in the county who were allowed to
design their own patterns, and left exactly at the right moment.

"By the way, Mrs. Morland," said Mrs. Watson as she opened
the outer door for her guest, "do you know anything about Mr.
Adams, the man who owns the engineering works at Hogglestock? He is taking some rooms in the New Town these holidays
for his daughter and her governess, from a widow, a Mrs.
Merivale. My husband does her little bits of business for her and
he wants to know if they will be nice tenants for Mrs. Merivale,
who is far too kind and simply asks people to impose upon her.
I don't mean on the money side, but just personally. We
wouldn't like her to have the wrong sort of paying guest."

"Adams," said Mrs. Morland. "No, I have never come across
them. But I believe Mrs. Belton knows them. Yes, I'm sure I've
heard her talk about them. One of her sons saved the girl from
being drowned in the lake last winter, I think. She is at the
Hosiers' Girls' School."

"Oh, well, if Mrs. Belton knows them, that ought to be all
right," said Mrs. Watson, and went back to her work.

Mrs. Morland then continued her almost royal progress to
the Rectory where Dr. Dale showed her all her books in a neat
row on his study shelves, and she was able to ask him whether
two Latin words which she proposed to incorporate into her
next book were really spelled like that. She then visited Robin's
class where she made a great success with the little boys by
telling them about the dreadful day when her youngest boy
Tony and a school friend put all the peas they had shelled down
the bathroom basin so that it was stopped up, and then dropped
the spanner with which they had unscrewed the U-joint out of

the window into the water butt; also how he and that same friend had climbed out of a skylight onto the vicarage roof and there played the mouth organ while the vicar raged below.

Having told this story, she was assailed with doubts as to whether a school housed in clerical stabling was quite the right place for it. The joyful shrieks of the little boys reassured her to a certain extent, but she did not feel quite at her ease till she had privately consulted Robin, who gave it as his opinion that if she had said a rectory, he might have felt obliged to raise a protest, but as it was a mere vicarage where Tony played the mouth organ, the Church of England could stand it.

Master Watson then approached her.

"I've got three rabbits at home," he remarked.

Mrs. Morland said how lovely, and half of her thought with a pang how very nice little boys were with rather dirty hands and a bandage on one knee and wished her own four sons were still in that state of innocence; though she knew well with the other half that she could never go through it all again even if so doing would stop the war.

Master Watson looked at her and said nothing.

"What have you done to your knee?" she inquired.

"Fell off my bike," said Master Watson. "I'll show you the place if you like."

Before Mrs. Morland could pull herself together Master Watson had undone the not over-clean bandage and showed her the knee, which was at the least attractive stage of healing.

"It's ravel gash," said he proudly.

"He means gravel rash," said Frank Gresham. "I had much worse gravel rash when I fell off the tool shed. Tom's only just eight. I'm going to be nine in December. Would you like to see Tom's rabbits? Come on, Tom."

He put his hand into Mrs. Morland's and began to pull, which proof of confidence so affected her as nearly to make her cry; but her better self again coming to the rescue and informing her that Jane Gresham's little boy was being both presumptuous and patronizing, she regarded him for the moment with almost as cold a dislike as her own adored sons had frequently roused in her, and said she was very sorry she couldn't see the rabbits, but she must get back to lunch at the Fieldings'. Although she said this with a courageous aspect she was secretly embarrassed by Master Gresham's vicelike grip and wondered if she would have to go about with him attached to her for the rest of her life, when luckily Robin intervened, told the little boys to go home, and said he would walk down to Hall's End with her if he might.

"I'd love it," she said, "if you are sure you can."

"We don't have lunch till a quarter past," said Robin.

"But oughtn't you to rest," said Mrs. Morland, giving herself a kind of general shake with the intention of tidying her clothes, hat and hair, though with very poor results, "I mean put it up, or something."

Robin suddenly realized what her misplaced compassion was driving at. She looked so anxious—almost damp with worry, Robin thought irreverently to himself—that he hastened to reassure her.

"If you mean my stupid foot," he said, concealing very well the annoyance, unreasonable perhaps but inevitable, that such well-meant thoughtlessness always caused him, "it's perfectly all right. I really hardly think about it at all now. We'll go out by the stable door, shall we, and get around into the High Street by Little Gidding—nothing religious, only the name of a lane, pre-Domesday as far as my father knows."

They went out by a wooden door in a dark red brick wall, ivy-grown, and came into the little cobbled lane which curled around and came into the High Street at Mr. Pattern's corner.

"People do do *wonders*," said Mrs. Morland.

Robin said he was sure they did; in almost everything, he added, hoping to cover by this his complete ignorance of what his gifted companion was talking about.

"There's that man who played polo," said Mrs. Morland. "And I believe there's one who rows. And someone who used to climb mountains, though whether he really could afterwards, I am not quite sure. And I had an old friend whose leg stuck straight out in front of him when he sat down, and he had to hit it, and then it doubled up and no one would have noticed. And he had perfectly ordinary trousers."

Whether to take off his foot and kill the celebrated authoress with it, to shake the breath out of her body, to burst out laughing in her face, Robin was undecided. But being a level-headed young man in most things, pluming himself on an eighteenth-century delight in characters and oddities, and having, not without many bitter moments, decided that an artificial foot was something to be taken metaphorically in one's stride, and that what people said really didn't matter, he choked down his rising irritation.

"All those fellows were splendid," he said generously, "but they had a great advantage over me. To lose a leg is on the grand scale. A mere foot is just rather ridiculous."

Mrs. Morland said she was very sorry indeed. And by the way she said it Robin guessed that she was also sorry for her well-meant and quite idiotic way of expressing sympathy, and was furious with himself for having so far betrayed his feelings. So to make amends he asked after Tony Morland with whom, as we know, he had been at Southbridge School, though senior to him.

Tony, Mrs. Morland said, was quite well when last heard from, and wanted the most extraordinary things that no one in England had been able to get for ages, like fountain pens, and wrist watches, and razor blades and pretense gold safety pins to fasten his collar flaps down. Also he wanted a lot of extra underclothes, and as he was fighting he couldn't get any coupons, so she had to spend all hers on his requirements, but she didn't mind, as she had quite a good stock of clothes herself and if spending coupons would annoy the income tax people she was all for it.

Robin said he hadn't much hope of their minding anything,

and then they talked about old Southbridge friends and Robin told Mrs. Morland that Philip Winter, his predecessor as classics master, had just managed to marry Leslie Waring, the niece of the people, at Beliers Priory, by the skin of his teeth on twenty-four hours' leave, and was now somewhere in Holland.

"Then I expect he will see Tony," said Mrs. Morland, who evidently considered this the chief object of anyone under General Dempsey's command.

And then she told him that the Carters had another baby, called Noel, after Noel Merton who had married Mrs. Carter's sister Lydia; and he told her that the headmaster's elder daughter, the lovely Rose Birkett who had thrown Philip over for Lieutenant, now Captain Fairweather, R.N., an old Southbridgian, had also had another baby, her third he thought, and was in Portugal with all her children and her husband, who was on a mission there, and had made great havoc among the Portuguese with her exquisite English fairness.

"Well, good-bye, and thank you very much for letting me see the school," said Mrs. Morland, when they reached Hall's End.

"Oh, I thought I might as well look in for a moment," said Robin, opening the front door which was never locked in the daytime.

"Hullo, my boy," said Sir Robert, emerging from his library in a very holiday frame of mind. "Come and have some sherry. We didn't finish it last night. Will you join us, Laura?"

"Oh, thanks most awfully, sir," said Robin, suddenly and surprisingly gauche.

"We needn't share it," said Sir Robert. "Dora can't touch it, and Anne and Miss Bunting have gone to lunch with the Pallisers—with the Admiral and Jane I should say, though it's difficult not to think of her as Jane Palliser with her husband missing so long, poor girl."

"Oh, thanks most awfully, sir," said Robin, "but I expect Father will be wanting me. I didn't know it was so late."

He ran off with very little perceptible limp towards the Rectory. The bell of St. Hall Friars sounded one.

"I thought the Rectory had lunch at a quarter past," said Sir Robert, thoughtfully. "Well, all the more for us, Laura. Come into the library."

After lunch Lady Fielding had to go to High Rising for a W.V.S. meeting, so she and Mrs. Morland went off together, and were able to have a delightful talk about Mrs. Morland's new novel, of which a number of intellectual pink young gentlemen who were mysteriously free from the galling chains of the fighting or industrial forces, had written in weeklies that Mrs. Morland represented the effete snobbery of a capitalist society, comparing her unfavorably with the great mid-European woman writer, Gudold Legpul, whose last book (said to have been smuggled at the risk of patriots' lives to England via Barcelona, but really composed in the comparative seclusion of her home in Willesden), I Bare my Breasts, had so courageously attacked the Fascist Government of our so-called Empire; while other and older men, who had long ago given up worrying about politics on account of having to read twelve novels every week and write intelligently about them on Sundays, said Mrs. Morland had again given us of her best, and retold the plot of her story slightly wrong. But as Mrs. Morland knew nothing about reviews, having like the gentlemen just mentioned quite enough to do to earn her living honestly, unless friends were kind enough to tell her about the nasty ones, the world went on much as before.

As was perhaps natural, their talk gradually shifted to their children. Here Mrs. Morland showed great magnanimity in not deploying her four sons against Lady Fielding's one daughter.

"Of course it would have been very nice, Dora," she said to Lady Fielding, "if we could have married some of our children, but it doesn't look like it."

"If you mean Robin Dale," said Lady Fielding, who had the good professional chairwoman's habit of going as straight to the point as possible, "I think you are wrong. If he is attracted by anyone, it's poor Jane Gresham—no harm in it, but they have known each other all their lives, and it's easy to feel sorry for a girl in her position—she's only four years older than he is."

"I daresay you are right," said Mrs. Morland, reserving her own opinion.

"Anyway, Anne is too young for us to worry yet," said Lady Fielding.

"Of course," said Mrs. Morland, going off on one of her usual snipe flights, "my elder boys can't marry anyone, because they are married."

"There are still Dick and Tony," said Lady Fielding not very seriously.

"Dick is probably engaged by now," said Mrs. Morland placidly. "He wants me to send him some of the old photographs of himself as a horrid little boy to Australia, which is where his ship is now, and there's only one person in the world that could want to look at that sort of thing. As for Tony," said Mrs. Morland letting down the window, for they were coming into High Rising, and it was the sort of railway carriage which can't be opened from the inside, thus causing sufferers from claustrophobia and pyrophobia to go mad, "it would be delightful and nothing I'd like more, but I'm afraid Anne isn't common enough for him."

The train stopped, Mrs. Morland opened the door and they got out.

"I do admire your way of looking straight at things more than I can say, Laura," said Lady Fielding. "I don't know another woman who could say that. Come again soon."

Perplexed but gratified, Mrs. Morland got out of the train and was at once pounced upon by her old friend and ex-secretary, Mrs. George Knox, the W.V.S. secretary, who had a little petrol when on official work and had come to meet Lady Fielding and was able to take Mrs. Morland part of the way home.

As Anne's parents were taking a well-earned week's holiday,

except when one or other of them had to go into Barchester, which happened far too often, Miss Bunting had graciously waived the question of lessons for the time being. Some governesses would have been under these conditions a confounded nuisance to put it mildly, but Miss Bunting had not for nothing spent many years of her life avoiding being a nuisance to His Grace, or the Marquess, or his mere Lordship. Indeed among her most cherished recollections was the skill with which she, with the ladies Iris and Phyllis, then under her charge, kept out of the way of the Marquess of Bolton during the week when the Budget came out; though even this was perhaps eclipsed by the tact with which she had effaced herself, Lord Henry Palliser and the ladies Griselda and Glencora Palliser after the Derby when the Duke of Omnium's Planty Pal was unplaced. Frequently had she told her various pupils that time should never hang heavy on their hands, as there was always plenty of work to be done, and conversely, that there was time enough to do everything if only you used method. This was no idle phrase-making, for her whole life had been founded on and still consisted in never being idle and never being hurried. She did permit herself a short and lady-like nap after lunch, it is true, but she had earned it by some fifty years of patient, conscientious devotion to pupils, most of whose children and in many cases grandchildren were now caught up in the whirlwind of war.

Anne spent the morning with her father, watching him trim a hedge and plant some more pea-sticks and do a bit of digging and talking to him in a very agreeable and intelligent way. Miss Bunting got out her much-worn writing case and wrote a number of letters to old friends and pupils in her clear flowing hand, read the *Times* quietly from beginning to end, made up a bit of velvet ribbon into a new evening bow, heated her curling irons on the gas ring upstairs and recurled her spare fringe, and finally gave Gradka an hour's lesson in English humor. That industrious young woman had prepared a lunch, part of which was cooking itself in the oven while the rest was sitting in the refrigerator, and as she possessed the invaluable faculty of being able to concentrate on one thing at a time, they got through a lot of work. Byron's satiric poems and the Ingoldsby Legends she had now mastered for all examination purposes and it merely remained to correlate the art of Sir William Schwenk Gilbert with that of Samuel Butler before writing her essay.

Miss Bunting's opinion of public examinations of any kind was so small as to be practically invisible, but she was quite aware that in the world as it is most of us have to conform, and will have increasingly to conform, so she determined to do her very best for Gradka, whose pertinacity she admired though she found the student herself and her complete self-satisfaction something of a trial. The Bab Ballads are not perhaps the book we would choose to try to explain to a foreign refugee with little knowledge of their historical and literary background, but Miss Bunting did not know the word impossible. Having explained to Gradka that the likeness between Gilbert and Butler must be sought in their great facility and ingenuity in finding rhymes rather than in their philosophical outlook (which gave Gradka a low opinion of Gilbert at once), she proceeded to take these poems which, in her almost infallible judgment, would be chosen as typical by the examiners, and gave Gradka a short lecture upon their meaning with explanations of various topical allusions. All of which Gradka took down in notes and appeared to understand, having the cleverness of book-educated foreigners at grasping the form of a joke combined with their total inability to laugh at it.

"So, I thank you very much indeed," said Gradka at the end of Miss Bunting's explanation. "There is one more poem which I shall ask you about, 'Captain Reece.' It is a satire, is it not?"

Miss Bunting said not exactly. It was, she said, more in the nature of a fantasy.

"A fantastic poem I shall say then in my essay, yes?" said Gradka.

Miss Bunting said not quite. She would herself call it on the whole a humorous poem: light humor, she added.

"I now pretty well understand oll the English humor," said Gradka, "but this poem, no. I read it as a satire upon your navy, which is pampered. It is ollso a satire upon democracy when the Captain marries the washerlady, yes? The humor is because she is a widow. Widow is very humorous in English, like mother-in-law or dronk man. But one thing is very admireable that is the duty theme. In Mixo-Lydia we are all against duty, but here the duty-spirit is awfully popular."

Miss Bunting said doubtless Gradka meant that devotion to duty was an essential trait of the English character; popular, she added, did not have quite that meaning. To say that an actor, for instance, was popular meant that the people liked his acting; not that his acting was expressive of the people.

"Aha!" said Gradka, an exclamation into which she was able to put a wealth of whatever meaning she chose—usually a sinister one. "In Mixo-Lydia all our actors are expressive of the people; they are ollso popular as you say it. I ollso note in 'Captain Reece' the repetition theme which drives the symbolic nail to its home by the act of repeating. 'It is their duty and they will,' followed by 'It was their duty and they did.' It is the Nelson touch. It is very striking. I find it very English."

Miss Bunting was over seventy, but her well-trained brain, except in the hour after lunch, worked as well and swiftly as ever. For an instant she thought of trying to explain to Gradka that Gilbert was not really thinking of Nelson or duty or democracy, or indeed anything except amusing himself and his readers in light witty verse. Even as quickly she decided that this would be governess's labor's lost, and that the examiner would probably be much more in sympathy with Gradka's attitude than with her own, which was incidentally that of the few widely-educated people left. And here she was perfectly right, for it was Gradka's ponderous exposition of these very points that turned the scale between a Beta plus and an Alpha minus, which was the mark she was finally awarded.

So Miss Bunting folded her pince-nez and put them in their case, and Gradka collected her books.

"One moment, there is something I shall ask you, Prodshkina Bunting," said Gradka. "You know a gentleman called Adams perhaps? An ironmonger, very, very rich, at Hogglestock."

"We do not use the word ironmonger for a person who employs labor on a large scale," said Miss Bunting. "We say ironmaster. Mr. Govern who keeps the shop in the High Street is an ironmonger."

"I thank you," said Gradka, whose eager willingness to absorb information on any subject under the sun was one of her many less-endearing qualities. "So, now I know Mr. Govern is the ironmonger and I know he is the tinker for he tinks kettles. Do you know of the ironmaster Adams?"

Miss Bunting said she had heard of him through common friends.

"Mr. Adams is perhaps common too?" said Gradka, with no wish to be like that gentleman, but always ready to learn.

"A common friend in good English, means a friend of two or more people," said Miss Bunting, wishing Gradka would go away but impelled by her life's training to give information where it was desired. "For instance, Dr. Dale is a friend of Sir Robert's and a friend of Admiral Palliser's. One could therefore say that he is their common friend."

"Aha," said Gradka thoughtfully. "Which you ollso say mutual friend. It is a synonym, yes?"

"No, Gradka," said Miss Bunting, roused like an old soldier by the distant trumpet. "We do *not* say mutual friend when we mean common friend. That our great author Charles Dickens uses the word in this way is a fact you may note, but not copy. He was a law to himself. A common feeling is a feeling about some person or subject, shared by two or more people. A mutual feeling is an identical feeling in each of two people about the other. There could be a mutual friendship between two people. A mutual friend is nonsense."

"So, I thank you again very much," said Gradka. "It is now quite clear to me grammatically, ollso for speaking or literature, the difference between common and mutual. I shall perhaps put this in my essay, for I think the examiner will not know it and he will be so ashamed he will have to give me good marks. So this will be to our mutual advantage. To say our common advantage would be wrong here, yes?"

Miss Bunting praised Gradka's grasp of what she had just told her. She also reflected that not one of her English pupils would have even tried to understand what she had just said, and would have thought it broadly speaking rot, and wondered why heaven had implanted in so many unattractive Central Europeans such a passion for barren accuracy. It had all been tiring and she wanted to get ready to take Anne to lunch at the Pallisers'.

"I shall tell you," said Gradka, "why I wish to know about the ironmaster Adams. I have a friend Prodska Brownscu from Mixo-Lydia like me, and she has told me how Mr. Adams has tricked a dirty Slavo-Lydian who has tried to get some money for the Slavo-Lydian Red Cross last year. And I wish to see the man who has done this. And Prodska Brownscu has told me he has taken a lodging in the New Town, so I think I shall see him there, yes?"

Miss Bunting told Gradka she had better go back to her lunch now, or everything would be late. Gradka made a little bob and went downstairs. Miss Bunting sat back for five minutes, her eyes shut, her hands folded: a custom which she had found of great value in helping her to prepare for a fresh lesson or engagement. The name Adams; everyone seemed to know him or know about him. Not at all the kind of person one would wish to know, she thought, but the world was changing too quickly for her and she was old and tired, and if the world was to belong to the Adamses, one must accept them, always keeping one's private integrity. At the end of her five minutes she got up, washed her hands, put her hat and gloves on and went to find Anne.

That young lady had already come in from the garden and was ready for Miss Bunting in the hall. Her great week of pleasure was indeed well underway. She had met her parents at the station, had a new dress, assisted at an exciting dinner party, had her book signed by Mrs. Morland, spent a lovely morning with Daddy, and now had in prospect the further treats of lunching at Hallbury House and then going down to the station again to meet Lady Fielding on her return from High Rising; for such was the afternoon's program. Small enough beer one might say; but to a girl without brothers or sisters, growing up during the war and having led until lately a rather invalid existence, such pleasures, scorned by her more sophisticated contemporaries, were very real. Sir Robert and Lady Fielding, people themselves of a simple and in some ways almost austere manner of life, were sensible enough not to expect their only daughter to grow up in their likeness, but very glad to find that she was not a slave to the spirit of this restless age.

Miss Bunting had a few errands at the post office, so she and Anne left the house before one o'clock, passing the end of Little Gidding a few minutes before Mrs. Morland and Robin Dale came down it. The business transacted, they went on to Admiral Palliser's where the old parlormaid Freeman told them the Admiral was around the back of the house; a misleading terminology, but clear to the meanest intellect. They found their host and his grandson, who was just back from school, engaged in the delightful task of clearing out the scullery waste pipe with a bit of stout wire. The Admiral had his coat off and his shirt sleeves rolled up. Frank had faithfully copied his grandfather, and both being of much the same build, square and strong, they made a pleasant couple. As Miss Bunting and Anne came around the corner the Admiral was probing for the obstruction, while Frank gazed with rapt attention.

The Admiral having grappled his prize, sheered off, hauling

as he went, and with a sickening greasy plop, out came a horrid shapeless mass covered in gray soapy slime. Frank joggled up and down to express his pleasure.

"There," said the Admiral, straightening himself. "Why the maids have to put rubbish like that down the sink, I don't know. Good day, ladies. If you will excuse me I'll go and wash. I can't shake hands in my present condition. Frank, take Miss Bunting and Anne into the drawing room, wash your hands and tell Freeman we're ready for lunch."

"Can I bury the slosh, Grandpapa?" said Frank, eyeing longingly the stinking mass.

It is just possible that the Admiral, though he prided himself on being a martinet, would have given in to this request, for he hesitated. But even as Frank spoke Miss Bunting had looked at him. There was nothing particular in her look, she did not presume to criticize a distinguished Engineer Admiral's method of bringing up his small grandson, but such was the command of the eye that had quelled the heir to many a peerage or landed estate, that Frank said: "All right, Grandpapa," and stood on one leg.

"How *do* they make that mess?" said the Admiral.

"I should say," said Miss Bunting, putting on her pince-nez and regarding the mess with cold scientific interest, "that they never used the sink basket and never put boiling water and soda down the pipe, and probably had very old dishcloths."

"Well, well, I'll speak about it," said Admiral. "Jane ought to be back from her camouflage work now," and he went indoors by the kitchen passage, while Frank conducted the ladies through the side door into the drawing room. Here he was about to put Miss Bunting through a searching interrogatory about the slosh or muck of which she appeared to have so profound a knowledge, but Miss Bunting remarked that his grandfather had told him to wash, and such was her authority that he quite forgot to make an excuse till he was in the bathroom and wiping his imperfectly washed hands on the clean towel. Being a conscientious little boy, as little boys go, he then industriously tried to wash the marks of his dirty hands off the towel, which led to an interesting experiment as to how far one could stuff a towel down the wastepipe of the basin. It would not go very far, even when prodded with a toothbrush, because the corner, so neatly rolled to a point, rapidly developed into the main body of the towel, large and unmanageable. The gong sounded, his mother's voice was heard calling his name up the staircase. Frank hastily withdrew the towel, not at all improved by being forced down a soapy pipe, draped it in a negligent way over the towelrail with the dirtiest part to the wall and ran downstairs.

A nice bit of fat boiled bacon off the ration (which for the benefit of any readers from another planet we will explain to mean not that the bit of bacon in question comes off your ration, but that it isn't and never was on it) with young potatoes and peas from the garden is not to be despised. Frank did not despise it, by which happy chance his elders were able to talk in peace for a time.

The talk, as in many a previous summer, was about going away for the holidays, though as no one was going, the discussion was purely academic. The Admiral spoke wistfully of the pleasant sequence of grouse, partridge and pheasant. Jane wistfully mentioned motor tours through France or the Tyrol with friends, or sailing a very small uncomfortable yacht with her husband. Anne's eyes lighted as she said how she had been to Devonshire with Mummy and Daddy, and bathed every day when it was warm enough. Miss Bunting who, we regret to say, was not enjoying her fat bacon as much as she used to before she acquired a complete set of upper and unders, took advantage of a lull in the conversation to say that one of her few disappointments when at Gatherum Castle was that the schoolroom party never went to the Scotch place as Her Grace preferred them to go to Littlehampton; which ducal memory slightly damped the other members of the party. But, said Miss Bunting, she was luckier than many other people this year, for Lady Graham had kindly asked her for a week in August.

"You are the only one who is going away from Hallbury this summer," said Jane Gresham, though not complaining. "I'm doing August and September at the camouflage to let the people with more than one child get away. Frank is going to his other grandfather at Greshambury for three or four weeks before school begins again. It makes a change."

"I'll ride Roger's pony," said Frank, suddenly swallowing his last mouthful in a way that should have choked him, only it didn't. "Roger's afraid to jump. I jumped over a ditch."

"Go on with your lunch, Frank, you are all behindhand as it is," said Jane, putting his pudding in front of him.

"Mary's afraid to jump too," said Frank. "I like ponies that rear. I'd like to ride a buckjumper. Mother, could Mr. Dale ride a buckjumper with only one foot? If I had only one foot, I'd always ride. Oh, Mother, Tom said if people's feet were shot off before they were too old, they could grow again. Could they, Mother?"

His mother said no; and to put his knife and fork together as Freeman was waiting.

"Oh, Freeman, look here," said the Admiral. "Tell cook the scullery pipe is all right now. She's been putting kitchen stuff and old clothes down it."

Freeman, although it was meat and drink to her to know that cook was at fault, was bound by the fine, if exasperating staff loyalty which prevents any servant giving another one away while she is in the employer's service. When the cook has been given notice and gone to a fresh place with the excellent character that her employer is too frightened to withhold, then is the moment when her fellow servants proffer the ominous words: "I think, madam, you ought to know—" followed by a catalogue of crimes before which Moses would have blenched. But while she is still in residence kitchenware may be broken and hidden, fat sold, spirituous liquors from Hooper's Stores put on the family account which will not be sent in till the following month, even a pair or so of silk stockings abstracted from the wash, and the rest of the staff will look the other way. So Freeman, who had more than once had words with cook about the silly way she acted, not putting her glasses on while she was doing the wash-up when it stood to reason you couldn't get the mustard off the plates if you didn't see it, at once assumed entire solidarity with the kitchen front, and said she was never one to meddle; throwing in as an afterthought a "Sir" whose tone should have warned the Admiral.

Oh, if only Father wouldn't quarterdeck the maids in public, thought Jane, half-amused, half-annoyed; for to her would fall the task of somehow smoothing things down.

"Lady Pomfret told me," said Miss Bunting to Jane, with the air of one changing the conversation altogether, "that she simply could not get good dishcloths at the Towers. She said," continued Miss Bunting with deliberate untruthfulness, "that it was disgraceful that the Government couldn't give us better dishcloths."

"Oh, dear!" said Jane, doing her best to take up the cue that she felt Miss Bunting had offered her. "What can one do?"

"I knitted some for her with some nice coupon-free thick gray cotton," said Miss Bunting, "and there was no more trouble."

"Oh, Miss Bunting," said Anne, who had hardly spoken till now. "Couldn't I knit some for the Admiral? I'm sure Hooper's have got gray knitting cotton in the window this week, without coupons. Do you think cook would like them?" she added, turning her head towards Freeman, for she was young enough to be on good terms with the kitchen and not yet afraid of them.

"I daresay cook wouldn't mind, miss," said Freeman in the gracious language of her caste, and indeed of most people's castes now. And putting the pudding on the table she went away.

Jane looked gratefully at Miss Bunting, who was again slightly preoccupied with raspberry pips in her dentures and did not see, for she had simply done her duty and for the ten-thousandth time helped an employer out of a difficulty.

Lunch being over, Jane very kindly took Miss Bunting to the drawing room, established her in a comfortable chair, and gave her old Lady Norton's book on gardens, *Herbs of Grace*, by which means Miss Bunting had a peaceful sleep, while Anne and Frank dug a hole and had a funeral for the slosh before Frank went back to school. Anne helped Jane to bottle raspberries while cook was upstairs, and then Jane suggested early tea before Miss Bunting and Anne went down to the station to meet Lady Fielding. It was assumed that Miss Bunting had been reading Lady Norton's book all afternoon, to which assumption Miss Bunting gave tacit consent by comparing it unfavorably with similar books by other gardening ladies of higher rank.

"Well, come again soon, both of you," said the Admiral who had escorted his guests to the front gate. "A good idea of yours, Miss Bunting, about the dishcloths and I'll see that cook puts boiling water and soda down that pipe."

"For goodness sake don't, Father," said Jane. "You know how horrid it was after you told her about the scullery not being properly blacked out. I'll try and find a good time to mention it."

"All right, my dear, all right," said the Admiral, rather impatiently, for an old sailor does not lose the habit of command easily. "I'll tell you what the trouble is, Miss Bunting, one can't get the right wire to go through these pipes. You want something thicker than I can get, but very flexible. I dare say there's a good reason that we shouldn't have it. Mr. Churchill knows best. But I *would* like a good long piece of stout wire with a hooked end," said the Admiral wistfully thinking of the days when he had the engineers' stores under his thumb wherever he went and could indent for any delightful bit of metal he wanted.

"Nice girl, Anne Fielding," he said to his daughter as they watched Miss Bunting and her pupil walk down the High Street. "Who *are* all the girls going to marry, poor children? There's not a man about the place except poor Robin."

"Perhaps they will be just as happy if they aren't married," said Jane, which made her father blame himself for reminding her of

Francis Gresham. Poor Jane. There was little Frank, it is true, but it looked as if Frank would be an only son, an only child. And even if Francis came back at last, how would he and Jane settle down; what would be the end? Then he told himself not to be an old fool and went to his library where he found occupation enough in getting the accounts of the local Soldiers' and Sailors' Families Association into shape for the annual audit, for he was treasurer for Barsetshire and took his duties very seriously.

Would they be just as happy if they didn't marry, Jane wondered, as she went upstairs. By the landing window she paused and looked over the garden and paddock at the lovely Barsetshire landscape before her, with the woods of Gatherum Castle in the distance. If she were not married; if there had never been a Francis Gresham, and she were still Jane Palliser, would it be better? No one here for her to marry either, except Robin, she thought, laughing without much mirth at the idea, even if she were free. Did she want to be free, she tried to ask herself. Would she be glad or sorry if Francis came back; if she had certain news that he was dead, poor Francis.

A spot of raspberry juice on her frock suddenly roused hot anger in her.

"Oh, what is the *good* of it all?" she said aloud, and went to the bathroom, telling herself, as her father had just done, not to be a fool.

The bathroom was, not to put too fine a point upon it, in a mess. Water was slopped on the floor, the soap was sitting in a puddle of water on the ledge of the basin. She turned the hot tap on, hoping it might run really hot if cook had remembered to make up the fire before retiring to her room for the afternoon, and while it ran she picked up the towel from the rail. The rail was cool, which presaged ill for the water: the towel was wet and the side of it that had been nearest the wall filthily dirty. Her odious son again, of course. How often she had told Frank to rinse the dirty soap off his hands before he dried them she could not guess: ever since Nannie went on to the Greshambury nursery two years ago, certainly. Well, thank goodness the laundry still called, though at irregular and ill-ascertained intervals. She was about to throw the towel into the basket where the week's dirty towels were put, when she reflected that being wet it would make everything else wet and possibly—if the laundry left as long a gap as it did last time—grow green mold. With controlled rage she folded it and hung it on the rail again, hoping that in cook's good time the water would be hot.

"And that's about all I'm fit for," she said scornfully, to her own reflection in the mirror over the basin. The face that looked back at her gave her no help at all. Indeed, it looked so disagreeable that she couldn't help laughing as it and then she thought of Frank and how very much nicer he was then all the other little boys she knew, how tight his hug, how affecting the nape of his neck and the way he sprawled over the bed in his sleep. Her face softened as she came to the reasonable conclusion that she was being of some use in helping to bring up a happy, intelligent little boy who appeared to find her quite satisfactory. And then Frank came dashing in to his tea bringing Tom Watson with him, and she stopped thinking about herself.

When Miss Bunting and Anne got to the station, the train from High Rising was not yet signaled and they were able to enjoy such familiar but always interesting sights as a lot of mysterious wooden boxes being put into a van in the little siding, several hens going mad in a crate, the village hunchback who sold newspapers, chocolates and cigarettes in a little booth, creeping out of it by a flap under the counter rather like Alice when she had at last made herself the right size to open the tiny door, the stationmaster coming down to the station from his house in a bowler hat, going into his office and emerging in his gold-braided cap, the porter having a heavy Barsetshire flirtation with a Land Girl, two dogs tied up in the parcels office getting their leads entangled and a tabby cat walking about on the line, with that indefinably down at heels and slatternly air

that cats have when out of their proper surroundings. So what
with one thing and another the time passed very pleasantly till
the train came in and Lady Fielding got out of it. The only other
passengers for Hallbury were a short, vigorous, rather roly-poly,
brisk woman and a large ungraceful girl.

"Mummy!" said Anne. "Do look. That's Miss Holly."

"Do I know about her?" said Lady Fielding in whom the
name struck no chord.

"Yes, Mummy, I *told* you," said Anne eagerly. "Miss Sparling's secretary, that was with Miss Pettinger and they hadn't
enough to eat. Oh, Mummy, you *do* remember."

Lady Fielding dimly remembered something Anne had said
about the headmistress of the Hosiers' Girls' Foundation School,
and her secretary being the guests for a time of the headmistress
of Barchester High School who was famed for her chill hospitality, but the whole affair had very little interest for her, she did
not want to stare at complete strangers, and moved towards the
exit with Anne hanging on her arm.

"Excuse me," said a voice to Miss Bunting, who was a little
behind the Fieldings, "but aren't you Miss Bunting? Dr. Sparling, my chief, met you at Lady Graham's and she told me you
were staying at Hallbury. Holly is my name, Dr. Sparling's
secretary."

Miss Bunting graciously acknowledged her identity. Each
lady was secretly comparing the other with her description as
given by a third person. Miss Bunting, remembering Anne's
definition of Miss Holly as rather like a plum pudding, only very
quick, admitted its correctness. Miss Holly, to whom Dr. Sparling had mentioned meeting an old governess who was exactly
what a good ex-governess ought to look like, felt that she would
have recognized the original anywhere, and that if the place
of their chance meeting had been Timbuctoo, Miss Bunting
would have been just the same, her skirt unfashionably long, her
hat unfashionably high on he head, her withered throat en-

circled by a black ribbon, yet unmistakably a lady of birth, breeding and intellect.

"This is Heather Adams," said Miss Holly. "Her father has engaged me to give her some coaching before she goes to Newton College for which she won a very good scholarship. He has taken rooms here for the holidays and wanted us to have a look at them."

The large girl shook hands with Miss Bunting, who congratulated her. By this time they were all at the gate and at such close quarters that it would not have been civil to ignore the newcomers, especially as Anne had claimed Miss Holly as an old acquaintance, so Miss Bunting introduced Miss Holly to Lady Fielding and then Heather Adams's name was mentioned.

"I think Heather's father knows Sir Robert slightly," said Miss Holly. "Mr. Adams who owns the Hogglestock works, you know. He did mention that he had had some correspondence about the Friends of Barchester Cathedral Fund."

Lady Fielding made a suitable and polite reply, feeling slightly annoyed with Miss Bunting and incidentally with her daughter Anne, for letting her in for acquaintance whom she did not think her husband particularly wanted.

While they were speaking, the New Town taxi was seen coming up the ramp. It drew up and disgorged Mrs. Merivale.

"What *will* you think of me being so late?" she said. "Miss Holly, isn't it? And Heather Adams—how do you do, dear? I had ordered Packer's taxi as soon as I got Mr. Adams's phone call saying you were coming to look at the rooms, and I told him to come around by Valimere and the time was going on and no sign of him and I felt quite upset, so I phoned up the garage and they had forgotten the order, just fancy! But most luckily Mr. Packer was there himself and he was quite upset and said it was a mistake in the office because the young lady was out this afternoon, but he would come himself. So now, do get in and Mr. Packer will drive us out to my house and wait to take you back to catch the Barchester train. Mr. Adams liked my rooms and I thoroughly enjoyed our little talk and if you see anything you would like altering you must be sure to tell me."

In a flutter of kindly excitement she herded her guests into the taxi and they drove away.

"Isn't Miss Holly nice, Mummy?" said Anne, when they had crossed the footbridge and were mounting the High Street.

Lady Fielding was rather tired by a troublesome meeting at High Rising where even Mrs. George Knox's tact had not been able to prevent Lady Bond putting several people's backs up, for her ladyship, though Staple Park was let to a school and she and Lord Bond were living in a small house on their estate, had not abated one jot of her viceregal domineering. Also she saw with resigned despair that this chance encounter had the seed of an annoying amount of social intercourse in it and would more than likely lead to a nearer acquaintance with both Mr. Adams and his not very prepossessing daughter. So she did not respond with her usual enthusiasm to her daughter's artless remark, and then blamed herself and felt a beast.

Miss Bunting, whose life as a highly valued governess had made her very sensible to fine shades, had a pretty good guess at what Lady Fielding was thinking, and was sorry for her. Her own conscience was clear; the most ordinary good manners had forced her to speak to Miss Holly and Heather Adams, and even to introduce Miss Holly to Lady Fielding. She could do no less. Miss Holly was a pleasant and capable woman, secretary to a woman of unusual distinction as teacher and organizer in the scholastic world, who was holder of an honorary degree at Oxbridge, and the only woman upon whom the freedom of the Hosiers' Company had ever been bestowed. So far so good. But the introduction of Heather Adams was not so good. Miss Bunting knew what Sir Robert felt about her wealthy and rather pushing father without being told; just as she had known that the Marquess of Bolton would never allow the Marchioness to ask that dreadful Mr. Holt to come and see the garden; just as she had known how the Duke and Duchess of Omnium, kind and easy-going people on the whole, would see to it that Sir Ogilvy Hibberd never got his foot within their doors, even before his shocking attempt to buy Pooker's Piece for building land, and his discomfiture at the hands of old Lord Pomfret.

However, it had been impossible to avoid the unexpected meeting, and as she was in no way to blame, she with her usual clear common sense did not blame herself. Lady Fielding's spurt of ill humor subsided before Anne had realized it was there, and it was a very happy party that sat down to dinner at Hall's End.

"Daddy, isn't it lovely, we've still got tonight, and Friday, Saturday, Sunday, Monday, Tuesday," said Anne. "Everything has been lovely and *long* since yesterday. I do hope it will go on being long."

"So do I," said Sir Robert, smiling. "But not all Tuesday. We have to go to Barchester on Tuesday."

"Oh, *Daddy!*" said Anne reproachfully. "You came on Wednesday and you said a week."

A complicated discussion then took place as to what a week really was. Lady Fielding said seven days might mean seven whole days with a day at each end for coming and going which would make it nine. Miss Bunting said if people invited one to come on Tuesday for a week, it was difficult to know whether they expected one to go on the following Tuesday, or on the Monday just preceding it. She herself, she said, always took care when she received similar invitations to have the days of the week in writing from her hostess. Sir Robert said he had always wondered why the French, who were supposed to be logical, called a week a semaine and a fortnight a quinzaine, as no amount of logic could make twice seven be fifteen. It was, he said, just what you would expect from the French, and for his part he thought we ought to have Calais, which really belonged to us, and then there wouldn't be so much nonsense. Lady Fielding then pleaded for Aquitaine and Normandy, and everyone fell into the delightful game of remaking the map of Europe on purely personal prejudices, without the faintest regard for history, geography, or (quite rightly) race, for as Gradka said, who came in at the end of dinner, put everything onto the trolley and wheeled it away with slightly scornful competence,

"If it is of races you speak, Mixo-Lydia will never tolerate Slavo-Lydia. You have an English proverb which says 'Blood is thicker than water,' but I shall tell you that Slavo-Lydians have pigs' blood, *un point c'est tout.* Pouah!"

"They must be dreadful people," said Lady Fielding, far too sympathetically. "Good night, Gradka."

"I shall tell you," said Gradka to Miss Bunting, pausing in the open door with the loaded trolley, "of sommthing very humorous."

"Very well, Gradka, but shut the door," said Miss Bunting. "These summer nights are so cold."

"You know, everybody," said Gradka, standing with one hip thrown out and an arm akimbo in a rather truculent way, "that I have stoddied English humor, as exemplified in Butler and Byron and the Ingoldsby Legends and W. S. Gilbert. But there is one very fonny thing which I shall tell the examiners. It is a piece of inconscious humor."

"*Un*conscious," said Miss Bunting.

"So, thank you very much," said Gradka. "You know the names of Sir W. S. Gilbert, what they are. They are William Schwenk. And what is Schwenk?"

"Probably a family name," said Sir Robert, who was bored.

"Family! That would indeed be humorous. As well you might say Christian, for no English are truly Christian," said Gradka crossing herself fervently in the Mixo-Lydian form, which Mrs. Morland had once described as very upside down and un-Christian. "No. I shall tell you Schwenk. It is what we call the Slavo-Lydians. It means a vermin which is died and becomm eaten by maggots. Ha-ha! That is what we call those pig Slavo-Lydians and it makes us laugh till we burst."

"That is enough, dear," said Miss Bunting. "Good night, Gradka."

Gradka recognized the voice of authority and withdrew to the kitchen where she washed up and then resumed her studies.

"Foreigners," said Sir Robert in a kind of mild despair. "And to think that we have to study their feelings. Much study any of them give to ours."

CHAPTER 4

The rest of Sir Robert and Lady Fielding's holiday was not so long as the first two days. This is a mathematical phenomenon so well known that no comment need be made, just as during a weekend Saturday teatime to Saturday bedtime is a pleasant eternity, and the whole of Sunday an express train. But a great many nice things happened, like Hallbury House coming to tea with Hall's End, Hall's End going to tea with Mrs. Watson and there meeting Hallbury House, Mr. and Mrs. Watson and Master Watson going to tea and tennis at the Rectory and there meeting Hallbury House and Hall's End. Tennis was not very serious, for though the Watsons and Jane Gresham played really well, there was no good fourth. Robin was still not quite sure enough of his foot and Anne was too coltish and not up to Mrs. Watson's slashing balls. But she was a promising player; and while they were having tea Jane Gresham, a county player for two seasons before the war, offered to give her some coaching, if they could get a court, for the Admiral's court had been made over since the second year of the war to geese and rabbits, the theory being that they would keep the grass down and then prove a succulent addition to the larder. In practice their lawn eating was of a sporadic nature, so that bare muddy patches alternated with thick tufts of Jacob's ladder and clover, nor did they fatten much unless their diet was supplemented. But no one minded, for the Admiral had never been a player, his sons were married and away, and Jane too busy to get up parties; besides which, as we know, really good tennis players there were few within the wartime radius of Hallbury. As for the old gardener, he looked upon all tennis courts and indeed flower beds, grass walks and pleasure lawns as a flying in the face of Nature, who intended them for vegetables.

The Watsons, always ready to promote the pleasure of their young friends, at once offered to lend their court, and it only remained to settle the days. What with Anne's daily routine and Jane's camouflage work and other activities, not to speak of the times when the Watsons wanted the court themselves, it was not easy to arrange a time, but finally Tuesday after tea and Saturday morning were provisionally fixed.

"You'd better come, Robin," said Jane to the Rector's son. "It'll be good practice for you."

Robin, chafing under his disability, for he had tried one set and not done well, was inclined to refuse. But Jane quite truthfully said that she was sure she could help him and Anne said three would be much more fun than one."

"There, my child, you show your ignorance," said Robin. "Three-handed tennis is a poor game. If only we could get someone else, just about as rotten as I am, we might make a do of it."

Jane agreed that they ought to find a fourth, though certainly not a rotten one, and Robin was not to talk in that silly way.

"Mummy," said Anne to her mother who was talking to Dr. Dale, and in any case took little interest in tennis. "Oh, Mummy, Miss Holly used to play tennis when she was at Miss Pettinger's. She beat Cynthia Dandridge that was the captain of tennis in singles once."

"Did she, darling?" said her mother. "You do look hot. Where is your cardigan? Put it on."

Anne loosened her cardigan which had been on her shoulders with the arms tied around her neck and put it on properly.

"Couldn't we ask her to come and play tennis, Mummy?" she said.

Lady Fielding, who now remembered who Miss Holly was, and did not, as we know, much want to be implicated with that lady, or rather—for she had nothing against her personally— with her pupil Heather Adams and even more her pupil's father, said something noncommittal. Anne, who was never good at asserting herself, looked a little disappointed and took refuge in a fruit cake sent by an old pupil of Dr. Dale's from Australia. Lady Fielding turned to Dr. Dale, relieved to have got rid of the subject so easily, when Mrs. Watson's rather brisk voice was heard asking if that was Cicely Holly.

"I don't know," said Anne. "She used to teach a kind of very high up arithmetic at the Hosiers' Girls' School, and she is Dr. Sparling's secretary."

"Stout woman, runs along the hockey field like winking?" said Mrs. Watson.

Anne said some of the girls called her Roly-poly, but she did run very fast.

"That's old Cicely," said Mrs. Watson, who was one of those jolly women that never forget old school friends and enjoy nothing more than the Annual Reunion of Old St. Ethelburgians. "Well, wonders will never cease. I wonder if she remembers Molly Glover. Where is she now?"

As Anne was suddenly taken shy, Lady Fielding, hoping to scotch the unwelcome subject, left her talk with Dr. Dale and said to Mrs. Watson that Miss Holly was still with the Hosiers' Girls' Foundation School, now at Harefield Park.

"Harefield? Oh, bad luck!" said Mrs. Watson, sympathizing with herself. "Only eight miles, but what I say is without petrol it might as well be eighty. We'll have to think again."

Lady Fielding drew a silent breath of relief. If, without telling a lie, or even really implying one, she could leave Mrs. Watson under the impression that Miss Holly was at Harefield Park, all would be well, and thank goodness Anne was in her shy mood.

But Lady Fielding had not allowed for the persistence of a girl, however retiring, who had a moth-like devotion for a schoolmistress.

"Mummy," said Anne, reproachfully. "You know Miss Holly is going to be in the New Town in the holidays."

As Lady Fielding could not publicly kill her daughter, she smiled and said nothing.

Mrs. Watson, all agog for news of her old fellow student, pounced upon Anne and elicited from her the information that Miss Holly was taking a holiday job to coach the daughter of that Mr. Adams that gave all that money to the Friends of Barchester Cathedral Fund.

Mr. Watson said rather ponderously that, feeling a certain responsibility for his client Mrs. Merivale whose rooms Mr. Adams was engaging, he had made a few inquiries in Barchester about him.

"They say he's a hard nut," said Mr. Watson, "but you get fair treatment if you stand up to him. I saw the daughter once—just like her father, reddish hair, heavy build, didn't seem quite all there."

"Now then, Charlie," said his wife, "don't be horrid," and there was some good natured, heavy banter between them about Molly being jealous of pretty girls, which had the effect of making Lady Fielding feel glad that they didn't always live in Hallbury and then be ashamed of herself for the feeling.

"And to think of Cicely Holly being in the New Town," said Mrs. Watson. "I'll phone her up and get her to come to tea one day and bring the girl with her. What's her name? She'll be nice company for Anne, make a change."

Anne volunteered that it was Heather.

Poor Lady Fielding, who had always quite liked Mrs. Watson, though so seldom at Hallbury that there was no intimacy, felt her mild liking turn to gall. A woman who could say "phone up" would be capable of anything and was indeed deliberately encouraging Anne to thwart her father's and mother's wishes.

Then she blamed herself for being unfair. Anne was a darling, good, confiding girl and could not suspect the depths of social currents. In fact, Anne was being nice and polite to Mrs. Watson and she, Dora Fielding, was divagating far from her own standards of behavior.

"What a good thing Mrs. Merivale's rooms were empty," said Mrs. Watson. "She's a good little soul and had quite a fight for it after her husband died, I believe. But her people were very good church goers, and what I say is, the background always tells."

"They nearly weren't empty," said Jane. "At least, she had a lodger who went to see about them."

"Not that dreadful Captain Hooper, the Hush-Hush man," said Mrs. Watson. "Nearly everyone in the county has had him and got rid of him. He started with the Villarses at Northbridge Rectory and tried to get into Beliers Priory but General Waring wouldn't have him. Intelligence does throw up the most peculiar objects. What I say is, it's a wonder we're winning the war at all when you see the kind of lodgers people get."

"I don't know who it was," said Jane, "but she said it was nice to have him."

Dr. Dale, who owing to a life's work on Haggai and his age, which was just going to be considered by the Oxbridge Press when war broke out, thus giving them an opportunity to shelve various scholarly works which would obviously never sell, was apt to have his mind elsewhere, suddenly came back to A.D. and asked what was wrong with Intelligence. He understood, he said, from the Archbishop's last speech in the Lords that Our Leaders were proving their quality in the furnace of war.

There was a moment's silence.

"Isn't the rector an old darling," said Mrs. Watson, beaming upon the company. "But what I always say is that all those books do make a frightful difference and give people a wonderful outlook."

This remark, though profoundly true in its essence, again turned everyone to marble.

"I expect," said Anne, and then stopped, suddenly overcome with embarrassment at finding herself addressing so large a company on so large a theme.

"Well, Miss Anne," said Mr. Watson, who affected this mode of address for young unmarried ladies, which his wife said was a scream, "what do you expect?"

"Oh, I only thought," said Anne, "that Mr. Churchill would know if the Intelligence was really funny. I don't mean funny exactly, but what Mrs. Watson said. I expect it is really to deceive German spies, like that play, Mummy, where the silly young man is really the clever detective."

She stopped, crimson with nervousness and feeling that she had made a fool of herself and her family. But her audience, who were all fond of her, thought none the worse of her and Robin smiled in a way that Anne found strengthening.

"Well, what I say is," said Mrs. Watson, summing up the situation in a masterly way, "that if Mr. Churchill put Captain Hooper into Hush-Hush to put the Germans off the scent, he never did a better day's work. And now," she continued, having disposed of Captain Hooper, "let's have a good talk about Haggai, Dr. Dale. Did you see he was in the *Times* the other day?"

"Haggai? I did not notice it," said Dr. Dale. "I usually read my *Times* very carefully. I cannot understand this. We have got our old *Times*es, Robin, I hope."

Robin said that he put them on the study shelf himself and only let them go for kitchen use or salvage after four weeks.

"If it was by the Bishop, I can understand its not attracting my attention," said Dr. Dale, who in common with the whole body of Barsetshire clergy regarded his Bishop as specially sent to try him and to encourage the Disestablishment of the Church. "But if it was Crawley, I should have spotted his style at once." For Dr. Crawley, the present Dean of Barchester, was an excellent

clergyman of the Moderate school, and something of an authority on the prophetic writings. "The only matter in which I may
be to blame," he continued, while everyone listened respectfully
or made a respectful appearance of listening, "is that little article
which appears at regular intervals, I believe, near the Court
Circular, I do not know what there is about it, but I cannot bring
myself to read it. If the article on Haggai was there, it is a lesson
to me to prove all things."

"By the time one has done the Court Circular and the
marriages and the funerals and the engagements," said Lady
Fielding, sympathetically, "which is really the only way one has
of keeping in touch with old friends now, one simply doesn't feel
equal to any more on that page."

"Don't worry, father," said Robin, "I'll look through the
*Times*es tonight. The article wasn't very long ago, you say," he
added, addressing Mrs. Watson.

"I never said an article, my dear boy," said Mrs. Watson
laughing heartily, "It was the crossword," at which the rest of the
party couldn't help laughing too.

"Crossword? I never do them, I don't understand them," said
Dr. Dale. "When Buckle was editor there weren't any crosswords."

"You ought to," said Mrs. Watson. "They are quite educational. I learn ever so many words I didn't know."

If Dr. Dale, the most courteous of pastors, could have brought
himself to cast a venomous and contemptuous look at a respected female parishioner, this would have been the moment.

"Now, what was the clue?" said Mrs. Watson.

"As far as my memory serves me," said Sir Robert, also a
confirmed addict, "it ran something like this: 'The old woman
was lively in French.'"

"Old woman?" asked Dr. Dale, indignantly. "Haggai was *not*
an old woman. The term might, though I would deprecate such
a use, be applied to one or two of the minor prophets; but most
emphatically not to Haggai."

"It's only a kind of play on words, Dr. Dale," said Lady Fielding. "The Hag part of Haggai sounds like an old woman; like a hag."

"A fool, Lady Fielding," said the Rector with Johnsonian echo, "would not consider such an etymology. The most ignorant tyro would tell you that."

Lady Fielding meekly said that she did not mean that exactly.

The Rector then fell into paroxysms of apology for having treated Lady Fielding as he would have treated a fellow scholar; as he would have treated the Master of Lazarus, whose little book, *The Economic Outlook of Israel under Zerubbabel*, he had had the pleasure of reviewing with the contempt it deserved in the Church Times. He then felt that he had not improved his case and looked unhappy.

"I do quite understand, Dr. Dale," said Lady Fielding earnestly; and seeing that he still looked distressed she added: "And if you would lend me the review, I am sure I would understand even better."

Dr. Dale, much gratified by such a request, and anxious to make amends for any unintentional discourtesy to a guest whom he liked, rose, went to a bookcase, took down a small pamphlet and looked at it lovingly.

"This is an off print of my review," he said, half to himself, half to the company at large. "I had fifty made at my own expense and still have a few left. If I may have your permission to write your name in it, Lady Fielding, I shall feel you have forgiven my want of courtesy."

Sir Robert, rather maliciously, said that to appreciate fully Dr. Dale's review, his wife ought also the read the Master of Lazarus's book, but luckily the Rector did not hear this remark, being fully occupied writing Lady Fielding's name in his beautiful and still firm writing on the flyleaf of the pamphlet.

"Well," said Mrs. Watson, "what I always say is the Bible's a wonderful book. You never know *what* you will find in it."

Luckily this piece of Biblical criticism did not reach the

Rector's ears either, for he might have been seriously distressed by it, and then Lady Fielding began to say good-bye. Jane said she must collect Frank, who was somewhere in the garden with Master Watson. Robin said he would come with her and the rest of the party went to their homes.

There was no particular hurry. Double Summer time was dragging its slow length along in a land where it was always chill, gray, unfriendly afternoon. As they sauntered down the gravel walk against the old brick wall where apricots, that almost lost fruit, still grew and ripened, Robin said one of the worst things the war had done was to make that awful after lunch feeling go on till supper time, or even later, and if he were the Peace Conference, he'd make Germany have triple summer time forever and ever. Jane said the Japs too.

"Quite right," said Robin. "And if there were a quadruple summer time they'd deserve it. I say, Jane," he added in a kind of desperation, "I never know if I ought to mention the Japs or not, because it's so *rotten* for you about Francis. So if you don't think me a beast I want to do the right thing. I mean, does it make it worse if people talk about them? Don't think I'm trying to be sympathetic or anything, but we do all feel most awfully sorry about Francis."

Jane walked even more slowly and finally stopped.

"I don't suppose I mind anything very much," she said, examining a beetle-eaten rose leaf with great attention. "I expect I mind just about as much as you mind about your foot. I mean one knows the horribleness is there, but quite often one forgets it. I suppose you do."

"Oh, Lord! yes," said Robin, vaguely feeling that the higher he set his own standard of courage the more valiantly Jane would reach towards it. "Sometimes I forget for ages, especially in school hours. And the boys do so enjoy my sham foot. One does wake up at three in the morning sometimes, of course."

"Quite," said Jane. "But there's one thing, Robin, you can't get your foot back. I might get Francis."

She paused and there was a silence again while Robin considered his statement.

"What a beast I am," he said suddenly. "I never thought. If there were a chance that I could grow a new foot, or at least have the old one back again, I'd be twice as sick as I am. Knowing's better than not knowing."

"Or you might think," said Jane in a somber voice, gently ripping the beetle-gnawed leaf to pieces, "that it would be better to know that your foot was all blown to bits than to imagine that it was wanting to get back to you and couldn't, and that you mightn't know what to do with it if it did come."

The silence grew. If Jane did feel that to put one's head on someone's shoulder, almost anyone's shoulder, would be an anodyne: if Robin felt that one might cheer a person up by putting an arm around their shoulders and giving them an encouraging and impersonal hug; whatever their feelings might have been, neither really liked being demonstrative, so they walked on again in the direction of a noise which had gradually been forcing itself upon their attention.

"I don't think a tank *could* get into the stable yard," said Robin, "but if one has, your child is at the bottom of it."

"Or Molly Watson's," said Jane impartially, though she knew and Robin knew that Frank was the ringleader in all his and Master Watson's doings.

As they entered the stable yard the noise resolved itself into the old garden watering-cart, for we do not know how otherwise to describe the kind of iron boiler on two wheels with a third dwarf wheel to steady it when not being pushed and a kind of perambulator handle to propel it. This interesting machine used to be pushed by the gardener's boy in a happier age and from it the undergardener would fill his watering can and water the flower beds. For a good many years a hose had made it almost unnecessary, though the old gardener still used it for his more delicate plants, leaving it in the sun so that the chill was taken off the water. At the moment it was obviously some engine of destruction. Both little boys were pushing it across the cobbles with loud shrieks and bellows, and appeared by their red and perspiring faces to find it heavy work. On its side some letters or figures had been chalked by a youthful hand.

"Hello, Mother; hello, sir," shrieked Frank, his shrill voice overtopping the clank of the water-cart, "this is V13, the tram the Yanks filled with dynamite and sent it at the Germans. Look, Mother! That's the Germans! Come on, Tom!"

With more loud encouraging yells the little boys pushed their clanking machine towards the slight depression in the stable yard where the water used in washing down carriages used to drain away. Here they had set up an old and battered wooden stump, black beyond recognition. With a final whoop they gave the machine a push down the slope. It crashed into the figure, both fell over, and a quantity of garden rubbish such as broken flower pots, pieces of tile edging, rusty bits of wire and a large round stone ball, was shot in all directions.

"Look, Mother!" "Look, Mrs. Gresham," shouted the little boys in chorus.

"Good lord!" said Robin, "it's our old Aunt Sally that we used to have at mothers' meetings and school teas. Hi, Frank, where did you find her?"

Frank said in the loose box where all the trunks were.

"She must have been there for about twenty years," said Robin thoughtfully, "because I can just remember her with pipes in her nose and eyes and ears, and I don't think father had any school teas after my mother died. Give her a lick of paint and she'd be as good as ever. But I don't suppose those wretched children know what an Aunt Sally is, and I don't suppose there's a clay pipe in the world now."

The little boys, not quite understanding, but somehow scenting sadness in the air, stood watching the grown-ups.

"I didn't think you needed it, sir," said Frank. "We found it behind a box of croquet things. Oh, Mother, we had a splendid game of being blacksmiths. Look, Mother! Come on, Tom!"

Before the horrified eyes of the grown-ups, Messers. Gresham and Watson rushed to the ci-devant loose box, now a kind of repository for unwanted house and garden furniture, returned with a mallet apiece, and improvising a kind of forging song, swiped in turn at the stone mounting block.

"Frank! Frank! stop!" cried his agonized mother, while his schoolmaster with a hearty oath strode over and wrenched the mallets from the amateur blacksmiths' grasp. One was chipped, the head of the other was loose.

"I *am* so sorry," said Jane.

"It's not your fault," said Robin. "It's those young devils. The Women's Institute have the loan of our old croquet set occasionally; otherwise it wouldn't really matter."

"Sir," said Frank in dulcet tones, picking up the mallets which Robin had laid on the horse-block, "could we play at crutching then? Here you are, Tom."

Putting a mallet under one armpit, each little boy began to limp about the yard, the end of the mallet handles banging heavily on the cobbles.

"No, you couldn't," said Jane with sudden violence. "Give me those mallets at once; *at once* I said, and don't ever touch them again. Oh, Robin, I could kill them with pleasure."

"Well, I wouldn't if I were you. You couldn't get two more the same in a hurry," said Robin reasonably as he took the mallets from her.

The little boys, rather sobered by the sight of an angry mother, an unusual experience for either, began to tidy away their rubbish. Robin, with sudden suspicion, asked where the stone ball came from. Master Watson said it was on the top of the rockery and somehow it got rather loose.

"It's only one of the old stone balls off the pillars of the coach-house gate," said Robin, with the resignation of despair. "One was cracked and my father has rather a fondness for the one that wasn't, so he got the gardener to make a kind of rockery with the ball on top. I'll tell him to put it back tomorrow."

"Good-bye, Robin," said Jane. "I don't suppose you'll want to see us again for quite a long time. Come along, Tom. I'm going to take you home before you and Frank can do anything worse. I can't tell you how sorry I am, Robin."

Robin accompanied them to the gate and saw them on their way down Little Gidding, telling Jane not to be silly and worry, because it didn't matter a bit. Then he came back to finish the tidying. Just as he was lifting Aunt Sally to restore her to her home in the loose box, his father came into the yard and asked him what he was doing.

"I may as well tell you it's those boys of Jane's and Molly Watson's, Father," said Robin, holding Aunt Sally upright while he spoke. "They were playing at Germans and got the stone ball off the rockery, but it's all right, and old Chimes can put it back tomorrow. It's funny to think that lots of children have never seen an Aunt Sally and never will. Lord, Lord, how much valuable knowledge is going to be lost by the time the war's over."

He began to hoist Aunt Sally up, to carry her away.

"Wait a minute, Robin," said Dr. Dale, gazing earnestly at that lady's black face and almost obliterated features, with a streak of dirty white or red here and there to show that she was human, a scrap of dirty muslin, once a bonnet, clinging to a nail in her head, and an old broken pipe stem sticking out of one ear.

"It makes me think of your mother, Robin," said Dr. Dale at length, with a sigh. "All right; put it away." And he continued his walk around the garden remembering school teas and mothers' meetings and Robin's young mother presiding.

Robin laid Aunt Sally in her box, thinking with amused wistfulness that she appeared to be his only link with a mother he could hardly remember. Then he collected the mallets, but decided that the loose head had better be secured and if possible a band put around the chipped end before they were used again. So he took them up to the house, regretting that he was too tall to swing along between them as he would have done some twenty years ago. Then he thought of Jane's sudden anger when the little boys wanted to play at what they called crutching. Not like Jane to have such an outburst. And suddenly he went hot with shame as the thought struck him that she had been angry on his account, that she had thought the little boys crutching might remind him of his foot, that he might resent it, feel hurt, or unhappy. Women all over. You try to explain to them till you are black in the face that you don't really mind having an artificial foot, and then they work themselves up into thinking that you do. Good old Jane: but too many women about every-where. Perhaps he would do better to accept Mr. Birkett's suggestion and go to Southbridge. But even there he believed they had a science mistress and a junior classical mistress. Probably even monasteries had some unattractive female monks now to keep up their numbers. Even the army couldn't escape them. Only the lucky, lucky ones in the real fighting line. Robin had done his best to school himself against his fighter's longing to be in the forefront of the battle, but bitterness would still break in.

He put the mallets in the hall and set himself to work at his classics till supper time.

The rest of the exciting week ran quickly away. Sir Robert and Lady Fielding went back to Barchester and Anne was left to Miss Bunting and the routine of lessons. Lady Fielding before she went had a short conversation with Miss Bunting on the subject of Mrs. Merivale's lodger.

"I don't want to be *too* snobbish," she said. "At least, to be truthful I really do, and though I am sure Mr. Adams is a much more useful member of society than I am—or at least I don't honestly think that, but I suppose I ought to think it—I don't frightfully want to be implicated. It all sounds so horrid, but with Anne I expect you see what I mean."

Miss Bunting, who was freer from illusions than most people, took no notice at all of her employer's foolish and well meant efforts towards democracy.

"Certainly Heather Adams," said Miss Bunting, snapping her pince-nez shut and letting their cord run up into the fascinating little spool which she wore pinned to her attire (for the vagueness of this word seems suitable to her dignity), "certainly Heather Adams is probably not a suitable companion for Anne. The Hosiers' Girls, though the school has an excellent record of scholarships, are not quite what one would wish."

Lady Fielding might have thought that her daughter's governess had stopped short before the end of her sentence, as indeed occasionally happened owing to difficulty with her uppers, but she didn't; appreciating the fine shade conveyed by the lacuna.

"So many people aren't," said Lady Fielding, piteously. "And I know one oughtn't to be stuffy about it, but Anne is so easily impressed by people and her father doesn't really want to meet Mr. Adams much apart from business. And now Mrs. Watson is going to ask the girl and her schoolmistress to tea and wants Anne to go. One can't very well refuse in a small place like this. Oh dear, it's very awkward."

"We must move with the times," said Miss Bunting, to Lady Fielding's great surprise. "When I first went out as a governess, no girl was allowed to walk out alone, not even around Belgrave Square. But the whole world has changed. I find Anne has a very kind nature and, I think, good principles. It would take more than a Hosiers' girl to harm her."

She did not add: "And stop being silly and leave it to me," but Lady Fielding could almost hear the words, and took heart and told herself that Miss Bunting was right, and it was only because Anne had been an invalid that she worried so much. And, to be logical, why should a delicate girl be more easily influenced for bad than a robustious type? And then she got into such a muddle of confused maternal hopes and fears that she decided to leave everything to Miss Bunting and Anne; which was probably the wisest thing she could have done.

Mrs. Watson was as good as her word, as indeed she always was, which was one of the reasons for her success as a local organizer, and rang up Miss Holly at Valimere. Miss Holly remembered Molly Glover quite well and was glad to hear of a friend in the neighborhood. Her tennis was rather rusty now, she said, and Heather Adams was not very good, but they would love to come up to tea. Saturday week was fixed with tea at half-past four and tennis afterwards, so that Mr. Watson could join them.

Miss Holly then reported the invitation to Heather Adams while they were having coffee after supper in what Mrs. Merivale called the lounge, and Miss Holly, with equal determination and possibly more reason, the sitting room. During the few days that she and her charge had been at Valimere, a friendly feeling had sprung up in them both towards their kind, pretty, cheerful, worn hostess. They had begged her to drink her coffee with them after the evening meal, an invitation which Mrs. Merivale, after twisting her hands in agony, had accepted with pleasure, making the stipulation that this was only to be when Mr. Adams was not there. Heather, rather a lonely only child who had never made friends at school till her last year, was much interested by the lives and careers of the Misses Merivale, and though too apt to appraise every other young woman by her scholastic achievements, was genuinely impressed by the excellent positions Mrs. Merivale's daughters, with nothing but the Barchester High School behind them, had achieved.

"That call," said Miss Holly coming back from the telephone, which was clearly audible in every corner of the jerry-built house, "was from a Mrs. Watson in Hallbury. We were at school together. Do you know her, Mrs. Merivale?"

"Well, I really haven't had much time to know anybody," said Mrs. Merivale, "what with Mr. Merivale dying and the girls to educate and the lodgers to cater for; especially in the Old Town.

It's really much further than you'd think at the end of a day's work and you have to push your bike all the way up the hill. But I had a very nice friend of Mrs. Watson's here for a month once, and then Mrs. Watson came down to see her and had a really lovely fox fur. The girls always say they'll give me a fox fur, but I say: 'Put the money on your legs, girls, not around my neck,' for you know how all these young people go through their stockings and it's bad enough with no coupons without having to pay for them as well."

Miss Holly saw, from the look in her pupil's eye, that she might be about to give Mrs. Merivale a short lecture on economics and the total want of connection between coupons and cash payments, so she hastily said that Mrs. Watson had asked them to tea on Saturday week and tennis afterwards. Mrs. Merivale was much gratified, for Mrs. Watson was a well known local character and what was called "respected" in Mrs. Merivale's circle, and she liked her lodgers to go to the right houses because it did them, and her, credit, though she was not in the least ambitious socially for herself, reserving her real interest for the various friends her daughters brought home for holidays or on leave.

Heather, without any great enthusiasm, but with a mild willingness to oblige which had only come upon her in the past year, said then Daddy had better bring down her tennis things when he came at the weekend, and he could bring Miss Holly's too; and so it was arranged.

Those who knew Heather Adams in the early days of her career at the Hosiers' Girls' Foundation School, were amazed and pleased by the way she had improved. When she first came to the school she had been as nearly unpopular as a girl who is not actively unpleasant or malicious can be. Her ungainly shape, her scanty reddish hair, her total want of interest in games or the honor of the school, her real affection for all forms of mathematical study (a thing obviously against nature), her incapability of making friends, nay, her evident desire not to make any,

her general lumpishness and her scorn of everybody and everything, were so boring to the other girls that they all gave up
trying to make friends and left her to her own life; which was
exactly what she wanted. Miss Sparling (for she had not then got
her D.Litt.), the admirable headmistress, had devoted a good
deal of anxious thought to her uncouth pupil, only child of a very
wealthy self-made manufacturer, motherless, without any background at all as far as Miss Sparling could see. Then at the
beginning of the first winter after the school had moved to
Harefield Park, Heather's sluggish nature had had two very
salutary shocks. The first was that she fell in love with Lieutenant Charles Belton, R.A., during church on Sunday, and remained violently in love with him till five-thirty P.M. on the
same afternoon, at which hour he, by deliberately backing out
when she was offered to him as a partner at a small informal
gramophone dance at the school, turned her love to gall, worm-
wood, hatred and the fury of a woman scorned. The second
shock was that even as her love for Lieutenant Belton died, a
greater, deeper and purer love for his elder bother, Commander
Belton, R.N., who had gallantly taken pity and danced with her,
was born. This secret passion, with its outward concomitants of
contempt for her fellow pupils and the sulks in general, was
nourished on nothing for a term and a half, and then as suddenly, it passed away. But not in hatred; far otherwise. It died
because Commander Belton fished her out of the lake where she
had deliberately skated over the place marked DANGER, made
her run as fast as she could to his parents' house in Harefield
where she was dried and put to bed, and then, having discovered
to his annoyance that he was her ideal, had with considerable
courage and unselfishness told her that his true love, a Wren,
had been killed in an air raid. Upon which Heather, overcome by
the pitiful romance, proud of sharing a secret only known to
himself and his mother, at once stopped being in love and
became a much nicer girl.

This change was apparent to everyone. Her mistresses attributed it each to the particular activity in which Heather came under her charge. Her father told several friends at the County Club (to which it had become quite impossible not to elect him), in the iron and steel world, and on the Bench, that there was nothing like a good school, whatever the expense, for a motherless girl like his little Heth, and would have defrayed a large part of the cost of the school's new site (on the Beltons' land, along the Southbridge Road) had not the Hosiers' Company stopped him. Mrs. Belton, partly because she was sorry for so unattractive a girl with so much money, partly because anyone who had been cared for in her house had a claim on her kindness, partly because she suspected Heather's calf-love for her elder son and knew its hopelessness, had gone on taking an interest in her and letting her come to Arcot House on half-holidays instead of nature walks or a visit in a motor bus to the Barchester Museum; and at Arcot House Heather observed a gracious manner of life still surviving among wreckage, and what is more, observed that there was something in it.

We do not wish to imply by this retrospect that Heather Adams suddenly became handsome, slim, attractive, unselfish, an ornament to Society and the Home all in a breath. Far from it, even in a great many breaths. But that she tried very hard to be nicer there is no doubt at all; and this effort happening to synchronize with a turn for the good in her circulation, complexion and health in general (for which Dr. Perry was largely responsible, and to which his female assistant Dr. Morgan made absolutely no contribution at all), she also found herself very much happier and almost liked by the larger part of the school. Finally she had won the best open mathematical scholarship for Newton College, beating all other candidates in Duodenal Sections and Impacted Roots by several marks, and this success, as often happens in the case of a being convinced by circumstances of its own deep inferiority, gave her an assurance hitherto lacking and a pleasant feeling that though Love was not for her, Fame and the Common room of Newton were. So that when Mr. Adams, incited thereto by Dr. Sparling though he never knew it, nervously suggested the holiday coaching, Dr. Sparling's efficient secretary and trusted friend, Miss Holly, had no objection to taking on the job of duenna coach for the holidays.

"I hope you won't find it too dull," Dr. Sparling had said while the question of terms was still under consideration; the consideration being chiefly how to beat down Mr. Adams, who was prepared to pay Miss Holly about twenty pounds a week and was distinctly dejected when less than half that sum was proposed as a maximum.

"Not a bit," said Miss Holly. "I like Heather and it's a pleasure to teach a girl with a clear head. And it's pretty country. I might say that I hope you won't find it dull at Bognor," for Dr. Sparling was going to spend a month of the summer holiday with the mother of her great friend, Mr. Carton. Old Mrs. Carton had seen and approved the lady her son so greatly admired, and this visit was a token that whenever Dr. Sparling felt her duties to the Hosiers' Company would allow her to retire to the decent obscurity of being Mrs. Sidney Carton, the door of "Enitharmon," Blake Close, Bognor Regis, would be as open to her as the door of Assaye House, Harefield, which was where Mr. Carton lived when not in his rooms at Paul's.

Practically the whole of the New Town did its going about on bicycles. As nearly all the bicyclists were women, who do not believe that any machine needs cleaning, oiling, or any attention whatsoever; or children who had never been taught to do anything for themselves and took their bicycles to the garage to have a tyre mended or pumped up, there was outside the shops, the church (very high), the nasty little cinema, the Council Chambers, the W.V.S. room and all other places of congregation as fine an assortment of what looked the Lord Nuffield's backyard at Morris Cowley Station as one would wish to see.

To this higher carelessness Mrs. Merivale and her family

were no exception and when she kindly offered Miss Holly the use of any of the girls' bicycles during their stay, Heather was appalled by the state they were in. She wasted no time in regrets or expostulation, but quietly and determinedly overhauled each bicycle, cleaning, oiling, noting what spare parts were urgently needed. Mrs. Merivale luckily did not take this high-handed action as a reproach, but did say she was very upset that Heather should clean the girls' bikes as well as paying for her board and lodging. Heather, who had a passion for machinery, not altogether approved by her father, who though proud of her interest in his works did not want her to be in and out of the fitters' shops all the time, took no notice at all and continued her salvage work, being a very good amateur mechanic.

"There," said Heather, wiping her hands professionally on a bit of old bath towel that Mrs. Merivale had given her. "And if you oil them a bit and don't bang them about so much, and remember to pump up the tyres and put them tidily in the shed, they'll do very nicely for a long time."

"Thank you very, very much," said Mrs. Merivale, who was constitutionally incapable of putting anything back in its place, except things like her boarders' toilet articles or laundry, over which she showed meticulous care. "You really oughtn't to do all that work. I don't know what your father would say."

"He'd do it much better than I do," said Heather enviously. "He was always in the works ever since he was a boy, and I only get in at odd times because I'm a girl. It's too bad."

But Mrs. Merivale felt the obligation with all the strength of her upright, generous, obstinate little mind and even the phlegmatic Heather wondered if the subject would ever be dropped, till she had the good idea of asking if she and Miss Holly could borrow two bicycles that very Saturday for Mrs. Watson's tennis party. At the thought of doing a kindness Mrs. Merivale brightened at once, only regretting, at really very boring length, that the enamel on all the bicycles was so scratched.

"It's because you don't have a proper stand for them," said

Heather, to which Mrs. Merivale answered, possibly with truth that they'd take up more room in a stand than they would in a heap.

"So what I'll do," said Heather to Miss Holly later, "is to ask Daddy to get them to make a frame at the works, and he can bring it out on Saturday."

"A very good idea," said Miss Holly, "but you know what will happen."

"She won't use it," said Heather, with a perception that the pre-Belton Heather did not possess.

CHAPTER 5

Saturday dawned bright and fair, but observing that it was still Double Summer Time, took offense and relapsed into chill grayness. As no inhabitant of the British Isles has ever got used to the odious and so called summer weather which has always been their portion, and far less to the vagaries of D.S.T., there was a good deal of grumbling everywhere, which grumbling was gradually diverted to the less eternal grievances of the fish, the daily woman, that girl at the Food Office, the Government, that noise all night like a mouse just at the head of my bed, and I *must* set a trap as pussy doesn't seem much good at it, the way the laundry has ironed that nice tablecloth, and other daily food of human nature. At Valimere the ladies behaved with great restraint. Mrs. Merivale, who never bore a grudge, said no wonder the weather was like that with all the noise there was everywhere; Miss Holly was too busy with some Hosiers' business to notice the outside world; while Heather was absorbed in a delightful little book called Indifferential Relations, with a table of Kindred Affinities and graphs of Nepotic Constants.

However, it did not rain, the wind was not a gale, and Miss Holly and Heather set off for their tennis party, speeded from the front gate by Mrs. Merivale, who hoped they would thoroughly enjoy themselves and not to worry about supper as it could all be kept hot and if Mr. Adams came in before they were back she would give him a nice cup of tea. A few minutes' ride brought them to the level crossing and so to the foot of the High Street. Here Miss Holly dismounted, saying with truth that she was not so young as she used to be, but Heather, whose legs though ungraceful were extremely powerful, rode scornfully on, tacking from side to side, to the great alarm of an army lorry, two jeeps and a motor dispatch rider, none of whom were accustomed to keep the rule of the road and therefore deprecated such action in others. Miss Holly was not unduly anxious for her charge. She knew Heather had an excellent head and no nerves to speak of, and further she had on taking the job contracted out of all responsibility for her physical safety, knowing from experience that she had no fear of heights and a passion for climbing to the top of any high building and walking around it, preferably on the parapet. To this Mr. Adams had agreed, adding with ill-concealed pride that his little Heth had a will of her own, same as her Dad.

So Miss Holly pursued her way peacefully up the hill and when she got to the Watsons' house found Heather on the front doorstep, her face bright red, her sandy hair damp and clinging to her head. Miss Holly was no snob, and as we know she liked her pupil in her own businesslike way, but she did for a moment wish that she were not meeting Molly Glover with quite such an unattractive not to say temporarily repellent creature in tow.

"Well!" said Mrs. Watson, throwing open the door and beaming at her guests. "This *is* nice to meet you again, Cicely, after all these years. And this is Heather Adams? You do look hot, dear. Don't leave the bicycles outside or they'll be pinched. Charlie!" she shouted towards the back of the house.

Mr. Watson came into the hall from his study.

"This is my husband," said Mrs. Watson, presenting Mr. Watson to the visitors. "This is Cicely Holly, Charlie, that was at Fairlawns with me, only she was a great swot and I was a dunce. It was always tennis with me, wasn't it, Cecily, only in those days it was basketball. What a foul game, only they call it netball now. And this is Heather Adams whose father you know. Take the bicycles around to the back, Charlie, there's a good boy. He's got a kind of workshop with all sorts of things in it," said Mrs. Watson with all embracing in discriminating pride, "and the bikes will be quite safe there. And don't get any oil or anything on your flannels, Charlie," she added, as Mr. Watson took a bicycle handle bar in each hand.

Heather's rather vacant eyes had lighted up at these words.

"Have you got a lathe?" she inquired.

Mr. Watson said he had.

"Electric or foot-drive?" said Heather.

Mr. Watson said electric.

"I'll take one of the bikes," said Heather, and wrested her bicycle from his grasp. Mr. Watson, amused but not disconcerted, for not even the Lord Chancellor's death could do that, led the way around the house. Mrs. Watson shut the front door and took Miss Holly to the drawing room.

"Sit down and we'll have tea as soon as the others come," said Mrs. Watson. "Well, I'd have known you anywhere! And what I always say is, once you've been at school with anyone there's a little bit of the past in common that makes all the difference. Those were the days at Fairlawns. Do you remember Gwenda Hopkins? She married a very nice man in the Indian Civil and has three daughters all in the Forces. And Ivy Paxton? You know she died; a dreadful shock to her mother. And Hilda Cowman; she used to be rather a pal of mine but she got some sort of job in a factory and looks down on me because I'm married. And now do tell me all about yourself."

During these remarks and while Mrs. Watson took a breath for a monologue which would obviously go on until she had said all she thought of saying, Miss Holly sat plumb and upright in her chair, regarding her old school friend with scientific interest. That Molly Glover had recognized her was not surprising, for as Miss Holly freely confessed to herself she had been a plain stout girl and was a plain stout woman, and except that she now wore suits from a good tailor and not a gym tunic or a one piece frock, her round face with a good deal of color, her beady black eyes, her smooth black hair neatly brushed back and coiled, her round compact form, were almost exactly the same as in the upper forms at Fairlawns. She could not say the same of Mrs. Watson, the large, handsome, rather crumby woman before her, with her hair set in curls and rolls. Under what layers of change her old schoolfellow was buried: how unlikely it was that if they had met by chance she would have disentangled the tall almost gawky Molly Glover with her fair pigtail from the woman who had enveloped her. Not till Mrs. Watson patted a shining curl into its proper place did Miss Holly feel sure that it was the old Molly Glover with her trick of pushing a wisp of straggling hair behind her ear.

"I've never seen you at the Old Fairlavinian Reunion," said Mrs. Watson. "You ought to come some time. One of the old girls, you'd remember her, Pixie Macalister, she's games mistress at a mental home now, and does wonders with the poor things, teaching them all sorts of games with a soft ball and letting them have a free fight in the padded cell on their good days—it gets them uninhibited she says—and, where was I, oh yes, well Pixie belongs to a very nice club in the Buckingham Palace Road called the Ludo Club, from 'ludo,' I play, you know—do you remember Miss Stroke's Latin class, and how cross she used to get with gerunds and things—and she can get a room there for our meetings quite cheap. Last time I went to town specially for a reunion I spent the night at the Westmoreland, a splendid hotel with bed and bath and really *good* breakfast all included, and we had doodlebugs all night, only I didn't hear them. What I always say is, the one that's going to get you has your number on it, so why worry? But Charlie says, 'It's not the one with your number on it that worries me, Mollie. It's the one that says, To Whom It May Concern.' So I've not been to town again since, because I hate him to be worried."

At this point Miss Bunting and Anne arrived, and Mrs. Watson, having blown off steam, relapsed into her normal self as a kind hostess. Miss Bunting and Miss Holly had not met, but they had a kind of liaison through Dr. Sparling, and each conceived a respect for the other as an expert in her own line, while Anne talked quite happily to Mrs. Watson, who always got on very well with young people.

"What has happened to Charlie and Heather?" said Mrs. Watson, suddenly noticing that her husband and her guest were missing.

"If your husband is showing her an electric lathe, she won't come till she is fetched," said Miss Holly, but at that moment they came in, Heather with a black smear across her white tennis skirt. Had Miss Holly been an ordinary governess she might have felt impelled to remark on this; but being a remarkable woman in her own way, she simply absorbed the fact and made no comment.

Heather, who was by now not so red in the face, had passed a most agreeable quarter of an hour with Mr. Watson in his workshop, examining the lathe and entering into a highly technical conversation with him about bushes and chucks. Mr. Watson was both amused and interested by her artless talk. No woman, in his experience, knew anything about machinery or would ever want to; for being able to drive a car was simply a trick one learnt. Regarded with friendly tolerance by his wife as an enthusiast who spent on machinery and things time that would be far better employed on the tennis court or the golf course, he had in Hallbury no one to share his simple joys. To find a young woman—for Heather's imposing figure and large face somehow took her out of the category of girls—who could argue with him as man to man about turret lathes, poppers, precision work, repetition work and such homely subjects, was a perfect godsend. Had he not been almost as fond of tennis as of his tools they might have stayed there all afternoon, but it was tea time so he took his reluctant guest to the drawing room.

It has not, we hope, escaped our readers notice that Heather Adams, though much improved in person since she fell in love and into the Harefield lake, had very little social experience. Her father, self-made and slightly suspicious of what he called "society," had plenty of friends, or what passed for such, in his business world, but even in his wife's lifetime he had never brought them home. She had died some seven or eight years previously, and Heather had led a solitary life, attending the Barchester High School where she made no friends, her sole companionship at home being the housekeeper of the moment. None of these had been very good, none was bad, and she was well enough fed and clothed; but for recreation and talk she had drifted towards her father's works where the hands were friendly to her on the whole, especially the older men in the fitters' shops who had found her as useful as any boy and far more intelligent and less cheeky. When at last her father realized that his daughter was growing up, he had packed her off to the Hosiers' Girls' Foundation School, then evacuated to Harefield Park. Here Mrs. Belton had seen her and been kind to her and Heather had picked up a good deal, as had her father, who had pursued a curious unequal friendship with Mrs. Belton, whom he looked upon (rather unfairly for it was her elder son, not she, who had picked Heather out of the lake) as a kind of tutelary genius. Mrs. Belton had accepted this new responsibility as she usually accepted what came her way, and though she made no conscious effort to change or improve Mr. Adams, her influence with him had been considerable. His taste in clothes had become a little quieter, he had dimly realized that there were people to whom it didn't matter if you were rich or poor so long as you behaved like a gentleman, a word to which he now attached some favorable connotation.

But miracles are not expected and mostly do not happen. Mr. Adams did not turn into a Belton, nor did his daughter. The aboriginal Hogglestock was deep in them; they conceived a slightly suspicious attitude to unknown people, ready to heave half-bricks; but they had also seen and admired another world, and could feel fairly at ease in it when sure that its intentions were good.

So Heather, who a year or two earlier would not have been invited to a tennis party in the rather close society of a small country town, or if she had, would have glowered at her hostess, been sulky with the older people and rude to the younger, was now almost at her ease, quite ready to continue though not to initiate a conversation, and pleased with her host and his hobby. Her visits to the Beltons had made her fairly conversant with the county and Barchester types to which Mrs. Watson's party belonged, but Miss Bunting was something she had not yet come across. That Miss Bunting was old fashioned in dress, insignificant in appearance, rather precise in manner, was patent enough and from that point of view hardly worth study. But her newly awakened perceptions told her that this small elderly lady, whom any of her father's housekeepers would have scorned to resemble, was something that mattered. One does not have a scientific brain for nothing. Heather saw before her a fascinating problem which she meant to solve; and here she was well ahead of her father, who would have seen Miss Bunting's outer insignificance, but probably missed the significance behind it. What Miss Bunting thought about Heather no one can say: for Miss Bunting had been keeping her thoughts to herself for some half-century, and only to those whom she knew to be really interested would she open her store of a slow-garnered wisdom.

Mrs. Watson, saying that they would not wait for the others, now marshalled her party to the dining room, where there was a good sit down tea. Heather and Anne were placed together and told to make friends, such being Mrs. Watson's simple and direct method, while the grown-ups talked about the topics of the day, notably the sudden rebirth of glycerine, which everyone thought had left the world forever.

The two girls looked at each other. Anne's chief feeling about Heather was that she was alarmingly strong, yet curiously undefended, though she could not have put this into words. Heather saw a peaky girl, all eyes and nose, who looked as if one could knock her over by blowing, but somehow gave her an impression of living in a very safe world of her own. Each thought, though without formulating the impression, that the other needed some protection or help. Anne, being more used to Hallbury tea parties than Heather, opened the conversation by asking Heather if she liked tennis. Heather responded and though nothing very brilliant was said, both young ladies were getting on nicely, when Jane Gresham came in, apologizing for being late because Frank had been poking about in the scullery waste pipe again with a bit of old sponge on the end of a stick and the sponge had stuck and no one could get it out and of course it was Saturday and they'd have to wait till Monday to get it cleared. She then sat down by Miss Bunting, opposite Heather, and smiled at her.

The smile was merely general friendliness to include a strange girl who must be that Heather Adams they had talked about, but to Heather it appeared that the sun had risen, a very good firework display was taking place, peacocks with the voices of nightingales were swinging in cedar trees, their jeweled tails drooping over flower-edged, gold-sanded streams, and a full moon was filling the world with throbbing rapture. This is, of course, putting it rather mildly.

"You're Heather Adams, aren't you?" said Jane. "Isabella Ferdinand told me about you. I know her aunt."

As Heather did not reply, she smiled again and turned to Miss Holly. And then Robin arrived to whom Mrs. Watson said: "Better late than never."

"It nearly was never," said Robin, making a bow to the company and sitting down by his hostess. "I cleaned my tennis shoes and left them on the bathroom windowsill to dry, and one of them fell out into that horrible elder tree outside the pantry window and got stuck. I couldn't get at it with a stick and I daren't climb, so there it was. Luckily the cook's grandson was there, so in the end he got it."

"Is that Alfie?" asked Mrs. Watson, who was very strong on people's connections.

"No, Wallie," said Robin. "Adenoids, mentally defective, quite an intelligent child though if you show him twopence; even more intelligent if you show him sixpence. Do you suppose one could cure real full blown tonsils by bribes? Can I have some of that cake?"

The cake was in front of Heather.

"Will you cut it, Heather?" said Mrs. Watson. "This is Robin Dale. Heather Adams, who is staying at Mrs. Merivale's with Miss Holly; Robin's father is our Rector so you'll see him on Sunday."

Now, we cannot account for these things, but while Heather, for no reason at all, had at once taken to Anne with a kindly protective feeling, and had seen in Jane's entrance the veritable goddess appear, her almost immediate reaction to Robin was scorn and dislike. Perhaps his easy manner reminded her of Lieutenant Charles Belton, who had so brutally and unconsciously won and broken her heart on that fatal Sunday; perhaps she felt that a young man must be a softy if he couldn't climb a tree; perhaps she thought his attitude to mental deficients stupid and irritating, that he ought to be in the army. In any case the demon of gaucherie and ill breeding who had been so long exorcised came rushing back with outspread wings and fiery claws and caused her to say, quite against her own better judgment and with a voice she hardly knew: "I'm Chapel, so's Dad." After which she wished she was dead.

Luckily no one heard her. Except Anne, who felt so frightened that she almost wished she was dead too. But being a courageous creature for all her shyness, she decided that more than ever must she stand by her new friend, and asked her if she liked Shakespeare. Heather, burning with shame and anxious to make amends, said she liked him very much and told Anne all about the school performance of part of *As You Like It*, in which she had acted Audrey; and Anne's eyes grew larger and darker with interest and admiration. So tea came to an end, and stuffed with cake the party went into the garden.

*   *   *

As Anne had already, according to arrangement, had some coaching with Jane that morning, Miss Bunting had asked Mrs. Watson not to let her play too much. Mrs. Watson therefore arranged a four of Jane, Miss Holly, herself, and her husband. Miss Holly, the unknown quantity, proved unexpectedly good, bounding about the court like a hard rubber ball, sending a forehand drive with terrifying speed and pouncing on one or two backhanders like a cat on a mouse. So much did the four enjoy itself that by the time the score was thirteen fourteen, the onlookers lost interest and the two girls went to pick raspberries, while Miss Bunting and Robin sitting on the veranda, from which they could see the court but were out of earshot, talked about the subject near to both their hearts, little boys; approaching it from very different ages and points of view, but always with the welfare of those exhausting and pleasing beings in mind.

"What is so sad," said Miss Bunting, "is that so many little boys will go to school improperly prepared for communal life, because they will be only children. Mrs. Gresham's boy, for instance."

Robin admitted that it was hard on the children. Hard on the mothers too, he said. There was Jane who always meant to have a proper family, but with Francis away so long, what could she do?

"You know her nurse gave notice because there wasn't another new baby," said Robin, crossing his legs and nursing his unreal foot. "It's a bit stiff. And I must say it's a bit stiff for Francis too. He can't have any more children and he can't see the one he's got."

Miss Bunting's face grew very stern, for too many of her ex-little boys had no boys of their own, or would never see them again; or, like Francis Gresham, were perhaps alive, perhaps dead, and no one could know.

"I suppose," said Robin, thoughtfully, "I ought to get married and give a hand with the good work, but I'll have to get a proper job first. Six little boys in a stable isn't going to be good enough to marry on and my father, though eighty-two, is quite capable of living till ninety. Not that I grudge him the pleasure, if pleasure it is, dear old chap," he added.

"You will forgive me," said Miss Bunting after a silence, "if I look at things from a practical point of view. I always have: also a common sense one. Many excellent preparatory schools have been greatly assisted by a headmaster's wife with kindness, energy and money."

"But I can't be a fortune hunter, Miss Bunting," said Robin, alarmed. "And anyway, who wants a man with a wooden leg?"

The bitterness in his voice went to the old governess's heart, but it was never her policy to let her pupils suspect any weakness in her, so she merely said:

"Mr. Dale, you are talking in an exceedingly foolish way. You must pull yourself together."

Having said this she recrossed her hands with great composure and looked at Robin. He flushed angrily, made as if to speak, but apparently thought better of it. Presently he said:

"I'm sorry, Miss Bunting. And I wish you'd call me Robin. Mr. Dale isn't so friendly."

"Thank you, Robin," said Miss Bunting. "I will. All my old pupils," she added, "call me Bunny."

Robin flushed again, but this time with overpowering gratitude for her condescension. Not too awkwardly he took her chilly, withered hand, kissed it with an air and laid it respectfully on her lap. At the same moment the set finished and the Watsons, frankly rejoicing in having beaten their guests, brought the tennis players back to the veranda. Heather and Anne were recalled from the raspberry nets and with Jane and Robin went onto the court. Neither of the girls was very good; Robin, though once expert at the game, was hampered by his foot, and the set proceeded with more laughter than skill.

It is possible that Heather, who had worked pretty hard at

tennis during her last spring and summer term, would have played better had she not been overcome by the dazzle and glory of playing against Jane Gresham. Anne may have thought Miss Holly very nice, but there her admiration stopped. For Heather, the whole world was shaken by a new star, a Gresham Sidus, blazing in the empyrean. Not only was this shattering enough in itself, but she was also suffering from split personality, one half of her wishing to play so well that Mrs. Gresham would utter some such epoch-making words as: "Oh, well taken, Heather"; the other wishing to lose every stroke and then die at Mrs. Gresham's feet. The result of this dual control was that she hit more and more wildly, became as red and damp as when she had bicycled up the hill, and cannoned into Robin several times, nearly throwing him off his balance and making him swear under his breath. Anne, acutely sensitive to mental currents though she did not know it, was less and less happy. That she had made several good strokes and remembered what Jane had told her about foot-faulting that morning, counted for little with her in comparison with seeing poor Robin being buffeted and Heather looking so cross and almost horrid. However, the set must be played.

Meanwhile, the Watsons and Miss Holly joined Miss Bunting on the veranda. All were intelligent and Mrs. Watson was almost educated, so their talk roved in a gentlemanly way through a variety of subjects.

"Was that the bell?" said Mrs. Watson, interrupting her husband in his description of the Bishop entertaining some colored bishops at the palace with ostentatious want of profusion.

"You'd have heard it if it was," said Mr. Watson; which appears deplorably illogical but is plain to any householder.

"No, I wouldn't," returned his wife. "You remember that time it was Lady Pomfret and I was in the scullery."

The argument, if so it can be called, was proceeding along

these rather devious and irrelevant lines when a scrunching was
heard on the gravel at the side of the house.

"It *was* the bell," said Mrs. Watson, whose chain of reasoning
will at once be apparent, and even as she spoke a powerfully built
man in almost well cut gray tweeds came around the corner.

"Pardon me," said the newcomer, addressing himself to Miss
Holly, "but am I right?"

Miss Holly, recognizing her charge's father and correctly
interpreting his words, said to her hostess:

"Oh, Mrs. Watson, this is Heather's father. Didn't Mrs.
Merivale give you my message, Mr. Adams?"

"She did," said Mr. Adams. "As soon as I arrived back she said
you and Heth had gone to play a tennis match with Mrs.
Watson up the hill and you had said to give me a cup of tea. But
it's a bit late for tea so I said I'd push on a bit and see my little
Heth playing. Mrs. Watson, isn't it? I'm glad to meet you, Mrs.
Watson, and to thank you for your kindness to my little girl."

Mrs. Watson said she was so glad to have Heather, who was
on the court at the moment, and introduced her husband.

"Mr. Watson and I are old acquaintances," said Mr. Adams,
sketching a kind of salute to his host. "Clubmen, as you might
say. There's not many a Thursday I don't see Mr. Watson at
lunch at the County Club."

"So that's how Charlie spends Thursday," said Mrs. Watson
who, as she afterwards penitently told her husband, could not
help talking to people as she thought they would like to be
talked to, to which her husband replied that she would do it once
too often if she weren't careful. She then, to cover her lapse,
quickly introduced Mr. Adams to Miss Bunting, who greeted
him civilly and was quite obviously suspending judgment.

Mr. Watson quietly went into the house.

"Did you walk up, Mr. Adams," said Mrs. Watson, "or bicycle
like Miss Holly and Heather? It's a good pull up the hill."

"I don't bicycle," said Mr. Adams, "not unless I must, though
I've bicycled as far as most people in my young days before I

could afford a car," which piece of autobiography rather depressed his hearers as showing clearly that he regarded them as, on the whole, effete plutocrats. All but Miss Bunting who simply sat, accumulating evidence, waiting the right time to weigh it, unbiased, clear of mind.

"And I don't mind telling you, Mrs. Watson, that I wouldn't ride up that hill of yours for five pounds. No; my sekertary phoned up a taxi to meet me at the station. Now, it's a rule of mine, when you take a taxi, don't dismiss it till you're sure you've done with it. I've seen more than one good deal slip through my fingers before I learnt that. So when we got to Mrs. Merivale's house I said to the driver, 'Wait a minute, I may be going on.' And in I went and got Miss Holly's message and so I said to myself, Sam Adams, that's my name, Sam; you take the taxi to Mrs. Watson's and you'll kill two birds with one stone. You'll see Heth playing tennis and you'll see her friends. So I came up. Packer's waiting for me outside."

"Packer!" said Mr. Watson, who had come out with such drinks as the times could afford on a tray while Mr. Adams was finishing this soliloquy. "He won't come out for anyone on a Saturday afternoon, let alone wait for them. He always goes to the bowling club."

"He mayn't do it for anyone—thanks, lime and soda if it's all the same to you," said Mr. Adams, "but it isn't anyone or everyone who's got Packer's son in his nuts and bolts shop; and a very good apprentice he's making. Well, here's fun."

He took a deep draught of his innocuous beverage and looked around. The impression he made on most of his audience was overpowering size. Mr. and Mrs. Watson were tall and on a generous scale; Miss Holly, though short, had a good cubic content, but Mr. Adams reduced them all three to mediocrity. Only Miss Bunting, small, spare, almost insignificant to the eye, kept her value unchanged, as indeed she did whatever the circumstances.

A confused sound of talking now heralded the arrival of the

tennis party. Largely owing to Heather's love smitten condition, Jane and Anne had won the two sets and Anne, with quite a pink face, pleased and excited, looked a different creature. At the unexpected sight of her father Heather's face cleared and she flew into his arms with a rapturous shout of "Daddy!"

"And, Daddy," she continued, "this is Mrs. Gresham. She lives here with her father—your Admiral Palliser."

"A fine old gentleman, Mrs. Gresham," said Mr. Adams. "We think a lot of him on my board. You can't pull the wool over his ears, get up when you may."

Jane smiled at this tribute and Heather thought so did the angels smile.

"And this is Anne Fielding, Daddy," she went on. "She's awfully keen on Shakespeare. Daddy, couldn't we go to Stratford and see Shakespeare? Anne's never seen him, only read it. You know her father, Daddy."

"So you are Sir Robert's young lady," said Mr. Adams, taking Anne's hand and looking down kindly on her. "Well, him and I have had more than one tussle, but no bones broken, and he's a man I have a regard for."

After paying which tribute he looked so huge and important that Jane thought of the Frog and the Ox, and said so to Robin, who grinned.

"And Mr. Dale," said Mrs. Watson completing the introductions. "He has a school here and my younger boy and Mrs. Gresham's go there."

"Dale?" said Mr. Adams. "Seems familiar, but I can't exactly place it. Glad to meet you. I never got much schooling myself and dare say if I had I wouldn't be where I am now. Still, it's a good thing for them that can stand it. You aren't any relation of the Reverend Dale of the Barsetshire Archaeological by chance?"

"That's my papa," said Robin. "Eighty-two and going strong. I've heard him mention your name. You are coming to the Archaeological's meeting here, I hope."

Conversation now became general and the party soon broke up. Mrs. Watson, whose youngest son was spending the afternoon at Hallbury House with Master Gresham, asked Jane to send him home at once, as it was high time he had his bath and went to bed, so that she and Charlie could have their supper in peace.

"Daddy!" said Heather in an urgent undertone to her father, as he was talking to Mr. Watson, "couldn't you take Mrs. Gresham back? She hasn't got a car."

"That's an idea," said Mr. Adams, "and have a chat with the old Admiral. And what about you, girlie? I'll tell Packer to tie your bike onto the car if Miss Holly doesn't mind."

Miss Holly being consulted was agreeable to anything her employer proposed, and said she would walk her bicycle as far as Hall's End with Anne and Miss Bunting, and then ride back to Valimere. Robin, finding that no one wanted him, went back to the Rectory, thinking what a hideous lump that Adams girl was and pitying Jane who was saddled with her and her father for at least half an hour longer.

So Mr. Adams said goodbye to the Watsons, took his ladies in tow and found Packer sitting in the driver's seat reading the *Barchester Evening Sentinel*, to whom he gave instructions to convey the party to Hallbury House, return to Mr. Watson's house, fasten Heather's bicycle to the car and pick him up again at the Admiral's. Mr. Packer, without removing the cigarette from his mouth, said "O.K.," and what did Mr. Adams think of United Steel Products; up half a point they were. Mr. Adams said he didn't think, he knew, and all his spare cash was going into Government Loans. Mr. Packer looked dejected.

"Gambling," said Mr. Adams to Jane and Heather as soon as Mr. Packer's overdriven gears let talk be audible. "If I've told my hands once I've told them twenty times, small men must play for safety. And mind you, it's the British Empire we're backing, and if that isn't safe, no one knows what is."

"Except shares in an undertaker's business," said Jane.

Mr. Adams looked almost bewildered, then began to laugh with sudden uncontrolled amusement and Jane realized, and was slightly ashamed of it, that her remark had established her in his mind as a wit.

"Daddy's *frightfully* patriotic," said Heather admiringly, and Jane again felt ashamed that the word 'patriotic,' which heaven knew was what we all were, or ought to be, or wished to be, should make her feel uncomfortable and hoped her new friends would not notice it. But she might have spared herself the trouble, for Heather said she supposed we'd all be buried on a Beveridge plan now; and during the few moments that their journey lasted she and her father indulged in a joke of their own, almost unintelligible to Jane, about the actual calculations for such a scheme. It was a world she did not know and she suddenly felt lost, and thought of Francis with a pang of longing such as she had schooled herself not to encourage. But these things come upon us indirectly, sideways, and our defenses are vain.

The taxi stopped at Hallbury House and they all got out. Jane led the way to the garden, where she knew her father would be working. The Admiral was in his shirt sleeves among the beans and rather surprised to see his visitors, especially Heather whom he had never met and by whom he was much struck and that not very favorably, as he had always liked his womenfolk good-looking or smart, preferably both. But they were guests in his garden, so he showed them all his vegetables, his joy and pride, and discussed United States Products with Mr. Adams, while Jane showed Heather the fowls and the rabbits and the runner ducks and let her collect the eggs, and Heather walked in a roseate mist and hoped the visit would never end.

Her father's voice calling her to say good-bye then shattered her crystal globe, and they all walked around the other side of the house, where they found Frank Gresham and Tom Watson sitting on the back doorstep eating raspberries and cold rice pudding.

"I'm giving Tom his supper now, Mother, in case he doesn't

get enough when he goes home," said Frank, who was obviously being Harry Sandford to Tommy Merton.

"You must go now, Tom," said Jane, unsympathetically. "Your mother wants you."

"But, Mother," said Frank, casting a noble and protecting glance towards his friend, who was hastily running his spoon around the rice pudding dish to get the last bits of skin, "he *needs* his supper. Mother, if you'd been trying to unstop the scullery pipe, *you'd* need some supper."

"His supper is waiting for him at home," said Jane, rather annoyed to find herself arguing with her son over Master Watson's uninterested head. "Go along now, Tom, and you'll see Frank after church tomorrow. You can come to lunch if your mother says yes. Only go at once, or I won't ask you."

Master Watson got up with a satisfied expression, shook hands and said good night to everyone present, known to him or unknown, and disappeared. The Admiral, who had been looking at the scullery drain, now turned upon his grandson and asked if he had heard him say that pipe was not to be touched and what the dickens had he been doing. The eyes of all were then turned upon the mouth of the pipe, from which protruded a piece of decayed rubber.

"It's only one of the tires off that old pram in the Watsons' garage," said Frank in an aggrieved voice. "Tom and I got it off on purpose to help, and we poked it up the pipe and it got stuck, because bits of it kept breaking."

"Did I or did I not say that pipe was NOT TO BE TOUCHED?" said the Admiral.

"Oh, dear," said Jane, "Frank, you are very disobedient and we can't get a man till Monday. Go and get washed."

"Pardon me," said Mr. Adams, "but have you tried the U-joint?"

The Admiral indignantly said of course he had, but the obstruction was lower.

"Well, Admiral, what you want is a length of our pliable one-

and-seven-sixteenths annealed spang-rods," said Mr. Adams, kindly, as a keeper might reason with an elephant.

"Good God! you needn't tell me that, Adams," said the Admiral. "And where am I to get a spang-rod? Might as well try to get a razor blade."

"Good God! Good God!" said Frank, performing a small dance as he looked admiringly at his grandfather.

"Go and get WASHED!" said Jane, desperately.

"If Packer hasn't got one in the garage I'll have one sent out tomorrow from the works," said Mr. Adams. "Packer can run over and fetch it. Don't you worry, Admiral. We'll have that pipe cleared by lunch time tomorrow. Well, it's been a pleasure to meet you, Mrs. Gresham. That's a fine youngster of yours. What's your name, sonny?"

Frank, who had taken advantage of Mr. Adams's diversion not to go in and get washed, said he was Francis Gresham and he was going to be a sailor like his father.

"I didn't know your husband was a sailor, Mrs. Gresham," said Mr. Adams to Jane, "but of course he would be with your father an Admiral. He must be proud of this young man."

Jane, ever determined above all things not to allow her anxiety to cloud any friend's mind, said with a brilliant smile that he was very proud.

"But he can't see me," said Frank, "because the beastly Japs won't let him come home."

Jane could have killed her son; though, being a mother, one felt grateful and in an unreasonable way almost proud that Frank could speak without a shadow of his mythical father. Most luckily her father, whose sympathy, loving though it was, she shunned above all, was angrily wrenching at the pram tire and had not heard.

"Mrs. Gresham!" said Mr. Adams, shocked. "You'll excuse me. I hadn't an idea. I wouldn't for worlds—"

"You couldn't know," said Jane, summoning her smile and

speaking fast and low. "I've heard nothing for four years. No good speaking of it." And she looked towards Frank.

Sam Adams, as he would have said of himself, could take a hint with any man, once he knew where he was.

"I take you, Mrs. Gresham," he said, "Heather, come along, we mustn't keep Mrs. Merivale's supper waiting."

They went to the front gate.

"Good-bye, Heather," said Jane. "We must have some tennis again soon. I'll get Robin and Anne."

"Mr. Dale isn't very keen, is he?" said Heather. "He wouldn't even go up a tree to get his tennis shoe."

"Poor Robin," said Jane, not much noticing the dislike in Heather's voice. "His foot is still a trouble."

"Did he hurt it?" asked Heather, disturbed.

"Oh, it was blown to bits at Anzio," said Jane. "He manages very well with his artificial one. Good-bye, Mr. Adams."

She stood at the gate till the taxi had gone. Then, shutting her mind more firmly than ever against remembrance or hope, she went to see that her son gave himself more than a surface wash.

The taxi journey to Valimere did not take ten minutes, but into that time the Adams family packed a great deal of useless regret for spilt milk.

"Oh, Daddy!" said Heather. "It's too awful. I was beastly about Mr. Dale because I thought he was lazy and stupid, and all the time it was an artificial foot. And Mrs. Gresham will hate me for being so beastly."

"She'd be more in her rights to hate your old Dad for making such a fool of himself about her husband," said Mr. Adams ruefully. "I suppose I had ought to have known, but the old Admiral never said anything, and it stands to reason you don't know these family affairs by instinct. Well, well. Don't you worry, girlie. She's a fine woman and what you say isn't going to worry her one way or the other."

"Nor what you say neither, Dad," said Heather gratefully. "Do you like her, Dad?"

Mr. Adams said he'd like anyone who was good to his little Heth, if it was Hitler himself, though in saying that he thought he was pretty safe. And then Mr. Packer drew up at Valimere and received certain instructions about a spang-rod, with a tip which staggered even his views, nourished by subalterns on leave and Barchester magnates in a hurry, on that subject.

CHAPTER 6

On Sunday morning Heather, who had not slept for thinking of Jane Gresham; or rather, had thought of her quite often when she was not asleep, which is not exactly the same thing, would fain have persuaded her father to take her to the parish church in Old Town. But this he would not consider for a moment and indeed spoke to his dearly loved child very strongly on the subject of not getting above herself and thinking what was good enough for her dad and his mother before him, for the old man was never a one for going to any kind of service, not holding with being preached at not by Mr. Gladstone himself, wasn't good enough for her. If Heather had burst into tears and said: "But Dad, I want to see Mrs. Gresham," it is possible, though not probable, that he would have yielded, for he also felt that it would not be unpleasant to see that lady again. But he had his own plans for Sunday.

Mrs. Merivale, like many New Town dwellers, would have liked to go to the parish church, but after a week of housework and cooking and queues, and mostly lodgers and children as well, they felt they simply could not go more than a mile uphill either on foot or a bicycle, especially in one's Sunday clothes. So some of them said they would go next Sunday if it didn't rain, or at any rate on Christmas Day; some went to the New Town place of worship, which was so High that whenever it saw the words "Anglo-Catholic" it crossed out the "Anglo," and owing to lack of funds was a Petra-like temple, all front and practically no back, where they sat in gloomy disrelish of the clergyman's long cassock and peculiar ways, so gaining merit: and some again stayed in bed or mowed the lawn or pottered about in the little glasshouse or took the motor bike down.

If Mrs. Merivale was alone, her habit was to make herself a cup of tea and go back to bed, unless she had a daughter on leave who wanted a proper breakfast, though we must say for the girls that they were very good about putting the alarm clock forward an hour and taking a tray up to her for a surprise. But when she had lodgers she behaved just as if it were a weekday, so she gave Mr. Adams and Heather and Miss Holly a large filling breakfast, after which Miss Holly mounted her bicycle and rode away to Harefield to spend the day with a friend in the village, and have a talk with the caretaker at the school, while her employer and his daughter partook of the ministrations of the Reverend (by courtesy) Enoch Arden in a small red brick edifice with Anglo Saxon dog-tooth molding in yellow brick around the top of its front door, called Ebenezer.

In the Old Town, which had been there in some kind of form when the New Town was a wolf-infested swamp, there was not this variety of religious experience. You went to church or you didn't. Mostly you did, for the Old Town as a whole was fond of its Rector. There were many points in his favor. He was old, he had been there for thirty years and become part of the landscape; his young wife, so much younger than he, had died and he had with much propriety remained a widower, though as a matter of fact, if he had seen anyone he liked enough he would not have felt bound by his late wife's memory, deeply as he had loved her. And perhaps more than all these claims on his parishioners' love and respect, he had stuck to the old forms, so that everyone knew where they were. The Dearly Beloved Brethen was re-hearsed at length; the marriage service said what it has always said, without mealy-mouthed circumlocutions; the proper psalms for the day were sung; and Hymns Ancient and Modern were used, from a reasonable sized book, without the additions that have more than all the demerits of the older hymns and none of their warm familiarity. He also had the organist, who was the Hallbury stationer and lived with a half-witted brother, well under his thumb. There had been a terrible week, before the memory of the younger generation of Hallburians, when the organist, flown with three days at one of the Three Choir Festivals and the lordly talk of cathedral organists, knights too, some of them, had begun to intromit, as the Rector very alarmingly put it, with the simple chants to which the congregation were accustomed. He had furthermore essayed to give an extra touch of holiness to some of the sung responses by dragging their slow length along as unconsciousably as Charles II's death, so that the congregation's breath ran out. The Rector, sorely displeased, had yet bided his time, till on the twenty-fifth Sunday after Trinity the organist had surpassed himself in slowness on the response *And take not Thy Holy Spirit from us.* Several of the congregation looked about them with troubled faces, saw no help, and stopped singing in despair; while the Admiral, who was senior churchwarden and had a powerful voice, sang it at the pace at which he considered it should be sung, and then looked around with contempt on those timeservers who were bursting themselves over semibreves.

After the service the Rector had spoken his mind to the organist, smiting him with blasting and with mildew and with hail in the labors of his hands, after the manner of his favorite prophet, winding up by accusing the unfortunate stationer, in Haggai's own words, of earning wages to put them into a bag with holes. It was easy enough for the organist to demolish the Rector's arguments over his supper, telling his half-wit brother that a bag with holes in wasn't no argument at all, and all his savings went into the post office savings bank, but in face of his Rector he was dumb. Next Sunday the Rector preached a very powerful sermon about the wrath of Moses when he came down from Mount Sinai and found the Israelites worshipping the golden calf; and though the exact application of the sermon was not evident, it was felt that the Rector had scored a point. The responses were played after the old manner, the Rector invited his organist to come in and have a glass of excellent sherry, and when two days later the half-wit brother tried to throw himself out of the window, it was the Rector who sat with him till doctors and police could come and take him away to the County Asylum. Since that day there had been no further rebellions or innovations at St. Hall Friars.

On this Sunday morning Dr. Dale awoke with the calm and happy anticipation that Sunday never failed to bring him. From seven o'clock on this summer morning to after seven o'clock in the evening, he would be constantly in his beloved church, saying alone or in communion with his flock the words he loved, in charity with all men. All through the early service he moved and spoke in this golden mood, rejoicing in such of his flock as came, full of compassion rather than reprobation for those who did not. Among these was his son Robin who, more tired than he liked to admit by the tennis party, had passed a restless night till the early morning, when he had fallen into a deep sleep which his father had not disturbed. Waking at eight o'clock he had come down full of remorse, to find his father breakfasting alone.

"I'm very sorry, Father," said Robin. "I just didn't wake up."

"I am very glad you didn't," said Dr. Dale. "It would have been a good thing if you had slept all morning."

He then groaned.

"It's all right, Father," said Robin, though in a very general way, as he had not the faintest idea what his father was groaning about.

The Rector said he was an old man.

Robin, still in darkness and feeling his way carefully, said no one was old now.

"Whom the Lord loveth He chasteneth," said Dr. Dale. "But if it were His will to chasten us in ways we could understand, it would make life very much easier. I cannot, with all reverent submission, feel I have deserved this."

Robin, who was by now well into the excellent breakfast which the Rectory cook, ably seconded by the Rectory hens, had supplied, said with some indignation that his father didn't deserve anything; not *anything*, he said; and anyway what was it.

"I know," said the Rector, "that my lines are laid in pleasant places, but at times one is apt to forget. I had forgotten, I am ashamed to say, till Freeman reminded me this morning."

Robin, who knew that the verger was a walking church calendar, asked what Freeman had reminded him of.

"It was his duty," said the Rector. "Marmalade, please, Robin."

"And he did," said Robin, pushing the marmalade towards his revered and rather wearing sire. "Have you forgotten to marry someone, sir?"

"I hope not," said the Rector, anxiously. "I don't think Freeman would allow that. No. It is the Mothers' Union service this afternoon."

"Shall I write a sermon for you, Father," said Robin, who had partly for fun and most sincerely with a wish to help his father, dabbled from time to time in occasional sermons, not unsuccessfully.

"Thank you, Robin," said his father. "Thank you, my boy. It is very kind of you. The address is all right. I was correcting it only last night. It is that banner, Robin. I cannot away with it. In my church. In St. Hall Friars. An abomination of desolation. A greenery-yallery abomination. When I was a young man," he continued, talking half to himself as he often did, "I thought of an old church with regimental colors in the nave. Old colors with tattered ends and honorable scars. The gods are just and of our pleasant vices Make whips to scourge us. The old church was granted to me; and the banner. A just reward for presumption doubtless. I am glad your mother never saw it."

Robin, who though he sometimes wished he had a mother and then again after seeing Mrs. Tebben at Worsted or Mrs.

Rivers at Pomfret Towers, to which the Earl and Countess found it impossible not to invite her, was quite glad he had not, was not sentimental about it, said it was a jolly good thing mother never saw it and he was sure she would have loathed it. Anyway, he said, to make a person a saint because they'd let the pigs starve in Lent, didn't seem fair.

"Roast pork and crackling," said the Rector, gazing into space. "Yorkshire hams. Trotters. Pig's face and young greens. Gammon rashers. Everything."

Father and son were silent for a moment in contemplation of these raptures.

"And pork pies with lots of jelly," said Robin in a low voice. "No, Father, be a man. Think of Spam."

"Anathema maranatha," said the Rector without heat. "You are quite right, Robin. We must face facts. And I must not be selfish. The Mothers' Union almost worship that banner. When I say worship," he added, hastily, "I do not mean it in any derogatory sense. They are all good church women. Perhaps 'venerate' is the word I should have used."

"I wouldn't, Father," said Robin. "I don't think the Venerable Bede would like it. They just think it is a lovely banner and such artistic coloring," at which the Rector looked perplexed and Robin felt a little ashamed and told himself for the hundredth time that he must remember his father was of an older generation and might with luck and an earlier marriage have been his grandfather. So he got up, patted his father's shoulder reassuringly and went off to his own affairs. Dr. Dale then opened the Sunday paper which had just come and fell forthwith into such a transport of fury over the week's religious article which, hoping to reach the general public who never read that particular organ, made a so very unconvincing comparison between the Kingdom of Heaven and Big Business, with a hierarchy of managers, secretaries and accountants, some faithful in great things, some in small, as quite drove St. Ælla's banner out of his mind.

*   *   *

Morning service passed off peacefully. The Rector, fortified partly by prayer, partly by a very good Sunday lunch and a glass of port from one of a half-dozen given to him at Christmas by his old friend Lord Stoke, president of the Barsetshire Archaeological Association, addressed the Mothers' Union with kindness and sympathy, even going so far as to sketch a kind of blessing over St. Ælla's banner, which though carefully wrapped in blackout material was beginning to tarnish, thus adding a sickly browny green to the general effect. The Mothers' Union all said the Rector was a lovely man and went back to a tea party at Mrs. Freeman's cottage, each one bringing her own milk and sugar, the hostess supplying the tea and cakes. All of which Mr. Freeman duly reported to the *Barchester Chronicle*, where it appeared next Friday. By a careless mistake of the compositor, aged seventeen and a half, and with an eye on a reserved occupation, the names of the host and hostess appeared as Trueman. This led to unpleasantness, Mr. Freeman saying he wrote it plain enough for anyone as had learned his alphabet, the compositor maintaining that if people didn't give their "F's" a proper tail nor take the trouble to write clear, it was a pity there wasn't evening classes for adults at Hallbury, and didn't he know there was a war on. To which Mr. Freeman replied he'd thank the compositor not to talk like that to a man who was in the Mons Retreat long before his (the compositor's) father had to marry his mother, and he'd find there was a war on soon enough himself when the next call-up came around.

To turn to more peaceful scenes, Dr. Dale and his son then went to tea with Admiral Palliser. As Master Gresham was spending the afternoon with Master Watson and his rabbits, there was no interruption to a pleasant interlude. The weather was, as usual, too chilly to sit about outside, but after tea they strolled comfortably in the garden, the Rector and the Admiral discussing local matters, while Jane and Robin picked gooseberries in a desultory way.

"I went up to town last week to see old Thing," said Robin, apropos of nothing; thus irreverently alluding to the brilliant young orthopedic surgeon, Mr. Omicron Pie, whose grandfather Sir Omicron Pie had been a well known consultant, often called in by Barchester doctors.

"Had he anything to say?" said Jane.

"Not much," said Robin. "Blast those red gooseberries, they go off like a bomb at you."

"Tom Watson told Frank that people's feet grew again if they weren't too old," said Jane who, hard with herself, was sometimes deliberately hard to others. Not from unkindness. Perhaps from a feeling that it might brace them, as it sometimes braced her.

"He would," said Robin, not noticeably flinching. "Old Thing didn't say that. He said I was a very excitable case and not to overdo it."

"I suppose that's why you played tennis yesterday," said Jane.

"I suppose it is," said Robin. "But if it's any pleasure to you, I had a rotten night."

"I don't know that it's a pleasure," said Jane. "But it may teach you sense."

Robin said he didn't think so. Nothing, he added, taught one sense, not the kind of sense that meant not overdoing things, except getting so old that one jolly well couldn't. He then blasted another gooseberry and Jane said if he put more in the basket and ate less, that wouldn't happen. She then went on picking up the row while Robin picked down it, and not till they had got to the end and started on the next row did they meet again.

"Getting on?" said Jane.

Robin showed his basket.

"Not so bad," said Jane. "There was a fresh lot of people from the Far East last week."

"Repatriated?" said Robin.

"Repatriated—rescued—escaped," said Jane, as one who might say it's all one and doesn't interest me.

"Anyone know anything?" Robin asked, with no outward appearance of interest.

"Not a soul," said Jane. "Why should they?"

"People do hear of people who are missing quite ages afterwards," said Robin, doing his best to be as impersonal as Jane, but not succeeding so well.

"Yes; and they don't too," said Jane. "You can't count a man who had seen someone two years ago who thought he had heard of Francis a year before that. How I *hate* these gooseberries," she added with cold fury, holding up a finger gashed and bleeding from a long thorn.

"Suck it," said Robin.

"I am," said Jane rather mumblingly. "Beastly things, gooseberries. Spikes and bristles and pips."

"You look rotten," said Robin, stating a fact without emotion.

"I *hate* those bits of news that aren't news," said Jane. "One thinks about them at night. Come on, we'll give the gooseberries to Cook and you'll want to wash before evening service. Give me your basket and I'll go in the back way. No, empty it into mine."

She held her basket above the prickly gooseberry bush and Robin poured his gooseberries into it. Their eyes met. Each saw in the other an image of desolation, well chained and subdued. Jane laughed and went away towards the kitchen.

Robin could not laugh. Her lot was harder than his, for he knew the very worst. She had never known the truth, might never know it. He had his school, the offer of a job at Southbridge with a life of useful work. She could never make a certain plan again in her life, unless Francis Gresham returned or was proved to be dead. All useless. Everything was useless. He took his empty basket to the house, put it in the little garden room, washed his hands and joined his father and Admiral Palliser, who had come to anchor at a wooden seat on the flagged path which ran under the drawing room windows, and were enjoying some temporary sunshine. The elder men continued their talk about parish matters. Three quarters chimed from St. Hall Friars tower. Evening service at half-past six. Supper. Books. Bed. School next day. So it all went on. So it went on for poor Jane.

The noise of a car drawing up outside was heard. The door in the wall was opened and in came Mr. Adams and his daughter. No one can say that the Admiral was enthusiastically pleased to see his Chairman of Directors on that day and at that hour, but he put a good face on it and asked them to sit down.

"If it's all the same to you I'll stand," said Mr. Adams, who was holding a long thin parcel. "I've been sitting most of the day one way and another, what with the chapel and lunch and an afternoon with the papers. I'm putting on weight, and Sam Adams can't afford that. I have to get about a bit in my business. But that's not what I came to say, Admiral Palliser. What I came to say is this. You remember what I said about that scullery waste-pipe of yours was giving trouble."

Admiral Palliser said he did, and his grandson had managed to get it stopped up again.

"He'd get a good tanning if he was mine," said Mr. Adams, not vindictively, but as a matter of business. "But that's his mother's affair. Shall we have the pleasure of seeing Mrs. Gresham, Admiral? My little Heth here thinks the world of her."

Robin, near whom Heather was standing, saw her unattractive face go a dusky red and wondered what was up. She had been so deliberately disagreeable to him at the tennis party that he was rather frightened of her; for a well-bred young man has no weapon against the rudeness of a young woman. So he made no comment.

Admiral Palliser said his daughter was somewhere about, and would certainly be with them soon, as evening service was at half-past six.

Mr. Adams, undoing his parcel, said Sam Adams could take a

hint with any man and he had something to say on that subject, but one thing at a time was always his motto. He then extracted from its wrapping a metal rod which he pushed toward his host, who eyed it intently.

"It's a spang-rod," said Admiral, reverently.

"Same as what I said," said Mr. Adams. "Don't you touch it. It's a bit oily and I'm used to oil. Same as what I said; our pliable one-and-seven-sixteenths super-annealed spang-rods. I sent Packer over to the works same as I said. I'm sorry I couldn't get it before lunch, the way I said, but he had the car out for taking people to church this morning. But I said to myself, Better late than never, so me and Heth thought we'd come up and see about that pipe. And here is Mrs. Gresham. As I was just saying to the Admiral, Mrs. Gresham, I've brought the spang-rod, not that that's a subject ladies know much about, unless you call my little Heth a lady who was in and out of the works before she could speak, as the saying is."

"It reminds me of the old Ironsides," said the Admiral. "She was the supply ship for the Flatiron and all that Iron class. I've never had a ship with such first class stores. The chief engineer was a North-country man called Outhwaite, with a broken nose. I've never had a man under me who knew his job so well."

Mr. Adams, who had hardly been able to wait for the end of the sentence, said the way things turned out was something you wouldn't hardly credit, and did the Admiral know that Outhwaite was now the owner of the works at Newcastle where they got all those special castings done last year. Upon which the Admiral forgot time and place, plunging into technicalities with Mr. Adams. Six o'clock chimed. The Rector began to look uneasy.

"I fear I must leave you, Palliser," he said. "It is already six o'clock."

"Good God!" said the Admiral. "Sorry, Adams, but we are going to church at half past, so I can't see the spang-rod work. We must have another talk."

"Well," said Mr. Adams, looking around at the company who were now all at the disadvantage of being seated, "that is what I was coming to, but one thing at a time is my motto, and that's what I say in season and out of season as they say."

If his hearers felt that his remarks were not in season, they bore them well; all except the Rector, who with an apology to Jane Gresham got up and went away to meet his verger at St. Hall Frairs.

"Fine old gentleman," said Mr. Adams, following the Rector's progress to the garden gate. "But what I had to say concerned him as much as it concerns me. You see," he continued, "we went to chapel this morning, my little Heth and me, and it wasn't altogether what we meant. The reverend may have meant well, but all this politics in religion I don't hold with, and as good as communism which, believe me or not, does no good in my line of business, and so I told him afterwards. 'Look here, Mr. What-did-you-say-the-name-was,' I said, 'Adams is my name, Sam Adams. You may have heard of me,' I said, 'most people around Barchester have, and I don't grudge the pound I put in the plate,' I said, 'because a pound isn't worth more than seven and sixpence now, if that. *But,*' I said, 'if you think Jack's as good as his master, and believe me or not I know what I'm talking about, he's *not,*' I said. 'I've gone to chapel all my life,' I said, 'but it's a long lane that has no turning and this is where it comes and it's taking me to the Old Town this evening to the church.' So being a business man I said to Heth: 'We'll kill two birds with one stone and take the Admiral his spang-rod and go to evening service at the church.' Well, that's that."

This general confession left his hearers quite overpowered, and there was an exhausted silence till Jane, seeing her father turned to stone with the oily spang-rod in his hand, jumped up and said it was after the quarter, and they would be late and drove her father in to get the oil off his hands. Any awkwardness there might have been was then overridden and intensified by Mr. Adams, who cordially invited Jane to come with him and his daughter in the car. Before Jane could say yes or no, she found herself in Packer's car and within three minutes at the church gate, so there was nothing for it but to take her new friends in and settle them in the Palliser pew, which, as we know, was well provided with prayer books, if a trifle out of date; and here they were shortly joined by the Admiral who had walked up with Robin. It is not surprising that Jane had felt misgivings about letting the Adams family loose upon the church, but with her usual good sense she accepted them as guests of Hallbury House for the time being.

During the events we have just related, Heather Adams had not said a word beyond the usual greetings. To anyone who had known her a year or so ago, this would have seemed so normal as not to attract any attention, but since the Belton family had come into her life, Heather had acquired enough social polish to pass muster. But the sudden irruption of Jane Gresham upon a heart at the moment unoccupied had been cataclysmic, throwing her back into a schoolgirl stage of dumb adoration exhausting to all concerned, and very apt to be confused with the sulks. This Jane could not know, and merely thought that for so large a girl, brilliant at mathematics, well educated at the Hosiers' Girls' Foundation School, she was uncommonly gauche and heavy in hand. Jane was not sentimental, but a kind of practical compassion had made her befriend Heather at the tennis party and made her feel under an obligation to befriend her now, and as long as she and her father were Hallbury House guests. By which kind resolve she did, had she but known it, rivet the unlucky Heather's chains yet more strongly.

Heather, who was conversant with the order of the Church of England service owing to her attendance at Harefield Church with the Hosiers' girls, was next to her father and guided him efficiently through the prayer book, so that Jane, much occupied with her own thoughts, did not notice the occasional hesitations or mistakes of her father's chairman. At times she lost herself in the familiar words of the liturgy and the worm ceased to gnaw at her heart. Then with warlike phrases in the psalms, with the prayer for prisoners and captives, she was brought back to the old round of hopes and despairs, not knowing what she wanted or what she prayed for, longing to lay down a burden of doubt and self-torture that only she could bear.

Dr. Dale had a kind habit, encouraged by his doctor and his congregation, of giving the shortest of sermons at the evening service, so that before half-past seven, his hearers were at liberty to disperse. The attendance had not been large that evening, after the morning services and the Mothers' Union so that the unusual sight of strangers in the Hallbury House pew was very generally noted. The Watsons, who had brought Frank Gresham with them to return him to his mother afterwards, recognized Heather and her father. Sir Robert Fielding recognized Mr. Adams from their business meetings and hoped he would not have to introduce him to his wife. Not that he was more of a snob than most of us are, but he foresaw possible social complications for his extremely busy wife which were, to his mind, quite unnecessary. And they had heard enough from their daughter Anne about Adams's girl, for whom she seemed deplorably to have taken a liking at the Watsons'. Probably that girl in the Palliser's pew was she. Lady Fielding, one of the rare people who when worshipping do not at once become more than usually perceptive of their neighbors, simply registered the fact of strangers and thought no more of them. Anne Fielding, sitting away from her parents beyond Miss Bunting, recognized her new friend with pleasure and the protective feeling for which she could not account and wondered, with the slowly developing social sense that had lately begun to flower in her, if Mummy and Daddy would mind if she asked Heather Adams to tea one day. As for Miss Bunting, very little escaped that lady, but she had accustomed herself to observe, to classify, and suspend judgment until she knew, through some inward monitor, that she was right.

As the little congregation moved into the porch and onto the stone path that led to the churchyard gate, it was impossible not to greet friends.

"Mummy!" said Anne Fielding, pulling at her mother to attract her attention, "It's Heather Adams. I told you we played tennis at Mrs. Watson's. You remember her at the station, with Miss Holly. Hello, Heather!"

Heather was pleased to see Anne, who looked so fragile yet gave her such a sense of security; of poise, Heather might have said, had the word been familiar to her vocabulary; and in her turn she pulled at her father's sleeve.

"Daddy," she said, "it's Anne Fielding that I played tennis with at Mrs. Watson's. You remember her."

After this there was nothing for it but that Mr. Adams should renew his acquaintance with Sir Robert and be introduced to Lady Fielding, who with real kindness said how nice it was for Anne to have a friend of her own age, and asked if he and Miss Bunting had met.

"We have," said Miss Bunting, showing no disposition to shake hands yet acknowledging Mr. Adams's existence with a gracious bow of the head. Mr. Adams was conscious of embarrassment mingled with awe, feelings almost unknown to him, and was for a moment tongue-tied and afraid that he might be found wanting. The Watsons with the two little boys joined the party, and there was a general mixing after which it was obvious that Mr. Adams would forever be part of Hallbury Society, at any rate for so long as he and his daughter were in the neighborhood.

"Hello, sir," said the voice of Frank Gresham at the level of Mr. Adams's lower waistcoat buttons.

"I hear you've blocked the scullery drain again, sonny," said Mr. Adams, shaking the rather dirty hand that was offered to him.

"It was all the fault of the sponge," said Frank in an aggrieved voice. "It all got stuck in the pipe. People don't seem to understand about things getting stuck. Tom saw it, didn't you, Tom?"

he added, pulling Master Watson forward. "This is Tom Watson, sir. He is only beginning Latin. Do you know Latin, sir?"

"I don't," said Mr. Adams.

"Frank!" said his mother in an agonized undertone.

"But I'll tell you what I do know," said Mr. Adams, who had not heard Jane's interjection. "I know how to get the scullery pipe clear. I've brought a spang-rod for your grandfather."

"What's that, sir?" asked Frank.

"Something *you* don't know, sonny," said Mr. Adams, good humoredly. "Look here, Admiral," he continued as his host joined the group, "suppose I drive you and Mrs. Gresham back and we'll clean that scullery pipe here and now. It'll be a lesson to this young man. It's not half-past seven yet and I'll have the pipe clear by a quarter to eight, and then Heth and me must be off, or Mrs. Merivale will be wondering where we've got to."

Frank danced violently to express his approval.

"Come on, Tom," he said.

"No, Tom, you are not going back with Frank," said Mrs. Watson, who had overheard. "What I always say is, get two boys together and there's bound to be mischief. Come along."

"Now, I've a suggestion to make," said Mr. Adams. "Say I take your young man along to the Admiral's and as soon as that pipe is cleared I'll run him back in the car."

"Let him go," said Mr. Watson, who had been talking to Heather. "Heather can come back with us and look at a new chuck and Adams can pick her up when he brings Tom back."

Mrs. Watson gave in, saying that Charlie always had an eye for the girls.

"Well, good-bye, Lady Fielding," said Mr. Adams. "Pleased to have met you, I'm sure. I'm glad the girls have made friends. They'll have a lot in common, being only children. Send Miss Anne along to Valimere any time you like and I hope Miss Bunting will come too. Her and Miss Holly will have a lot to talk about, education and all that, and it'll do my Heth good. I'll

give you a ring when I'm down, Sir Robert, and we'll thrash out
that matter of the memorial window. Come on, young men."

Enveloping the Admiral, Jane and the two little boys, he
carried them off to Packer's car. His late audience looked at one
another, but could not well discuss him in front of his daughter,
so the Fieldings went back to Gradka's excellent supper and the
Watsons took Heather off to talk machinery with Mr. Watson.

It struck both Admiral Palliser and his daughter, when talking in the evening, that Packer, who was difficult to get, what
Mrs. Merivale called "choosy," making a favor of accepting high
payment for his rattle trap old car, changing people's appoint-
ments mercilessly, refusing (broadly speaking) to go out before
ten or after six, on Saturday afternoons or Sunday mornings,
was perfectly content to sit idle for hours while Mr. Adams
changed his mind and his plans. Not because they were what
Packer would call capitalists, for Mr. Adams was a capitalist on
a very large scale; not because they made or ever had made
unreasonable demands, for never would they have dreamed of
treating him or dared to treat him as Mr. Adams did. And
regretfully they came to the conclusion that Packer preferred
Mr. Adams because he was not a gentleman and ordered him
about. It did not pay, the Admiral said, to ask people politely if
you wanted anything done. The Adamses gave their orders and
took it for granted that they would be obeyed; just as he, the
Admiral, had done in his flagship. Why had the leadership
passed from the Admiral and his like? There was no satisfactory
answer; but the Admiral considered Mr. Adams in a battleship,
and felt that there at least he would find his level pretty quickly,
which comforted the old seaman.

"You know, Father," his daughter had said, "it isn't really so
bad. Mr. Adams may be a J.P. and even an M.P. in time, but I
don't think the county would stand him as Lord Lieutenant. All
the same there's something rather nice about him. A kind of
person who gets things done."

At which the Admiral had glared at his daughter over his

spectacles, and said Adams wasn't the only one who got things done, and it was probably people saying things like that about Hitler that had got him where he was.

But leaving these social changes, let us return to Hallbury House, outside which Packer was sitting in his car, reading the Sunday paper folded very small, thus betraying his standard of intelligence to anyone who cared to take notes. Though why to read the *Times* with the sheets flapping about like animated bedclothes should be the mark of cast, as against reading other organs which it would be invidious to mention very neatly packed into what almost becomes a cube, we cannot say. Are we to judge our fellow creatures by their capacity to read rapidly, with the eye rather than the mind, as against reading line upon line with practically no mind at all? The answer would appear to be that a good many of us do.

While Packer was mastering the details of L.-Cpl. Hackett, L., 43537201, coming back from Burma after three years to find his wife with twins of two and an idiot baby all of whom were taught to call the sergeant at the local Hush-Hush camp "Daddy," and shooting the whole lot of them, and then giving himself up to the police with the words, "All right, mates, I done it," Mr. Adams, a small boy grasping each hand, led the way to the back of Hallbury House, followed by Jane and the Admiral, who was lovingly carrying the oily spang-rod. It did occur to Jane and perhaps to her father that it was as a rule the host who took his guest to any given part of a house or garden, not the guest who took the host, but Mr. Adams being obviously an elemental force, they resigned themselves to fate.

"Now," said Mr. Adams, shaking himself free of the little boys and taking off his coat, "we'll see who's master. Got the spang-rod, Admiral? Thanks. What you want is some cotton waste," he added, as the Admiral rubbed his rather oily hands on the grass edge.

"Cotton waste!" said the Admiral, angrily. "Good God! Man,

do you suppose I can get any? And when I think I could have it in the bale when I was at sea. Well, well."

"Here you are," said Mr. Adams, pulling a lump out of the pocket of his discarded coat. "Never without it. I'll tell my sekertary to see they send you some from the works. Now, you boys, here's something you haven't seen."

From another pocket he extracted a kind of small rubber dome, set on a wooden handle.

"See this, young men?" said Mr. Adams. "This is first-aid for scullery pipes. Press it down over the hole in the sink, then pull it up. You'll have to pull, because—"

"I know, sir," said Frank, eagerly, and (to his mother's ear) pretentiously. "It's a vacuum. Vacuum is Latin for empty. Did you know that, sir? Tom hasn't got as far as that yet. He's only doing first declension, aren't you, Tom? *Vacuus, vacua, vacuum, vac—*"

"That's all very nice, sonny, but it won't unblock your grandad's pipe," said Mr. Adams, who appeared to be becoming a close relation to the whole family. "Now you listen to me. Next time the pipe gets blocked, I don't say by the cook, I don't say by one of you young men, try the squeegee first. And if that doesn't work, try the spang-rod. Here, what's your name, Frank, you go into the scullery and when I say 'Go,' turn the tap full on."

"Oh, Mr. Adams," said Jane, "I don't want to interfere, but cook," at which name she involuntarily dropped her voice and looked around nervously, "is very difficult and—"

"That's all right, Mrs. Gresham," said Mr. Adams. "That's why I sent that lad of yours in. Cook won't mind him, and what's more he won't mind cook. Besides I'll lay an even sixpence that she's out. They always are on Sunday evening, with cold tea for the family. If I had my way I'd have a good big hot meal every Sunday evening. That'd teach them."

With which highly undemocratic words Mr. Adams began to push the spang-rod up the pipe. It went up like Aaron's rod, twisting obediently to its master's hand. In a moment he appeared to be satisfied, withdrew the rod and called out "Go!"

At once the roaring of water coming off the main was heard, and down the pipe came an avalanche of mixed filth with a core of sponge.

"Stop her," Mr. Adams called to Frank.

The roaring ceased.

"Is there a kettle boiling?" said Mr. Adams.

"Yes, sir," shouted Frank.

"If you'll pardon me, Mrs. Gresham, I'll just finish the job," said Mr. Adams, turning to the scullery door, when he felt something pulling him and looking down saw Master Watson.

"Well, sonny," said Mr. Adams.

"Oh, sir, can I see the evacuee?" said Tom.

Mr. Adams looked perplexed, then laughed and told Tom to come inside. In a moment or two boiling water with heaps of soda in it came rushing down the pipe. Mr. Adams and the two little boys, now in a state of simmering hero worship, emerged, and Mr. Adams put his coat on and said he must be off. The Admiral and Jane escorted him to the gate, the general progress rather impeded by the affection of the two little boys for their new patron, an affection expressed by hanging heavily on any parts of him they could reach, and getting among his legs; but Mr. Adams took it all in good part.

"Get in, Tommy," he said to Master Watson, not so much as an affectionate diminutive as a comprehensive name for small boys. "Well, good-bye, Admiral; good-bye, Mrs. Gresham; good-bye, young man."

And he already had one foot in the car when Dr. Dale came up, for it was that gentleman's habit to partake of a cold supper with Hallbury House every other Sunday or so, to give his staff a free evening, while Robin went to one or another friend, or to the Omnium Arms, where they still had a fairly good dinner. Much as the Admiral and his daughter loved their Rector, they could have wished that he had arrived even one minute later, for being now rather exhausted by the way Mr. Adams had taken over the house and the little boys, they were thoroughly glad, though in a grateful way, to be seeing the last of him. Mr. Adams withdrew the foot he had placed in the car.

"I fear I am late," said Dr. Dale. "Freeman detained me about the Barsetshire Archaeological next week. We are having some of them at the Rectory, you know."

Mr. Adams, taking the role of both host and hostess upon him, greeted the Rector warmly and said that was the kind of sermon he *did* like. Not a lot of communistic claptrap like the reverend down in the New Town, he said, but what he *called* a sermon; short, sweet, and to the point, at which the Rector, who had simply filled up seven minutes in an adequate way, was surprised and flattered.

"Chapel I was born and Chapel I was bred, you know," said Mr. Adams, to the despair of his audience who neither knew nor cared, "but me and Heth—that's my daughter, you know, Rector—heard such a bellyful of nonsense if you'll excuse the expression down at the chapel this morning that we said we'd try C. of E. and very pleased we were."

The Rector, who was not used to such manifestations, said he was but a humble instrument in the hands of One who moved in His own mysterious ways.

"His wonders to perform," said Mr. Adams. "Quite right, and if you asked them at Hogglestock they'd tell you it *was* a wonder to find Sam Adams—that's my name, Sam—in a church. Well, good-bye all. Good-bye, Mrs. Gresham. My little Heth is quite taken with you. Mr. Watson's."

These last words were spoken to Packer, who had after long and intensive study, got to the place where L.-Cpl. Hackett had been remanded in custody. He folded the paper even smaller and put it in his pocket. During his short delay Dr. Dale was greeting his Hallbury House friends for the third time that day, and said he had brought the church accounts with him as they were even more confusing than usual, and he hoped the

Admiral, his senior church warden, could get them unentangled.

Telling Packer to wait half a jiffy, Mr. Adams, to the ill-concealed horror of the speakers, put his large head and powerful shoulders out of the car, looking rather like Mr. Punch when in vacant or in pensive mood.

"Excuse me, I'm sure," said Mr. Adams, "but hearing the word 'accounts,' I couldn't help hearing what you gentlemen said. You gentlemen need someone to do the accounts for you. It's my motto, never do anything yourself unless you can do it better than the man on the job, and that's why I've never so much as looked at a column of figures, not to add them up, since I got into a big way. Give me a company report and I know my way about as well as any man, as anyone in Barchester will tell you. But I don't keep a dog and bark myself. I pay my accountants to do their work and do it well; and it pays them to do it well. You didn't ought to be doing those accounts, Rector, not at your age. You gave me and my daughter a most gratifying experience in your church tonight. Sam Adams never owed any man anything and he's not going to begin. I'll send one of my men down to run through those accounts of yours any day you like to name, and he'll have everything so that the Pope himself couldn't find fault, balanced to the last penny. Well, that's a bargain. Good-bye everyone. Right, Packer; Mr. Watson's."

The car moved away. A deep religious hush fell upon the survivors.

"Good God!" said the Admiral.

"I'd say so myself if I wasn't a clergyman," said Dr. Dale.

"Good God! Good God!" said Frank Gresham, dancing on one leg, and quite unable to understand why the three elders, excluding Dr. Dale who had never been known to say a harsh word except about the Bishop of Barchester, should all pounce on him with such fury that he was for once quite subdued and ate his supper in complete silence.

CHAPTER 7

It must not be thought that Miss Holly and Heather Adams were idle during these weeks. We have only numbered the serene, or fairly serene hours, but Miss Holly and her pupil worked very hard, and such was Heather's application and her native intelligence that Miss Holly foresaw that she might take a very good place in the mathematical tripos, and was sometimes only just able to keep ahead of her. For though mathematics was Miss Holly's subject, she had of late years rather deserted them in favor of general secretarial work for Dr. Sparling at the Hosiers' Girls' Foundation School.

Anne Fielding had of course got permission to ask Heather and Miss Holly to tea, during which Miss Bunting, who saw no sense nor usefulness in pure mathematics, had introduced Heather to The Loves of the Triangles. Heather, whose sense of humor was rudimentary, owing its bare existence mostly to Mrs. Belton, read this work with stupor, with dawning apprehension and finally aloud to Miss Holly, though almost inaudible because she laughed so much.

At Hallbury House there had been a serious consultation about Mr. Adams's offer, or rather threat, of an accountant. It seemed ungracious to refuse, yet very difficult not to accept after the tacit consent that Mr. Adams had taken for granted. The Admiral and the Rector so havered and hairsplit over the matter that at length Jane Gresham, rather impatient with men, offered to see Mr. Adams about it herself, an offer which the men in a cowardly way accepted. No time must be lost. Mr. Adams was a man of deeds as well as a man of an exhausting number of words, and the accountant might descend, unheralded, upon St. Hall Friars at any moment. The following Saturday was the Barsetshire Archaeological meeting and everything would be in turmoil for two or three days beforehand, so Jane rang up Miss Holly and put the matter to her. Miss Holly, who combined perfect loyalty to her employer with an aloof and amused sense of his peculiarities, quite understood the position and said he would be at Valimere on Wednesday for the night, and if Mrs. Gresham would like to come to tea, he would arrive soon afterwards and would she like to bring Frank. Jane said that though she loved Frank very much, she did not particularly want to take him anywhere, as he was going through a stage of boasting that made her feel ashamed of him, but if Miss Holly didn't mind——Miss Holly said she had not been the elder sister of five brothers for nothing, and by all means bring him along.

So on Wednesday when Frank got out of school he went back with Master Watson and picked up his mother at the camouflage netting.

"Mother, can Tom come with us to tea with Heather?" said Frank. "He wants to come, don't you, Tom?"

"Certainly not; he hasn't been asked," said both mothers with one breath.

"I only thought it would be a treat for him," said Frank in an aggrieved voice. "He gets lonely without me, Mrs. Watson."

"Not a bit," said Mrs. Watson cheerfully. "And you've got to clean your rabbits, Tom."

"Oh, Mother; oh, Mrs. Watson, can I stop and help Tom to clean his rabbits?" said Frank. "You need someone to help you, don't you, Tom?"

Both mothers squashed the suggestion.

"I've got a bulgineer," said Master Watson confidentially to

Master Gresham whom he looked upon as a sensible sort of fellow, more or less his own age.

"What *is* he talking about?" said Jane to Mrs. Watson. "Does he mean an engineer, and if so why?"

"I don't think so," said Mrs. Watson doubtfully, "though he does mix words up dreadfully. What is it you've got, Tom?"

"Bulgineer," said Master Watson in a fatigued voice. "Bulgi-neerbuk; *you* know, Frank."

"Mother!" said Frank reproachfully. "Belgionair—a buck— *you* know."

"Your Belgian hare you mean," said Mrs. Watson, which remark appeared so stupid to her son, who had been saying the same thing with all his might, that he scowled softly at his mother and went off to clean his rabbits' cages.

That day was a lost day to Miss Holly and Heather Adams so far as work was concerned, for the idea of Mrs. Gresham, the Admiral's daughter, which sounded like Happy Families, coming to tea was such an event to Mrs. Merivale that she had to discuss the arrangements for their reception from breakfast time onwards. Miss Holly and Heather would willingly have had their breakfast in the bright kitchen with their hostess when Mr. Adams was not there, but she was adamant on what was due to paying guests and gave them excellent breakfasts in the dining room where the Elle-woman's head always had fresh flowers. Once or twice it had been warm enough to have it on the little veranda, but more as a gesture than anything else and they gladly went back to the dining room and Mrs. Merivale said a lodger was very nice; a generalization which they were glad to hear.

"Miss Holly," said Mrs. Merivale, putting a tray with coffee jug and milk jug on the table that morning, "which tea cloth do you think Mrs. Gresham would like?"

Miss Holly, suppressing a desire to say that it wouldn't matter in the least as Mrs. Gresham probably wouldn't notice, said which one was Mrs. Merivale thinking of.

"Well, there's the one with the violets embroidered on it," said Mrs. Merivale, pleating the edge of the breakfast cloth as she spoke, "only they're a bit washed out. The one with the ecru lace is nice, if it weren't for the darn in the middle; that was where one of my guests put a cigarette. She was a *dreadful* woman. I used to lie awake at night and wish she were dead, which was very ungrateful as she paid punctually every week, but she used that nasty-scented soap and the bathroom simply *reeked.*"

Miss Holly said the darn wouldn't show a bit with a vase of flowers on it.

"But I'd be upset all the time," said Mrs. Merivale, trying not very successfully to flatten the pleats, "thinking she would notice the darn."

Miss Holly said she expected Mrs. Gresham's linen was all darned by now. Everyone's was.

"Or the little one with the waterlily border," said Mrs. Merivale, "that Annie embroidered for me when she was twelve. She was always so clever with her hands. And there's the open-work one, drawn thread you know, but it's gone nearly everywhere. I used to have everything so nice, Miss Holly, when Mr. Merivale was alive, and it upsets me to see everything falling to pieces. Which do you think Mrs. Gresham would like? I'm sure she's used to having everything dainty about her at home."

Miss Holly, with admirable patience, said she thought the waterlily-bordered cloth would be very nice, and she was sure Mrs. Gresham would be interested to know that Mrs. Merivale's daughter had embroidered it, and Mrs. Merivale went away temporarily satisfied. But not for long. At intervals during the morning a light tap at the door would be followed by an agitated appeal for guidance on some essential point such as did Miss Holly think Mrs. Gresham would like China or Indian; would Mrs. Gresham like cucumber sandwich or jam or both; did Miss Holly think Mrs. Gresham would like the little doilies with the picot edge or the green linen ones with the hemstitch only they were a bit faded. Miss Holly gave calm and she hoped soothing answers while Mrs.

Merivale twisted her hands and her overall and her feet more desperately.

"Oh, just one more thing, Miss Holly," said Mrs. Merivale, coming in without knocking, her hair curling more than ever in her tribulation. "About guest towels."

Miss Holly had just been trying to explain to Heather, who was getting sulkier and sulkier, Widdowson's Law of Inverse Relations, about which she was not quite sure herself, not having paid much attention to it when she took her degree. She looked up with a rather strained patience and said, "What about them?"

"Oh, I *beg* your pardon," said Mrs. Merivale, with the alarming refinement that occasionally overtook her. "You are busy, Miss Holly."

"Not really," said Miss Holly, who was fond of their kind, silly hostess in her own practical way and did not at all wish to seem brusque, or in Mrs. Merivale's phrase to upset her: "Tell me what's the matter."

"It's the guest towels, Miss Holly," said Mrs. Merivale, twisting a duster that she was carrying into a kind of rope. "I *would* like to have everything nice in the bathroom if Mrs. Gresham wants to wash her hands, and I was wondering if she'd like the real Irish linen towel, only it's getting so thin, or the little fancy towel with the ducklings in couch stitch. She has got lovely ones at Hallbury House I expect, and I'd like to give her the best."

"The Irish linen one," said Heather, who had not hitherto taken any part in these discussions.

"Oh, *thank* you," said Mrs. Merivale, and went away.

"And she wouldn't care which one really," said Heather, barely waiting for the door to close behind their hostess. "People like that don't have guest towels. Mrs. Belton didn't. Lady Fielding doesn't. It's like fussing about doilies and things. Proper people just don't. Mrs. Gresham wouldn't notice anything. All she thinks of is being kind to people."

And the unhappy Heather flushed deeply.

Miss Holly continued her exposition of Widdowson, up to his famous "Friction of Constants," which Heather at once seized and mastered. On what had just occurred Miss Holly made no comment, for it had for some time been plain to her practiced schoolmistress's eye that Heather was in for a bad attack of heroine worship. They all had to have it, and it had to run its course. But Miss Holly did devoutly wish that Heather Adams had contracted this form of mental measles while still at school, where it would not have given much trouble, instead of saving it up till the vacation before she began college life. Still, a good attack now might inoculate her against much further trouble, and Mrs. Gresham was a far more suitable object for adoration than a female don of any age, in Miss Holly's opinion. She felt sorry for Mrs. Gresham if this heavy devotion was to be hung about her neck, but that was really no business of hers, so they did some exercises on the "Friction of Constants" and the "Laws of Relations" and then it was time for lunch. And after lunch they had a few sets of tennis on the New Town courts and came back to get tidy for tea.

Miss Holly, with calm and fatal prescience that her charge was going to give trouble, had taken the precaution of asking Mrs. Merivale if she would join them at tea, saying, most untruthfully, that she knew Mrs. Gresham would like it. Mrs. Merivale, after objecting that her hair needed washing, that she was sure they didn't really want her, that she did want to keep an eye on the cakes, that she wouldn't know what to say to Mrs. Gresham and would be so upset if Mrs. Gresham noticed anything, though what kind of thing she did not particularize, ended by accepting and thereupon falling into a frenzy of cake-and scone-making, for which she was famous even with rationing, and so was upstairs putting on her best afternoon frock when Jane rang the front doorbell and was admitted by Heather. The result of this was that after the three ladies and Frank had sat in the drawing room, or lounge as Mrs. Merivale preferred to say, for a few moments, she herself opened the door, showed a pale and streaky face and saying, "Your tea's all ready, Miss Holly," vanished.

"Oh, dear," said Mrs. Gresham, who guessed that something was wrong.

"I think it's because Heather opened the front door to you," said Miss Holly. "Mrs. Merivale may think it was meant as a slight, because we didn't think she was good enough to open the door, or a reproach because she wasn't down then. You never know."

Jane very sensibly said the best thing would be to go into the dining room and hope for the best. So they went to the dining room where tea was to be laid, trying to pretend that all was well, but as far as Jane and Miss Holly were concerned, slightly nervous. For to those who do not live in a world where to take offense is almost a social duty, the atmosphere can be very frightening.

However, by great luck Mrs. Merivale came out of the kitchen with a very special silver jam spoon she had forgotten, and before she could retreat Jane Gresham had greeted her warmly and shaken her hand and said how glad she was that Mrs. Merivale was in, otherwise she wouldn't have seen her. An idiotic, nay a fatuous remark; but it served its turn, for Mrs. Merivale, who had a very high sense of duty towards lodgers, couldn't possibly leave them without the special jam spoon. So, without quite knowing how, she found herself seated at the table and Miss Holly, with a kind of apology for being hostess in Mrs. Merivale's own dining room, was asking her how she took her tea.

"Oh, after Mrs. Gresham, *please*," said Mrs. Merivale, unfolding the green linen doily with the hemstitch, and at once making a cocked hat of it.

So Jane with great composure accepted the first cup, while Heather sat and gently glowered, which was her way of expressing her admiration of her idol's social gifts. Frank behaved with exquisite politeness, passing cake and sandwiches to everyone with ceaseless courtesy of a fatiguing nature. In front of Mrs. Merivale and Frank and Heather, the great subject of Mr. Adams's offer of an accountant could not be approached, so Jane and Miss Holly worked very hard at finding topics of conversation, a task which was not made easier by Mrs. Merivale's abnegation, not to say self-abasement, before every subject that was introduced. If it was a concert she said she wasn't really musical like Mrs. Gresham; if it was a novel she said she couldn't read highbrow books like Miss Holly; if the Royal Family (an almost sure card in most cases), she said she hadn't been to Court like Mrs. Gresham, which drove Jane, who had not been presented, and though full of loyalty had never particularly wanted to be, into a kind of inverted snobbism; if a film, she said she could never seem to have the time to go to the pictures now, as she was glad to get to bed as soon as she had washed up the supper things, thus making Jane and Miss Holly feel like Legree. And all this with such writhings and twistings of her fingers and hugging of her elbows and, as Miss Holly well knew, twistings of her legs under the table as made her friends almost as sorry for her as they were for themselves.

Frank, having by special invitation eaten the last of everything as Mrs. Merivale said it upset her to see anything left in case it was nasty, now turned his powerful mind upon his hostess.

"Do you live here alone, Mrs. Merivale?" he asked. "It's a very nice house."

Mrs. Merivale colored most becomingly.

"I've got four little girls," she said, suddenly becoming quite human. "Annie and Elsie——"

"And Tilly and Lacey," said Frank, giggling at his own wit.

His mother sat aghast, praying that Mrs. Merivale would not take it as an insult.

"No, Evie and Peggie," said Mrs. Merivale, adding, "but they don't live in a treacle well."

The answer was so unexpected, so out of keeping with Valimere, that Miss Holly and Jane were left speechless and ashamed of themselves for having snobbishly underestimated their hostess. On comparing notes afterwards they found they had both expected her choice in fairy stories to be the nauseous and popular series of Hobo-Gobo and the fairy Joybell. And all the time Mrs. Merivale had been a highly educated woman.

"Do they wash up?" said Frank.

Mrs. Merivale said they did when they were at home, but they were all away now in the A.T.S. and W.A.A.F. and W.R.N.S., or in America.

"Shall I help you to wash up?" said Frank. "I help Cook and Freeman, and Cook says I polish the glasses like a real butler."

Mrs. Merivale seemed delighted by this proposal, and after a purely formal protest against visitors giving a hand, she lost interest in the grown-ups and dismissed them to the sitting room, while she and Frank piled the tea things onto a trolley and wheeled them away. Heather then said she was going to walk up to the station and come back with her father, so Jane and Miss Holly were left alone, when, casting delicacy to the winds, Jane asked Miss Holly if she could give her any help. Mr. Adams, she said, had been so extraordinarily kind, and it was going to be very difficult, she feared, to refuse his kindness without hurting his feelings. What did Miss Holly think?

Miss Holly, who thought Jane Gresham a very sensible young woman, expounded her views of her employer's character, formed during the last year or two.

"Like most of us," said Miss Holly, "he has changed a good deal as the war went on. If that silly Heather hadn't fallen into the pond and been pulled out by Commander Belton, we would never have heard of him except as a parent. He was quite content in his own station. I say this without feeling," said Miss Holly, "for I haven't any particular station myself except what I can make. But he formed a kind of reverent attachment for the Belton family—I really don't know how to put it otherwise—and has paid great attention to Mrs. Belton. He isn't a fool socially and if he wants to get on that way he will learn. So will

Heather up to a point. But whether they'll be happier or unhappier for having immortal longings in them, I couldn't say. He admires you, because you are Mrs. Belton's sort. So does Heather. And what you say will probably carry weight. But if he did take it the wrong way he can be nasty. I don't think he will, though."

"Oh, dear," said Jane. "But I must save dear Dr. Dale from an accountant. He might have a stroke, or go mad if anyone came and interfered, poor darling. Someone has got to do it."

"Well, my money's on you," said Miss Holly, in an unexpectedly dashing way. "I do quite a lot of betting through the Harefield butcher," she explained calmly, seeing the surprise that her guest could not quite conceal. "Only in half-crowns. But it's my vice, and a great comfort to me."

Jane was much interested in this sidelight on a distinguished mathematical scholar and would have liked to pursue the subject but for delicacy; and also from a slight fear that she might find that Dr. Sparling was implicated in the Black Market and Mrs. Belton a secret drinker. So she thanked Miss Holly for her advice and they went into the once pretty, now overgrown garden and pulled up some weeds, though nothing short of a motor plow would have made any real impression, and talked of other things, and Jane tried not to feel frightened of the impending interview. Then Heather came back with her father, clinging affectionately and heavily to his arm, as Frank was accustomed to cling to his mother's; but the arm was a very massive one and its owner did not appear to feel his daughter's weight an encumbrance.

Having brought her two idols together, Heather Adams was quite prepared to stay and watch them, but Miss Holly on some adequate pretext drew her into the house and Jane felt slightly sick. A rickety garden seat stood in the sun against a little glasshouse and here it seemed warm enough to sit down, which Jane gladly did. For though the daughter of a long naval line, she could have wished that her knees felt less like cotton wool.

With all the tact she could muster she spoke of Heather and

how proud her father must be of her, a tribute which Mr. Adams accepted with great complacency not untinged with pride. She then spoke of Mrs. Merivale and how glad she was that Mr. Adams had such a pleasant hostess for his daughter and how nice it was for Mrs. Merivale to have such pleasant guests: all of which Mr. Adams again accepted as his due.

"Though mind you, Mrs. Gresham," he said, "it's all your doing that we came here and that's a thing I can't thank you for enough."

Jane disclaimed any responsibility beyond having been to Mr. Pattern and sent details of the house to Mr. Adams by her father.

"That's what I say," said Mr. Adams. "You put yourself out, Mrs. Gresham, for people you didn't know. And it's just the sort of thing you would do," he added with a kind of friendly ferocity which Jane did not quite know how to take. So she reverted to Mrs. Merivale, her charms and her domestic virtues.

Mr. Adams agreed. But he was just as glad that Miss Holly was with his little Heth, he said, as she was a very sensible woman and wouldn't let Heth go too far. Not but what Mrs. Merivale was very nice, said Mr. Adams, and a wonderful cook, and the house so clean it was a treat, but after all it was only for a couple of months and it was just as well all Mrs. Merivale's girls were away.

"You mean they might distract Heather from her work," said Jane.

"Well, I do and I don't," said Mr. Adams. "My Heth knows she's got to work hard, and do well at her college, and it takes a lot to turn my Heth when her mind's made up; like her dad. But what I was thinking of was Heth's future. She's going to go much farther than her dad. It was all very well for me, Mrs. Gresham, starting at five shillings a week as I did, to hobnob with every Tom, Dick and Harry. But Heth is starting from where I've got to and I shall see that she doesn't forget it."

Jane produced a few commonplaces from her social armory and heard Mr. Adams's voice going on, but what he was saying she really did not know, so stunned was she by the implication of his last words. It appeared, not to put too fine a point upon it, that to Mr. Adams's mind Mrs. Merivale and her daughters were not quite good enough for his daughter. The terrifying and to her almost unexplored hierarchy of the great mass of English people rose before her with all its gins and snares. Belonging as she did to a level upon which the Duke of Omnium at one end and, say, Robin Dale, the crippled schoolmaster, at the other, were in essentials equal, being, though a duke was always a duke, gentlemen, she had never really troubled to conceive the gradations, far greater than those between peer and private gentleman, which seamed and rent the sub-middle classes. Evidently Mr. Adams, while not wishing to conceal his humble beginnings, considered himself and even more his daughter, a good deal above Mrs. Merivale and her daughters. What Mrs. Merivale and her girls, all with good high school education and all doing good war jobs, would think of the wealthy manufacturer and his girl with little background and few graces, she couldn't guess. That is to say, she had a pretty shrewd idea of what Mrs. Merivale would feel; though as for the younger generation, probably its easy, perhaps too easy tolerance, its war experience of all sorts and conditions of women, would make Elsie and the rest of them accept Heather good-humoredly as one of themselves. But the Merivale girls would far more likely marry well than Heather Adams, for all her brains and her father's money, and that Mrs. Merivale would, if unconsciously, realize. Mr. Adams, she felt, could not realize it, and she would be sorry for the person who tried to explain it to him. And this brought her back with an unpleasant jerk to the fact that she had somehow to explain to Mr. Adams that his kind offer of an accountant for Dr. Dale could not be accepted, and she heartily wished that she had shown less temerity and her father and the Rector more courage. But a daughter of the Royal Navy has courage in her blood and Jane gave herself a mental shake and began to listen to her companion.

"That's a fine youngster of yours, Mrs. Gresham," said Mr. Adams. "What's he going to do?"

Jane said he was going into the Navy, rather surprised that anyone should ask the question.

"My father was chief engineer in Admiral Hornby's ship," said Mr. Adams. "The father that was of Captain Hornby that married Miss Belton. Quite a coincidence."

Jane said, with idiotic fervor, that *indeed* it was, though not till later did the thought strike her that Mr. Adams had evidently considered this as a kind of blood-bond between them.

"Both my brothers are sailors," said Jane, maundering nervously on, "and so are their wives; I mean naval families. My people have always been Navy. They used to live in what is now the Rectory, where Dr. Dale lives."

Having got so far as the name of Dr. Dale, her throat became constricted and her mouth unpleasantly dry.

"Fine old gentleman he is," said Mr. Adams, while Jane prayed that he might continue the subject. But as he appeared to have said his say, she plucked up her courage which was at the moment running out of the heels of her boots, and asked Mr. Adams if he had been in earnest when he suggested helping Dr. Dale with the Church accounts.

Mr. Adams said Sam Adams's word was as good as his bond, a statement which custom did not stale for him.

"My best man's up in the North at the moment," he continued, "but I've got a man in the costing department who is up to all the tricks. Hundreds of pounds he's saved me one way and another. I'll make it worth his while to come over on Saturday afternoon every quarter or so and get things straight. Then the old gentleman can sit back and take things easy."

This was getting worse and worse.

"He rather *likes* muddling about with his accounts," said Jane weakly.

"He's a fine old gentleman," said Mr. Adams, as if this were an entirely new idea, "but muddling the accounts doesn't make them balance, Mrs. Gresham. I wouldn't be worth—well, I won't say what, but what I am now—if there'd been any muddling with my accounts. Two and two makes four, and you can't get away from it; not nohow."

Jane nearly said "Contrariwise," but pulling herself together she said she thought the Rector really enjoyed trying to get the accounts right, and her father was always glad to help him.

"Well, that's very friendly of the Admiral, Mrs. Gresham," said Mr. Adams, "and he's a fine old gentleman. But, take it from Sam Adams, it may be ten thousand pounds, it may be tenpence, it needs a man that's been brought up to it. If there's any hurry, Mrs. Gresham, say the word and I'll have my man back from Sheffield tomorrow. You want the best for the old Rector. Well, you're right. Always aim at the best and you won't get the worst."

Even worse.

"It is so *very* kind of you," said Jane in desperation, "but I think Dr. Dale would be so worried by a real accountant that he would be quite ill. I know he would. You see, he is very old and has always done it in his own way. I can't bear to seem ungrateful, but if you won't take it unkindly, it would be most kind of you to leave things as they are."

Mr. Adams's massive face became an unpleasant dusky hue, and the large hairy hand which lay on his knee assumed a form uncommonly like a fist.

"All right, Mrs. Gresham," he said after a pause of a few seconds which felt to Jane like an eternity in Purgatory, "Sam Adams can take a hint with any man. I'm not wanted. Right. I shan't be there. I don't know that Mrs. Belton would have treated me like that. Me and Heth won't be here long and she's got plenty to do studying her figures. I'll speak to Miss Holly."

The worst. What Jane had feared all along and hoped, though not too hopefully, would not occur. She was quite certain that if she stood up her knees would bend the wrong way and darkness shot with colored flashes come before her eyes. But the Navy does not surrender.

"We didn't in the least wish to be ungrateful," she said. "But the Rector is so old, and he doesn't explain things very well, and we thought——"

"Who's we?" said Mr. Adams, his fist unrolling itself on his knee.

"Father and Dr. Dale," said Jane. "They didn't want to seem ungrateful——"

"So they put you onto the job," said Mr. Adams, not unkindly. "See here, Mrs. Gresham, if you'll say the word we'll call the whole thing off and forget it. I dare say if anyone tried to run my works his way I'd feel the same."

"We would be"—Jane began trying to express her gratitude.

"Never mind about we," said Mr. Adams. "What I said was, you say the word and we'll forget it all."

At this moment Jane would willingly have thrown her glove in his face, except that she had left it with its fellow in Mrs. Merivale's lounge. But being level-headed enough she reflected that a change of wording would be a very small sacrifice to make to redeem the happiness of her father and the Rector, and then suddenly thought of Monna Vanna and began to laugh. Mr. Adams looked at her with a kind of suspicious, unwilling admiration.

"Well, then," said Jane, standing up and suddenly feeling quite unfrightened, "you will do me a great kindness if you don't send your accountant, and I'm most grateful. Thank you very much indeed. And now I really must collect Frank or he will have talked Mrs. Merivale to death."

Mr. Adams also got up and began to make the gesture of shaking hands, but Jane was already a pace ahead, so he merely dropped into pace beside her, and Jane asked if he was coming to the Archaeological Meeting on Saturday, and he said he was. And by this time they had reached the house where they found

Mrs. Merivale and Frank sitting in the veranda shelling peas into a colander.

"Mother," said Frank, "I'm eating all the peas that go through the holes. Look, Mother!"

He jiggled the colander in the air. Five or six very small peas fell out onto the veranda floor. Frank picked them up and crunched them, dust and all.

"Come along, Frank," said Jane, observing her hostess's agitation as a good deal of grit and a strand of coconut matting went into her young guest's mouth. "I hope he hasn't been a bother, Mrs. Merivale."

Mrs. Merivale said she had enjoyed having a butler very much and the worst of lodgers was they got dirty so quickly: a remark about whose meaning Jane did not bother to inquire. Her son, though not exactly a lodger, was certainly as dirty as a small boy needs to be, and the sooner he was home and in his bath the better. And then Heather and Miss Holly came out and they all said good-bye, with promises of meeting again on Saturday at the Archaeological, and Jane and Frank walked back to the Old Town.

"Daddy," said Heather when the guests had gone. "Why didn't you get Packer's car and take Mrs. Gresham home?"

"Well, why didn't I?" said Mr. Adams thoughtfully. "Suppose I'm not as quick as you, Heth, at thinking up those things. Why didn't you tell me?"

"Oh, well, never mind, Daddy," said Heather. "Miss Holly and I are going to play in some mixed doubles down on the courts. Come and watch us. Mr. Pilward is playing and his son that's on leave."

"Righto, girlie," said Mr. Adams. "I wouldn't wonder if Pilward is Mayor of Barchester next year. In fact, I don't wonder at all." For Pilward & Sons Entire with the horse-drawn drays that it still managed to keep going was a powerful name in Barchester business circles. "He did about eight thousand pounds' worth of business with us last year one way and another. It's all good for trade, eh, Heth?"

"Daddy," said Heather. "We are going to the Archaeological Meeting on Saturday, aren't we? Mrs. Gresham asked Miss Holly and me to have tea with her. Oh, and Anne asked us to tea at Hall's End too, Daddy. Which shall I say?"

"Well, girlie," said her father, thoughtfully, "I'd go to both if I was you. Miss Anne's a nice girl and I've got a few words I'd like to say to Sir Robert. And you listen to what Miss Bunting says, because though she mayn't be much to look at, there's very little she doesn't see. And we'll go and see Mrs. Gresham too. I may have something to say to her myself. Some of my pals are well in with the Red Cross and I might hear of something about her husband. I've got my feelers out. And I'd like to show her all's friendly," said Mr. Adams, half to himself. "Well, run along and get ready for your tennis. Your old dad'll come down. It's as good a place as any other for having a word with Ted Pilward about those chromium taps. Have a look at young Ted, too."

Heather turned to go upstairs, whither Miss Holly had preceded her. In the doorway she stopped and stood in ungraceful irresolution, one hip well thrown out and fiddling with the door handle.

"Daddy," she said.

"Eh?" said her father, looking up from the evening paper. "Old Uncle Joe's going strong in East Prussia. What is it, girlie?"

"Daddy," said Heather. "Do you know who I think Mrs. Gresham is like?"

"She must be a good-looker whoever she is," said Mr. Adams. "And all her wits about her too. *And* plenty of pluck."

"I think she's like Queen Guinevere," said Heather, with the pleasing agony we all feel when avowing our feelings for the adored object. "Anne lent it to me."

"Lent you what, Heth?" said her father.

"Tennyson, Daddy. He's wonderful," said Heather, her face

transfigured, or shall we rather say, shining at the romantic thoughts suggested to her. "I wish I was Sir Lancelot."

"Always wishing you were somebody, aren't you, Heth?" said her father good-humoredly. "Run along now. I don't want to miss old Ted Pilward."

So Heather went upstairs, hugging the thought of riding with Mrs. Gresham through a green forest on May Day morning and subsequently rescuing her by lance and sword from enemies, finally to renounce her in favor of Captain Gresham, R.N., miraculously back from the Far East, and becoming a hermit.

Mr. Adams sat in thought. He then went to the telephone, rang up his secretary at her private address, and told her to get a copy of Tennyson's Poems for him.

"Good metal," he said aloud to himself. "As good a job as I could turn out at the works and then something. Best stainless steel."

Over which loverlike words he fell into a muse till Miss Holly and Heather came down in tennis things, and they all went over to the New Town tennis courts.

CHAPTER 8

The Barsetshire Archaeological Society is a body of very respectable age, having been founded in 1759, thus adding, as nearly all its presidents have said at the annual dinner, something more to this wonderful year. Its originator was Horatio Palmer, Gent., an ancestor of Mr. Palmer at Worsted. He was a gentleman of considerable property in the Woolram Valley and believed that anything he dug up was a Roman remain. He was succeeded in the presidency by Sir Walpole Pridham, whose descendant Sir Edmund Pridham is still a hard working servant of the county. Sir Walpole believed with fervor equal to Mr. Horatio Palmer's that whatever he dug up was British, and since then the presidentship had been divided pretty evenly between the Roman and the British enthusiasts, and had gradually become the blue ribbon of Barsetshire, having been held by the Duke of Omnium, an Earl de Courcy, an Earl of Pomfret, Dean Arabin, Mr. Frank Gresham (little Frank's great-grandfather who married a fortune), and in fact by all the county's most noted peers, landed proprietors and spiritual leaders. The office, which is held for life, was at present represented by Lord Stoke, a very energetic old peer, almost stone deaf, who had slightly varied the nature of the post he held by his conviction that everything he found was Viking. Over the remains excavated a few years previously in Bloody Meadow, on his estate, feeling had run very high, but Lord Stoke, having on his side the

Icelandic antiquary Mr. Tebben from Worsted, had borne all before him. It was well known in the county that Lord Bond at Staple Park coveted his honorable post, but he was of the first creation and though he was liked, his wife, Lord Stoke's half-sister, was of an overbearing nature and his chances were not favorably considered. Also Lord Stoke, though over eighty, was very well preserved, and showed every sign of living forever.

The treat or bait offered by this year's summer meeting was, as we already know, to examine the disused well in the grounds of the old Rectory, and decide whether any of the brickwork was Roman; much to the annoyance of Lord Stoke, who had to admit that the probability of anything Norse, or even Danish, was extremely remote. Feeling was running very high. Each side hoped to smash the other in the Journal of Archaeological Studies in Barsetshire. But the person who perhaps looked forward to the day's meeting more than anyone was Mr. Freeman, the verger, who was going to get a whole column about it into the *Barchester Chronicle* or die in the attempt.

In happier days the little town of Hallbury could hardly have held the cars that would have rallied from all over the county. But times were changed. Not only was petrol severely rationed, but many people were shy of appearing in a car at all and did not like to stretch their Red Cross, or County Council, or any form of compassionate allowance for what was so obviously a pleasant outing and of no particular use towards winning the war. Those who proposed to attend were mostly coming by train from Barchester. Some would come in the morning and lunch with friends; some would come after lunch and stay to tea with friends. Lord Stoke proposed to ride over from Rising Castle on a useful cob which was still up to its twenty-five or thirty miles a day, and had sent his brougham to fetch his champion, Mr. Tebben from Worsted, thus causing Mr. Tebben a good deal of irritation, as it was now impossible for him not to bring his wife. The Dean of Barchester was coming by train. Mrs. Morland was coming with her old friend and ex-secretary, Mrs. George

Knox, wife of the famous biographer, for Mrs. Knox had W.V.S. petrol, and had, rather cunningly, arranged to take a large parcel of harsh, stringy knitting wool and a bale of very nasty sham flannel to the Hallbury W.V.S. who were making clothes for liberated Central Europeans, and serve them right. Lord Bond and Lady Bond and their tenants the Middletons from Skeynes were going by train to Barchester, lunching with the Bishop and coming on after lunch. The Pomfrets hoped to come with the estate agent, Roddy Wicklow, who was on leave from Belgium and could have petrol for three hundred miles, and so the rather wearisome list of ways and means went on. But the whole company about to be present was united in despising such people as Sir Ogilvy Hibberd, who just because he was a trade expert though no one quite knew of what, or why, had free quarters at a very expensive London hotel and all the petrol he wanted. There is a snobbery of doing without luxuries—or what one used to call ordinary necessities—which binds a great many good people together against those who profit by the condition the world has got into.

Hallbury House, Hall's End, the Rectory, the Watsons' and other houses were having simple lunch parties, and there would be open house everywhere for such teas as could be given, and everyone was looking forward to seeing friends and acquaintance and getting, even for so short a time, outside the very small circle in which we now all perforce live. No one was looking forward to the day more than Anne Fielding, whose opportunities of seeing people during the past year had been very limited. To her mother's great delight she was, though pleased, not over-excited about the day. A year ago she would have had a temperature, or had to go to bed feeling sick from sheer over-excitement. But now, thanks to Dr. Ford's directions and perhaps even more to Miss Bunting's vigilant care, she was so well that the daily rests were almost a thing of the past. In fact, at the last consultation, Dr. Ford had said he saw no reason why she should not go back to Barchester in the autumn and take up a normal life with classes, so releasing Miss Bunting. This lady, though she had enjoyed her task of helping Anne to widen her mind and strengthen her body, was not sorry at the prospect of leaving Hallbury, where she saw very few people, and returning to the Marlings after her visit to Lady Graham. For at Marling Hall there was still a certain amount of coming and going, and though she would have died sooner than admit it to anyone, the Marlings were the kind of family to whom she was accustomed, while the Fieldings, kind, delightful and intelligent people though they were, could not be called county: not possibly.

An amicable division of the more important guests had been made among the houses in question. Dr. Dale, as of right, had Dr. Crawley and his wife. Admiral Palliser was entertaining the Pomfrets and their agent. The Watsons had invited the George Knoxes. The Fieldings had offered to entertain Lord Stoke, whose groom and horse could go to the Omnium Arms, Mr. Birkett, the headmaster of Southbridge School with his wife, and Mrs. Morland. To these they had kindly added Lord Stoke's friends Mr. and Mrs. Tebben. And when we say friends, Mrs. Tebben's rule in life was that wheresoever her husband went, there (if humanly possible) went she also; which meant she had to be asked, because if not asked, she came.

A lunch party of ten, six of whom are guests, is more than most housekeepers would care to face, but to Gradka it was but an occasion to show her skill and her art. Also the news from Mixo-Lydia had of late been very good. Powerful Russian forces had entered it from the northeast, driving the Germans before them with great slaughter, had beaten off all counter-attacks and freed nearly all the country, and were now rapidly penetrating Slavo-Lydia before the Germans could re-form. The Mixo-Lydian flag, which being composed of bands of blue, white and red was very difficult to distinguish from a lot of other flags, had been hoisted on the cathedral of SS. Holocaust and Hypocaust, and there had already been several highly enjoyable clashes on the Mixo-Lydia frontier and some cattle-maiming on both

sides. All this Gradka had read in the newspapers and heard on
the wireless; also at Mixo-Lydian House, the headquarters of
her nation, near Southbridge, where Monsieur and Madame
Brownscu had had a frightful quarrel about Mixo-Lydia's post-
war policy. Though as this policy was the simple one of exter-
minating all Slavo-Lydians there would not seem to outsiders to
have been very much to quarrel about.

At half-past twelve the pleasant and unwonted sound of a
horse's hoofs at a spirited trot were heard in Hallbury High
Street as Lord Stoke came smartly up the hill on his cob,
followed by an elderly groom in livery. Old Mrs. Freeman, the
verger's mother, who was ninety and annoyingly active in the
body though weak in mind, came onto the pavement and called
out, "God bless your Grace," under the impression that it was
the great Duke of Omnium who died in the '60's. A number of
women who were still doing bits of shopping said what a sweet
horse it was, and all the children within earshot rushed along
with desultory cheers, hoping it was going to be a circus. Lord
Stoke, owing to his deafness, could not hear them, but was
pleased by their attention, and reining in his cob, let him
proceed at a foot-pace to Hallbury House. Here his groom
dismounted and held the cob's head while Lord Stoke, who at
eighty was beginning to feel an occasional touch of stiffness,
climbed down. The groom then walked the horses slowly to the
Omnium Arms while Lord Stoke, finding that the front door in
proper county fashion was not locked, went in and was lost to
view.

Now one of Lord Stoke's amiable eccentricities was an inor-
dinate interest and curiosity about all his friends' domestic
concerns. Whenever possible he entered their houses by the
back entrance. When he did not know the house an infallible
instinct directed him to the kitchen quarters, and so it was that
Gradka, giving her finishing touches to the cold lunch she had
arranged, was startled to see an old gentleman in a shooting

jacket, riding breeches and gaiters, wearing a flat-topped brown billycock, standing in the kitchen doorway.

"Morning, morning," said Lord Stoke, seeing what was obviously that foreign girl someone had told him the Fieldings had.

Gradka, at once recognizing a proper nobleman when she saw one, made a kind of curtsy.

"That's right, my dear," said his lordship. "And how are the Poles?"

Now if there is one thing a Mixo-Lydian cannot bear, it is to be confused with a Pole, for every Mixo-Lydian child knows that Mixo-Lydia utterly defeated the Poles in twelve hundred and fourteen in a great battle, where no less than five Mixo-Lydians were left dead upon the field, and seven Poles and a boy. So Gradka stared contemptuously.

"That's right, that's right," said Lord Stoke, evidently under the impression that she had answered him. "What are you giving us for lunch, eh? All sorts of good things? Well, that's very nice. And where is Lady Fielding? No, don't you trouble. I'll go and find her."

His lordship went off, followed by a glance of intense scorn from Gradka which he did not see and would not have noticed if he had. And then by good luck Anne came downstairs and with an aplomb that the Anne of a year ago would have hopelessly envied, bellowed her own name to him (having been previously instructed to that end), stood over him while he put his hat, gloves and whip in the hall, and took him into the drawing room, where her parents welcomed him and he was soon engrossed in Barchester gossip with Sir Robert, whom he heard very well: as indeed he could always hear if he really wanted to.

A curious sound as of shrill cheering drifted into the drawing room.

"What a funny noise, Mummy," said Anne. "Can I go and look?"

She sped to the front door and looked out. To the infinite joy of the Hallbury children, Lord Stoke's carriage had just made its appearance, walking at a funeral pace up the hill to save the horse who was rather old. A gentleman on a horse had been a fine beginning to the day's festivities, but this spectacle was entirely eclipsed by a brougham, an object which none of the children had ever seen. In a less degenerate age all the small boys would have turned cartwheels beside it in the hopes of a half-penny, but children are entirely uneducated now. The old weather-beaten coachman, who was used to making a sensation wherever he appeared, smiled grimly as he drove slowly and carefully up to Hall's End, while the children shrieked and yelled, some saying it was the woyreless man, others that it was the funeral, and when auntie doyed she had a lovely royde in a cowch. For English remains undefiled in much of Barsetshire, and any child who said wahless, or dahyed, or keeoch would have been mocked and flouted by its fellows. (Phonetics are incapable of expressing what we wish to express, but the intelligent reader of a certain age will know what we mean, without things like ə and ø which do but darken counsel.)

Anne, brimful as always with her latest readings in English literature, thought it was very like the election at Eatanswill. And when Mr. Tebben with his scholar's stoop and his gray hair got out of the carriage amid friendly hoots, she said to herself, "He's kissed one of 'em." And when Mrs. Tebben in her usual state of peasant-arts and hand-woven disarray followed him, such was the ecstasy of the young populace that Anne said half-aloud, "He's kissing 'em all." The coachman then touched his hat, gave a friendly flick to the horse, and drove off towards the Omnium Arms, amid shouts, relics of an older and better civilization, of "Whip behoynd, mister," of which he took no notice at all.

With the kindness that was natural to her and the elegance that Miss Bunting had unostentatiously inculcated, Anne received the Tebbens and assisted Mrs. Tebben to get out of a very draggled tussore dust-coat like a relic of Edwardian coaching days, and to unwind herself and her hat from a dingy art-green scarf. She also offered to put Mrs. Tebben's mauve raffia basket with a bunch of faded raffia flowers on it, and its handles tied up with string, into the cloak room with the other outdoor things but Mrs. Tebben refused, saying there was something in it.

So they all went into the drawing room where Lord Stoke received them as if he were at home at Rising Castle, cast Mrs. Tebben at Lady Fielding and pushed Mr. Tebben into a corner to talk Viking shop with him.

Lady Fielding had never met Mrs. Tebben before, and was much impressed by that lady's earnest manner, her flowered dress with a good dip on one side and her straw hat covered with a very faded wreath of artificial cornflowers.

"Do let Anne take your basket, Mrs. Tebben," she said.

"I did try to, Mummy," said Anne.

"It is kind of you," said Mrs. Tebben, sitting down with the basket firmly held on her knees, "but I have some things in it."

This seemed probable, as being what baskets are for, and Lady Fielding, feeling that Mrs. Tebben was quite capable of having brought a cap in a bandbox said something polite about would she care to go upstairs and change.

"No, no; not a change of attire," said Mrs. Tebben, in what was evidently a literary allusion. "It's only something for lunch. I think it is quite dreadful to accept anyone's invitation to a meal nowadays, for really one becomes a plague of locusts."

"How kind of you," said Lady Fielding, "but you really mustn't. I do assure you we are quite well off here, and my Mixo-Lydian help, or whatever one calls her, is a wonderful manager."

"I always say how Brave the women of England are," said Mrs. Tebben, which made Lady Fielding want to say that she was not brave, nor a woman, nor English. "But we housekeepers know. And we must all bear our part. I have just brought," she continued, pulling several small parcels untidily wrapped in newspaper from her bag, "a little piece of goat's-milk cheese—I have kept a goat since our donkey Modestine died, not that he gave any milk of course, but I do like a four-footed animal about the place and it doesn't matter how bad goat's milk goes, because you can always let it go a bit worse and make cheese with it. And two tinned salmon fish cakes that Gilbert wouldn't eat for his breakfast. And here is a morsel of marge. And oh dear, it has been upside down all the time but never mind, it wasn't very wet—a little bowl with the remains of last night's shape, only I fear Gilbert ate all the jam that should have been on it. I'll just keep this bit of newspaper; it will do nicely for salvage."

So speaking she thrust the unpleasant packages into Lady Fielding's hands, her face gleaming with patriotism.

"Anne, darling," said Lady Fielding, "please take these to the kitchen at once. And for goodness' sake don't let Gradka see them," she added in an undertone which was covered by the rustling of Mrs. Tebben putting a greasy piece of the Sunday *Times* back into her bag.

Anne with great presence of mind hid the odious parcels, by now in a state of considerable deliquescence, in a far corner of the downstairs cloak room behind her father's golf clubs, and was just in time to open the front door to Mrs. Morland and the Birketts.

"Dear Anne," said Mrs. Morland, kissing her affectionately, "Anne Knox drove me over and we passed the Birketts on the way up the hill, so we picked them up, though I believe it is strictly forbidden. This is Anne Fielding, Amy," she said presenting Anne to Mr. and Mrs. Birkett, who had heard of her through Robin Dale and were well disposed.

With the arrival of the Birketts the party was complete. Anne went to tell Miss Bunting, who preferred to remain in her own room till the fuss of receiving guests was over. For Miss Bunting, whether it was the long cold windy summer after the dry windy spring, or a slight homesickness for county surroundings, or her years, had been feeling very tired of late and thought with regret of a more ordered life when well trained servants announced the right people and the wheels of life ran easily. Anne found her sitting in a chair, taking her infallible refresher of closing the eyes and letting the hands lie in the lap for five minutes and suddenly felt sorry for the omniscient, the all-perfect Miss Bunting. But lunch must not be delayed, and in a very short time both ladies were downstairs. Gradka, faithful to her principle of not appearing before guests till a meal was over, sounded the gong, and the company passed into the dining room.

Say what you will, a cold lunch however good is not so good as a hot one; at least not for those who no longer find cold meat and pickles or hard-boiled eggs and salad what they would wish. Not that cold meat could have been offered, for not only had the weekly joint been very small of late, but even tougher and more shapeless than usual, consisting of a large bone with splintered ends, a layer of gristle and some rather clammy grayish flesh. But in Gradka's capable hands the meal was as excellent as it could be, and far nicer than any other lunch in Hallbury.

The arrival of the Birketts had been a great comfort to Lady Fielding, who had found two such characters, in the fullest English sense of the word, as Lord Stoke and Mrs. Tebben, not to speak of her dear friend Laura Morland, a little too much for her and was afraid her husband might be bored, or even worse, show it. Sir Robert was a Governor of Southbridge School and had always liked and esteemed the headmaster and his wife, more than once standing up for them against the Bishop who was apt to promulgate a kind of Rescript or Episcopal Recess without waiting to consult the other governors.

"One of the reasons I came over today," said Mr. Birkett, "Roman brickwork not being exactly in my line, was to see young Dale. We want him back at Southbridge. Have you any idea what his views are, Lady Fielding?"

Lady Fielding said she didn't know, but Anne might be able to tell him.

Anne rather nervously said that she thought Robin liked his

little school very much, but she didn't know what would happen when his present little boys went to their prep. schools, as there didn't seem to be any more just now.

"H'm," said Mr. Birkett, much to the interest of Anne, who had often seen the word in books but never heard anyone say it. "That's the worst of this war."

"What he means," said Mrs. Birkett, "is that there won't be enough school-fodder soon, and then what will happen to the schools?"

"All be State schools then," said Lord Stoke, to whom Anne had obligingly bellowed the gist of the Birketts' remarks. "Bad thing for the country. There isn't a boy at a State school that knows a Friesian from a Holstein."

As none of the company present knew what either of these animals were like, there was a respectful pause.

"My old governor sent me to Eton," said Lord Stoke. "He was there and so was his governor and all his uncles."

This remark so paralyzed the conversation that Lady Fielding felt no one would ever speak again, when Mrs. Morland, who was famed for a kind of desperate courage, suddenly shouted across the table that Lord Stoke ought to put that in his life.

"Oh, are you writing your life, Lord Stoke?" said Anne, to whom anyone who wrote anything was a phoenix.

"Just jotting a few things down," said Lord Stoke with apparent detachment, but secretly pleased and flattered. "Haven't got to Eton yet. There's a lot of stuff about my old governor—he married twice, you know, and Lucasta Bond is only my half-sister; Bond's breaking up now, sadly changed—and the old days at Rising Castle. When my old governor was a boy the footmen all slept two in a bed, in those little rooms beyond the servants' hall—you know the old basement, Mrs. Morland—well away from the maids," he added in a kind of stifled bellow which his hearers understood to be a tribute to the Young Person. "Ever read Pomfret's book?" he inquired of his host, alluding to the late Earl's memoirs, *A Landowner in Five Reigns*, whose success surprised its author as much as it surprised his publishers.

Sir Robert said he had.

"Too much about going abroad and all that," said Lord Stoke. "What people want is books about the land. People are interested in the land. Don't go abroad and all that now," said his lordship rather unfairly, as Lord Pomfret's book had been written several years before war was thought of. "Heaps of farming fellows writing books now, but they haven't been at it as long as I have. When my old governor was a boy his father's laborers got seven shillings a week and a cottage. We'll never see that again, not in my time."

Such was the power of Lord Stoke's personality, and we may add, his voice, that everyone present heaved a kind of sigh in memory of the happy days when laborers had fifteen children and very small wages and looked forward to the workhouse when too rheumatic to work. All, that is, except Miss Bunting, who considered that laborers' wages were, like everything else, in the hands of Providence, and that it was not for her to judge.

"Of course," said Mrs. Tebben, who had done economics at Oxford and had a passion for boring and useless accuracy, "we must take the value of their cottages into consideration, and what they grew in the garden. By the way, Sir Robert, I must tell you about a delightfully economical vegetable dish I have found. When the peas are getting a bit over, I put them in a casserole with a little water and some meat extract cubes and let them simmer all day, and by the evening you hardly know they are tough at all. I sometimes, rather daringly, steal a bay leaf from the Manor House—my daughter married the Palmers' nephew you know, so we are almost related and a bay leaf will never be missed—and add it to the savory mess. You have no idea."

Sir Robert courteously said he hadn't, and how were her children.

"Ah, you remember that I am a grandmother, Sir Robert," she

said, which Sir Robert had not remembered in the least because he didn't know it, and vaguely thought that her children, whom he had only mentioned to get away from savory messes, were in their late 'teens. "My Margaret and her little brood are very well and happy. Her husband is on a home job at present, so that is very nice. And Richard," said Mrs. Tebben, her voice softening as it always did at the mention of her only son who would really have been quite fond of his mother if she had not insisted on understanding him, "is out of the army too, with a stiff knee. He was in Margaret's father-in-law's engineering business, Mr. Dean, you know, but he doesn't want to go back to the Argentine and I believe he is getting a job with a Mr. Adams at Hogglestock. Have you ever heard of him?"

Sir Robert said he had and that Anne had rather made friends with his daughter in the holidays and they would probably be at the Archaeological.

"Good news! good news!" said Mrs. Tebben. "Gilbert! Mr. Adams will be at the Archaeological and I shall find or make an opportunity to mention Richard to him. Every word helps."

Mr. Tebben made no comment, but his eye met Sir Robert's with such deliberate long-suffering blankness that Sir Robert heartily wished he had never embarked upon the subject of Mrs. Tebben's family at all, and at the same time he felt sorry for Mr. Tebben without knowing why. With as much haste as was compatible with the courtesy due from a host to a guest who has been invited through no wish of his own, he turned to Mrs. Morland and told that worthy creature all the story of the row in the Close about the Precentor's extra petrol, which she much enjoyed.

After they had eaten several kinds of excellent pastry, cakes and tarts, miraculously extracted by Gradka from the fat ration, and were drinking their coffee, Anne said to her mother that they must ask Gradka to come in as she would expect to be thanked.

"I am so sorry," said Lady Fielding to the company, "but do

you mind if our Mixo-Lydian help comes in? It seems to be a custom of her country that the cook should be thanked by everyone. It won't be long. And I feel we ought to thank her, because she has let us have lunch at a quarter to one on account of the Archaeological."

Everyone said How nice, especially Mrs. Tebben, who had a weakness for Central Europeans and often thought she would like to dress like one herself.

"I haven't any wine today, Dora," said Sir Robert nervously. But Anne said that was all right and Mixo-Lydians didn't drink wine at midday.

As before, Gradka came in, accepted without interest the thanks of the guests, despised their praise, and evidently had the poorest opinion of them all. Lady Fielding thought she would then go away, but Gradka, leaning carelessly against the sideboard said, "I shall now tell you some news."

All the ladies present were certain she was choosing this moment to give notice, and wished they were somewhere else.

"Today," said Gradka, rather loudly, having been warned by Anne that the English lord was deaf, "owing to your lunch being at a quarter to one I listened to the radio in the kitchen."

As there was no reason why she should not have the wireless on, whatever the hour of lunch, this statement was most unfair, carrying as it did an implicit slur on Lady Fielding's consideration for those in her employ.

"Listening to the one o'clock news, eh?" said Lord Stoke. "And how are the Czechs getting on? Nice place Carlsbad used to be, but they pronounce it all wrong now."

"Czechs?" said Gradka. "Gob! Czy pròvka, pròvka, pròvka."

"Eh?" said Lord Stoke.

"Oh, Lord Stoke," said Anne, speaking right into his ear for fear of hurting Gradka's feelings. "She isn't a Czech. She is a Mixo-Lydian. She said, 'God! No, never, never, never.' I know a bit of Mixo-Lydian that she taught me."

"Well, Gob isn't any worse than Bog," said Mrs. Morland. "I

have nothing particular against the Russians apart from not liking them, but I do think to call God Bog is just silly."

A hum of agreement confirmed her views.

"You are perfectly right," said Gradka. "To say Bog is silly. Oll that the Russians say is silly. So is oll the Poles say, and the Czechs and all that bondle of rubbish. But I shall now tell you about the one o'clock radio. The government of Mixo-Lydia is overthrewn——"

"Overthrown, Gradka," said Miss Bunting.

"So; I thank you," said Gradka. "It is overthrown and we have no longer a President which was a man entirely of no value, but we have a Krasnik. Oll Mixo-Lydia will be in a fermented state tonight."

This epoch-making news was received with a poor show of enthusiasm. Few of the company knew who had been a President, and none cared.

"Dear, dear," said Sir Robert, feeling vaguely responsible. "And what is a Krasnik?"

"What you call a president," said Gradka. "Aha, I olready see you will object: Then why coll him a Krasnik? You would not understand."

"Was there anything else in the news?" said Mr. Tebben.

"Olso, there is a revolution in Slavo-Lydia," said Gradka. "And now Mixo-Lydia is free from the Germans we will march into Slavo-Lydia and kill oll the men and seduce oll the women. And oll the children shall work for us and live on the food of pigs and cows. So oll shall rejoice that Peace is at last come, and be grateful to the Russians which bring us that heaven's gift and then we shall say to them, 'Oll right, Mister Russians, you can now make yourselves scarce.' And oll those that linger on the road, our Mixo-Lydian plastroz, which is what you call militia or guerrilleros, will slit their necks. God wills it so."

At this remarkable picture of the millennium no one quite knew what to say. Gradka, looking like Charlotte Corday and the Vengeance rolled into one, stood with a hand on her hip, surveying in her mind's eye a distant and delightful scene of unrepressed carnage, till Lord Stoke, whose ear had been caught by a word familiar and dear to him, thought he recognized a kindred spirit and asked her what kind of cows they had in her parts.

Lady Fielding felt she could bear no more and thanking Gradka warmly for the excellent lunch and the good news, withdrew her company, while Anne helped Gradka to clear away. Sir Robert was then able to talk to Mr. Tebben, who looked as if he needed cheering up, about the excavations near Brandon Abbey, while Mr. Birkett cornered Mrs. Morland to talk about Southbridge School and various old boys; which, as he lived, breathed, slept and ate school, not to speak of organizing and still doing a good deal of teaching in the upper forms, was a very pleasant relaxation for him.

"And how is Tony?" he asked, for Mrs. Morland's youngest son had been right through Southbridge from the day when he arrived at the preparatory branch, with a bowler rather too large for him and an apprehensive expression, to the day when he had left in a cloud of evanescent glory as a prefect, the Captain of Boating and holder of a formaship, pronounced formayship (as being supposedly sued for *in forma pauperis*) or scholarship to Paul's College, Oxford.

"I cannot say," said Mrs. Morland, angrily pushing her hair and her hat off her face simultaneously in a very unbecoming way, "how *furious* we both are. There he was, perfectly happy, though of course they never tell me if they are happy or not, and perhaps happy is not quite the word, but at any rate he was killing Germans with great satisfaction; though I must say," said Mrs. Morland, making an obvious effort to be broad-minded, "that to mow Germans down with very large guns in tanks is not quite the same as *killing* them; and then what must the War Office do but send for him in an aeroplane, by which means he had to leave nearly all his kit behind and arrived quite unexpectedly at High Rising to say he was going to India at once, with two bottles of champagne which were bought, not stolen, and a bunch of perfectly filthy clothes to be washed and mended."

"I presume," said Mr. Birkett, "that it was a kind of compliment to send him to India. They don't pick one subaltern out like that for fun."

"Compliment or no compliment," said Mrs. Morland, pointing her remarks with her face-à-main which she had suddenly remembered that she was wearing, "to India he went, in a bomber, in thirty flying hours: though whether flying hours are longer or shorter than other hours I do not know, any more than which weighs more, a pound of lead or a pound of feathers."

Mr. Birkett said he thought it was the number of hours during which you were actually in the air; not refueling, or coming down somewhere to have lunch with a friend.

"And that," said Mrs. Morland, ignoring his explanation, "is what I cannot abide. Why send him to India in thirty hours when it will probably take him weeks and weeks to get back? Unreasonable, I call it, and if I were the Peace Conference I'd stop people flying at once. It only makes people nervous, just like the wireless."

"I quite agree with you," said Mr. Birkett. "The reason we all had such good nerves during the Napoleonic wars and Miss Austen was able totally to ignore current events was that communications were slow. A corvette with dispatches from Spain, which had probably had to beat out as far as the West Indies and then run up the Channel and round the coast like the Armada and make her landfall at Grimsby, left people, except those personally affected, singularly unmoved. It's a devil's age, Laura, and it is, I can assure you, no pleasure to me to have to send my boys out into it. But I wish Tony the best of luck."

"I hear from him quite often," said Mrs. Morland. "In fact he writes as much as he did from D-Day and France and Belgium and Holland and Germany, and about exactly the same things."

"His guns and his men, I suppose," said Mr. Birkett.

"Oh, *no*," said Mrs. Morland. "Asking me to find something

that is at the bottom of one of his drawers or trunks, he doesn't know which and send it to him: or to buy him something that simply doesn't exist, like a wrist watch or a fountain pen. But it seems to make him feel a bit nearer," she added with a touch of melancholy which she would never have shown but to so old a friend.

And then she asked about friends at the school, and Matron, and the Edward Carters and their brood, and the Birketts' daughters Rose and Geraldine, and Kate Carter's sister, Lydia Merton and her small Lavinia: and so they ran pleasantly through the gamut of common friends till Lady Fielding said they ought to be starting, as the proceedings were to begin at two-thirty.

Miss Bunting then bade a formal farewell to the guests, showing no favor, and went upstairs for her rest, and there was a great collecting of impedimenta by Mrs. Tebben and in a lesser degree by Mrs. Morland and the whole party set out for the meeting, though in no violent hurry, for as they had Lord Stoke the President with them, nothing could happen till he came.

The well which was to be the scene of the proceedings was, as may be remembered, in the cellar of the Old Rectory destroyed by fire some two hundred years ago. By degrees its stones had been taken for building; the farmer nearby had converted some of its outhouses into wagon sheds and stabling, but the foundations of part of the house still remained, just outside the churchyard. They were by now in most places level with the ground, or so covered with earth and weeds as to be unrecognizable, being a kind of No-Man's Land over which various people interested, such as the Duke of Omnium, the Cathedral Chapter, and the Court of Haphazard litigated at intervals in a meaningless way. This last was a very old ecclesiastical tribunal over whose derivation antiquaries had long and fruitlessly squabbled, some saying that it was old Norman-French, though what it meant they could not precisely explain; others that it was a corruption of Ampersand (itself a corruption, so that, as the Dean had wittily said, it was a case of *corruptio corruptionis pessima*), mean-ing perhaps that the church was *per se* the possessor of anything it could get hold of; and yet others that it had been called that in Gramfer's time and what was good enough for him was good enough for anyone else as he'd a been a hundred and forty-two if he'd a lived till the war and that was more than old Hitler could say.

The well had of course been bricked up for safety long ago, but owing to some very necessary repairs to Hallbury's water supply it had been temporarily reopened and the Barsetshire Archaeological Society had taken advantage of this to apply for permission to hold their summer meeting at Hallbury and investigate the brickwork before the well was filled in and lost. A strong fence within which ten or twelve persons could move about had been erected around the mouth of the well, and by courtesy of the contractors and the prospect of some heavy tipping to come, a workman had been down the well on the end of a rope most of the previous day, cutting out specimens of brickwork at different levels. And as there was a chance of some difficulty with a deep spring in the event of filling in the well the contractors, a local firm who at bottom believed more firmly in unseen forces than in any amount of boring and surveying, had obtained the services of Ed Pollett. This character, a half-wit or a natural genius, as you may choose to look upon him, was the illegitimate son of a virago of a mother and one of Lord Pomfret's keepers and had begun his career as under-porter at Worsted Station. From this he had gone, having as some may remember a genius for mechanics without knowing what they were, as temporary chauffeur to Lord and Lady Bond one summer. When motors were put down for the war he had been transferred to Marling Hall where he managed the tractor and did odd jobs, and a year or two previously had married Millie Poulter, niece to Mrs. Cox at Marling who let rooms. As Millie was nearly as half-witted as Ed, though without any of his genius, they led a very happy, skittish life and had already had a couple of nice healthy children, decidedly wanting. Now one of Ed Pollett's many gifts was a water-sense. With or without the hazel twig Ed could always feel water and after the epidemic of measles at Grumper's End the summer old Miss Brandon died, he had successfully diagnosed a forgotten cesspool in the Thatchers' backyard that no one had ever suspected.

As the party from Hall's End arrived on the scene of the excavations, Ed was standing on the edge of the well talking to the laborer at the end of the rope and, we are glad to say, both being local men resistant in the highest degree to so-called education, their talk, consisting of short remarks exchanged at long intervals and about nothing in particular, would probably have been quite comprehensible to Gurth or even Hereward the Wake.

At the sight of Ed Pollett Lord Stoke, with no apology, broke from his party and went over to the well. For ever since Sir Edmund Pridham had saved Ed from the conscription which would certainly have driven him really mad within a month, besides the chance of his running amuck and using his idiot's great strength against his fellows, and had told the story to Lord Stoke, that nobleman had taken Ed so to speak under his baronial wing, and enjoyed nothing more than a chat with him.

"Afternoon, Ed," said Lord Stoke.

Ed turned slowly, saw his patron, grinned and pulled his forelock, a piece of atavism which Lord Stoke said was well worth fifty guineas.

"Well, Ed, looking at the well, eh?" said Lord Stoke.

Ed smiled again seraphically.

"Who's down there?" said his lordship, whose curiosity in all local matters was unbounded. "One of the Duke's men?"

Ed looked doubtful.

"It's Purse," he said at length.

"Percy who?" said Lord Stoke. "One of Dudden's boys?"

Ed said he didn't rightly know. Purse it was, and Purse was going to stand him one at the Omnium Arms afterwards."

"Never mind," said Lord Stoke. "Children all right, Ed?"

Ed smiled broadly.

"Millie's expecting again," he said. "March."

As it was now mid-August this artless remark might have shocked a peer less wide-minded than Lord Stoke. But his lordship, who conserved a good eighteenth-century flavor, poked Ed with his stick to the intense pleasure of the onlookers, and said he'd be a grandfather before he could turn around.

He then approached the well, squatted on the edge, called down it and asked who was there. A voice from the depths said it was Percy Bodger my lord.

"Is that old Bodger's grandson; old Bodger over at Harefield?" said Lord Stoke.

The voice said it was, my lord.

"Fine old fellow your grandfather," said Lord Stoke. "Got rid of all my rats for me the year the river came up in the Castle cellar. Tell him I asked after him."

The voice said it thanked his lordship and grandfather would be main pleased.

"Getting some bricks for us, eh?" said Lord Stoke.

The voice said yes, my lord.

"Much water down there?" asked his lordship.

The voice said maybe two feet and a stinking dead cat if his lordship didn't mind, and went on with his chipping.

By this time a crowd of twenty or thirty people had collected and were looking at the well with the faith of the people who looked through Mr. Nupkins's back gate, hoping persons to have sight of Percy Bodger rising from its curb, or see Lord Stoke fall down it. As neither of these delightful occurrences took place, it began gently to melt again and look for its friends.

At the Rectory Dr. Dale and his guest the Dean had had a very pleasant conversation, chiefly on ecclesiastical affairs, while Robin spoke when he was spoken to and wondered what old Birkett wanted to say to him, for the headmaster had taken the precaution of ringing up and saying he hoped to see him during the afternoon. They touched lightly on the affair of the Precentor's extra petrol, the Dean giving it as his opinion that though the Precentor was quite in the wrong, if not actually breaking the laws, yet the mere fact of the Bishop's reprobation made him, as it were, guiltless in the eye of heaven; with which Dr. Dale heartily agreed. The Rector then inquired after Dr. Crawley's very large family of children and grandchildren and was glad to hear that they all were well and Octavia's husband now had an excellent artificial arm and the baby was a fine little fellow. Dr. Crawley then asked the Rector how Haggai was getting on and was delighted to hear that he was well into the second chapter. Dr. Dale said he was getting old and the grasshopper was becoming a burden.

"Never mind, Dale," said the Dean, who was fond of the old man and did not like to see him cast down. "It is a great thing that you have Robin with you."

"It is," said Dr. Dale, looking affectionately at his son. "Don't wait for me, Robin, if you want to go down to the Old Rectory."

Robin thanked his father and said that as all his young scholars were going, with the firm determination of falling down the well, he thought he would be more usefully employed in helping to keep them away from this innocent occupation.

The Dean said they would meet again at Philippi and dismissed Robin with a kind of decanal salute, and Robin went off, quite understanding why the Dean's family sometimes felt that their family was going it more than they could bear. After a silence his host said,

"I know I am lucky to have Robin with me, Crawley, but in the good Scotch phrase, I am apt to sin my mercies. When you are as old as I am you will know what it is to want to be quiet. I can be alone in my study with my books for days quite happily, and my housekeeper brings me meals on a tray. Robin is a good son and a brave and hardworking boy, but there are so many years between us. My wife, as you know, was thirty years my junior. Robin can hardly remember his mother. He should have been my grandson. I get very tired, Crawley, very tired, and it's dull for him."

Although the Dean was not very sensitive to find shades, he quite sympathized with the Rector's point of view. Much as he loved his many daughters and his two sons, now all married, all with children, he sometimes, and especially at Christmas and during school holidays when his wife's exuberant grandmotherhood filled the Deanery with children and nurses and odd parents, echoed from his heart the cry, "Oh, for an hour of Herod." While the grandchildren were all young it had been bad enough, but at least the evenings were free. Now, with half of them sitting up to the evening meal and the eldest using his study as if it were a sitting room, he often thought enviously of anchorites and people who—in a better climate—lived on the top of a pillar. So he quite sympathized with Dr. Dale in his secret wish to be alone with his books and his memories, and was about to say so when he saw that his host had fallen asleep, upright in his chair, sleeping lightly as old men do, but rapt away from the world. So he got up quietly, told the housekeeper he was going down to the Old Rectory and left the Rector to his dreams.

As he approached the scene of the meeting he ran into the Fieldings and the Birketts, all old friends, and they had the story of the Precentor's extra petrol all over again, with such additions as their fancy suggested. Mrs. Birkett asked after the Rector, for she remembered every parent that had ever been through her hands and Dr. Dale was a not undistinguished parent. The Dean said he had fallen asleep after lunch so he had left him and come down to the Old Rectory.

"And how is Robin?" said Mr. Birkett. "I wish we could get him for Southbridge, but I suppose he will feel he ought to stay with his father."

"To tell you the truth, Birkett," said the Dean, falling behind a little with the headmaster, "I don't think his father much wants him."

Mr. Birkett looked interested.

"I don't mean that they aren't fond of each other," said the Dean, "for anyone can see they are. But from what Dale said to me I think he would be happier alone. He is getting on and lives mostly in the past and his books and, as he said, Robin is really the age of a grandson to him. He has a very good housekeeper and if Robin were away I don't think he would notice it much. To tell you the truth, Birkett, I believe the old man lives with the memory of his wife and as Robin can hardly remember her he is rather a third person."

"H'm," said Mr. Birkett, though this time Anne was not there to admire. "Thank you, Crawley, I shan't rush it, but I'll keep what you said in mind. He must be a good age."

"If it comes to that, we are getting to a pretty good age ourselves," said the Dean. "I wonder that the people who try to write the Bible in modern language don't alter the threescore years and ten."

Mr. Birkett said that judging from the bits of Basic English he had seen, there would certainly be no word for threescore and probably not for ten. One and one and one would be the best they could do."

"Come, Birkett, be fair," said the Dean. "Even the Romans knew no better than to say ten-fifty when they meant forty. Or if they didn't say it, they wrote it and carved it, which looks as if they meant it."

"And those dreadful French say four-twenty-thirteen for ninety-three," said Mr. Birkett.

"And look at the Germans, saying half-eight when they mean half-past seven," responded the Dean.

"Or those foul Italians thinking that quattrocento means the fifteenth century," said Mr. Bickett in antistrophe. "I wonder what Lord Stoke is saying to Ed Pollett. Let's go and look."

*   *   *

The lunch at Hallbury House went off quietly. Lord and Lady Pomfret were pleasant guests, but Lord Pomfret never had very good health and his Countess, taking more than her share of all county activities, was always a little anxious about him. Their agent, Roddy Wicklow, the Countess's brother, was also an excellent fellow, but not much given to speech, so when Jane had asked after Lord Mellings and Lady Emily and the Honorable Giles and Mr. Wicklow's wife and two children, there wouldn't be much more to say.

"Mellings is going to a day school in Nutfield now," said Lady Pomfret. "I wish Southbridge had a pre-preparatory house. He is going to the prep. school when he is eight."

"Lady Pomfret," said Frank, "I'm going to Southbridge. If your little boy comes I'll take care of him. I'm very good at taking care of people. Tom Watson wants to go to Southbridge when I do, mother. I told Mrs. Watson I'd take care of him. Do you think he'll go, mother?"

Jane said she didn't know and to hurry up with his dinner.

"Where do we go to school?" said Lord Pomfret to Frank, which was very kind of him, for he was frightened of children and would often have been frightened of his own only his wife wouldn't let him.

"With Mr. Dale, sir," said Frank.

"Any relation of the Allington Dales?" said Lord Pomfret.

"That old Miss Lily Dale was his great-aunt or something of the sort," said Admiral Palliser; but Lord Pomfret had never heard of her.

"She was engaged to some man, then broke it off," said the Admiral, "and I gather she lived on the romance till she was well over eighty. A real Victorian heroine."

"I have heard Gillie's aunt speak of her," said Lady Pomfret, who had become very good friends with her predecessor before old Lady Pomfret died. "The man married someone—one of the Gazebees, wasn't it, and died abroad."

No one contradicted her; and so are history and memoirs written.

"It is a nice school?" she continued, doubtless with Viscount Mellings's pre-prep. education in mind.

"Very nice," said Jane. "The only trouble is that there are so few people here. When Frank and his lot have gone to boarding school I really don't know what Robin will do. There's a kind of gap and the next lot won't be ripe for two or three years."

As Lady Pomfret naturally did not take much further interest in what was apparently a moribund school, the conversation, such as it was, languished politely through dessert from the garden and coffee. Frank then brought his mother to shame by boasting of his horsemanship to Roddy Wicklow, who was quite well known in a quiet way as a gentleman rider before the war. Lady Pomfret, both seeing and feeling her hostess's infanticidal feelings, broke across Frank's talk by asking her brother what the name of that man who was going to stand for the County Council.

"Adams," said Roddy. "He has a works over at Hogglestock. One of the new men."

"You wouldn't have heard of him, Admiral," said Lady Pomfret. "I did see him once, at the Hosiers' Girls' School prizegiving. Not very attractive."

The Admiral said he was on Mr. Adams's Board of Directors.

"Sally always took her fences without looking," said Roddy. "What do you think of him, sir?"

The Admiral said he didn't know. Business, he said, was one thing and Adams was a remarkably good business man, and pleasure was another.

"But probably," he added, "Jane could tell you more. She seems to have a way with her where he is concerned. He wanted, in all kindness, of course, to send down one of his accountants to help our Rector, Dr. Dale—the father of the young man we were talking about—and it would have worried the old man into a fit. It was all very awkward, but Jane managed to make him see sense."

"Oh, he is all right," said Jane, suddenly attacked by that form of self-consciousness that makes us belittle someone we rather like; possibly just for the pleasure of talking about them. "Not quite what Hallbury is used to though. And he has a large, very plain girl called Heather who is going to Cambridge. But it's only for the holidays, till whenever Cambridge begins. He will call her 'my little Heth' and she weighs about twelve stone."

Lord Pomfret, who though as nice and hard-working as he could be had not much sense of humor, laughed politely at Jane's rather unkind words and said seriously that what really mattered was how the fellow was going to vote. If he was the right sort they could do with a man like him on the County Council; someone who understood the growing class of industrial workers in and around Barchester, as well as old fogies like himself and Pridham, who thought more of the agricultural interest.

"I think," said Jane, "he will be at the meeting this afternoon with his daughter. If I see him would you like to meet him?"

Lord Pomfret said he would and then it was time to start for the Old Rectory. The Admiral escorted Lady Pomfret, and Frank, slipping his hand into Roddy Wicklow's, told him all about the pony at Greshamsbury and how his cousin Roger was afraid to ride it. To which Roddy made answer that he'd met a lot of horses he was afraid to ride himself, and Frank though usually impervious to fine shades felt a little subdued. So Jane fell to Lord Pomfret, and as he had not much small talk and they knew each other well enough not to bother, she reflected upon the way Mr. Adams seemed to crop up everywhere, and had an uncomfortable feeling that she had not been quite ladylike in making mock of him and his daughter before people who didn't know them. But the scene which met their eyes as the Old Rectory banished all thoughts, except those of keeping the children of both sexes, both gentry and non-gentry, from falling down the well. Robin, who in his schoolmaster capacity felt rather responsible, had arranged with the verger for a relay of well-watchers to keep children out of the enclosure, while he volunteered to take not more than two children at a time, one in each hand, to see what was happening. Lord Stoke's groom, the Rectory gardener and the elderly old man from the Omnium Arms were co-opted, Ed was warned, and everyone waited for the proceedings to begin.

CHAPTER 9

It now became apparent that the Society's President was lost. The Fieldings had not seen him as they were talking to the George Knoxes. Ed said he couldn't rightly say nothing. His lordship was argying with Purse, he said, and then his lordship got up and went away and Ed hadn't seen him anywheres, no he hadn't. Lord Pomfret said he might have fallen down the well, but this explanation, in view of the fact that Percy Bodger was down there all the time and must have noticed something, was poorly received, though the Admiral maintained that any Bodger was capable of ignoring entirely such an incident as an old gentleman falling down the well onto his head, having a rooted and feudal belief that the gentry were privileged and that it was not for the likes of them to ask.

At this moment Lord and Lady Bond and the Middletons, who had been lunching at the Palace and come on by train, appeared in the field. To Lady Bond, as his half-sister, appeal was made. She had not yet seen him anywhere, but was not at all anxious.

"It's so like Stoke," said Lady Bond, who had a dashing way of mentioning her half-brother and her husband by their baronial names without any prefix, a habit which many of her friends envied but were too modest to copy. "Of course it's a cow. Who farms here?"

"Old Masters," said the Admiral. "He rents my field and has his milking-shed over there."

He pointed to the converted outbuildings of the Old Rectory some fifty yards away.

"That's where you'll find him," said Lady Bond. "Here, Ed!"

Ed Pollett came shambling up and took his cap off.

"Go and see if his lordship is in the cowshed and bring him here," said Lady Bond.

Ed looked frightened.

"There's that old Daisy in there. She dropped a fine little bull calf last night, she did, and they say it's unlucky to go in more than once," said Ed. "Millie wouldn't rightly like me to go, my lady."

"Don't be a fool, Ed," said Lady Bond. "You needn't go in. Just go to the door and tell his lordship to come at once."

Ed went off at his own slow countryman's pace.

"The ancient Norsemen," said Mr. Tebben, who had been listening to the conversation with some interest, "had a very similar belief. I was reading the other day in Grettir Halfbone's interesting twelfth-century gloss on the Laxdaela Saga that when the female salmon——"

But what Mr. Tebben in his gentle scholarly way was going to say we shall never know (nor in any case would we have cared), for at that moment the Watsons with Mr. and Mrs. George Knox came up and overheard the last words.

"The Laxdaela Saga, my dear Tebben," said George Knox, burst into the conversation like a shell. "The Laxdaela Saga," he repeated, to give himself time to bludgeon all present into being an audience. "How I long to reread it, no one knows. Even you do not know, Tebben. When I was a boy," said George Knox, raising his voice as he saw the Middletons approaching, "my days were not long enough for reading. Well," said George Knox, fixing the unfortunate Mr. Tebben with his eyes till that Icelandic authority felt like the Wedding Guest, "well, I say, do I remember long summer days, lying on my stomach as little boys do," continued George Knox with a smile which his loving and unimpressed wife knew to be meant for a whimsical one, "in the long grass of an orchard, absorbing every word, every word, I say, of the great Sagas of the North: the Skyrikari, the Reaping of Magnus Trollbogi, Haelfdan Hogsister, the great lament for the burning of Gunnar Pedderdotterssen's barley rick. You, Tebben," said George Knox, as one who condescendingly pats a well-meaning dog on the head, "will better know than I the true, the heroic pronunciation of these names, but let that pass," he said, though Mr. Tebben had shown no symptom of taking up the challenge. "Even at that age the little boy among the orchard grass knew what was essential. Little did the names matter to him. It was the story he loved; ay, Tebben, and loves still. You scholars may burn the midnight oil, but we romantics know."

"When Richard, my son, was quite a little boy," said Mrs. Tebben, breaking into George Knox's speech with a mother's pride, "he had the same difficulty with proper names that you have, Mr. Knox. He had a book he was very fond of which he always called From Cursy to Agronaut. You will never guess what it really was," said Mrs. Tebben looking proudly around her for support. Not getting any she added gaily, "It was From Crecy to Agincourt. It amused us so much and we have never forgotten it."

Several mothers present, headed by Mrs. Morland, gave examples of similar mistakes, bearing the marks of genius, made by their own children, while George Knox stood champing and pawing the ground, occasionally taking a deep breath as if to continue his extempore lecture and then having to let it out again in a most mortifying way, owing to the total want of interest from his fickle audience. Just as he saw an opening Mr. and Mrs. Middleton joined the group.

"Ha! Knox," said Mr. Middleton, with a kind of crusading fervor for which there was no reason at all.

Mrs. Middleton greeted the company in general, and particularly Mrs. George Knox, for there was a firm though undemonstrative friendship between these two ladies. Neither was young, neither had children, and both had a deep untiring affection for their rather overpowering husbands and not the faintest illusions about them.

"George has been talking, I suppose," said Mrs. Middleton.

"He has," said Mrs. Knox. "And what's more he will again, at any moment."

"About anything particular?" asked Mrs. Middleton.

"Sagas," said Mrs. Knox. "And why I really don't know, as it all began with a bit of folklore from Ed Pollett about not going into a cowshed more than one at a time. I mean one person at a time, not one cowshed. Sometimes I wonder why language was ever invented when I think of the extraordinary things it makes one say."

"I know," said Mrs. Middleton sympathetically. Or so an acquaintance would have said; but the few whom she allowed to know her well, Anne Knox among them, sometimes felt that while her voice expressed deep interest, her eyes were always looking a little way from the point of discussion towards some distant object unknown to her friends, barely suspected by herself. Then Mr. Middleton, having greeted the rest of the ladies with a touch of Versailles and the Grand Monarque, in his turn inquired what they had been discussing. Lady Fielding said that Mr. Knox had been telling them about the old Norse sagas, upon which George Knox once more took a breath and began.

"You, my dear Middleton, will bear me out——"

"I will bear with you, Knox, but cannot promise to bear you out——" said Mr. Middleton.

His wife said Jack was being Shakespearian.

"——until I know what line you were taking up."

"You flatter me, Middleton," said George Knox rather irritably. "There is no question of a line, my dear fellow. I was merely sharing, or shall I more humbly say, trying to share with our

friends the emotions roused in me as a boy by reading the great
Norse stories, the Skyrikari, the Reaping of——"

"Not again, George darling," said his wife.

"AH," said Mr. Middleton, leaping into the conversation like
a salmon up a waterfall in his anxiety to get in ahead of George
Knox, "the sagas. Wonderful tales of heroes and of men. How
often, Anne," he continued, addressing his wife as a focus from
which the whole company might be brought within his circle,
"how often have I told you of my great walk over the country of
Njal and Gunnar of Lithend, all through the long days of a
sub-Arctic summer."

"I don't know, Jack," said his wife impartially. "A great many
times."

"Tramping alone and on foot," said Mr. Middleton, to the
intense annoyance of Mr. Knox, who had never been to Iceland,
"for these things, Bond," he said, suddenly addressing his land-
lord, who jumped and tried to look as if he were listening, "must
be experienced alone; alone, I say; over the Snorrefell, down
Hormundsdale, across Grimmswater—I give the English ren-
dering of these names. I tell you, Bond, no one who has not seen
that country in its majesty, imbued with the spirit of the Heroic
Age, can begin to understand the saga."

He paused.

" 'Only those who brave its dangers,'

'Comprehend its mystery'," said Anne Fielding in a small
but distinct voice.

"You remember Anne," said Lady Fielding to Mr. Middleton,
glad of this excuse to break what threatened to be an intermi-
nable monologue. "The Marlings' old governess, Miss Bunting,
has been reading with her all this year. I think I see Lord Stoke
coming back."

"Not Longfellow," said Mr. Middleton, "an thou lovest me."

His wife said dispassionately that he must really stop thinking
he was Shakespeare.

"A poet, if you choose to call him such," said Mr. Middleton, "who brought into the sagas an atmosphere of middleclass New England. Away with such a fellow from the earth."

"No, George, you are *not* the Pilgrim's Progress," said Mrs. Morland, who had been occupied in tucking some bits of hair under her hat and suddenly came to life.

"I don't agree with you, Middleton," said Mr. Tebben in the mild voice of the scholar who will go to the stake for his self-formed convictions, the fruit of study and thought and not taken from the Press or a voice prancing with supercilious earnestness out of a box. "To my mind Longfellow gives the feeling of Norse literature as well as anyone, besides making it accessible to those who cannot read the language."

"Oh, Mr. Tebben," said Anne gratefully, "I do *love* Longfellow. Next to Tennyson he's my favorite poet."

Mr. Tebben said she might do far worse, which gratified Lady Fielding very much. For though she was not much of a reader herself, she quite realized Mr. Tebben's worth as a critic and was pleased that her daughter had been encouraged.

"I am silent; I am silent, Tebben," said Mr. Middleton rather crossly.

"No, you aren't, Jack," said his wife, "and even if you are, you won't be. Lord Stoke, how are you?"

"I wouldn't have missed the meeting today for worlds," said Lord Stoke shaking hands with Mrs. Middleton and then, to the reverent joy of all his old friends, taking a large red bandana with white spots out of his coat pocket, removing his brown flat-topped billycock and mopping his head. "Finest little bull calf I've seen since Bond's Staple Jupiter. What happened to him, Bond?"

Lord Bond said he had gone to the Argentine with Staple Hercules.

"Bad thing all those Dagoes getting our bulls," said Lord Stoke. "Come and have a look at this fellow. Pity Palmer isn't here. He'd have liked to see him. Do you remember, Bond, when your man was taking a bull over to Palmer and it got away?

I always said your man wasn't fit to be trusted with a good animal. Poor Palmer; he's aging sadly."

Mr. Knox and Mr. Middleton, neither of whom knew anything about bulls, then plunged into the conversation and everyone wondered if the meeting would ever begin.

"I wish a bull would bellow," said Anne Fielding to Mr. Tebben, in whom she felt she had found a friend. "Then those Skroelings would stop talking and run away."

"What do you know about Skroelings?" said Mr. Tebben, amused at this girl's interest in Icelandic matters.

"Out of Kipling," said Anne. "It's called 'The Finest Story in the World.' It's marvelous, Mr. Tebben. You would love it. It's all about reincarnation."

Mr. Tebben was disappointed by this secondhand approach to Icelandic literature, but he thought Anne Fielding a nice child, reminding him a little of his own gentle Margaret of whom since the war he had seen very little, occupied as she was with children and war duties. Anne, thanks to Miss Bunting, was overflowing with subjects she wanted to talk about or ask about, from the books she had read during the last year, and they fell into a very friendly conversation.

"It's nearly three o'clock," said Lady Bond to her half-brother, who oblivious of his duties as President of the Barsetshire Archaeological Society was about to take his ignorant and unwilling audience to see the bull calf.

"God bless my soul, Lucasta, so it is," said his lordship. "Where is the well?"

"If your Lordship will be so good as to come this way," said the voice of Dr. Dale's verger.

"Certainly, certainly," said Lord Stoke, good naturedly.

"Who are you, eh?" he added as Freeman led him towards the enclosure.

"The Rector's verger, my lord," said Freeman.

"Yes, yes, yes. But what's your name?" said Lord Stoke.

The verger named himself.

"Freeman. Now why the deuce—yes; I've got it," said Lord Stoke, who had a knowledge of that part of the country only equalled by Sir Edmund Pridham and surpassed by none. "Your father was under-keeper at Pomfret Towers. I remember him about the time of King Edward the Seventh's Coronation. Foxy-faced man with a wart on his nose. Married—now, wait a minute; yes. I've got it. He married the sister of that Wheeler that used to clean the chimneys at the Towers. Any children?"

"Yes, my lord," said Freeman. "A girl."

"That all?" said his lordship.

"Yes, my lord," said Freeman.

"Pity to let good stock die out," said Lord Stoke.

"Yes, my lord," said Freeman. "This was if your lordship doesn't mind."

He led his patron into the enclosure, whither they were followed by most of the party we have just met, and some other people of county or local importance with whom we are not concerned. Mr. Tebben and Anne Fielding, now deep in the Brontës, sat down outside on a bit of foundation and went on with their talk.

The secretary, a youngish clerk in a Barchester lawyer's office, unfit for service owing to his defective eyesight, but full of zeal for Barchester antiquities, then came up and spoke to his President, having been too frightened to do so before.

"This is the well, Lord Stoke," he said. "We've had a man down it all morning and he has brought up pieces of brickwork from various depths. Perhaps you would like to look down the well yourself first and then say a few words to the Society."

"Oh, sir, can I look down too?" said a voice beside Lord Stoke and not on his level.

Lord Stoke looked down and saw a small boy, holding another small boy by the hand.

"Can't hear you, my boy," said Lord Stoke. "What's your name?"

"Frank Gresham, sir," said the boy at the top of his voice.

"And this is Tom Watson. He's not so old as I am, but he would like to look down the well if I hold his hand. Oh, sir, can we?"

By good luck Frank's voice was of a pitch that happened to suit Lord Stoke's deafness.

"All right, my boy," he said. "But you've got to hold my hand."

"Oh, sir! thank you," said the little boys. Pushing Master Watson's right hand into Lord Stoke's left hand, Frank went around to his lordship's other side and took his right hand. They moved to the edge of the well and looked down. There was nothing to see, for the well was so deep that the water at the bottom lay in darkness.

"Oh sir, can I throw something in?" said Frank and dropping Lord Stoke's hand he picked up a small piece of brick from the rim and threw it down the well. After what felt like five minutes there was a dull plop.

"I told you to hold my hand, boy," said Lord Stoke. "Off you go now."

The little boys, with regretful looks at the well, went back to their mothers, who were just as glad to have them away from their rather risky pastime, especially Mrs. Watson who had overheard Freeman telling a friend it was no use any of the Society falling in, for nobody'd fetch 'em out, as Percy Bodger had said he wouldn't go down there again, not with that stinking cat about and anyway the rope was too short by six feet.

The secretary then approached Lord Stoke with a tray on which were a number of fragments of red brick or tile, all neatly labelled.

"These are the pieces, Lord Stoke," said the secretary.

"Eh?" said Lord Stoke.

"These are the fragments of brick, Lord Stoke," said the secretary, more loudly.

"All right, young man. What's your name? Henry, eh? Is that your Christian name or your surname?"

"My surname, Lord Stoke," shouted the secretary.

"All right, all right, no need to shout like that," said Lord Stoke. "And you needn't Lord Stoke me all the time. 'Sir' will do quite well. And what do I do with these, eh?"

The secretary, who secretly felt that Sir was not a sufficiently polite mode of address for a baron whose title went back to the Wars of the Roses, said they were to make a speech about. He would have said they were for his lordship to make a speech about, but being obedient to authority he did not like to use the word lord again, and in default of such a word as sir-ship had to fall back upon a circumlocution.

"Where's the Rector?" said Lord Stoke. "He knows more about this than I do."

No one had thought of the Rector and everyone felt slightly ashamed. When we say no one, the verger had thought of his spiritual overlord, but as he said afterwards to Mrs. Freeman it seemed a shame for the old gentleman not to have his after dinner sleep; with which Mrs. Freeman quite agreed. When we say no one however, this must not include the Rector's son who thought of his father mostly as a kind of very nice grandfather that needed looking after. He had noticed that the old man was tired by dinner time if he did not rest after lunch, but very cross by dinner time if he had dozed too long, and whenever he could he arranged to wake his father after an hour or so. And today, shortly before Lord Stoke and his party came to the enclosure, he had asked one of the village men to take his watch while he went home, roused his father and brought him down to the Old Rectory.

Dr. Dale's arrival was the signal for an almost regal reception, everyone coming forward to express respectful pleasure at seeing him and quite forgetting the well. Dr. Dale was gratified, but being of an honorable nature he dealt quickly with his friends and went up to Lord Stoke with apologies for being late. Lord Stoke showed him the fragments of brick which Dr. Dale touched with his elegant old hands.

"Most interesting," he said. "Most interesting. And what do we do now?"

Several people, like a stage crowd, asked each other the same question, which gave the secretary his chance to call upon various speakers who had been chosen beforehand. The day was fairly fine, but the eternal wind of that bad summer was blowing, there was nowhere to sit, inside the enclosure one was squashed, outside it one could not hear, so the audience gradually melted, leaving the President, the secretary and the Rector to deal with the enthusiasts, who finding no public were enabled to quarrel among themselves with much greater freedom.

A silly afternoon thought Jane Gresham to herself. All very aimless and waste of time, but one had to get through the time somehow. It didn't much matter if the brickwork was Roman, British, Saxon, Danish, Norman: the well was condemned, a dead cat was at the bottom of it, Frank thank goodness had not fallen down it. Presently there would be tea in the Watsons' big room, more talk with friends and then people would go and there would be supper and bed and Sunday morning. And so on forever and ever. And somewhere, if he was alive, life was going on for Francis Gresham and there was no power on earth that would tell either of them anything about the other. She thought, as she had often thought, that she could bear being in ignorance of Francis' fate if she was sure he had not been deceived about her. She imagined fake news coming to him, wherever he was, of London burnt and bombed to ruins, of all trade and traffic at a standstill, of death, slavery or deportation for everyone in England. Could he help believing these things? Would he not be in anguish for his wife and son? And even if he were dead, which might be the best fate for him, how could one truly believe that he was happy if he knew how unhappy she was. If going to heaven meant not minding if people we loved were happy or not, she did not look forward to heaven and knew Francis would be most indignant at finding himself there. And new inventions made everything far worse. What was the use of people being able to fly to the Far East within forty-eight hours when to get back might take forty-eight days, months, years, eternity. This wouldn't do. She shook herself angrily and went to see if Frank was in mischief. Both he and Master Watson were innocently occupied in building a railway station from bits of the ruins and quite good.

From across the field she heard archaeological voices. Presently there was a clapping of hands and she realized that the meeting was over and the fate of the well decided. Robin Dale came over to where she was sitting near the boys.

"Well, what is the verdict?" she said.

"I haven't the faintest idea," said Robin. "Father spoke very charmingly about anything but brickwork, with a passing reference to the Prophet Haggai. All the experts spoke rather uncharmingly about their own hobbies. Lord Stoke was annoyed because Mr. Tebben who was sitting on a stone capping verses with Anne and couldn't be found till too late. The secretary was all put out because a special piece of brickwork was missing. The only person who really enjoyed himself was Freeman, because he is reporting the names of the guests for *Barchester Chronicle*. And what have you been doing?"

"Robin," said Jane, not directly answering his question, "have you ever wondered if your foot, the bits of it that were shot off, misses *you*?"

"Well, yes, I have occasionally," said Robin, half wondering where this would lead, half sure that it would lead to something that would need quick thought and a convincing tongue. "But I don't now. After all it's buried quite comfortably at Anzio. At least I suppose they buried it. I really don't know. Anyway it can't talk, so that's all right."

He then fell silent, conscious that he had been talking too much, and foolishly, to cover his own unease.

"Still, I suppose a foot is different from a person," said Jane, in whom Robin recognized a savage wish to hurt herself. "It wouldn't care for one when one was alive, so why should it miss one when one's dead? Robin, if you couldn't ever see or get news of a person you were very fond of, would you feel miserable?"

"Like hell I would," said Robin bracingly. "Poor old Jane." And he put an encouraging arm across her shoulder.

"It's not poor Jane," said the lady, taking no notice of the arm and speaking with her face averted. "It's poor Francis. I don't mind missing him so much—I don't know *what* I feel about him. But it does kill me to think he may be missing me."

"Supposing he is dead," said Robin, knowing that Jane had always faced this possibility.

"Well if you, or Dr. Dale, or the Bishop—not that he's any good—can make me think that just being dead would make Francis not miss me——" said Jane, speaking with such arrogant confidence that her sentence did not need finishing.

"Mother," said Frank, appearing suddenly at his mother's elbow, and as if this were a very reasonable request, "have you any chalk?"

"I have," said Robin, withdrawing his arm from Jane's shoulder and feeling in his coat pocket. "Here you are."

"Oh thank you, sir," said Frank and returned to Master Watson.

Jane looked at her watch.

"Come along, boys," she said.

"Oh but *Mother*," said Frank, "Tom hasn't finished his ticket office; have you Tom? Oh Mother, can't he stop and finish it?"

Jane asked how long it would take.

"Not long, Mother. Oh, Mother, do let Tom finish it. One of his back teeth came out this morning. Tom, show Mother."

Master Watson obligingly opened his mouth and pointed with a dirty finger at a gap in his upper jaw.

"Mrs. Watson made him rinse his mouth, Mother, and the water was all bloody," said Frank. "I wish I'd seen it, Mother."

"With pydrogen hoxide," said Master Watson.

"He means hydrogen poxide," said Frank scornfully. "Did it fizzle, Tom?"

Tom nodded his head violently as Jane said they must really come now. So Frank wrote STATIO CLAUSA on a piece of flat stone with the chalk and set it up against the building.

"Third conjugation," he said loftily, "but Tom doesn't know it yet. Never mind, Tom. I'll help you with your prep. when we go to Southbridge."

"Odious, condescending child," said Jane to Robin as they walked towards the Watsons. "He does need a father."

"Speaking as a schoolmaster, my limited experience of fathers is that they are, if possible, even less use than mothers," said Robin, who knew that Jane was again her usual self and wished to join her in forgetting her short loss of self-control.

The Archaeological Society's tea was to be held, by kind permission of Mr. and Mrs. Watson, in the hall where the camouflage netting was done. The big frames had been pushed against the wall: the tables were spread with food instead of patterns and strips of green and brown material. An urn had been lent by the Women's Institute, and Mrs. Freeman with a few friends from the Mothers' Union had volunteered to serve the teas. At one end of the room was a special table where the President with some chosen guests of honor was supposed to sit, but anyone who knew Lord Stoke would have known that his insatiable curiosity about people in general would never allow him to remain seated. Dr. Dale however was glad to sit there quietly, and the Pomfrets joined him with Admiral Palliser and the Birketts. Dr. Dale beckoned Jane to make one of them but she said she ought to move about a little and see that everyone was being looked after and brought Mrs. Knox up to take her place.

Before she could give her mind to the guests there was one pressing duty; that of catching Masters Gresham and Watson and disposing of them in such a way that they would not be a nuisance to the grown-ups, and their mothers could at the same time keep an eye on them. With Mrs. Watson's wholehearted cooperation a round table with an iron top was rescued from an old summer house, placed in a corner of the hall and heaped with food, Frank and his friend were then ordered to get a chair each and try not to be a bother and their mothers returned to the guests.

The success of most learned societies is measured by their teas. The Barchester Archaeological had been accustomed to do its members very well in this matter, but each successive summer of the war had reduced the quality of the food and increased the amount of substitute milk. This summer the food fell well below even the previous years' averages, being mostly dry looking cakes with no color and no smell, or sandwiches of grayish bread with various proprietary "spreads" in them. As for the milk, it was just powdered milk beaten up with water and very nasty too, though released as a great favor by the grocer who was Mr. Freeman's cousin. But nothing has yet stopped people eating nasty cakes or drinking greedily cups of tea of an unknown and powdery brand flavored with artificial milk and everyone was in very good humor, saying perhaps next summer the war would be over.

"Over next summer?" said Mr. Knox to Jane. "Speaking as a historian which I am not, for biographies of historical persons do, do *not*, I say constitute history as I, alas, am the first to confess; speaking, I say, as a historian however unworthy, I say to myself: what is the lesson history has taught us?"

He glared at Jane, defying her to guess the riddle.

"Nothing, I should think," said Jane. "If it had people would have a bit more sense."

"The lesson of history?" said Mr. Middleton coming up on the other side of her, much to Mr. Knox's annoyance. "Had you, Mrs. Gresham, walked as I have over the fields of Waterloo, and Quatre Bras and Ligny too——"

"And died at Trafalgar," said Jane, and then wished she hadn't, for it was but too evident that Mr. Middleton did not recognize the allusion and she feared he would want it explained. Luckily, however, as she afterwards told Robin Dale, he tanked right over her without so much as noticing what she said.

"——you would realize," Mr. Middleton continued, holding his cup in one hand and pouring all the tea that had slopped over his saucer into an empty cup that the secretary had just put down, "that history has no lesson at all."

"Nay, Middleton," said Mr. Knox, attracting by this striking and unusual opening the attention of all those near him, "nay," he repeated, pleased with his success, "there I join issue with you. Wait though. May I," he said thrusting his cup across the table to Mrs. Freeman, "crave another cup of this excellent tea?"

With a smile of pitying toleration for the peculiarities of the gentry, Mrs. Freeman served him, carrying on the while an animated conversation with the Mothers' Union secretary about 2-ply navy wool without coupons at the Barchester Co-op.

Mrs. Middleton approached, saw her husband replunge into the fray, smiled abstractedly and moved towards the door seeking fresh air, for the room was hot with humanity. Jane, who had always liked and admired Mrs. Middleton but did not know her very well, followed her, said a few words about the day's entertainment, and hoped she was not tired.

"Oh no," said Mrs. Middleton. "I don't get tired, or hardly ever. One can't afford to when my husband is about. He needs all the tiredness for himself."

Jane could not decide whether this was simplicity or sarcasm and hardly liked to ask. Mrs. Middleton remained silent, looking over the garden, apparently quite content and not at all embarrassed by the silence; which Jane found somehow reassuring, as if there were suddenly a strong arm to lean on.

"Good day Mrs. Middleton," said Lord Stoke, whose perambulation of the room had brought him to this point. "We don't often meet nowadays. Do you remember that famous meeting at your house about Pooker's Piece, when that bounder Hibberd was trying to buy it and enclose it?"

Mrs. Middleton smiled, always with her look of seeing a little farther than the place where she was, and said she did remember it, and how old Lord Pomfret had bought the land and given it to the county.

"Poisonous fellow," said Lord Stoke. "Well, he's a Liberal M.P. now and poor Pomfret's dead. And what's happened to that young man that played the piano. Lanky young fellow with a face like nutcrackers."

"Oh, Denis Stonor, Jack's nephew," said Mrs. Middleton, "at least Jack's sister's first husband's son: no relation of ours at all. He is in America I think."

"Ballet dancer or something, wasn't he?" said Lord Stoke.

"Not exactly a dancer, Lord Stoke," said Mrs. Middleton. "He wrote music for ballets and Lord Bond very kindly lent him some money to finance a new company and it was a success and then he went to America and was caught by the war. I believe his music is played a good deal."

"America in wartime, eh?" said Lord Stoke, with less than his usual good humored tolerance. "Thought they rounded all the fellows up."

"Not SHIRKING," said Mrs. Middleton raising her voice. "He had a weak HEART and was always rather an INVALID and the army wouldn't LOOK AT HIM."

"Poor young man," said Lord Stoke. "Is he married?"

Jane idly thought that Mrs. Middleton's distant gaze was directed upon something unattainable which for a moment had come nearer to her. Mrs. Middleton shook her head, possibly exhausted by the effort of shouting.

"Ah well, perhaps it's a good thing," said Lord Stoke. "Doesn't do to have a family if you're an invalid. Bad for the stock." He then inquired after Mr. Middleton's three cows and went off in search of more gossip.

It had never before struck Jane that Mrs. Middleton was particularly good-looking, but whether it was the sun falling through the leaves of a large walnut tree, or some thought or quiet vision that transfigured her, Jane suddenly saw her as an enchanting woman.

"Mr. Stonor must want to get back to England sometimes," she said, just to say something.

"Perhaps," said Mrs. Middleton abstractedly. "But sometimes it is better if people don't come back."

This she appeared to say for herself alone, but her words struck an unreasonable chill to Jane's heart as she thought how she had sometimes wished for the certainty that Francis would never return rather than the relentless uncertainty and anxiety that underlay her daily life. As Mrs. Middleton continued to gaze upon this unknown point beyond the horizon, Jane pulled herself together and finding the secretary disengaged introduced herself and congratulated him on the delightful afternoon.

At this the young clerk was delighted, for the Archaeological Society was his method of escape, not only from being in a solicitor's office when he would rather have been a Death's Head Hussar, but from his mother who knew him through and through (or so she said) and never stopped trying to know more.

"Do tell me," she said with an interest that would only have deceived a mother-ridden young man, "what the result of the meeting really was. I had to keep an eye on my little boy and a friend of his and couldn't hear all the speeches."

"Well, Mrs. Gresham, that is difficult to say," said the secretary. "Our speakers differed considerably, but if you ask me, some of these old gentlemen haven't really *studied* the subject; not what you'd *call* studied," he added.

Jane said she didn't suppose any of them were exactly experts, but they did know a lot about the county. Lord Stoke, for instance, had lived at High Rising all his life, as his forebears had since about 1400, and knew everyone and every inch of the country.

"Admitted, Mrs. Gresham," said the secretary. "But to know a bit of Roman brickwork takes more than that. I may seem a bit dogmatic to you, Mrs. Gresham, but it happens to be quite a hobby of mine. We lawyers must have our little hobbies you know, or we get quite dissected as you might say."

Jane felt she might more probably say desiccated, but smiled and said "Yes, of course."

"But there was one unfortunate occurrence," said the secretary, getting nearer Jane and lowering his voice, "which I wouldn't mention, except to you Mrs. Gresham, because we lawyers have to be careful what we say."

Jane said perhaps he had better not tell her then.

"A lady like you," said the secretary gallantly, "is as safe as well I won't say houses for tempora have mutantur, but as safe as," he continued, obviously searching his mind for something stable in this world of flux, "well, as safe as *anything*."

"Rather double-edged," said Jane and then wished she hadn't, for the secretary mistaking her meaning, said he was sure he hadn't meant it in that spirit and was obviously prepared to take offense.

"And what was it?" said Jane with frenzied eagerness.

"Well," said the secretary relenting, "it was this, Mrs. Gresham. I had looked at all the samples of brickwork myself and labelled them as the man brought them up from the well, and there was one that, in my poor opinion for what it's worth, absolutely clenched the matter. Now I labelled that bit myself and put it on the side of the well just as Lord Stoke came up. I was going to put it on the tray with other specimens, but Lord Stoke had some little boys with him——"

"One of them was mine," said Jane, that the secretary might be forearmed against indiscretion.

"——oh really, a fine little fellow," said the secretary with no enthusiasm at all, "——and when he turned around to speak and I looked on the parapet of the well, the sample was gone."

"Oh dear," said Jane.

"Mind you, I do not say those boys done it," said the secretary, his grammar rather affected by his enthusiasm. "They weren't that sort. But I have my strong suspicions, Mrs. Gresham, that one of our members, I won't say who, deliberately took that specimen, Mrs. Gresham, while my eye was off it. Preferring not to make unpleasantness, I said nothing, and I name no names, but I am morally convicted that a certain person not a hundred miles from here deliberately pocketed that sample."

Jane asked why.

"Ah, well you may say why, Mrs. Gresham," said the secretary, edging Jane up against the table till she thought she would fall over backwards into the teacups. "That person, whose name I would prefer not to mention, may have wished to withhold valuable evidence, or he may, you'll observe I only say *may*, propose to put it as an exhibit in his local museum and say he dug it up."

Jane said it was a really shocking story, repeated how grateful they were to the secretary for arranging such a delightful afternoon, and continued her progress.

Pausing before the little table where Frank and his friend were still hard at work, she asked if they were having a nice time.

"Yes, please," said Master Watson with his mouth full.

"I liked the well best, mother," said Frank, pushing a large mouthful into one cheek with his tongue. "Mother, did you know I threw a stone down and it took about ten minutes to plop in the water. Ed says there's a stinking cat down there. I expect the cat stinked like anything when my stone fell on it."

"It wasn't a stone," said Master Watson, in the brief pause necessary between finishing the cake he had in his mouth and taking a fresh one. "It was a brick. I saw it with a bit of paper on it."

"Well, get on with your tea," said Jane, only thankful that the secretary of the Archaeological Society had not overheard the conversation.

Now at intervals during the afternoon, when not entertaining guests or keeping an eye on the little boys, Jane had vaguely wondered if the Adams family were coming. It hardly seemed a treat that would interest them, but she remembered Miss Holly saying something about it and felt that she would miss no opportunity of improving her young charge's general information. In the turmoil of tea and talk all this had entirely gone out of her mind and it was with almost a start that she suddenly found herself face to face with Mr. Adams.

"I dare say," said Mr. Adams, holding out a hand to be shaken, "you were wondering why Heth and I weren't here. Well, the answer is I was kept."

Jane, stifling an intense desire to say "Pleased to meet you," shook the proffered hand, and said she was sorry he and Heather had missed the discussion.

"About some brickwork, wasn't it?" said Mr. Adams. "Not much in my line nor Heth's. If it had been about chromium steel now, or high mathematics, me and Heth would have had a word to say. But we can't all be interested in the same things, and that's a fact."

Jane said it was and rather wished Mr. Adams would go away, for her duty was to the company in general and she had a sensation of being forcibly monopolized. But it was very easy to offend the Adamses of this world and Jane hated unpleasantness, so she asked after Miss Holly.

"Remarkably fine woman, Miss Holly," said Mr. Adams, "with no nonsense about her," at which Jane looked quickly at him. But the borrowing was obviously unconscious, and he went on, "Heth and she came to the meeting and went back to Mrs. Merivale for tea. But I dare say you are wondering why I was kept."

There was no way of expressing how little she wondered or indeed cared, so Jane said not bad news she hoped.

"I wouldn't like to say," said Mr. Adams. "No, not bad news exactly. More what you would call uncertain news. It might be bad, it might be good."

So peculiar was his rather ill-assured way of speaking, so unlike his usual confident self, that Jane wondered for a moment if he had been drinking. As far as she knew he was remarkably abstemious and there were certainly no signs of drink about him. So she felt slightly uneasy.

"Now, I don't want to upset you, Mrs. Gresham," said Mr. Adams, "But I've got a pal who is pretty high up in the Red Cross and goes to meet all those repatriation ships."

"Jane dear," said Mrs. Morland at her side. "I am dreadfully sorry but I must say good-bye. The Tebbens are going in Lord Stoke's brougham and will drop me at the station. Here they are."

"Do you know, Mr. Adams?" said Jane, introducing him to Mrs. Morland and the Tebbens.

"Is it the Mrs. Morland that writes the books?" said Mr. Adams much to Jane's surprise.

"How very nice of you to ask," said Mrs. Morland, dropping a glove which Mr. Adams gallantly rescued for her. "Do you like them?"

"Well, Mrs. Morland, I'm not a reading man," said Mr. Adams, "but I like a good book now and then. There was one by you my little girl brought back from the libery this summer—Heather, that's her name; Heth I call her—about a lady dressmaker that gets trapped in a foundry by the German spy. Now, I've some works at Hogglestock, and I do some pretty big castings myself, and I must say the scene where the villain is going to throw her in the furnace and the hero comes along in the overhead crane with the big magnet and picks her up by the steel chain the villain has wrapped round her—well, it was hardly credible it could really happen, but I thought, 'Whoever thought that up wasn't a fool.'"

Mrs. Morland, always the most modest of creatures about her own works, pushed a hairpin into herself and knocked her hat rather on one side before expressing her great pleasure that Mr. Adams had enjoyed the book.

"Enjoyed I wouldn't hardly say," said Mr. Adams, "for that's not the way I look at books. But there's not one in a thousand, I said to myself, would think up a thing like that, and a thing that is, making allowances for everything, quite feasible. If ever you want to know anything about the shops or the foundry for a book, Mrs. Morland, just you ring my sekertary and I'll tell her to see you get all the information you want. Now, don't forget; for Sam Adams won't forget."

Before Mr. Morland could thank him properly, Mrs. Tebben had burst to the front and shaking Mr. Adams by the hand said that as a mother she must thank him for having been so wonderful to Richard.

"Well, madam," said Mr. Adams, puzzled but master of himself, "I don't know who it is you are reluding to, but I always do my best to give everyone a fair do."

Mrs. Tebben was about to explain that her son Richard was a difficult character but wonderful when you came to know him, when her husband said Lord Stoke's horse would catch cold if it waited and Mrs. Morland would miss her train, upon which Mrs. Tebben, with a long handshake and earnest gaze, intended to exhibit to Mr. Adams the depth of a mother's love and the brilliance of her son Richard's qualities all in one breath, hurried her party away.

"More people know Tom Fool than Tom Fool knows," said Mr. Adams philosophically. "But now, Mrs. Gresham, you will be wondering what it was my pal had to say."

Then the Birketts came to bid good-bye to Jane and had to be introduced to Mr. Adams, and other friends came up one after the other as the party dispersed. And all the time they were talking Jane half wondered what Mr. Adams's pal had to say and half wished he would go away and not bother her. And all the time she was impressed, against her will, by the calm and almost masterful way in which Mr. Adams took the County and the Close; how he did not try to appear their equal, but was obviously well seated in the position he had made for himself. She also noticed how almost everyone, from Mrs. Morland (who was neither Close nor real County) to the Dean and Lord Stoke, who represented both, had points of contact, usually of a useful and civic kind, with Mr. Adams, and that he appeared quite often to be in a position to do some small favor, to help them over some small difficulty. What all the wives thought she did not know, but her impression was that Mr. Adams was what is called a man's man.

There was no reason why she should stay in his neighborhood, except indeed that when people began to say good-bye and leave the hall they would naturally come to speak to her. And if where she was standing happened to be in the neighborhood of Mr. Adams, it could not be helped.

Gradually the guests melted away. The Mothers' Union, who had cleared and washed up the tea things some time ago, now pushed the big tables back into their places and began to remove the camouflage frames from their temporary place against the walls. Frank and Master Watson, who had helped with the washing up and broken the lid of the biggest teapot, were suddenly apparent.

"Come along, Frank," said his mother, who sometimes felt that these words would be found on her heart when she died; which was at least better than the word "Don't," which would certainly have been found somewhere inside her if she had died a little earlier. "We'll take Tom back to Mrs. Watson. She said he could stay here as long as we did."

"I'll run you all down," said Mr. Adams, "I've got Packer outside."

Jane thanked him and said it was only a question of walking down the garden to the Watsons' house.

"So it is," said Mr. Adams, who had not realized that the hall, which he had approached in Packer's car from the back lane, was in the Watsons' grounds. "I'll walk down with you, Mrs. Gresham, and then I can run you and your little boy home."

Jane, who wanted a little fresh air after standing so long in the stuffy tearoom, thanked him and said she and Frank would really rather walk, to which he replied that he would walk with them, and Packer could pick him up at Hallbury House. It was all rather a bore, but the Archaeological always was a boring day, thought Jane, and one might as well be civil. So they all went down the garden and delivered Master Watson at his back door and then, without entering the house, went around into the street. Here Frank Gresham became absorbed in the game, mysteriously compelling at almost any age, of walking on the pavement in such a manner that he never trod on the joining of two flags, which made his progress a matter of concentration.

"Well, to return to the subject in hand," said Mr. Adams, "I'd like to tell you what my pal said. He meets those ships and sees the repatriated men before anyone else can get hold of them and gets a lot of useful information about people who are missing."

Jane looked quickly at him.

"Now, don't you commence to worry, Mrs. Gresham," said Mr. Adams. "I told you it was uncertain news. It's not good; it might be worse. There was a petty officer my pal was questioning and he mentioned a Commander Gresham. Now, there wouldn't be another Commander Gresham, would there?"

"I never heard of one," said Jane. "Commander Francis Gresham."

"That was the name," said Mr. Adams, glancing at her and seeing no signs of discomposure. "Well, this petty officer said he had seen him somewhere in the jungle on an island out there——"

Jane looked swiftly at him again.

"——about two years ago," pursued Mr. Adams. "He heard of him again from another man, about a year ago. He was down with fever then and pretty bad. Now, if I've done wrong, Mrs. Gresham, I'll apologize. It's not much news, but it may be better than none."

"Thank you very much," said Jane.

"Well, I'll be going on now," said Mr. Adams, for the short walk to Hallbury House was over and Packer was sitting in his car outside the gate. Jane stopped and put out her hand.

"Please don't tell anyone," she said. "They'd only want to talk about it."

"I get you, Mrs. Gresham," said Mr. Adams. "And I've got that pal of mine on the job good and proper. Any news that we do get you will hear. And if Sam Adams can do anything for you, you've only got to say the word. My little Heth, she thinks the world of you, Mrs. Gresham, and her and I see eye to eye in most things."

He then got into the car. Mr. Packer put into his pocket the newspaper he had been reading and the car went away. Jane collected Frank, superintended his bath, ate his supper with her father and her son, answered a number of Frank's questions, bore with more patience than her father the way Frank boasted about having looked down the well, sat with her father till about ten o'clock and then went to bed.

"Delayed shock," she said aloud to her reflection, which looked at her from the mirror in its usual way. "You'll begin to think presently and then you'll be sorry."

With which vindictive words she got into bed, read for a little, and was soon asleep.

Between two and three in the morning the long heavy pulsation of airplanes passing over the country with drumming persistence gradually penetrated her sleep. As she woke, every nerve and every dark thought sprang to life, taut and strained. The hope she had forbidden herself to feel had come to life again; and with it all the terrors and agonies that she thought she had buried beyond reach of plummet. Francis; alive two years ago, ill with fever one year ago, still free. Had he died? Had he been taken prisoner? Did he still live on that island, hidden in the jungle? Could he escape? Was he as anxious and wretched for her as she was for him? So her thoughts battered her all through the dark and the dawning hours. She might have spoken of them to Robin, but Robin was not here, and it was not of him she thought, it was of Mr. Adams. Hateful, hateful of him to disturb the peace she had made for herself, to crack the thin ice that lay over the deep lake of forgotten things. People who meant well, who tried to help, always made it worse. She would have liked to stand before him and rail like a fishwife, blaming his busybody interference and if possible hurting him a good deal.

Now would begin again the waking every morning with a sense of a crime committed, a crime unknown, which passed but too quickly into remembrance of her loss, of her uncertainty, of her misery lest Francis should also be fearing for her in a bombed and burning England. Then she would pull herself together, go about her duties, play with Frank, forget. But she could not put the enemy off the scent. The pangs, the contradictory passions that ravaged her would not be stifled. And so it would go on and on. And now, to add to her self-tormenting, she thought she had not been polite enough, grateful enough to Mr. Adams, who after all had tried, in his own way, to do what he could for her.

The growing daylight brought her back to common sense, to a resolve to accept his well-meant kindness as he meant it. And after all, in these horrid days when every man's hand had to keep his head more or less, and most of one's friends were too deep in their own anxieties to do very much for one, it was in a way comforting to think of a man who, even if not one's own sort, was ready to help and in a position to know and do a good deal. There was something about Mr. Adams that made it impossible to dislike him, and he was a person upon whom, she felt certain, she could rely for anything that he promised.

CHAPTER 10

Sunday spread its slightly depressing wings over all Barset-shire and the world outside. Most people went to church, ate too much wartime lunch, slept, played tennis, walked, wrote letters, and the day was over. By Monday the camouflage makers were at work again as if the Archaeological tea had never happened and Jane had herself well in hand again. Or if she had not, no one would have known it.

The great event of this week was Anne Fielding's seventeenth birthday, which was to be on Thursday. Her parents could not come down for the day itself and told her to ask her own party to tea and they would have a birthday dinner together at the weekend.

"It is rather difficult," said Anne to Miss Bunting, as they partook of a modest lunch together on Monday, "about asking who one likes, because one doesn't exactly know. I mean I'd like just to ask Mrs. Gresham and Robin and Dr. Dale—and Heather," she added a little dubiously.

Miss Bunting listened attentively, but made no comment.

"Only then," said Anne, "there are people one does like, only one doesn't want to ask them, like Mrs. Watson and Mrs. Merivale."

"Unless there is any very pressing reason, I would not ask people you do not wish to ask," said Miss Bunting.

"But they have asked me," said Anne. "And then there's Miss

Holly. She is awfully nice, but I don't want her for my birthday."

Miss Bunting gave it as her opinion that it was quite unnecessary for a young girl in Anne's position to consider the question of returning hospitality to everyone. Let Anne, she said, ask the people she wanted to ask and her mother would ask the people who ought to be asked.

"But I am glad," she said, "that you think of the duties of hospitality. When you have a house of your own, you will probably have to ask people who do not always interest you. Meanwhile, do as your mother suggests and ask your own friends. Mrs. Gresham and Dr. Dale and his son will be pleasant guests and Heather Adams will enjoy the treat."

If Anne noticed this distinction, we could not say.

"Oh, and there is one more person I would like to ask," said Anne.

Miss Bunting asked who that might be.

"Can't you guess?" said Anne.

Miss Bunting, who really did not much mind whom Anne asked, as all her little circle at Hallbury were well known to her, said she couldn't.

"You of course," said Anne. "*Do* come, Miss Bunting."

Whether Miss Bunting had meant to come to the tea party or not, we do not presume to state. Probably she had not thought very much about it. Her pupil's pressing and heartfelt invitation took her quite by surprise and a slight color appeared on her shriveled cheeks as she accepted the invitation.

The rest of Monday and whole of Tuesday and Wednesday were made rather difficult by Gradka, who in her enthusiasm for making a birthday cake such as her nation approved, was in and out of the garden, the drawing room, the dining room, and even Miss Bunting's and Anne's bedrooms, half a dozen times a day; sometimes to discuss the cake, and far too often to give them the latest wireless news about liberated Mixo-Lydia.

On the great Thursday morning, Gradka overslept herself, which had never happened before, for Gradka as well as being an excellent cook was an early riser. So early in fact did she rise that Sir Robert and Lady Fielding when in residence often wished she didn't. To the middle-aged the cheerful noise of brushing and sweeping, the crash of saucepans (for Gradka kept the kitchen door wide open till her employers came down), the sound of Mixo-Lydian folk songs which appeared to have only one tune and that a poor one, the loud and contemptuous conversation with the daily milk, the Tuesday, Thursday and Saturday bread, and the post, are not welcome till they have drunk their tea or their coffee. And worse than all these had been the devilish roar and whine of the electric carpet sweeper, which is far more like a siren than anyone who has lived near air raid warnings can like. Basely sheltering herself behind her husband's name, Lady Fielding had told Gradka that Sir Robert did not like the noise so early, and could Gradka do the carpet on the bedroom landing a little later.

"If needful, not at oll," said Gradka. "The devil sends the dust. God wills it so."

Lady Fielding said she didn't mean not at all in the least, but if it could be a little later, Sir Robert would like to have his sleep out.

"In Mixo-Lydia we say six hours of sleep for a hero," said Gradka, "seven for the Sczarhzy, what you call housemistress which is the hero's wife, either for the Sczarhzy-pskrb which is the housemistress parturiating, and nine for the Krzsyl, which is the old man, the dottard, as your Shakespeare says."

"Dotard," said Lady Fielding mechanically, passing over this reflection on Sir Robert, who was not quite sixty and remarkably strong and healthy.

"So; I thank you," said Gradka. "Then will I not sweep the landing. Why sweep today what you must again sweep tomorrow, we say in Mixo-Lydia."

Lady Fielding said she didn't quite mean that, but if Gradka could do it after half past seven, or perhaps just brush the carpet by hand and not have the electric cleaner running——

"Aha! it is the electric broom which you dislike," said Gradka, "I too, God! which noise, which tumult! In Mixo-Lydia we take oll our carpets into the street every day and beat them there while we gossip. So is everything clean. But here you nail your carpet to the floor and sweep it with this machine which shrieks like a damned up soul in devils' land. Ha! I would like to hear the jolly old Slavo-Lydians shriek when they are dead; ollso when they are alive too. Openly, I find quite detestworthy this sweeping machine, Prodshka Fielding, and for two lydions, which a lydion is one-sixtieth part of your farthing, I would crash it with the wood axe. So in future from now onwards I shall sweep with my hands and the machine may stand in the cupboard to think on his sins."

On the great Thursday morning in question the house was quiet. Anne was peacefully sleeping, being still young enough to wake slowly and easily with no interior alarm clock to make her wake with a vaguely conscience stricken jerk. Gradually a sound penetrated her consciousness. She woke up, listened, went to sleep again for an eternity, woke again after a third of a second, and heard the front door bell, which was a real one, not electric, pealing determinedly. As it didn't stop she dashed into a dressing gown and slippers and ran down to see if anything was the matter, though without any real apprehension, for misfortune had not yet touched her with the dread of a bell, a letter, a telegram, which most of us have, and had even before the war made every sound a menace.

As she ran downstairs the pealing stopped, then began again with renewed vigor. She undid the chain and bolts, which were more a token to burglars that they were not wanted than any real protection, for no side door or window on the ground floor offered any real obstacle to anyone wishing to effect an entry. On the doorstep was Greta Tory, one of the Hallbury post-women, niece of Admiral Palliser's cook.

"Many happy returns, miss," said Greta, who in her postman's cap askew on dirty, overpermed hair, her jacket imperfectly restraining what our cliché-ridden neighbors the Gauls would have called her budding charms, her legs in rather large trousers from below which her bare feet in toeless sandals peeped in and out, presented a very unattractive sight; but a nice, good girl, who gave all the wages she didn't spend on herself to her mother.

"Oh, thank you, Greta," said Anne. "How did you know?"

Greta said Auntie told her last night when she went around to supper with her at the old Admiral's, because Mrs. Gresham had said something to Auntie about having tea at Hall's End for Miss Anne's birthday.

"Nice lot of letters for you," said Greta, handing a fat bundle to Anne. "Where's that Gradka? Those foreigners ought to be made to work a bit, same as we. If she had to be round at the post office at half past five to sort the letters same as I have, she'd be all the better for it."

"I don't know," said Anne. "I was asleep and woke up when I heard you ring and no one answered it, so I came down. I say, Greta, would you like a cup of tea!"

Greta said she wouldn't mind if she did, so Anne shut the front door quietly, because of Miss Bunting, and the two girls went to the kitchen. As usual, Gradka had left everything in perfect order. The kitchen looked as if it had just been scrubbed, the little furnace for the hot water, well banked up, was quite hot and two kettles were sitting on it. Anne put one of them on the gas ring, got milk, sugar and crockery, and tea was soon made. Just as they were sitting down, there was a bang on the back door.

"That'll be Ernie Freeman," said Greta. "I passed him with the bread van in Little Gidding. He's early today. 'Xpect he wants to get off for the pictures. They're showing Inglorious Hampdens at the Barchester Odeon. Glamora Tudor's in it."

"What is it about?" said Anne, poised for flight to the back door.

"Ow, I dunno," said Greta. "Something about the war, I s'pose. They say it's ever so good and Glamora Tudor has a lovely song called 'What has my past to do with love?' You must have heard it, miss."

But Anne had fled to the scullery, and unbolting the back door opened it to Ernie Freeman.

"'Llo, Grad," said Ernie, who was looking into his basket of loaves. "On the warpath as per usual? Oh, I beg your pardon, miss, I thought it was that Grad. She ill or anything?"

"I think she must have overslept," said Anne. "I don't know what bread, but the same as usual, please."

"You'd better leave an extra sandwich loaf, Ernie," said the voice of Greta Tory from the kitchen. "It's the young lady's birthday."

"I'm sorry I'm sure, miss," said Ernie Freeman. "If I'd known it was your birthday, I wouldn't've knocked that loud, but I'm in a bit of a hurry on the round this morning."

"Oh, thank you," said Anne, as he put the bread on the scullery table. "You wouldn't like a cup of tea, would you? Greta's having one."

"Well, if you don't mind, miss, I will," said Ernie, putting his basket on the floor. "It won't hurt no one to wait."

Some very lively badinage then took place between Greta and Ernie, to which Anne listened, fascinated, till the milk came banging on the back door. Greta insisted on opening it and after a brief colloquy returned with the milk herself, who was a stout Land Girl from Northbridge. They all sat on or at the kitchen table, tea was drunk, Anne's birthday toasted and the new film discussed.

"What's it about?" said Anne to the milk girl, who had been there on her half-day off.

"I didn't really follow," said the milk girl. "Something about we're all heroes at home same as the boys at the front. Silly, that is. But Glamora Tudor's reely, well I can't seem to put it into words. And the dresses she has. It's all in Glorious Technicolor,

miss, and there's a closeup of her when she's working in a factory
in a mauve bath suit and ticks off the foreman that tried to make
the girls go slow because he's a German spy. We all hissed him
like anything. And then the hero, that's the R.A.F. sergeant only
he's a gentleman, comes back and thinks Glamora Tudor's been
false to him with—well I can't exactly explain," said the milk
girl hurriedly, seeing in Greta Tory's eye that Anne's want of
sophistication was to be respected, "but anyway she sings, 'What
has my past to do with love?' and all the girls join in and all the
machinery seems to work by itself like and join in the chorus and
the foreman comes in with a bag in disguise and they think it's a
bomb, but he's really the English Secret Agent that was pre-
tending to be a German spy so no one'd know he was a Secret
Service man and he has a big Union Jack in the bag and Glamora
and the R.A.F. sergeant sit on it and all the girls get out of their
overalls and they're reely wearing red brassieres and white knickers
and blue shoes and they lift the Union Jack in the air with Glamora
and her young man sitting on it and then it all fades out into a
photo of the King and Queen. I can't explain, but it seems to get
you somehow."

"Why's it called In Glorious Hampton?" said Ernie.

"I d'no," said Greta. "Isn't there an aeroplane called Hampton
or something?"

Before Anne could express her admiration of the film, there
was a knock at the back door.

"Oh, it must be the newspaper," said Anne.

"Don't you go, miss," said Greta Tory, "it's that Leslie, the
station master's nephew. I saw him go past the window. The
army's where he ought to be. Here Ernie, you run and get them,
there's a duck."

Ernie opened the back door, shut it again and was back in an
instant with the newspapers. A very nice sense of what was due
to the gentry prevented Anne's guests from opening them, but
as all but one had their headlines across the front page, their
self-control was not severely tested. The headlines, as usual,

were almost too large to read and far from truthful. The *Times*, which but rarely has any item of news on its front page, had been so far moved by the epoch making events of a world war as to announce to its subscribers at the top right hand corner in large type: "Peace Ballot in Guatemala."

"I think it's a shame," said Greta, who had been studying one of the lesser sheets without the law," old Winnie having to go about like that. He's ever so much older than the others. Old Roosevelt's got a bad leg or something so they say, but Joe Stalin's got all his arms and legs, lazy old blighter."

Ernie at once took up what he knew to be a deliberate attack on our Red Comrades, but before more than a few words had passed, a slight noise was heard; and looking round the whole party froze to respectful silence at the sight of Miss Bunting in a quilted silk dressing gown, her head covered by a neat little lace bonnet. So powerful was the effect of Miss Bunting's presence that the whole party got up and stood to attention.

"Oh, Miss Bunting," said Anne. "The bell kept on ringing and no one was up, so I came down. This is Greta Tory who brought the post and this is Ernie Freeman that does the bread round and this is Effie Bunce that works for Masters's dairy farm. She used to be with Miss Pemberton at Northbridge."

Miss Bunting took her pince-nez from a pocket, put them on, and looked searchingly at the intruders. Most willingly would they have bowed, scraped, curtsied, made a leg, bobbed, tugged a forelock; but civilization in its backward progress has eliminated all these forms of respect to age or position as uneducated, undemocratic and shameful. So they all went red in the face and looked up, down, around; anywhere but at the newcomer.

"You all seem to be having tea," said Miss Bunting. "Can you give me a cup, Anne? You may all sit down."

The guests sat down vehemently, so much overawed by Miss Bunting's calm and regal manner that they did not even try to giggle.

"Very many happy returns of the day, Anne dear," said Miss

Bunting. "And now," she continued, to the rest of her audience, "you will want to be going."

Glad to be dismissed from an awkward position, Greta, Ernie and Effie pushed their chairs back. The kitchen door opened again and Gradka appeared.

"You will wish to know why I am late," she exclaimed, "I am very sorry, Miss Bunting. I have been listening at midnight to the European news and there I hear a voice from Mixo-Lydia. Oh! how I rejoice to hear again that holy language. And such good news as makes me leap with joy. I shall tell you oll that Mixo-Lydia has burned the Town Hall of Slavo-Lydia's chief town with fifty people inside it. It was a great meeting for Anti-Mixo-Lydia and oll the head inhabitants were there. But could they treek Mixo-Lydia? This hero-land sends her brave sons. They steal petrol from a garage which is in Slavo-Lydia, they put the petrol in the Town Hall, they seize the Town Fool the idiot which is ollways in every town in Mixo- and Slavo-Lydia, they say to him 'Here are five lydions. If you set fire to this petrol we will give you the five lydions.' Ha! Well, oll goes as God wills it. Oll the chief men of Slavo-Lydia which is fifty men go into the Town Hall, very closely pressed together for it is not large. The fool lights the petrol. The Town Hall is of wood and poof! oll are burned. If any try to escape the brave Mixo-Lydians shoot them. And the fool is ollso burned, so they do not have to give the five lydions. And to express my pride when it says on the radio that my oncles and oll my cousins and oll my sisters' husbands and brothers-in-law were of those heroes! Bog! Which pleasure, which joy! Then I foll asleep so happily and do not wake till late. Excuse me, Prodshkina Bunting."

"Sit down and have a cup of tea, Gradka," said Miss Bunting, at the same time giving the other guests a nod of dismissal. "Anne dear, come upstairs and get dressed. Breakfast in half an hour, Gradka."

"Oh, Gradka," said Anne. "Here are the letters. Please will

you put mine on the breakfast table, because it makes it more exciting; I haven't looked at them yet."

"Willingly, Prodshkina Anne," said Gradka.

At the expiration of the half hour Miss Bunting and Anne met at breakfast. Miss Bunting made no allusion to the events of the early morning. This, in some governesses, might have been alarming, as indicating a saving up of wrath to come. But Anne knew Miss Bunting pretty well by now and understood that on a birthday all was condoned, her kitchen tea party passed over with a smile, even Gradka's atavistic outburst forgotten as a thing of no account. The post was most satisfactory for a war-time birthday, containing no less than four checks from relations, a pair of near silk stockings and a scarf which must have cost at least two coupons. Also very loving letters from her father and mother to say they would bring their presents on Saturday when they came down. By her plate there lay also a small parcel, addressed in Miss Bunting's elegant hand. Anne opened it and found a volume of Keats's poems in a handsome though faded binding.

"Oh! Miss Bunting!" she cried, getting up and giving the old governess a respectful kiss, "how heavenly! It is just what I wanted. Now I can read all Keats. I've only read the ones that come in poetry books. Thank you so very, very much."

"It belonged to the late Lady Pomfret," said Miss Bunting, looking away into the past. "She gave it to me one Christmas when I was staying at the Towers with my pupil David Leslie, her nephew. She told me it had been given to her by an Italian cousin—you know the Counts of Strelsa are connected with the Pomfrets—who had known Joseph Severn, Keats's friend, who was English consul in Rome."

"Might Keats have *seen* it, Miss Bunting?" said Anne, awe-struck. "Oh, but can you really give it to me? I mean, it is really yours. But I do *love* it."

"It is yours now, my dear," said Miss Bunting. "I don't suppose I shall be wanting poetry, or indeed any books, for very

long now, and I like my favorite pupils to have some remembrance of me. Now dear, we must let Gradka get on with her
work."

As she spoke, Gradka came in to clear away.

"There is yet more good news," she said complacently.

"Then I do not wish to hear it," said Miss Bunting. "Whatever it is, it will be in the *Times*, where it will not necessarily be
correct, but will at least be gentlemanly."

"It is not of massacring those dirty Slavo-Lydians," said
Gradka. "No, no, it is quite otherwise. I have a letter from the
Royal Society for the Promotion of English to say I have passed
my examination with honors. I wish to thank you, Prodshkina
Bunting, for oll your help and your assistance to form my style.
I kiss your hand," which she did very prettily.

> "'I kissed Maud's hand,
> She took the kiss sedately',"

quoted Anne, much impressed.

"You have worked very hard, Gradka; and I am gratified by
your success," said Miss Bunting. "And what will you do now?"

"As soon as possible I go back to Mixo-Lydia, to teach
English," said Gradka. "Then will oll my pupils get the better of
the Slavo-Lydians in oll examinations. But now I will take your
breakfast away and begin my preparation for Prodshkina Anne's
tea party. Prodshkina Anne, I offer you my best wishes, ollso
this little gift."

Anne eagerly opened the little parcel, which contained a clasp
of roughly worked silver with a very hideous face on it.

"He is Gradko, our national hero of which there are many
epopic lays," said Gradka. "He will remind you of me sometimes, when I am gone."

So Anne thanked Gradka warmly, did her share of the
household duties, wrote all her thank letters, and then fell
headlong into Keats, emerging reluctantly for lunch.

"Did you know my name was Maud?" said Miss Bunting as they sat at lunch.

"Oh no," said Anne respectfully, for it had never occurred to her that the old governess had a Christian name at all.

"You made use of a quotation from Tennyson this morning," said Miss Bunting. "When Gradka kissed my hand."

"Oh, Miss Bunting, I am dreadfully sorry," said Anne, all contrition. "It was only because it made me think of Tennyson. It must be *heavenly* to have one's hand kissed," she added wistfully.

Miss Bunting said there were unfortunately very few men who could kiss a lady's hand gracefully now. Her old pupil David Leslie could, she said, do it to perfection, though she feared it was more to show off than from any serious feelings of respect or affection.

"Perhaps he wasn't ever really in love with anyone," said Anne.

"I never knew him when he was not in love," said Miss Bunting. "That is why he did it so well. But it never meant anything. He is fundamentally selfish."

So exquisite and romantic a picture of a heartless gallant, probably with ruffles and a velvet coat, did this description present to Anne, that she could not contain her feelings and said she wondered if she would ever see him.

"If he is not killed flying," said Miss Bunting, "you very likely may. Your parents know his people."

"Miss Bunting, how old does one have to be before people fall in love with one?" said Anne, hoping secretly to hear that seventeen was exactly the right age. But her governess rather dashed her spirits by saying it might be any age between seven and seventy, and that the young people of today had very little understanding of the graces of life.

Then Miss Bunting went upstairs for her rest and Anne returned to Keats, managing to get through Endymion, Hyperion, The Eve of St. Agnes and a number of sonnets before Jane

Gresham came into the drawing room by the open french window.

"Many happy returns of the day, Anne," said Jane kissing her. "Here is a tiny present with my love."

The present was a small red leather jewel case with a lock and key and A.F. stamped upon it in gold. Anne was overcome by its beauty and its key and the extremely grown-up feeling of having a jewel case, even if she had nothing worthy to put in it.

"Oh! Mrs. Gresham," she said, finding no better word. "I shall put my little turquoise ring that Mummy doesn't like me to wear yet in it. Oh, and Gradka gave me a silver clasp this morning; I'll put that in it too. And my pearl brooch that granny left me. *Oh!* Mrs. Gresham."

"I'm so glad you like it," said Jane. "And now that you are seventeen, I think you had better call me Jane. Not all in a hurry if you don't feel like it; but any time you do feel like it, fire away."

To this Anne almost oppressed by the amount of grown-upness that was coming on her today, could only say *"Oh!"* once more; just checking herself from saying Mrs. Gresham, but far too shy to say Jane. This Jane quite understood and said no more on the subject.

"I do hope you won't mind if Frank comes," she said. "His visit to Greshamsbury is off because the children very selfishly have measles. So he made a special present for you and wants to bring it himself."

Anne quite truthfully said she would love it.

"Dr. Dale is coming," she said, "and Robin. And Heather, because I thought she would like a party."

Jane said it all sounded very nice, and understood at once that it was Anne's thoughtful kindness, though she was entirely unconscious of this charming gift, which made her add the outsider to her party of old and intimate friends. She wondered if Mr. Adams would come and fetch his daughter. Probably not, as he did not usually come down to Hallbury till Saturday. Why she felt a slight depression she deliberately did not inquire of herself.

Then Miss Bunting came down, the jewel case was admired, politeness and county news exchanged. Steps were heard outside. Dr. Dale appeared at the window and was warmly greeted.

"My dear child," said the Rector, taking Anne's hand. "I wish you many happy returns of this happy day with all my heart. Here is a little token for you. It belonged to my dear wife and had belonged to her grandmother. I would like you to have it."

A man less given to searching his own mind might have said, "And, I know, so would she." These words had occurred to Dr. Dale in the instant before speaking, and in that instant he had also thought, with that terrifying speed that outstrips time, that he could not truthfully say what his wife, so long dead, would have thought, or what she might be thinking now; for his faith did not seek to probe these mysteries. But of one thing he was certain, that she would have approved his decision, because whatever he did had always been right in her eyes.

Almost trembling with excitement Anne opened a little tissue paper parcel, took out a little faded green case, opened it and saw a ring set with six different stones in a row. As before with Miss Bunting's present and Jane's offer of a Christian name, she could say nothing but "*Oh!*"

"The stones," said the Rector, quite understanding her embarrassment and gratitude, "spell the word 'Regard.' Ruby, emerald, garnet, amethyst, ruby, diamond."

"Diamonds and rubies!" said Anne, half-incredulous.

"Let me try it on your finger, my dear," said the Rector.

Anne held out her hand. The ring slipped easily over her third finger. The Rector raised her hand and kissed it.

"You should not have given me your left hand, my dear," he said. "That is for your engagement ring. But it looks very pretty and I think you had better consider yourself as engaged to me for the present. When you are really engaged, you can put my little ring on the other hand."

Anne could not say a single word. The ring, the romantic thought of Robin's young mother whom she had never seen, the fact of having had her hand kissed for the first time, with a good substratum of Keats, made her feel almost faint for a moment. The Rector looked delighted. There was a little babel of friendly laughter and both Jane and Miss Bunting felt it would be very easy to cry. But they quickly pulled themselves together again and Miss Bunting, looking at her pupil who was embarrassed yet pleased, a pretty flush upon her cheeks, thanking the Rector with filial deference and a touch of the woman in it which the old governess much approved, felt with justifiable complacency that the year she had devoted to Anne Fielding had been very well spent. It had often been tiring; she had missed her own friends; she was old and felt old; but her work was as good as ever and she knew that in Anne she had made her final and not unworthy contribution to the society she had taught and molded in the person of its young for so many years. Anne would be able to stand on her own feet now. How very pleasant it would be to go and stay with Lady Graham when the holidays were over, to talk to Lady Emily about old days, to read to Agnes's children, perhaps to see her most loved and most undeserving pupil David Leslie. And then to go back to Marling Hall.

A noise was heard on the terrace outside. Robin stepped through the window.

"I say, Anne," he said, "oh, how do you do, Miss Bunting, hullo Jane, I didn't know Frank was coming. He and young Watson attached themselves to my coattails just as I came out of Little Gidding. They've got some secret together about your birthday. Shall I drown them both in your lily pond?"

"Sir!" said Frank pityingly, "I can swim. Tom can't swim yet because he's too little, but when we got to Southbridge I'll help him. They've got a swimming pool on the river at Southbridge. I can swim twice up and down the Barchester swimming bath. You won't need to be frightened, Tom; I'll hold your face up. Mother, Tom will be so disappointed if we don't stay to tea, because he wants to give his present to Anne. Oh Mother, can he?"

Jane said it was Anne's party, not hers, and Anne said she would love them to stay.

"Come on then, Tom," said Frank, pulling a folded paper out of his pocket.

Tom Watson, who had been lurking behind Frank, came forward with an untidy parcel wrapped in an old bit of newspaper, which he presented to Anne. Undeterred by the wrapping, which appeared by the marks of blood and scales on it to have been used by the butcher and the fishmonger, she undid the parcel. Inside it was a tight bunch of rosebuds, red, yellow, white, pink; their heads drooping from very short stalks, the whole bound tightly together with coarse string.

"How lovely," said Anne. "Thank you both very much. I'll put them in some warm water and I expect they'll come out."

"Mrs. Watson told Tom not to pick roses," said Frank, casting a pitying eye upon his friend, "so I told him to pick the smallest ones, then it wouldn't matter. Now I'll read you *my* present."

He unfolded the piece of paper and read aloud,

> "A happy birthday, Anne,
> As happy as you can,
> I hope you'll have a fan,
> And not be a man,
> And eat something out of a pan,
> And drink water that ran
> From where it began,
> And ride in a van,
> With love from Fran——

—k," he added.

Anne thanked him very much and asked if she might keep the poetry. Frank handed it to her.

"You didn't get 'tan'," said Robin.

Frank said it didn't rhyme properly enough, because it wasn't a birthday present.

"I did ask Tom to let me call him 'Tan' in the poem," he added, looking vindictively at Master Watson, "and then he could have come into the poem, but he didn't want to."

Everyone was getting a little bored and it was a relief to hear the tea bell.

"Oh, but Heather isn't here," said Anne. "I'd forgotten."

Miss Bunting said she could join them when she came, and swept the whole party into the dining room where Gradka had arranged a delightful birthday feast with a large birthday cake iced and decorated, and some delicious small cakes, all of her own confection, and fresh fruit from the garden. Anne fetched a bowl of warm water and put Master Watson's unhappy rosebuds into it, though it was obvious that they would never smile again. The little boys were put together and ate with great steadiness and application; the grown-ups, for as such Anne felt she was now truly ranked, talked and laughed.

"By Jove," said Robin. "I had forgotten my present."

He handed to Anne a small tight shapeless parcel which looked as if it might burst.

"Take care," he said. "It's a kind of a Jack-in-the-box."

And indeed it was, for the contents were a bath sponge of considerable size, which, though small compared with prewar standards was mentally priced by all the ladies present at a guinea at the very least, and would obviously be at least three times as large when in its natural element. Admiration almost obscured by envy appeared on every adult face. Anne offered heartfelt thanks to Robin and said the only sad thing was that she couldn't put it in her jewel box. Everything was very friendly and happy. Then the resounding front door bell was heard and Heather came in, hot and not very attractive.

"Sorry," she said to the company in general. "I missed the train from Barchester after lunch. I'd been to get you a present,

Anne. This is it with many happy returns from Daddy and me."

She put on the table some parcels which Anne at once undid. The contents were a large bottle of scent, a large box of powder, a powder puff with a huge satin bow on it and a box of bath salts. Jane and Miss Bunting and Robin knew that not only was the whole gift fantastically expensive, but most of its ingredients could only be obtained by luck, or by curious methods unknown to them. Anne did not know all this, but her instinct told her that it was not the present that anyone of her own age and roughly her own sort would have given or received, which made her thank Heather with all the more effusion.

Jane, guessing that Anne was a little shy of this guilty splendor, made room between herself and Robin for Heather, to whom everyone was particularly nice.

"How on earth did you get hold of all that?" asked Robin, to the secret interest of all present.

"It was Dad," said Heather. "He's got a friend in Barchester who has a kind of shop that isn't a shop, and he can often get you things. But he doesn't send them so I went in by train and fetched them, and that's what made me late. What a marvelous cake."

Anne said that Gradka had made it and they went on talking, but things were not quite so comfortable as they had been and Jane, feeling an unnecessary amount of pity for Heather, rather laid herself out to be nice, little knowing that she was heaping fuel upon the consuming flame of passion.

"When is your birthday, Heather?" she asked, trying to find subjects for conversation.

Heather said June the fifth.

"Bad luck it's over for this year," said Jane. "We must all send you a telegram next year. Perhaps we shall be having Greetings telegrams again by then."

"When's yours, Mrs. Gresham," said Heather, rapidly wondering what day, short of Christmas and all the Bank Holidays rolled into one, could be good enough for the idol.

Jane said Guy Fawkes Day, a flippancy which Heather thought hardly worthy of her.

"I wish I could be in Hallbury then," said Heather, "but I shall be at Cambridge."

Jane said she expected it would be great fun and lots of new friends.

"Just like the Hosiers I expect," said Heather gloomily, "only it'll be Honor of the College instead of Honor of the School. But when I've finished I'm going to help Daddy at the works."

Jane said how nice and felt bored, though she didn't show it.

Then Miss Bunting rose, compelling all to rise with her, and said it wasn't windy on the terrace. So to the terrace they went and sat in the sun in comparative warmth, and the little boys went to help Gradka to clear away and wash up while Frank tried to teach her the first Latin declension.

Though poor Heather was civil and willing, it could not be denied that her presence spoilt everything. She was just too much over life size to suit her company; all their talk had to be faintly watered down for her comprehension; in fact she was a bore to everyone. So all the more did they continue to exert themselves to make her one of them. All except Miss Bunting, who withdrew into herself and watched and said nothing.

Dr. Dale was the first to take his leave, thanking Anne very much for a delightful afternoon.

"Good-bye, dear child," he said to Anne. "Come and see me some day soon. Come to tea."

Anne said, truthfully, that she would love to, and kissed the old Rector affectionately, thanking him once more for her present.

"'From this day will I bless you,'" said the Rector, using the words of his favorite prophet and making all his friends love and admire him more than ever, although not quite at their ease. But he at once became his usual self again and saying a kind word to everyone went away by the garden door, refusing Robin's escort.

"My dear Papa," said Robin, looking after his father's departing figure, "is sometimes too like an elderly clergyman to be true," at which Anne became very indignant.

The doorbell pealed. The sound of Gradka's heavy tread in the hall was heard, then a man's voice. Heather said it was Daddy come to fetch her.

"I thought your father didn't come down till Saturday," said Jane.

Heather said he usually didn't, but when she told him it was Anne's birthday and Mrs. Gresham was coming, he said he must try to get there, which annoyed Jane more than she liked to confess, though at the same time her heart, most inconsistently, beat a little faster.

Mr. Adams came in, unheralded by Gradka who for some reason into which her employers thought it safer not to inquire always drew the line at announcing their guests, and made his excuses very civilly to Miss Bunting, who merely remarked with a very good imitation of the late Dowager Duchess of Omnium that it was Anne's party, in her parents' house, which caused Anne to be more forthcoming to the new arrival than she might otherwise have been.

"Did Heth bring you a little something?" said Mr. Adams.

Anne said she had given her a lovely present of scent, powder and bath salts.

"That's right," said Mr. Adams. "I told Heth not to spare expense and I hope she hasn't," at which Heather scowled in a very unfilial way. "But don't think that's all. Sam Adams isn't the man to do things by halves, and if my little Heth gave you something, you'll be expecting something from me."

In vain did Anne, crimson with embarrassment, try to expostulate and explain that Heather's present was marvelous and please, *please* would Mr. Adams not give her anything else. Her benefactor went into the hall and brought back to the drawing room a large flower pot containing the most flashy and revolting sickly green and purple spotted orchid plant ever seen in Hallbury. Miss Bunting, who was familiar with many hothouses, from the Duke of Omnium's three acres of glass to the Marling's modest lean-to against the garden wall, was nearly shaken out of her stoic calm by the sight of the leering and obscene plant, whose price she knew must be fantastic to her and the rest of the company's modest notions. Anne, extremely uncomfortable and thinking it quite hideous, thanked Mr. Adams very much and said she would keep it in her bedroom, which appeared to gratify the donor.

The arrival of this monster broke up the party. Robin said he would take Master Watson back to his parents, and went to collect the little boys from the kitchen. Jane went out onto the terrace and was followed by Mr. Adams.

"My pal in the Red Cross is well onto that job," he said. "And he's well in with the Intelligence people that meet the ships too. There won't be an avenue he'll not explore, Mrs. Gresham. I don't want to raise your hopes and we all know the Government and the Red Cross are trying their best to pick up news from the repatriated and rescued men, but sometimes the personal touch comes in useful. Now don't you worry. Sam Adams is here, and anyone in Barchester will tell you Sam Adams does not let a pal down. Now, that little Anne Fielding has been a good little pal to my Heth and she's a nice girl, and I don't grudge a penny I've spent on that plant, though I dare say it would surprise you what it cost. But if it was for you, Mrs. Gresham, I'd pay ten times as much and more."

Jane said something, she really hardly knew what, and suddenly nervous, a feeling she hardly knew, began to tweak off some withered heads from the climbing roses on the wall.

"Is there one for me?" asked Mr. Adams, with what she knew was meant to be polite gallantry, though she was keenly conscious of its being ridiculous and irritating. But the best thing to do seemed to be to treat it quite simply and offer him a rose for his buttonhole in a matter of fact way, which she did. As Mr. Adams did not take it from her hand, she came to the conclusion that in his circles it was etiquette for the lady to put the flower in the gentleman's button hole herself; and probably she thought, to be kissed.

Mr. Adams did not kiss her, but as she pulled the stalk through his button hole, he put his large hairy hand over hers and held it firmly.

"Anything I can do for you, Mrs. Gresham, you've only to say," he said. "I think the world of you, just like my little Heth does, and you've only to say the word."

Heather Adams came out of the french window and saw her father and her idol standing very close together, their hands touching, a look in her father's face that she had never seen. She would willingly have gone back, but it was too late, and the rest of the party were following her. Her heavy face grew black as night as for the first time in her life she felt jealous of a woman. Mrs. Gresham, the most wonderful person in the world; Mrs. Gresham who had filled her thoughts whenever mathematics left a crevice ever since she had met her, only a few weeks ago it was true, but it was like eternity; Mrs. Gresham for whom she would have laid herself down in a puddle to keep the adored one's feet from being wet, was making Daddy look at her in a way Heather did not understand, hated, and feared.

Mr. Adams said he and Heth must be going as Packer had another job to go on to, so they went off, each buried in private thoughts which in Heather's case had such an outward appearance of sulks at supper, that Miss Holly gave up trying to make conversation and went to the New Town Cinema with Mrs. Merivale, between whom and Miss Holly a cool friendship had grown during their association. It was not, said Heather rebelliously to herself, that she minded Daddy looking at Mrs. Gresham in that kind of way; but that Mrs. Gresham had fallen from her pedestal was a cruel blow to the worshiper. If Mrs. Gresham was going to be silly about Daddy, she would like to kill her and she wished they had never come to this beastly place, and she knew Cambridge would be beastly and everything was beastly. And then she sniffed so loudly that her father, who was busy over his E.P.T. figures and a few quite sound but rather daring suggestions his accountant had made, told her to have a hot bath and go to bed with an aspirin. Luckily he did not raise his eyes from his papers, so he did not see her sullen face with tears of rage making her eyes smaller than ever; so she was able to go to bed in complete and satisfactory misery.

The only other event of interest in this great day occurred after supper, just before Anne went to bed. A small procession was going upstairs. First Miss Bunting, then Anne, then Gradka who was carrying the orchid in its pot. At the landing window Miss Bunting paused and looked out. A half moon rode high in the sky. The terrace below shone white as marble and the scent of the night flowering stock was borne on the rather too cool breeze.

"Good night, Anne dear," said Miss Bunting. "Good night, Gradka. Sleep well and have happy dreams about your home."

"I thank you, Prodshkina Bunting," said Gradka, "but I hope I shall have dreams of those dirty Slavo-Lydians and that the Americans bomb them, and the Russians too. Aha! if I were an airman I would fly over Slavo-Lydia and drop my biggest bomb on it, like this."

With which words, Gradka, carried away by patriotism, threw the orchid in its pot out of the window. There was a crash below and then dead silence.

"Well, what is done cannot be undone," said Miss Bunting mildly. "Anne dear, tell the gardener to sweep it up tomorrow, before your parents come."

With which words she retired to her bedroom.

"Prodshkina Anne, I shall say I am very sorry," said Gradka. "I think of the Slavo-Lydian country—which country, my God! a land of pigs—and I am transported. Forgive me, I will pick it up and tend it with care."

Anne said with complete candor that it really didn't matter a bit and it was hideous and she hated it.

"Then you do not like this ironmaster, yes?" said Gradka.

Anne said not very much, but she was sure he was really very nice, and so convinced Gradka of her prejudice against the unhappy orchid that Gradka went to bed with a happy mind and we hope dreamed of Slavo-Lydians perishing by thousands.

CHAPTER II

A lthough Anne's real birthday was over, there was an after-math of excitement next day when her parents came down for the weekend bringing a little pearl necklace as a sign of grown-upness. Anne's joy and excitement over this gift were only clouded by the question of the jewel case. At present it was housing the silver clasp, the pearl brooch that had belonged to Sir Robert's mother and the turquoise ring that her mother did not like her to wear yet. The points that exercised her mind were first, whether the jewel case, which was obviously clamoring to be filled, would mind if she wore the pearl necklace; second, whether the turquoise ring which she didn't particularly care for would mind if it lived more or less permanently in the jewel case; third, whether her mother would let her wear the Rector's gift. After a long and most interesting family council with Miss Bunting as *arbiter elegantiarum*, it was decided that (*a*) the jewel case would like to house the pearl necklace during the day but would be delighted to release it for evenings and important occasions; (*b*) the turquoise ring, which was used to living in a small cardboard box with some cotton-wool, would be delighted to move to its red velvet boudoir; (*c*) that as Anne was only seventeen and all her friends knew she wasn't engaged she could wear the Rector's ring as much as she liked because he was such a dear, but if it fitted her right hand equally well she might in course of time transfer it to that position, as Lady Fielding felt sure the Rector wouldn't mind.

The sponge, now swollen by bath water and conceit to four times its original size, was much admired, as were the little volume of Keats and the silver clasp; which last was praised loudly whenever Gradka was about, to propitiate her. As for the scent, face powder, powder-puff and bath salts, Lady Fielding said how kind of Mr. Adams and reflected that the rather immortal smell of the last-mentioned was thank goodness in the bathroom Anne and Miss Bunting used, not in hers and her husband's. The orchid, which had been cleared away by the gardener who didn't hold with pot-plants not unless he knew where they came from, was hardly mentioned.

The unkind chilly August was succeeded by a worse September which made even the most determinedly seasonally minded people go back into coats and skirts and wonder if it would be worth while having their summer frocks cleaned before they put them away as they had worn them so little, though of course we might have an Indian summer. Or St. Martin's summer, said Robin after some Sunday afternoon tennis when he and Jane Gresham and Anne had stopped on to tea with the Watsons.

"Though why Saint, I do not know," he said thoughtfully. "To give a person half a cloak shows an entire want of common sense, or any real charity. I've often thought about it. Even if it was one of those huge cloaks like the ones Italian cavalry officers used to wear, whichever way you cut it in half what was left wouldn't be much use and so triangular."

Jane said it would be as bad as those paper patterns for dresses that show you so carefully how to fit all the bits of pattern into the stuff that you go mad.

"I always say," said Mrs. Watson, "that a lot of saints seem to be a bit subnormal. I dare say it's thinking of Other Things."

"Why do saints only read the *Times*?" said Mr. Watson.

His wife laughed loudly and said Charlie was very deep.

"I know what Charlie means," said Jane. "People only thank

St. Jude for things in the *Times*. At least I've never seen it anywhere else."

Mrs. Watson said thoughtfully that she supposed saints *would* read the *Times*.

"But," said Anne, her kind heart at once touched, "there must be millions of people who don't take in the *Times*, Mrs. Watson, and then they can't thank St. Jude or anyone, so he would never know how to tell them he was pleased because they thanked him."

Mr. Watson darkened counsel considerably by saying one could always have a box number.

"There's something in what Anne says," said Robin. "I don't know much about saints, but one doesn't quite see them with the *Daily Express*. I should have thought monthlies were more in their line than daily papers, anyway."

Jane said why.

"I don't know," said Robin. "I have no grounds for this belief. Direct inspiration if you ask me."

"What I always say," said Mrs. Watson, "is that there are a lot of things we don't understand. And talking of one thing and another, I suppose you know there is a Bring and Buy Sale in the New Town next Tuesday and I'm supposed to be collecting things for them here. Anybody got anything?"

Jane said the last one, the one for the Barsetshire Regiment Comforts Fund, had pretty well cleaned her out, but she would look around. What was it for, she said.

"I really don't know," said Mrs. Watson. "They've done the Blind and Cancer and Tuberculosis and the Red Cross and all the Allied Nations and Unmarried Mothers and the usual. Oh, I know, it's the Cottage Hospital."

It was unanimously agreed that to give things for one's own Cottage Hospital was *quite* different and Jane said she was pretty sure she could route out something. Robin said he didn't suppose some of his father's old sermons would be any good, which made Mrs. Watson laugh uproariously.

Anne began to speak, thought better of it and went pink.

"Out with it, Anne," said Robin. "Have you got half an earring, or a nasty bit of Oriental embroidery?"

"I was only thinking," said Anne, "about those bath salts and things that Heather gave me. I did just open them, but they smelt funny. Do you think I could give them to the sale, or would Heather see them? It was dreadfully kind of her, but they do smell horrid, all except the powder puff. I do like it, because I've never had a big one."

This was a poser and as such was seriously considered by the whole company. After a great deal of chatter, during which Anne had some difficulty in making her friends stick to the point, Mrs. Watson hit upon the brilliant idea of putting the bath salts into old coffee tins of which she had few waiting for some useful occasion, and selling them at famine prices. Mr. Watson said he would paint the tins different colors as he had a lot of odds and ends of paint in his workroom. As for the scent, Jane said the chemist wouldn't take back empty bottles now, so there were heaps at Hallbury House, and offered to stick fresh labels onto some and paint the words "Pre-War Scent" with Frank's paintbox, and then Anne could put the scent in them.

"Oh, thank you, Jane," said Anne, so much uplifted by this solution of her difficulties and everyone's kindness that she said "Jane" quite naturally, which Jane noticed with amusement, though she made no comment.

"By Jove!" said Robin suddenly. "No, I won't tell you why," he added, "but I have had a massive and original idea. I must speak to my father and then I'll tell you, Mrs. Watson. I believe for the Cottage Hospital, he'd do it, though he certainly wouldn't for anything else."

Then the conversation took another turn and presently Anne went home, accompanied by Robin as far as the door.

"I did want to ask you something, Robin," said Anne, one hand on the large brass door handle and holding out the other. "You don't mind about my having your mother's ring, do you?"

"Even if I did I wouldn't tell you," said Robin, "because the old man simply loved giving it to you and it looks very nice. As a matter of fact I can't sentimentalize about my mother, because I only just remember her. I get a kind of rush of sentiment to the heart occasionally when I think I've been half an orphan nearly all my life, but it doesn't mean anything. So that's that, and we will now proceed to the next subject on the agenda. Yes; very nice indeed."

Saying which he took Anne's gloveless, ringed left hand, raised it, deposited a light kiss on it, and went away with a backward glance of approval.

Excitinger and excitinger, Anne felt inclined to say. Twice had her hand been kissed since she had turned seventeen. True, no one had yet fallen in love with her, but that would doubtless occur in due course, perhaps when she was eighteen. And still the excitement grew, for her parents had a quite grown-up consultation with her after supper. As Gradka thought she could get a permit to return to Mixo-Lydia in October, said Lady Fielding, and Miss Bunting was to go to Lady Graham about the middle of September and then back to Marling Hall, she had decided to shut the house for the winter as soon as the old governess had gone. Anne would come back to Barchester and go to classes and help her mother in various duties, and the post-girl's mother, sister-in-law to the Admiral's cook, would as usual come in as caretaker, sleep in Gradka's room and keep things aired for them when they came down for weekends, but this, at any rate during the winter, would not be very often. Anne agreed wholeheartedly with all these plans, as indeed she mostly did with anything her parents suggested. She was a little sorry to be leaving Jane and Dr. Dale and Robin, but the thought of being grown-up in Barchester was too exciting for her regrets to be serious. The scheme of disguising the bath salts and scent was laid before her mother, who considered it and on the whole approved, provided the plan were so carried out that the Adamses had no suspicions; and on this matter the arrangements appeared to be sound enough. If Lady Fielding were to be truthful with herself, as she usually was, another reason for shutting up the house so early was to break off, without appearing to do so, the intercourse between Anne and Heather. It had been all right for these holiday weeks, but there was no reason why it should go on in Barchester. Heather would be at Cambridge before long and making fresh friends, so it was no unkindness to remove Anne. What Lady Fielding did not know, and would rather have liked to know, was Miss Holly's next move. Presumably she would have to go back to the Hosiers' Girls' School at the beginning of term and Heather would go home till the University term began. But if Miss Holly did arrange an extension of leave to remain at Hallbury and coach Heather after school had begun, well all the more reason to take Anne back. Lady Fielding did not dislike Mr. Adams and found Heather inoffensive, but the feeling of wealth, the extravagant presents, made her uneasy; it was a design for living too far removed from her own quiet standards for her to feel comfortable.

When Robin left Anne he went back to St. Hall Friars where the last bell for the evening service was ringing, and settled himself in the Rectory pew, from which place of safety he admired his father's appearance and voice and thought of many things while his tongue said its accustomed words. There were two important things to discuss with his father and he could not for the life of him guess how his father would take them. The first, in point of view of time, was the Bring and Buy Sale in the New Town for which he proposed to ask his father to sacrifice a small goat-carriage, a relic of Robin's childhood, which was still in tolerable condition and never used. The second and really important subject was whether his father thought he ought to keep on his little school. The numbers would dwindle to three, or four at the most, by the New Year and Southbridge School gaped for him, but if his father was going to miss him, Southbridge should gape till it was black in the face. One could probably get pupils to coach even if the supply of little boys ran short. Only pupils would have to live in the house, and how his father would hate boys at his quiet mealtimes and the inevitable slackening of the household discipline, Robin could well foretell. Still, one thing at a time, and the goat-carriage came first.

The service reached its appointed close. The Rector, as was his custom at the end of each Sunday, stood inside the church porch and said a word of farewell to all his flock. Then Robin walked home with his father, taking the back way by the near end of Little Gidding and entering the garden through the door in the stable yard wall.

"It used to be very different when I first came here," said the Rector. "I still had horses then."

This remark was dedicated to Sundays, for on other days the Rector accepted the present times as a necessary evil which there was no need to discuss.

"What fun it must have been," said Robin. "I'd love to have a dogcart with rubber tires and a fiery horse."

"Yes; I had the dogcart, and a brougham for evenings and wet weather," said the Rector. "I got my first car in nineteen-eight, I think, but I kept the horses till they died, and my old coachman. That was all before your time and before I met your mother."

He stopped by the mounting block and sat down in the sun to look at the quiet yard, with no sound of champing and jingling and hissing; no smell of horses and leather and oats and straw.

"The only carriage I ever had was the goat-carriage," said Robin. "What happened to the goat, Father?"

"We sold him to Lady Emily Leslie," said Dr. Dale. "She wanted a goat to go well in harness for one of her elder grandchildren, Martin Leslie, I think, the one who will come into the place. It was touch and go while he was in Africa, but he is at the War Office now. Dear, dear."

"Why didn't she have the goat-carriage too?" said Robin. "It seems awful waste to have it mouldering here where we haven't got a goat."

"Is it really mouldering?" asked the Rector anxiously.

Robin said not yet, and he had got the garage, which represented what was left of the blacksmith and wheelwright, to overhaul it not long ago and it was in quite good shape. As his father made no comment, he continued rather nervously.

"I suppose you wouldn't care to give it for a Bring and Buy Sale, Father? They are having one in the New Town next week."

"Certainly not," said the Rector. "You might as well ask me to give the old croquet set away, or your mother's Aunt Sally."

He got up and straightened himself.

Robin was not surprised by this outburst. One never knew when one's dear father, so heedless of possessions as a rule, would suddenly become suspicious and set a high value upon an old razor, or a worthless book, or a piece of furniture that had become not only shabby but dangerous.

"All right, Father," he said good-humoredly. "They can stay where they are. I only asked you because Mrs. Watson is collecting gifts. It's for the New Town Cottage Hospital."

His father said, "Oh" in a far from encouraging way and expressed a general opinion that the New Town did not need such luxuries. There wasn't a Cottage Hospital, he said, when he first came to Hallbury. And as for a New Town, no one had ever thought of such a thing. There used to be some of the best rough shooting in the neighborhood down on that marshy land before the old Duke's agent began to meddle.

So Robin said no more and they supped peacefully, and after their meal went to the study. Here after the labors of Sunday the Rector liked, when not supping with Admiral Palliser, to take his ease and read the various learned periodicals which had come during the week; for he was a corresponding member of more than one society dealing with Bible research (especially the later prophets) and antiquarian matters. On such evenings he liked Robin to be at hand though he paid no attention to him, and Robin, while secretly reserving the right to do as he pleased, scrupulously kept these Sundays for his father, explaining to his Hallbury friends that they had better ask him when his father was at Hallbury House. For although his father was extraordinarily well and keen-minded for his years he had of late often fallen into a muse upon the past from which he emerged rather uncertain as to who or where he was, and slightly indignant that Robin was a grown-up man and not a schoolboy.

Not that the Rector had anything particular to say to Robin, but he had a kind of patriarchal feeling that it was fitting for the son of his loins (for to Robin's ill-concealed shame his father used this scriptural phrase without any self-consciousness) should be with him in his old age on such Sundays as he was supping at home. Every now and then it did occur to Dr. Dale that he and Robin had little to talk about and how nice it would be to read in solitude, but his conscience told him, in the unnecessarily scrupulous way consciences have, that here was his only child, with an artificial foot, and what was he going to do about it.

On this evening, perhaps a little sorry for his fierceness about the goat-carriage, he felt more than ever that he must show a father's interest in Robin's affairs which, to his old mind, really seemed on the whole unimportant things. So he put down the Journal of Prophetic Studies and said to Robin,

"Well, Robin, how is the school to go next term? New pupils?"

Robin looked up from a letter he was writing and said that two of them were going to boarding school this term and two more, besides Frank Gresham, after Christmas, so the prospects were not very good at the moment.

"I am very sorry," said Dr. Dale. "You hadn't told me that, my boy."

Robin said, quite kindly, that there it was, and no good grumbling and he hadn't wanted to bother his father.

Dr. Dale asked rather indignantly what a father was for.

"I really don't know, sir," said Robin. "But whatever it is, you do it very satisfactorily. Still, it's what Rose Fairweather used to call foully dispiriting, I must admit."

"But there will be other boys," said Dr. Dale. "I have christened a number of small children this year. More than usual; which people tell me is somehow connected with wartime."

Robin said people would tell one anything, but the children his father had christened this year wouldn't be ripe until 1952 or so, and he doubted if he could wait till then. The intermediate vintages, he added, appeared to be very small and of poor quality.

"I believe," said Dr. Dale, looking rather troubled, "that you were offered a post at Southbridge School."

"Oh, don't worry about that, Father," said Robin, miraculously keeping all trace of irritation from his voice. "Mr. Birkett did ask me, but I expect he has found someone else now."

"But why should he find someone else?" said Dr. Dale indignantly. "I see no reason for him to pass you over and seek further. If my son, with the degree he has taken and his war experience is not good enough for the headmaster of Southbridge School, the world is in a pretty bad way."

Robin's heart leapt to a glimpse of freedom, but he had himself well in hand where his father was concerned. He could not think of the right reply, so he said nothing.

"I shall ring him up and speak to him myself," said Dr. Dale, rising majestically from his chair.

At this statement Robin nearly jumped. His father had always hated the telephone which he had only installed to please Robin's mother, and had never relented towards it. It was kept in the back passage where the servants, by shutting the green baize door, could gossip with their friends or the tradesmen without disturbing their master. This was annoying for Robin, whose conversations were all open to the kitchen if it cared to listen; but to do it justice it was usually talking so loudly in its own quarters, with the wireless on and the door shut, that he could have arranged to elope with Mrs. Watson or murder the Admiral without anyone being the wiser.

"Shall I get the School for you, sir?" he asked, seeing that nothing would stop his reverend papa.

"Thank you," said Dr. Dale. "Thank you, my boy."

So Robin and his father went to the back passage and there Robin asked for the headmaster's number. The telephone was answered by his invaluable butler, Simnet, who protected him against all his foes and rather too many of his friends, often intercepting messages which Mr. Birkett would have preferred to deal with personally. This Robin knew, and rather hoped Simnet would pretend Mr. Birkett was dead, or at any rate in bed.

But Simnet, on hearing that it was Robin Dale whom he remembered as an upper-school boy, at once fetched his employer, who was going through the timetables for the next term with his head housemaster Everard Carter and was rather annoyed with Simnet—and hence with Robin—for disturbing him.

"Good evening, Robin. What is it?" said the voice of Mr. Birkett.

"I'm sorry, sir, but my father insists on speaking to you himself," said Robin. "I've tried to head him off, sir, but it can't be done. Here you are, Father."

He handed the receiver to Dr. Dale.

"Good evening, Birkett," said Dr. Dale in his most resonant pulpit voice. "I wish to have a word with you. What is wrong with my son? . . . Nothing, you say. . . . Then what, may I ask, is the reason he is not going to your school as a classical master? . . . No, no; he cannot have said that. I do *not* wish him to stay at home. . . . No, I will *not* be responsible for what he may or may not have said, Birkett. . . . Yes, it is high time he got into the collar again. . . . What did you say? . . . No, of course you do not want him this term. . . . Yes, he will come next term. . . . Yes, that is all. . . . You will write and confirm this, of course. . . . Yes. . . . Yes. . . . My kindest regards to your wife, Birkett."

He hung up the receiver and turned to his son.

That same son's feelings may better be imagined than described. The freedom he had been pining for was suddenly within his grasp by the most unlikely means he could have imagined. He could wind up his little school by Christmas and in the New Year would be back among men and boys and books. No one would pity him there. A master with a pretense foot would simply be a master with a pretense foot to the boys. He might even become a School Character, like old Lorimer who taught classics till he died and kept a bottle of port in his desk. He might become a housemaster like Everard Carter, only then he would need a wife, which was a nuisance. Still, for the school even that might be accomplished. He looked around to thank his father as coherently as possible, but he had pushed the green baize door and gone away. Robin followed him to the study and found him winding the study clock, which could only be done at certain hours because of the way the elegant ornate wrought metal hands got in the way of keyholes for large chunks of the time people were about.

"A great deal of unnecessary fuss," said the Rector severely. "A few minutes' common sense on the telephone and everything is settled. Your father is not too old to know his way about the world."

Galling as his much-loved father's complacence was, Robin could not wish ill to any man at the moment and stammered some words of thanks.

"I can always come back for weekends when I'm not on duty, Father," he said.

"You need not have that on your mind," said Dr. Dale. "I have been alone most of the time since your mother died and I get on very well as I am. You will understand this as I mean it," said the Rector, looking keenly at his son. "Not that I don't like to have you here, Robin, for I do; but I can also do without you, and it will be better for you."

If instead of "like" his father had said "want," we believe that Robin might have made a protest. But he realized that he had heard what children rarely hear from their parents; how little his father really wanted a companion; how, in fact, he was in truth more contented alone. It was a draught with a bitter flavor, but Robin swallowed it and even as he did so reflected that he had felt exactly the same about his father, but lacked the courage, or the brutality, to say so. He sighed with relief, went over to his father, rubbed his face against his father's venerable head and said Thank you very much indeed.

There was then a short though not too uncomfortable silence, during which each wondered if something ought to be said about the late Mrs. Dale, who was possibly looking at them through the ceiling.

"I think your mother would say I was doing the right thing——"

"I'm sure Mother would have said you were most awfully kind, father——" said father and son simultaneously, and horrified by this display of emotion replunged each into his own occupation. Robin, who found it very difficult to concentrate on his letter, looked at his father from time to time, and noticed that old man's face, which had become quite strong and almost youthful in his excitement, was gradually falling back into its customary air of remote gentleness.

"Do you know, Robin," said Dr. Dale presently, in his usual kind, vague way. "I have had rather a good idea."

Robin, who by now would not have been in the least surprised if his father had rung up the Archbishop of Canterbury and told him to take a funeral service for him on Tuesday, asked what it was.

"They tell me," said Dr. Dale, "there there is a sale of some kind going on to get money for some good cause. Now, it occurred to me that there is that old goat-carriage in the stables.

You wouldn't remember it, Robin. It hasn't been used since you were a child. Now, with the shortage of perambulators, and so many people keeping goats for their milk, it struck me that the carriage might be sold at a very good price. What do you think?"

Robin, hardly daring to breathe lest this should be some baseless fabric of a vision, said he thought the plan first-rate, and he believed he had heard that the money was to go to the Cottage Hospital.

"A very good use for it," said Dr. Dale approvingly. "And another idea has just come to me. There is that old croquet set which we have not used for years. Do you think they would like it?"

Robin said he thought it would be a splendid idea.

"That is the kind of thing you young people don't think of," said the Rector, much gratified. "Can you arrange it, Robin? I should be at a loss whom to address on the subject."

He looked so anxious that Robin hastened to reassure him and said he would do everything necessary and his father was not to give it another thought. They then wrote and read in silence till the Rector took off his spectacles and said he was going to bed. Robin said he had some letters to finish and wouldn't come up just yet.

"Well, good night, my dear boy," said the Rector. "You *are* going to Southbridge School, aren't you?"

Robin again reassured his father, who walked slowly to the door, looking at the backs of his beloved books as he went. At the door he turned.

"I am in vein tonight," he said. "I have just got a third good idea, Robin. That old Aunt Sally. We don't really need her, do we? Good night, Robin."

"Good night, Papa dear," said Robin.

For the next thirty-six hours Robin went about holding his breath lest this bubble should break, but on Tuesday morning he received a letter from Mr. Birkett briefly expressing pleasure that he was going to rejoin the staff and suggesting that he should spend a few days of the Christmas holidays with him and his wife and discuss the next term's classical work with himself and Everard Carter. On reading this letter Robin felt that he was at last grown-up. Everard Carter, head of the top house, openly picked as the next headmaster, viceroy of Jove himself, was now going to turn into a colleague of Robin Dale, ex-soldier with a pretense foot. The fact was so overwhelming that he could not speak of it, having a primitive and quite unnecessary fear that no one must know or the whole affair would burst and he might find himself back in the Lower Third at Southbridge Preparatory School. He also routed out a lot of his old Latin and Greek text books and began to reread them and to try to remember where his own chief difficulties had lain, so that he might the better understand the chief difficulties of his pupils: which was well meant. To the world he was simply Robin Dale who has that nice little school where Alan, or Dick, or Michael goes; he has been very happy there but my husband and I really feel he must go to a *proper* school now, though Robin is a charming boy and so devoted to his father, and I think the dear old Rector would simply pine and die if he hadn't got his son with him. And the world noticed with approval that the Rector was sending some of the lumber out of the coach house down to the Bring and Buy Sale for the Cottage Hospital.

It would have been difficult for the world not to see this if it was about in the High Street on Tuesday morning. Robin, meeting Jane Gresham on the previous day, had heard from her that she was thinking of emigrating.

"Why?" said Robin. "Also where; not to speak of how?"

"I did think," said Jane, "that while Frank was at Greshamsbury I'd have a little peace. But now those odious cousins of his have measles, so I've got him on my hands for the rest of the holidays, and mostly Tom Watson as well. I feel like Mrs. Alicumpane. I wish you were Mrs. Lemon, Robin."

"So do not I," Robin remarked. But he thought of Jane's

words, and next morning caught both little boys and made them help him to get the goat-carriage out, dust it well, and polish its metal parts.

"Would you like to pull it down to the New Town?" he said.

"Oh, sir!" shrieked both little boys.

"Sir! I'll pull it," said Frank. "Tom's littler than I am, sir. He might get tired, mightn't you, Tom?"

Tom Watson looked rebelliously at his friend and said he wanted to pull it too.

"I'll tell you what," said Robin. "I've got to get Aunt Sally down too. Put her in the carriage and you can both pull."

The little boys screamed with pleasure. Aunt Sally was exhumed and placed in the goat-carriage.

"She does look a bit off-color," said Robin, eyeing the battered and rakish figurehead. "I wish we could paint her up a bit."

Tom Watson said his father had a lot of paint in the workshop. Robin, drawn in spite of himself into the spirit of the thing, said they would go around and ask Mrs. Watson, so the cavalcade went around by Little Gidding and into the Watsons' garden by the side door. Mrs. Watson was stringing beans for lunch on the back veranda and said they could use the paints with pleasure so long as they put them back tidily. So Robin and his pupils had a delightful and not too messy time giving Aunt Sally white eyes, nose and ears and a bright red mouth, and Mrs. Watson contributed a piece of old window curtain to nail on her dissolute head as a cap. A few touches of black paint were then applied to the more dilapidated parts of the goat-carriage, everything was put tidily away and the party moved off down the hill. Everyone who had the slightest claim to their acquaintance stopped to ask if that was really an Aunt Sally, and the old groom at the Omnium Arms produced a blackened clay pipe which was stuck into her mouth and looked very well, while Frank and Tom tried to adopt an aloof manner, as of people who habitually dragged Aunt Sallies about in goat-carriages.

At the station such a piece of luck befell as they might never have again, for the stationmaster, hearing that the carriage was going to the Bring and Buy Sale, said the Cottage Hospital had done wonders for his wife when she was taken so bad, and allowed the little boys to pull Aunt Sally down the ramp on the Up side, across the line where only porters were allowed to go, and up the ramp on the Down side. Both boys loudly expressed their desire that an express might come through at the same moment, but no one paid the faintest attention to their boasting. In another ten minutes the whole party had arrived at the Palliser Hall, a very nasty wooden affair with a corrugated iron roof, impossible to keep warm in winter or cool in summer, presented by the present Duke of Omnium to the New Town for civic and other meetings. As it was used almost ceaselessly for war work, whist drives, dances for the Forces, amateur theatricals, the Women's Institute, Flag Days, Grand Gala Concerts for the Allied Nations and twenty other activities, had no ventilation to speak of and no accommodation for making and preparing tea and other refreshments except one small lobby with a gas ring and a cold tap, it had acquired so rich a smell that Admiral Palliser, after presiding at a British Legion meeting, had said he now knew all about what England smelt like in the Middle Ages that he ever wanted to know.

Robin left his pupils outside and went in to look for someone in command. The hall was full of women arranging miscellaneous objects on the trestle tables used for refreshments, and pricing them. There was a shrill hurly-burly and Robin felt like Actaeon, but luckily the first person he met was Mrs. Merivale, to whom he explained why he had come.

Mrs. Merivale said she hadn't seen a goat-carriage since she was a tiny tot and her parents took her to Swanage to stay with auntie, and it would be quite like old times.

"I must tell Sister," she added, as a pleasant-faced woman in nurse's dress came up. "Sister, this is Mr. Dale, our Rector's son. Sister Chiffinch, Mr. Dale, who has taken over the Cottage

Hospital since Sister Poulter left. Mr. Dale has brought us a goat-carriage, Sister."

Sister Chiffinch greeted Robin kindly and said she had heard of him from Mrs. Belton at Harefield.

"I nursed Miss Belton when she had the 'flu about a year ago," said Sister Chiffinch. "Such a sweet girl, Mr. Dale. Mrs. Belton kindly asked me to her wedding which was a quiet affair, but Miss Belton looked a picture in white; quite one's ideal of a bride as you might say. You know her husband is some kind of Admiral now, and I think I may say without betraying professional secrets as you are a friend of the family, Mr. Dale, that I am reserving a certain date for a little visit to Mrs. Hornby apropos of a certain joyful event."

As Robin barely knew the Beltons and had found Elsa Belton, now Mrs. Rear-Admiral Hornby, rather alarming, he could not be much interested by the news so delicately adumbrated by Sister Chiffinch, but that lady herself he found enthralling.

"The Event itself was to be in the Land o' Cakes where they have a large estate," said Sister Chiffinch, "but as Admiral Hornby is at sea I do hope Hitler isn't listening and one cannot be careful enough, it is to be at her old home in Harefield. Such a sweet grannie Mrs. Belton will make. Really, Mrs. Belton, I said to her when we were discussing the Event, you look younger than any of us. But what is this I hear about a goat-carriage?"

All excitement she and Mrs. Merivale hurried to the door, outside which the carriage was drawn up, surrounded by a number of New Town children who had never seen an Aunt Sally before and were a little alarmed.

"How *sweet!*" said Sister Chiffinch rapturously.

This did not appear to Robin to be the *mot juste*, but Mrs. Merivale used the same words, so he supposed they were right. The question then arose where to put the carriage and its contents and how much to ask for it; or whether it would be better to have a raffle, only one couldn't *call* it a raffle said Mrs. Merivale who seemed to know all about these things because of the police, but it was really exactly the same. An arrangement was quickly made for the carriage to be on show outside the hall with a Boy Scout selling the tickets, but Aunt Sally was less easy to deal with, for clay pipes could not be procured. Robin said he must leave it to the ladies as he had to get those boys back by lunchtime.

"By the way, Mrs. Merivale," he said. "We've got an old croquet set that my father thought you might like, only I don't quite know how to get it down. It was too heavy for the boys to pull in the goat-carriage.

"Are these your boys?" asked Sister Chiffinch, looking at Frank and his friend.

Robin hastened to disclaim parentship and explained that they went to his little school.

"Well now, wonders will never cease," said Sister Chiffinch. "I was hearing about you from Mrs. Morland who writes the lovely books. She's quite an old friend of mine. Her youngest boy Tony was quite a mite when I first knew her—just about your age," she added to Frank.

"I know Uncle Tony," said Frank. "He's gone to Burma. Tom doesn't know him, do you Tom?"

Sister Chiffinch said East was East and West was West as the saying was, and it was quite funny the way people knew the same people and as she had some petrol for the Cottage Hospital and the car was there, she would run Mr. Dale and the kiddies home and fetch the croquet set, an offer which was gratefully accepted.

"We nurses do notice things, Mr. Dale," said Sister Chiffinch as she drove in a masterly way towards the station. "You have something wrong with your foot, haven't you?"

"I haven't got it at all," said Robin. "It fell off in Italy."

"Oh dear, *I am* sorry, perhaps I shouldn't have spoken," said Sister Chiffinch. "I had a patient once, a most delightful man whose name you would at once recognize, and he made quite a joke about the way he had left bits of himself in various wars. 'There's my appendix in South Africa, nurse,' for I was nurse in those days, he used to say, 'and my right kidney on the North-west Frontier and one eye at Cowes,' but that of course was a yachting accident not a war, ' and when I wake up in heaven,' he used to say, 'I'll find I've left the rest of myself in Kensal Green.' I assure you he was quite a scream. Is this the Rectory? How sweet."

"Round the next corner if you don't mind," said Robin. "The croquet set's in the stable yard."

Sister Chiffinch swung her car round the corner with great skill, remarked that there soon wouldn't be any horses left now, and drew up at the wooden door. They all went into the yard, where the Rector was looking at some croquet mallets that were leaning against the mounting block.

"I don't quite remember, Robin," he said anxiously. "Did I say I was going to give these to somebody? I got them out and then I forgot what it was all about."

"It's quite all right, Father," said Robin. "You said you would give them to the Bring and Buy Sale for the Cottage Hospital. And this is Sister Chiffinch who has kindly come to fetch them."

He then left his father with the Sister and with the help of the little boys put the croquet box and all its contents on the floor of her car. By the time this was done it was nearly one o'clock and he dismissed his pupils to their homes. In the yard he found his father and Sister Chiffinch deep in conversation.

"Now, isn't this a case in point?" said Sister Chiffinch, addressing Robin.

Robin said he was sure it was, but would she tell him exactly how.

"What I was saying about how funny it is the way people know the same people. Just by the merest chance as they say I

met you this morning, Mr. Dale, for a moment later and I would
have been hieing me homewards to the Hospital, and now what
do you think. Matron that I was under for a time at the
Barchester General, was nurse to Mrs. Dale in her last moments."

"You wouldn't remember her, Robin," said the Rector. "You
weren't born then."

Robin felt uncomfortable for his father, but was quickly
reassured by a glance from Sister Chiffinch which showed him
that she understood the whole case, and knew that the Rector
was not suffering from senile dementia, merely living for a time,
and in a rather addled way, in the past.

"That nurse was a very nice, kind woman," said the Rector,
"and this lady remembers her."

Sister Chiffinch said she would tell Matron when next she
saw her and Homeward Bound must be her motto. As Robin
shut the car door upon her she said,

"The Rector is a perfect old dear, Mr. Dale. I understand from
what he said that you are going to Southbridge School after
Christmas. I know the Matron there, not fully trained of course,
but quite a pal of mine. Now, you mustn't worry about the dear
old gentleman. He rambles a bit in the past, but his brain is as
good as mine. If you don't object I'll look in from time to time
when I'm up this way and keep an eye on him. And if I think
there's anything you *ought* to know, I'll let you know. So now a
sweet farewell till this afternoon."

With which words and without waiting for a reply she put
spurs to her car and drove away. Robin walked thoughtfully into
the yard and found that his venerable parent had already gone
back to the house, so he followed him. He was much touched by
Sister Chiffinch's kindness. People would probably say she was
trying to marry his father, but of this he felt sure there was not
the slightest danger on either side. And he was quite right, for
apart from some rather dashing flirtations of the "You did," "I
didn't" type, accompanied in her younger days by a certain

amount of mild scrimmaging and an occasional slap, she took little interest in men except as cases and had arranged with her friends Wardy and Heathy that she shared the flat with, that they would have a small nursing home after the war for very rich patients who needed unnecessary care.

CHAPTER 12

From two o'clock onward the Bring and Buy Sale was a magnet, drawing Old and New Town and any outsiders who had bicycles or a little petrol to use. Sister Chiffinch, dazzling in a clean uniform, cap and apron, presided over the goat-carriage, regarding from time to time with covetous eyes a large goat brought by no less a person than Miss Hampton, who had come from Southbridge on purpose with her devoted friend Miss Bent. Robin Dale, who had often met them in his later school days, went up and claimed acquaintance. Miss Hampton, in a neat tweed coat and skirt, ribbed stockings, monk shoes, a white stock and a very gentlemanly felt hat on her well-groomed, short gray hair, smoking a cigarette from a long ivory holder, was delighted to see him.

"I hear you are coming back to Southbridge," she said. "Bent and I had a little party to celebrate the news. Some people say you can't get gin. Don't believe them. Let people know you want gin and you'll get it. Must have gin."

Robin said in that case he would certainly make it his duty to call on them as soon as he got to the school, which made Miss Hampton laugh loudly and tell Miss Bent that was one up for Robin.

"You know," said Miss Bent, who was dressed in much the same style as her friend, except that her tweeds were baggy, her stockings slightly wrinkled, her feet cased in plaited sandals, the stock replaced by a loose greeny-blue scarf, and her hat of drooping raffia under which her home-shingled hair hung lank, "I don't think, Hampton, I still don't think we ought to let Pelléas go."

"Well, we've got him here and *I'm* not going to take the brute back," said Miss Hampton.

Robin asked how she had managed to bring a large goat a matter of ten miles cross-country.

"Lorry," said Miss Hampton. "All the lorry drivers know me. Learn a lot of facts about life from them while I stand them drinks. Stand still, Pelléas."

"Hampton's new book is founded on her Experiences," said Miss Bent, eyeing her friend with adoration.

Robin, who had read with much joy her best seller of school life, *Temptation at St. Anthony's*, inquired what the new book was to be called.

"*Chariot of Desire*," said Miss Bent reverently.

At this moment Sister Chiffinch came up with some raffle tickets.

"Let me introduce you," said Robin. "Sister, this is Miss Hampton and this is Miss Bent. They have brought a goat over from Southbridge for the Sale. This is my old friend Sister Chiffinch, head of the Cottage Hospital here."

"You'll excuse me, but are you the Miss Hampton that writes the books?" said Sister Chiffinch, her professional eye gleaming as she observed the newcomers. "I did so thoroughly enjoy that book of yours about the old lady and her housekeeper. Some of the nurses at the hospital were quite shocked, I do assure you, but I said, 'What Miss Hampton is thinking of, Poulter'—that was Nurse Poulter, quite a pal of mine but a bit antiquated in her ideas—'is not what you are thinking of,' I said, 'but something far otherwise, which is the *idea* behind it all; the *idea*,' I said."

"Shake hands," said Miss Hampton. "I like your sort."

"What a sweet goat," said kind Sister Chiffinch, gazing beneficently upon that very unattractive animal who was angrily eating some bits of stale cake he found on the grass. "Do you want a ticket for him, Mr. Dale?"

Robin took three and offered one each to Miss Hampton and Miss Bent, who refused them.

"Didn't bring Pelléas all the way here to take him home again," said Miss Hampton. "Can't stay long in any case. Bent and I have to go to Barchester to pick up some gin. We'll have to be off, Bent, to catch that train. Come and see us when you're settled, Mr. Dale. Sister Chiffinch too."

"I'm quite excited to have met you," said Sister Chiffinch, accompanying them as far as the road. "I've often thought of writing a book myself about some of the cases I've seen. Not till I retire of course."

"You'll be kind to Pelléas, won't you?" said Miss Bent. "He responds to affection."

"Rubbish!" said Miss Hampton. "Give him enough to eat and if he tries to stamp on your feet whack him with a stick. You won't have trouble. Not really a he, you know."

"Oh dear," said Sister Chiffinch. "Perhaps we could sell the kids," at which Miss Hampton laughed so loudly that several people turned around to stare. "Besides we don't know who will get him in the raffle."

"Doesn't matter who gets him in the raffle, dear woman," said Miss Hampton. "You'll have to have him, you'll find. Come on, Bent."

And the two ladies walked briskly away towards the station.

The Sale by this time was a mass of struggling buyers and bringers. Loud were the complaints for buyers that there wasn't anything left to buy. Loud were the complaints from bringers that they couldn't get near the tables with their gifts. The Old Town was well represented by most of the people we know. Sir Robert and Lady Fielding could not come as they were in Barchester during the week, but Anne had come with Jane Gresham and Frank, all the Watsons were there and, as the afternoon wore on, many of the tradesmen and cottagers. Mrs. Merivale, who was secretary of the Cottage Hospital Sale Committee, was enjoying herself rapturously, ordering people about in the kindest way, settling disputes, repricing goods whose tickets had come off, looking very pretty and receiving congratulations on every hand on the engagements of two of her daughters, which she had most dashingly put in the *Times*.

"Oh, thank you so much, yes, I am delighted," she said for the fiftieth time as Jane Gresham stopped to express her pleasure. "Elsie's fiancé is such a nice boy, I believe. You know she is in the Waafs and he is a Flight-Lieutenant, so it is really a coincidence. His mother wrote me a most charming letter and is going to have part of her house made into a flat for them for after the war. She was on the stage at one time, so she thoroughly sympathizes with Elsie's dancing. And Peggie's fiancé is perhaps a *little* old for her, he is thirty-two, but he is quite devoted Peggie says and very musical. He is a Paymaster-Lieutenant at Gibraltar and you know Peggie has been there with the Wrens, so it really seems as if it was meant. He has private means. And I don't want to anticipate, Mrs. Gresham, but I believe Annie will have some good news to announce very shortly. She is in the A.T.S., you know, abroad, and from what she says about a certain young man in the Signals I believe there is something in the air. Do come back to tea, Mrs. Gresham, I'm sure you're tired. Just any time you like. I shall be there from four o'clock for an hour. And bring your dear little boy, and anyone you like."

Before Jane could answer, more friends had come up to give their good wishes, so she went back to the tables and bought a few of the less revolting objects that had come in since she last made her rounds. At the home produce table she found Miss Holly and Heather buying jam. She greeted them both and asked Heather if her father was coming to the sale.

"But how silly of me," she added. "Of course he wouldn't on a Tuesday."

"Not as a rule," said Miss Holly. "But he said he would try to come before the end of the sale, didn't he, Heather."

Heather said yes in a fat, sullen voice. Her admiration for Jane was by no means dead, but she felt that a witch had come in the place of the real Mrs. Gresham who had been perfection. A horrible witch who was trying to enchant Daddy and make everything beastly. Half of her hated Jane and wanted to kill her; the other half still worshipped the now unseen goddess and longed passionately to find her again. And from all these jumbled feelings the result very naturally was the sulks, and even Miss Holly was getting rather tired of them and had gone so far as to allow Mrs. Merivale to say that if any of her girls got like that she would give them a good talking to. Still, Miss Holly was not Heather's mother nor, unfortunately, was anyone else, so the schoolmistress made Heather work twice as hard in lesson hours and rather left her to her own sulks during the rest of the day. And thank goodness the Hosiers' Girls' School would be re-opening soon for the autumn term and she would return to an ordered life.

Jane, who to tell the truth did not notice much difference between Heather in the sulks and out of the sulks, was tired and very ready for tea. Frank and Master Watson, under the eye of the old groom from the Omnium Arms, were grooming the goat with a scrubbing brush from the little lobby where the gas ring lived and a comb provided by Greta Tory, and each had a ticket for a rough and ready tea, so she told Frank she would come back to hear the results of the various raffles and walked slowly to Valimere, where she found her hostess alone.

"Tea is just ready, Mrs. Gresham," said Mrs. Merivale. "Now, don't say No to sugar, for I have quite a store."

Jane said she didn't take sugar.

"Now, are you *sure* you are not being unselfish?" said Mrs. Merivale, "for really I have *oceans*."

This point being settled, Jane was very glad to drink her tea and rest, while Mrs. Merivale expatiated on the excellence of her future sons-in-law.

"I must show you the photos, Mrs. Gresham," she said. "This is Elsie with her fiancé. It's only a snap one of the boys took of their crowd, but it gives you quite a good idea. That's her. It doesn't give her color of course, for she has quite glorious hair and her eyes are screwed up with the sun, but the expression is *just* like. And that's Peter as I must learn to call him, the one that's lighting a cigarette. It's a pity you can't see his face, but Elsie is going to send me a better one. And now I must show you this of Peggie and Don, short for Donald you know, because it's a proper studio photo. Don has three married sisters and they have all written lovely letters to Peggie and the eldest one wants me to go to her for Christmas, her husband is in the wholesale hardware and member of a very good golf club. Would you say any of the girls is like me? You never saw Mr. Merivale, but we all think Elsie is daddy's girl and Peggie is mummy's girl—in looks I mean."

As both snapshot and studio photograph were exactly like every other snapshot and studio photograph and Jane had never seen the originals, it was difficult to judge; but she said she did think Elsie's hair was like her mother's, only not so curly, and that Peggie had the same pretty eyes.

Much gratified, Mrs. Merivale said she was an old woman now, and what did Mrs. Gresham think of this? Jane said it was the Sphinx, wasn't it and what a beautifully clear print.

"Ah, but I mean what is going on under the Shadow of the Sphinx," said Mrs. Merivale.

Jane said it looked like a picnic and what fun; and then pulled herself up for showing so little interest and asked if they were friends of Mrs. Merivale's.

"You see those two," said Mrs. Merivale, pointing out a young man and a young woman in uniform whose heads were very close together. "That's Annie and her boyfriend in the Signals. They were having a joke about the old Pharaohs, that's why they're laughing. Her last letter said, 'Stand by, Mummy, for some galopshious news'; so I guessed."

Jane, with the painful struggle of one talking a foreign language without much practice, said he looked a charming boy and then despised herself for time-serving. But her kind hostess's pleasure was so obvious that she was glad she had made the effort.

"The girls say I ought to marry again," said Mrs. Merivale, "but that's only their fun. And one sees people like Mr. Adams. Not but what he is very nice and pays regularly and is really most considerate, but—well, you know what I mean, Mrs. Gresham, as well as I do."

Jane did know. She knew, as a fact of life not to be disregarded or avoided, that Mr. Adams was not of her class, nor even of Mrs. Merivale's. One might say nature's gentleman, but nature, to judge by the way people's teeth decayed and cuckoos threw young hedge-sparrows out of nests and cats played with mice, was not really a good judge. He had been very kind to her, going out of his way to help her about Francis, never putting himself forward; and she knew that she was more and more aware of his personality and was letting herself be attracted by it. Her nerves were sorely strained by the scraps of news Mr. Adams had brought and by the relentless ebb and flow of her hopes and fears. If Francis were known to be dead, she thought when off her guard of Mr. Adams's tweed-clad arm as something to hold by, to cling to. If Francis were alive—no, she would not think any more of the chances; she would think of other things. But every subject in the world led her exhausted mind back to Mr. Adams who was not a gentleman and never would be. And when she said gentleman, she meant what her father and friends would mean and all her own instincts knew.

"You look tired, Mrs. Gresham," said Mrs. Merivale. "Ought you to go back to the sale? Or what about the lodger?"

Jane looked stupidly at her.

"It's nice and sheltered if you'd like to stay here a bit," said

Mrs. Merivale, opening the door that led onto the little back veranda. "Mr. Merivale always called it that. He said it reminded him of the time he went to Italy with a Polytechnic Tour."

Jane's brain reeled slightly. So she told it not to, and said she must go back and find Frank.

The result of the raffles was to be made known at half-past five, in the faint hope that the prize winners would collect their booty before they left; a hope seldom realized, as ticket holders mostly lose their counterfoils, or go home leaving them with a friend who also has tickets, neither party having noticed her own numbers. When Jane got back to the sale, the tables were almost empty, the refreshment committee were washing up the tea things and the crowd was much less. The old groom from the Omnium Arms, who liked to see things done properly, had deeply disapproved the separate raffles of goat and goat-carriage and had said at least three times to every one of his acquaintance that a nice little turn-out like that ought to be sold as one lot. Effie Bunce, the Land Girl from Northbridge who worked for Masters the farmer, then said she had seen a set of harness in the loft that looked as small as anything. Masters, who had come down to see one of the Omnium keepers about some wire, was found and approached by the old groom. Masters was willing to oblige an old friend who had influence at the tap and in just as much time as it takes to bicycle up to the farm, find the harness, and bicycle back, the full equipment was there. Masters, entering into the general enthusiasm, said the harness had been there these twenty year, but he'd given it a good greasing from time to time and if they would like it for the Cottage Hospital they were welcome. Such of the Committee as could be found made an informal decision that the harness and goat should go as one lot, which led to frightful trouble when one or two more members found what was happening and said the harness ought to go with the carriage. The Reverend (by courtesy) Enoch Arden, who had been picking up a few books for the Ebenezer Chapel

Lending Library, said in a loud voice that thou (by which he was supposed to mean anyone who was listening) shalt not seethe the kid in its mother's milk; which statement, in view of the goat's status, was quoted as a rare bit of fun in the Omnium Tap for many evenings to come. It was then decided that the ticket holders who won respectively the goat and the carriage should have the option of purchasing the harness by tossing a penny, upon which Mr. Arden went home and prepared a powerful discourse upon animals that cleave the hoof and lead the weaker brethren into what is abominable before the Lord; only he delivered it as abhominable, which is far more frightening.

It was now half-past five. Several wastepaper baskets full of raffle tickets were produced and numbers drawn by the youngest Girl Guide present. Mrs. Merivale, to her great joy, drew the Elle-girl whom she had given for the Cottage Hospital in a rush of enthusiasm and whose absence, not to speak of the mark on the wall where she had been, she had since bitterly deplored. Sister Chiffinch, who had come back for the draw, had the egg-cozy made like a cock's head, and Master Watson, to his silent satisfaction, got a large homemade cake. Finally the tickets for goat and carriage were drawn. The crowd stirred excitedly. Jane became conscious of something looming behind her, turned, and saw Mr. Adams.

"I'm looking for my little Heth," said Mr. Adams.

Jane pointed her out on the other side of the crowd, in company with Anne Fielding.

"Ah, she's all right there," said Mr. Adams. "What's on now, Mrs. Gresham?"

Jane, vaguely conscious of an aura of dislike emanating from the far side of the crowd, said they were raffling a goat and a goat-carriage.

"Number forty-two," said the Girl Guide holding up a ticket. "A goat."

There was a short but pregnant silence while people scrambled about in their bags to see where that ticket had got to.

"Ow! it's my number," said Greta Tory. "I dunno what Dad'll say if I bring a goat back to tea. I *was* a big silly to take a ticket."

The Girl Guide, who quite rightly did not consider it her business what the lucky winners said, now drew another ticket, proclaiming, "Number eleven. A goat-carriage."

"Cripes!" said Effie Bunce, who had adopted this unladylike expression from some military friends at present quartered near Barchester, "it's mine. Dad'll create tonight; so'll Mum"; for old Bunce the ferryman at Northbridge was known far and wide as a wicked and foul-mouthed old man and his wife not much better.

There was another silence, this time of embarrassment. No one could force the girls to take their prizes; but no one else wanted the responsibility.

Then did Sister Chiffinch, suddenly emerging at Jane Gresham's side from among the crowd, like the Fairy Queen when the Demon King is at his worst, say in a clear and refined voice,

"Oh, dear! And I did hope the Cottage Hospital would get it."

Mr. Adams moved forward a little.

"I *am* disappointed for you," said Jane.

Mr. Adams took another step to the front.

"Sam Adams speaking," he said in a loud voice. "If those young ladies don't want their prizes, I'll have much pleasure in handing the Sekertary double the value of the tickets and presenting both lots to the Cottage Hospital. Anyone anything against it? Right. Tell me what I owe you Mrs. Merivale you are the Sekertary I think and I'll write you a check."

If a by-election had been in progress at that moment, Mr. Adams would certainly have been put in by the voters with no dissentient voice. Greta Tory and Effie Bunce, giggling loudly, handed their tickets back to Mrs. Merivale, who took them with a smile and said did Mr. Adams want the harness too.

"Oh, do have it," said Jane, almost forgetting in her excitement that it was Mr. Adams, and merely envisaging him as a benefactor.

"And I'll double that for the privilege of presenting Nurse oh, Sister is it, sorry—Sister I should say, with the whole outfit," said Mr. Adams without the slightest hesitation. "And I hope the kiddies that go to the Hospital will have many a happy hour with it."

The enthusiasm was frantic and Heather, pushing rather roughly past Jane Gresham, clung proudly to her father's arm. Frank and Master Watson besieged each his respective parent or parents to be allowed to help to take the goat to the Hospital.

"I don't know, Frank; *do* be quiet for a moment," said Jane Gresham. "Where are you going to keep them, Sister?"

"I've thought it all out," said Sister Chiffinch. "There's just room for the carriage in that shed outside where the wheeled chair lives, and the goat can go in the gardener's shed tonight and I'll get Old George that does our vegetables to knock up a partition for him. He likes animals and it will be a bit of interest for him," said Sister Chiffinch, who had found an old-age pensioner to keep the Hospital garden well stocked with potatoes and green vegetables. "I expect the boys would like to help, wouldn't they? And really, Mr. Adams isn't it, I can't thank you enough for your kindness. You must come in and see us some day. Such a nice bright place it is and the nurses, well they couldn't be nicer as the saying is, and our patients are so bright. Excuse me now," and she hurried off to superintend the harnessing of the goat, which was accomplished with the help of the old groom from the Omnium Arms, a good deal of zealous hindrance from the little boys and some businesslike advice from Miss Holly, who having lived for some time with an aunt who bred them had not a single illusion about those unfriendly animals. Jane then thanked Mrs. Merivale again for her tea and was just going when she felt a touch on her arm.

"Mrs. Gresham," said Mr. Adams at her side. "I only wanted to say don't you worry about things. My pal's well onto that business we were talking about and believe me he isn't one to draw back from going forward. Anything that comes through you'll know at once. Heth and I shan't be here much longer, but anything I hear in Barchester, you'll hear within the day and Sam Adams saying it," said Mr. Adams, who appeared for the second time that afternoon to be confusing himself with a golden-voiced announcer.

Jane thanked him.

"You're tired, that's what you are," said Mr. Adams. "Look here. Mrs. Gresham, I'll phone up Packer and run you up. No; no thanks. It's a pleasure I assure you. If you don't mind coming to Mrs. Merivale's I'll phone him up at once."

Jane was tired. She didn't want much to intrude on Mrs. Merivale again, but the thought of a car instead of the long drag up the hill alone, for Frank had got permission with Master Watson to see the goat home, was too tempting. Mrs. Merivale was delighted to see them and took Jane into the sitting room while Mr. Adams telephoned. The exchange were very slow in answering. The front doorbell rang shrilly and the knocker was banged, Mr. Adams raised his voice. Mrs. Merivale went to the door and came back with a telegram.

"Oh dear," she said to Jane. "It's one of those dreadful telegrams. I don't mind once they're opened, but it's the opening. You never know what's inside."

Jane knew the feeling well, though as the years had passed since Francis left her she had stopped fearing them, for they were never about what she longed to know.

"Shall I open it for you?" she asked.

"Oh, please, and do you mind looking if it's anything nasty," said Mrs. Merivale.

"It doesn't look nasty," said Jane, "but it doesn't make sense. 'Fixed episcopalian church today how's that mother in law letter confirmation follows constant evil custom.'"

"It must be for someone else," said Mrs. Merivale. "Nobody would ask me how their mother-in-law was. And what's all that about evil customs? I wonder the post office let people send such things. May I look?"

Jane saw no reason why Mrs. Merivale should not have her own telegram. She handed it to her saying, "Perhaps someone is sending you a present and wants to tell you the Customs will look at it."

"Oh!" said Mrs. Merivale. "It's not a telegram; it's a cable, only the place it comes from is too faint to read. I ought to have known, because when the girls cable to me from abroad it always comes like an ordinary telegram, only with the post as a rule, not by itself knocking at the door, which is war economy I suppose, but very stupid because if it were really important you wouldn't get it for much longer than you ought to. Besides——"

Even as she spoke, studying the telegram the while, her voice trailed away, her face became pink and her eyes brimmed. From the hall Mr. Adams's voice summoning Packer to get a move on became peremptory.

"Oh, Mrs. *Gresham*! It has suddenly come to me," said Mrs. Merivale. "Well, I always said Evie would be the first to get married though she's the baby. Oh dear! excuse me, I'm going to cry."

"Don't cry," said Jane, rather alarmed. "What is it?"

"I see it all now," said Mrs. Merivale, looking into the infinite with moist eyes. "It isn't Custom, it's Cutsam; that's Evie's American friend she's always writing about and I told you just before tea I thought there was something in the wind. It's from both of them. His Christian name, if Americans do have Christian names, is Constant—such original names Americans have."

"Is his name Evil too?" said Jane. "Americans do have funny names sometimes."

"That's the post office," said Mrs. Merivale loftily. "Of course it's really Evie. I dare say 'e' is rather like 'I' when you cable it."

"Packer will be here in a moment, Mrs. Gresham," said Mr. Adams coming in. "Am I intruding?"

"Oh dear me, of course not," said Mrs. Merivale. "And really, Mr. Adams, I have no right to be here when you are paying me for the use of this sitting room, but I was quite upset. I've had such a lovely cable from my youngest daughter in Washington, from her and her husband. They've just got married and cabled to tell me. I'll read it to you. It says 'Fixed,' well that's just American slang for getting married, isn't it, 'fixed Episcopalian Church today. How's that, mother-in-law'—he *is* a cheeky boy to call me mother-in-law in a telegram—'letter confirmation,' that means letter of confirmation of course, 'follows.' And then both their names, Constant and Evie Cutsam. I do wish I could have been there. Still, I dare say they'll come over with the baby later."

Jane, who saw that Mr. Adams, not realizing that Mrs. Merivale's utterance was merely prophetic, was rather nervous of what appeared to him a tardy act of reparation on the part of Mr. Cutsam, quickly said in an offhanded way that indeed it would be lovely if they had a baby some day and brought it to see its grandmother. Mr. Adams's face cleared.

"Packer's just come to the gate, Mrs. Gresham," he said.

Jane said good-bye to her kind hostess and again congratulated her warmly. Mrs. Merivale stood at the door while they got into the car. Just as Packer was starting the engine she ran down the little front path and laid her hand earnestly on the door of the car.

"Oh, Mrs. Gresham," she said, "excuse me worrying you, but I suddenly felt quite upset about that Episcopalian Church. You don't think it's R.C. do you," she added, looking around fearfully as if the Inquisition were on her traces.

Jane answered firmly that it was exactly the same as the Church of England. Mrs. Merivale's face cleared, she stood back and Packer drove off.

"A very nice little woman," said Mr. Adams, and Jane was amused to recognize in his voice the tone with which, a couple of generations earlier, her grandfather would have qualified Mrs.

Merivale's grandmother as respectable. "My Heth and I can't be grateful enough to you, Mrs. Gresham, for finding her. Everything has been most comfortable. Now, you look worn out," he added, looking solicitously at her. "Just lean back and don't worry."

Like so many of us Jane had almost lost the power of leaning back and not worrying. That she was better off than many of her sisters she would have been the first to admit, but the long strain of uncertainty, the many nights of restless, useless wondering and uneasy sleep, the self-control which she would have died sooner than betray, all these were so many cracks in her being, cracks which might widen. And like most of her sex she filled those cracks with unnecessary activities to stop herself thinking. But nothing will do that. She leaned back obediently, not like a comfortable house cat on a cushion; like a wildcat uneasy in captivity. Mr. Adams's tweed-clad bulk beside her seemed safe and comforting, and had the drive been longer she might have yielded to her fatigued impulse and leant against it. But they were at the gate of Hallbury House. Jane thanked him again and said how kind it was of him to give the goat-carriage to the Cottage Hospital.

"You asked me to," said Mr. Adams.

Jane looked at him.

"You said you were disappointed when the Sister didn't get it," said Mr. Adams. "And you said, 'Oh, do have it,' when the harness was going begging. I thought you meant it. If you didn't, well that's that."

Jane saw that he was hurt. Too tired to reflect, she laid her hand on his coat sleeve.

"Of course I meant it," she said. "Sister Chiffinch is so grateful, and so am I. All your kindness——"

"There's a lot of people," said Mr. Adams, not shaking off her hand but sliding away from it and getting out of the car, followed by Jane, "that would get the shock of their lives if they heard what you said, Mrs. Gresham. I'm a business man, Mrs. Gresham, and I have business ways. But you've been kind to my Heth and she thinks the world of you. And so do I," said Mr. Adams looking straight at her. "And that's why I'm doing all I can to make your mind easy about Commander Gresham. We'll hope for news soon. We'll hope for good news. If it's bad news, well, I know you'll take it much the same as good news. But good or bad, Sam Adams is here and he's never let a pal down yet."

Jane, looking at Mr. Adams and hearing what he said, idly wished that she knew how to faint. The afternoon had been so tiring; hope deferred was wearing her down, and to fall into those large arms and forget everything forever would be a relief past words. At the same time another Jane knew that this was not only weakness but quite silly. The two Janes stood for an instant measuring their strength. Then Mrs. Francis Gresham took command, noticing with a distaste she could not overcome Mr. Adams's large hairy hands and the rather overpowering clothes which never seemed to fit him by nature.

"I am more than grateful," said Commander Gresham's wife, "and I know Francis will be if he comes back. Thank you so much for the lift, which was just what I needed. Good-bye."

Mr. Adams said good-bye, got into the front seat with Packer and drove away, talking about some half-inch bolts. Jane went indoors and told her father all about the Bring and Buy Sale.

CHAPTER 13

The summer holidays, if summer could be called after the way it had behaved, said Robin Dale indignantly, were almost at an end. On Tuesday most of the schools were reopening, including the Hosiers' Girls' Foundation School and Mr. Robin Dale's Select Academy for the Sons of Gentlemen, as it sometimes pleased him to call it. Miss Holly was to go back on Saturday to meet Dr. Sparling and make various arrangements for the school year. Heather and her father were to leave Mrs. Merivale on Sunday. Anne Fielding was to go back to Barchester with her parents after the weekend and Miss Bunting was to go, as previously arranged, to Lady Graham at Little Misfit for a fortnight's visit before taking up her abode again at Marling Hall. For Robin there was the winter term at Southbridge to look forward to; for Jane her daily duties with the prospect of an emptier house when Frank also went to Southbridge after Christmas and a friend the less when Robin had gone, and her unceasing anxiety.

Miss Bunting, as we know, had not felt equal to the Bring and Buy Sale, and as the week went on she felt on the whole less equal to anything and spent a good deal of the day in her room, while Gradka waited upon her and asked such supplementary questions about the English language and literature as occurred to her active mind. Anne spent a good deal of time at the Cottage Hospital with Frank and Master Watson, in whose company she drove about the immediate neighborhood in the goat-carriage (by kind permission of Sister Chiffinch). Heather was not seen in the Old Town, being a good deal occupied with the New Town Tennis Tournament in aid of the Red Cross, in which tournament, to her own surprise and her father's intense pride, she got into the semi-finals, partnered by young Ted Pilward who had been given extended leave on account of an impacted wisdom tooth and was to go on a course the following Monday.

Ever since Sister Chiffinch's kind offer of keeping an eye on his venerable father, Robin had felt much easier in his mind about leaving him; but to be on the safe side he asked Dr. Ford from High Rising, an old family friend, if he would drop in to lunch one day and give a report of his father off the ration as it were. Dr. Ford, who did not fear any British Medical Association dead or alive, said he would certainly look in on Saturday round about lunch time, but what Robin meant was off the record. Robin said he hated to be disagreeable, but what he meant when he said off the ration was off the ration. So Dr. Ford drove himself over to Hallbury in his clanking old car on Saturday, called at the Rectory, was invited to stay to lunch by the Rector, accepted with just the right amount of unwillingness and remained till about three o'clock, talking with his old friend.

"Your father is remarkably fit," he said to Robin, who was lying in wait for him by the clanking car. "In fact I see no reason why he shouldn't live forever. Do you ever think he is going mad?"

Robin said he sometimes did, but really he didn't.

"Not a chance of it," said Dr. Ford, apparently deprecating this diehard attitude in his old friend. "You'll find he's a bit woolly at times and sometimes he'll be woolly on purpose, like a child, but it doesn't mean anything. Who looks after him?"

Robin said Dr. Shepherd.

"Old woman," said Dr. Ford, in defiance of all medical etiquette. "But he won't do your father any harm."

Robin then mentioned Sister Chiffinch's kind offer to look in from time to time.

"Not Nurse Chiffinch!" said Dr. Ford. "Bless that woman. She is a pearl. I'll never forget the way she handled young Tony Morland and his schoolfriend who never opened his mouth— Wesendonck, that was the name—when she was looking after George Knox's daughter Mrs. Coates and her baby. Lord! how Tony did talk. And now he's in Burma. Four sons Mrs. Morland has and all abroad somewhere. And you've got a gammy foot, haven't you," said Dr. Ford who had an insatiable curiosity about everyone. "Mrs. Morland said you had."

Robin offered to show it to Dr. Ford who was delighted and after a pleasant ten minutes' talk drove down to visit Sister Chiffinch, while Robin went off to Hall's End. Here he found Anne on the terrace with her father and mother who asked him to stay to tea, and they sat there talking while Sir Robert looked at a quantity of popular illustrated papers smelling of bad acid drops and as he flung each aside said what scandalous waste of paper the whole thing was.

"Go and get tea, Anne darling," said Lady Fielding presently. "Gradka is in a fervor of jam-making with our last raspberries before she goes, and I don't like to disturb her for tea. She doesn't mind Anne. What has happened to those Adams people, Robin?"

Robin said he hadn't seen them since the sale, but he thought from what Jane said that they were leaving tomorrow."

"Just as well," said Lady Fielding, dismissing people called Adams from her mind. "I was sorry for the girl. She seemed harmless enough, but Robert doesn't want us to get involved. Thank you, darling," she said, as Anne appeared at the french window with the tea trolley. "Robin will give you a hand."

Robin helped Anne to lift the trolley over the low sill and Lady Fielding told Anne to go and tell Miss Bunting tea was ready and ask if she would rather have it upstairs.

"Anne told me Miss Bunting had not been feeling well," said

Lady Fielding, "and I thought she didn't look very fit when I came down. This cold windy summer has done no good to anyone. I expect she will be happier at Lady Graham's where they are all old friends. Tea, Robert?"

Sir Robert threw down the last of the illustrated papers and said he couldn't think why people bought them.

"To look at, darling, I expect," said his wife. "Is Miss Bunting coming, Anne?"

"Mother!" said Anne.

Robin turned quickly to look at her, for her voice was urgent.

"I think she's ill or something," said Anne. "She was sitting in her chair having her kind of rest that she has, but she wouldn't answer me."

"You pour out Daddy's tea then," said Lady Fielding getting up, "and I'll go and see. I dare say she was asleep."

She left the terrace with the unruffled air that carried her through all her committees and various good works. Anne, already reassured by her mother's calm and confidence, poured out tea and asked Robin to admire her pearl necklace, worn in honor of her parents' visit. Robin thought what fun it would be to give Anne a really good present, not just a sponge, and determined to create a small sinking fund to be appropriated to her twenty-first birthday. So they talked away and Sir Robert joined in from time to time, and though they were all aware of Lady Fielding telephoning in the hall, they pretended she wasn't.

"Robert," said Lady Fielding from the french window. "Miss Bunting isn't at all well. I've just rung up Dr. Shepherd's house, but he is out and his assistant is away. It is a nuisance. I wonder what I had better do next."

"Oh, Lady Fielding," said Robin getting up. "Dr. Ford is down at the Cottage Hospital with Sister Chiffinch, I think."

"Thank goodness for a real doctor," said Lady Fielding, who had no more opinion than Dr. Ford of the Hallbury doctor. "I'll ring up at once."

This time there was no pretense of not listening from the party on the terrace. It was soon clear that Dr. Ford was coming at once and that Sister Chiffinch was mobilizing in case of need. Lady Fielding went upstairs again and the others sat rather subdued till Dr. Ford's car was heard. Gradka opened the front door and he went upstairs.

"Do you think Miss Bunting is going to die?" said Anne anxiously.

"I couldn't say, my dear," said her father. "I hope not, I don't know why she should. Dr. Ford will tell your mother what it is. Where's that new book of Mrs. Morland's, Anne? I cannot imagine how she goes on writing a book a year and all exactly alike. Thank you, dear."

And Sir Robert took the book which Anne had brought from the drawing room. Then Dr. Ford was heard at the telephone and then he went upstairs again and Lady Fielding came down.

"Oh, Mummy, is Miss Bunting going to die?" said Anne.

"I hope not, darling," said her mother a little too cheerfully. "Dr. Ford is with her and the ambulance is coming to take her to the Cottage Hospital, Robert. He thinks she will be better looked after there. It's a slight stroke, he says."

Robin and Anne, feeling very young and useless, went for a walk in the garden.

"It's like Angela," said Anne after a long silence.

"Angela who?" said Robin, who had also been immersed in his own thoughts.

"Keats. You know," said Anne.

"No, I'm afraid I don't know her," said Robin.

"But you *must*," said Anne rather impatiently. "The Eve of St. Agnes.

'Angela the old
Died palsy-twitched with meager face deform.'"

"So she did," said Robin. "But that doesn't mean that other people will."

"Besides, her name is Maud, she told me so herself," said Anne proudly. "I think hardly anyone else knows."

Robin said it was funny that some people never had a Christian name; at least one never heard it. Though he had known Miss Hampton and Miss Bent ever since he was in the Fifth Form at Southbridge School, he said, he hadn't the faintest idea what their other names were. Anne said she could not imagine Sister Chiffinch having a Christian name and was sure all her friends called her Chiffy; in which she spoke more truly than she knew, for ever since that excellent women had begun her training she had never been called anything but Chiffy, even by her pals Wardy and Heathy that she shared the flat with.

But in spite of light conversation they continued to feel young and useless, and also rather frightened and, in Anne's case, to feel rather cold. So cold in fact that she shivered as they stood looking at nothing in particular in the kitchen garden. Robin asked if anything was wrong.

"Only being cold," said Anne, looking at him with a mute appeal for help.

"Poor old silly, why didn't you put a coat on?" said Robin. "I'll tell you what we'll do. Go into the drawing room and light the fire. I'm sure your mother won't mind."

This excellent and practical idea made Anne cheer up like anything. Even as they were going back to the house a few cold spattering drops of rain were blown into their faces from a cold gray sky, and Robin said it was bound to do that after the way the Minister of Agriculture had said it would be a bumper harvest, and probably they would die of cold and starvation, while any food there was would be going to Mixo-Lydia; also any decent clothes and all the coal, he said rather crossly, for he did not like to see Anne shiver and was himself considerably disturbed by Miss Bunting's illness. For we are all apt to look upon our elders as permanent and to resent any sign on their part of derogating from this state; probably because it brings the thought of mortality too close to our own dear selves. But by the time they had shut the french windows and lighted the fire they both felt happier, and though the cold rain was pelting down on the terrace, it seemed much more probable that Miss Bunting would soon be better.

Robin, considering with quite fatherly care that Anne might be frightened when the ambulance came, began to talk to her about Southbridge and its glories, and drew so lively and pleasant a picture of a schoolmaster's life there, the bed sitting room he would have, the extreme niceness of the senior housemaster Everard Carter and his wife, the strong probability that he would himself be a housemaster some day that although the ambulance with its good St. John attendants, all Hallbury men, came to the door, steps went quietly upstairs and came slowly and heavily downstairs, and quiet voices talked in the hall, Anne felt much warmer and happier and was sure Miss Bunting would be quite well almost at once.

"You'll need a wife, won't you, if you are a housemaster?" said Anne, after considering the whole affair.

Robin said he supposed he would. One could be a bachelor housemaster, but then one might take to secret drinking or marry one's matron. And he happened to know, he said, that Mr. Birkett preferred married men, because they were less apt to want to move on.

"'High hopes faint on a warm hearthstone,'" said Anne thoughtfully. "I think Kipling's marvelous, Robin, don't you?"

Robin said on the whole he did. And then they had a silly conversation about wives for Robin, and Robin said he would marry Heather Adams and have six little boys exactly like their maternal grandfather, called Sam, Ham, Jam, Lamb, Pram and Ram, and Mr. Adams would give so much money to the school that they would make him headmaster. All of which silly conversation made Anne laugh so much that she stopped feeling cold. And when Lady Fielding came in, she said how sensible to light the fire and she was going to have done it herself, and Miss Bunting looked very comfortable in the ambulance and would Robin stay to supper. Robin said he would love to, but he thought he had better go back to the Rectory as his father was expecting him, and Lady Fielding said she was sorry, but he was quite right.

So Robin said good-bye, and after supper Sir Robert read aloud from Bleak House and Anne felt safe and warm. Sister Chiffinch telephoned about ten o'clock and said Miss Bunting was very comfortable and not to worry, and she would ring up again next morning. So Anne went to bed in quite good spirits.

If Anne had been a little older, she would have known that the expression "very comfortable" as applied to an ill person, means exactly what the relations, friends, or nurse in charge would like it to mean. From the patient's point of view it means more often than not a night of considerable pain, several bad nightmares, being woken when you least wish it and not knowing where you are when you wake up, so that you feel quite mad. Miss Bunting lay quietly enough at the Cottage Hospital. It was strangely difficult to speak, so she was silent. Her right arm felt unaccountably heavy, so she did not attempt to use it. Her self-control, learnt through a long lifetime, was unimpaired and Sister Chiffinch was entirely right in saying what she said about the Miss Bunting whom she could see.

But Miss Bunting was also living another life of which Sister Chiffinch knew nothing, of which even Miss Bunting's nearest friends were ignorant. For five or six years the old governess, so many of whose pupils had fallen in the last war, so many of whose older pupils' children were falling and would yet fall in this war, had had from time to time a dream that she flew—not in an airplane but with invisible wings—to Germany, and alighting in Hitler's dining room just as he was beginning his lunch, stood in front of him and said, "Kill me, but don't kill my pupils, because I can't bear it." The dream had always tailed off into incoherence, but it came again and again, and Miss Bunting had a sneaking feeling, which she condemned firmly as superstitious and even prayed against on Sundays, though with no real fervor, that if only she could keep asleep till Hitler answered, the war would somehow come to an end. But so far she had always woken too soon.

During the night, lying very still in her bed at the Cottage Hospital, unobtrusively but vigilantly watched first by Sister Chiffinch and then by the night nurse, Miss Bunting for the last time rose on invisible wings and flew over to Germany. Alighting in Hitler's dining room just as he was beginning his lunch, she stood in front of him and said, "Kill me, but don't kill my pupils, because I can't bear it," adding the words, "and if you touch David Leslie, my favorite pupil, I shall kill *you*." With an immense effort she remained asleep just long enough to be certain that she had won. Then Hitler swelled and swelled till the whole room and the whole world was full of him and burst, and all Miss Bunting's old pupils came running up to her. Her heart was so full of joy that it stopped beating, and kind Sister Chiffinch rang Lady Fielding up at half-past seven on Sunday morning to break the news.

The Fieldings were not altogether surprised, but truly distressed, for they had grown to respect and value the old governess during the year she had spent with Anne. There was very little to do. Dr. Ford and Sister Chiffinch were at hand, Mrs. Marling and Lady Graham were told on the telephone, and Lady Graham's mother Lady Emily Leslie sent word that if Mrs. Marling agreed, she would like the old governess to be buried in Rushwater churchyard, as David had always been so fond of her.

"I think," said Agnes Graham's cooing voice to Lady Fielding, "that darling mamma is going to design a tombstone with doves on it. Darling Emmy and James and Clarissa remember her quite well of course, so does darling John, but I think darling Robert and Edith are too small. We were all so fond of dear

Bunny. Darling David will be dreadfully unhappy when he hears, and my husband will be quite unhappy too," though whether Major-General Sir Robert Graham, K.C.B., would have subscribed to this statement, we do not know. Probably not.

But though all was arranged and no one was truly unhappy about Miss Bunting, a shadow of sadness hung over Hall's End. Not only was Miss Bunting's death the last of an excellent and faithful governess and companion, but with her, so the Fieldings and many other friends of the old governess felt, one of the remaining links with the old world of an ordered society had snapped. Nearly everything for which Miss Bunting had stood was disintegrating in the great upheaval of civilization.

"It almost makes me envy the Adamses of this world," said Lady Fielding to her husband.

"No need to, my dear," said her husband dryly.

"You know what I mean, Robert," said his wife. "They are on the top now and they don't miss what is gone, because they never knew it, and they are going to make a horrible new world just as they like it, with no room for us. We are nearly as dead as poor Miss Bunting."

"I don't altogether agree with you," said Sir Robert. "Adams is very wealthy and has a good deal of pull. But it will be quite a long time before he and his lot can do without us and our lot. He won't turn that girl of his into a lady."

Lady Fielding said she was rather glad that Anne had not seen so much of Heather lately, and then the subject dropped as it was time to go to church, and Lady Fielding said she had wondered about slight mourning, but as it was summer she thought it wouldn't matter. This may sound unreasonable, but all those readers who know how much easier it is to mourn in a fur coat which covers everything and a black hat, than in a summer frock, will understand. So Anne, who had fallen head over heels into a volume of Poe's poetry which she had taken to bed on the preceding night, was wrenched from her literary pursuits and accompanied her parents to St. Hall Friars, all in their ordinary clothes.

The news of Miss Bunting's death had spread to the few people interested in her, among them Jane Gresham, who felt as the Fieldings did that another piece of the pre-war world had gone and the tide of a Brave and Horrible New World was lapping a little nearer to her feet. Frank was going to church with the Watsons and back to lunch with them afterwards, so Jane and her father went to church unaccompanied. The Hallbury House pew was across the aisle from the Rectory pew, which prevented the occupants, unless they came in very late or behaved very badly and turned around to look, from knowing who was attending the service. So it was not until the Rector had blessed them and the congregation was going out into the churchyard that Jane saw Mr. Adams and his daughter.

It was not a welcome sight. Her conscience had upbraided her during the night for her weakness about Mr. Adams, telling her in no uncertain terms that she was letting herself be as silly as any other young woman whose husband was long away, or missing. Also, said her conscience, she ought to be ashamed of herself. Mr. Adams had been very kind, but he was probably kind to a great many people, and to him it was nothing to buy a goat with its carriage and harness to please someone—well, someone he liked, said Jane rather angrily to her conscience. But however she thought and argued inside herself, the fact remained that she had liked Mr. Adams more than she ever thought she could and had behaved in a way that neither her husband nor her father could approve. What Mr. Adams might do or say next she did not know, but now thoroughly frightened of her own folly, she would have given anything to have him safely in his works at Hogglestock.

But an admiral's daughter may not retreat, so she said good morning to Mr. Adams and Heather very pleasantly in the porch. Mr. Adams responded with what, to her guilty mind, seemed a curious manner, and Heather hardly answered at all.

"Good morning, Adams," said the Admiral. "I haven't seen you up here lately. And how are you, Heather?"

Heather, suddenly becoming the pleasant Heather she had been until lately, said quite well thank you. Mr. Adams walked on with the Admiral while Jane and Heather found themselves forced into one another's company, which was little pleasure to either. Heartily did Jane wish that anyone else were of their party, but the Dales and Fieldings went in the opposite direction, the Watsons were busy in talk with friends, so there was nothing for it but to follow the men toward Hallbury House, Heather suspecting and hating Jane, Jane rather frightened of Heather, who exuded an atmosphere of knowing more about Jane than Jane would like her to know. All very foolish we may say: a schoolgirl jealous of an attractive woman that her father liked, and an attractive woman with a scrupulous conscience feeling guilt where there was but a little folly. But so we are made.

Neither was Mr. Adams altogether at ease, for he had difficult things to say and was by now beginning to suspect his daughter's feelings. But to clear her doubts would mean acknowledging that what she imagined had some real existence; and that he was not going to do.

When they got to Hallbury House the Admiral asked his chairman of directors and daughter to have a glass of sherry, of which he had just managed to get a few bottles.

"I expect Mr. Adams will want to get back to lunch, Father," said Jane, hoping against hope that her father or his guest would back her. The Admiral said Nonsense, and Mr. Adams said Packer was waiting for him at the Omnium Arms and could wait a bit longer, so the sherry was drunk and talk touched on various topics and the discomfort grew.

But uncomfortable as it all was, it was even more uncomfortable and frightening for Jane when Mr. Adams, who was accustomed to facing all difficulties and bending them to his will, said to her.

"I've a little matter of business to talk over with you, Mrs. Gresham. If the Admiral doesn't mind, will you take a turn in the garden with me? I won't keep you long."

Instead of saying, "Avaunt, churl!" as Jane had rather hoped he might, the Admiral who knew that Mr. Adams had been busying himself on Jane's behalf, seemed to think this quite natural and said with naval gallantry that he hoped Heather would put up with his company meanwhile, to which Heather, who was fair-minded enough to bear no grudge against the Admiral for being the father of her fallen idol, said she would like it very much and would the Admiral tell her about the electric welding plant in his repair shop.

By this time Jane was almost shaking with fright, but she accompanied Mr. Adams to the garden and pointed out how well the anchusa was flowering this year.

"I've got something to say to you, Mrs. Gresham," said Mr. Adams.

Summoning all the Palliser in her, Jane stopped, faced him, and asked in what seemed to her a normal voice, what it was.

"You needn't be frightened, Mrs. Gresham," said Mr. Adams looking down at her, so that Jane, in one of those quick foolish thoughts that come to one at the gravest moments, thought of the great *San Philip* taking the wind from the little *Revenge's* sails. "What I'm going to say has nothing to do with anything concerning any ideas you may have had or I may have had about any feelings that may have passed in a temporary sort of way between you and I."

Jane felt her cheeks burning at this far too accurate description of her late encounter with Mr. Adams. She found it quite impossible to speak and looked very hard at a spider who was sitting in his autumn net, waiting for the tradesmen to call.

"My pal that I've told you about and his pal in the Intelligence," said Mr. Adams, "haven't been asleep, Mrs. Gresham. There was a lot of fresh news came in last week. I didn't like to say anything to you Tuesday, though I nearly did; for fear it wasn't correct. But it's absolutely OK'ed now. I think," said Mr. Adams, eyeing her more closely, as not knowing what the result of his words would be, "that you can take it from Sam Adams that Commander Gresham is all right. You'll be hearing from the Admiralty I expect before long, but I thought I'd give you a friendly word, and you needn't be afraid to believe it, Mrs. Gresham, because my pal and his pal have seen the man who had the news and it'll only be a matter of shipping till the Commander gets home."

The spider, sitting comfortably in his study, smoking and reading the *Daily Arachnoid*, felt his back door thread quiver. He put down his pipe and paper and went gently down the passage.

Jane went as white as she had been red. She tried to say something, but no sound came from her and the spider held her whole attention. He had by now ascertained that it was the butcher and was going cautiously to the back door to meet him.

"Well, that's all," said Mr. Adams, "I'm pleased to have done what I could, Mrs. Gresham, and now I'll say good-bye and all the best. My little Heth and I go home today. I know she'd like to thank you for your kindness, for she really thinks the world of you. Don't you hurry, Mrs. Gresham. I'll go and say good-bye to the old Admiral. He's a fine old man and we all have a great respect for him on the Board."

The spider, having removed his shoes and tiptoed to the back door, had tied the butcher up in a neat parcel, put him in the larder, and returned to the study where he picked up his pipe and went on reading a review of "An eight-legged Traveler in English Hedgerows," by Webly Spinner. Jane stared and stared at him and said nothing.

Meanwhile Admiral Palliser and Heather had a really de-lightful conversation about electric welding and manganese steel until Mr. Adams came back, when Heather's face fell into its late condition of heavy sulks.

"Well, Admiral," said Mr. Adams, "it's your lunch time and

we must be off. I don't want to make a mystery of what me and Mrs. Gresham have been discussing lately and I think you can guess that I brought some news of Commander Gresham. I may say that it's good news, and you can take it from me that the Commander will be coming back as soon as there is a ship. Sam Adams never says a thing if he can't prove it and back it, and that's that. And I may say I was seldom more gratified, not even when my little Heth here got her scholarship, than when I heard the news, for we think the world of Mrs. Gresham me and my little Heth. Don't we, girlie?"

The Admiral shook Mr. Adams warmly by the hand and with some difficulty thanked him for his interest. Heather stood with her mouth open, surprised, incredulousness, belief, mortification, chasing each other across her heavy face. It was all too like heaven to be true. Mrs. Gresham was still the most wonderful person in the world and her father was as perfect as he had always been. How she could have been wicked and horrible enough to think the wicked and horrible things she had thought, she did not know. Her only regret was that her father said they must go, and Mrs. Gresham was not there.

But as they walked down the flagged path to the gate, Jane came around the corner from the garden, looking as beautiful and kind and wonderful as ever and said good-bye to Daddy and thanked him very much for all his kindness. Heather had a romantic impulse to cast herself at Mrs. Gresham's feet, stab herself, and say as her life-blood welled from between her fingers, "I have misunderstood you, Mrs. Gresham, and this is my atonement." But her father said they must hurry along or they would keep Mrs. Merivale's lunch waiting, so Jane said good-bye to Heather and wished her the best of luck at Cambridge, the Admiral opened the front gate, and Mr. Adams and his daughter went down the street to the Omnium Arms, where Mr. Packer was waiting for them.

"Well now, girlie, you and your old Daddy must get down to brass tacks again," said Mr. Adams as they drove down to the

New Town. "No more holidays for us just yet. There's Cambridge first and then there's the works. Had a good time, Heth?"

"Oh yes, Daddy," said Heather. "I think Mrs. Gresham is different from everybody, don't you, Daddy?"

"I wonder what your mother would have thought of her," said Mr. Adams reflectively. "Many's the time I wish Mother was here, Heth. Still, you're Daddy's little partner, aren't you?"

"Yes, Daddy," said Heather. "Oh, and Daddy, Ted Pilward's going to be on a course in Cambridge till Christmas and he says there'll be some dances and he's going to ask me."

"Nice boy, Ted," said Mr. Adams. "Old Ted Pilward's a good sort too, Heth. Our sort."

Lunch at Hallbury House was as embarrassing as a lunch must be where father and daughter, both trained to suppress their emotions, both with emotion very near the brim, are alone together. But they managed pretty well and the Admiral knew that his daughter could look forward at last. For him it might not be so happy. Jane and Francis might want not unnaturally to find a home for themselves and Frank. To lose Frank would be hard. But all this was far in the future and for the moment he would think of Jane's relief from the long nightmare. That Mr. Adams could have made a mistake he did not think. He trusted, and on very good grounds, that his chairman would not make such a statement without very authoritative knowledge, and his hope of official confirmation before long was, we may say, amply justified. After lunch Jane said she was going to play tennis at the Watsons and might be out to tea. Then she let her father hold her closely for a moment, kissed him, and went upstairs to change.

The tennis at the Watsons' was not very serious, for now that Miss Holly had gone they no longer had a good fourth. So they rang the changes on Watsons, Jane, Robin and Anne, and there was a good deal of laughter while the little boys skirmished about and ate a huge tea. A passing reference was made to

Heather Adams, but the waters of Hallbury life had already closed over the heads of the summer intruders and flowed on their usual calm course. Then Anne went home, Frank was torn indignantly expostulating from the company of Master Watson and six new kittens which the kitchen cat had hidden behind a woodpile and guarded with very unladylike spittings and scratchings. Jane sent Frank ahead and said she would walk back with Robin.

"Do you know," said Robin, "that a great disgrace has occurred in my family. The raffle tickets for our Aunt Sally went very badly. I think people are so uneducated that they don't know what she is for. And no one would own to having a ticket when the winning number was drawn and the secretary can't read the name she wrote on the counterfoil, so she is back on our hands. She came up, like Boadicea, in the milk-float this morning. My father pretended he was pleased to see her again, but that was only showing off. He is really a good deal mortified. Here she is."

They had entered the stable yard by the wooden door and there, propped up against the mounting block, was Aunt Sally's matronly form. As they looked a sound of voices came down the garden path and two clergymen hove into view.

"Who has your father got with him?" said Jane.

"Oh, Lord, I'd quite forgotten," said Robin. "It's the Bishop."

"The *Bishop*!" said Jane, with a look of horror and incredulity difficult to describe.

"I don't mean *that* old woman," said Robin, thus irreligiously alluding to the present incumbent of the see of Barchester. "It's Bishop Joram. You know, that Colonial Bishop who did locum at Rushwater. He's got a job in the Close now, something the Dean found for him, and he does duty for other clergymen at odd times. He's taking evening service for Father and I think it will be a very good plan if he can come over once or twice a week, especially in the winter when I'll be at Southbridge. But don't say anything to Father about it."

By this time the Rector and the Colonial Bishop had reached the stable and introductions were made. The Colonial Bishop, who was highly susceptible, at once fell in love with Jane; as he had previously fallen in love with Mrs. Brandon and Lady Graham, and several other Barsetshire ladies.

"Bishop Joram, whom we have all been so glad to welcome among us," said Dr. Dale, entirely ignoring the fact that the Bishop had been in England now for some four or five years and was very well known throughout the diocese, "has given me the pleasure of coming to take the service this evening, and spending the night under my roof. I shall be proud to sit at his feet, for we have all heard of his fine work—where was it, Joram? Borrioboola Gha?"

The Colonial Bishop said not exactly; it was Mngangaland.

"Ah yes," said Dr. Dale, in a voice whose aged wisdom would have led anyone who didn't know him to think he knew where it was. "And what did you say the text was on which you propose to preach to us?"

"I don't think I did say," said the Colonial Bishop. "It is from the Book of Haggai, first chapter, fifth verse——"

"'Now therefore thus saith the Lord of hosts: consider your ways,'" said Dr. Dale triumphantly.

"I wish you were preaching, sir," said the Colonial Bishop. "I didn't know anyone read Haggai now."

"But my dear fellow," said Dr. Dale, forgetting in his enthusiasm the gulf of some thirty years that lay between him and his new friend. "My dear fellow! never did I think to meet a clergyman in these degenerate days who knew that great prophetic work. I have given much study to the subject and written largely upon it. You must come and look at some of my articles."

In his enthusiasm he was about to drag the Colonial Bishop back to the Rectory, but his son reminded him that the service was at half-past six and it was already ten minutes past.

"Thank you, my boy," said the Rector, rather downcast. "Never mind, Joram," he added, brightening. "The psalms are very short this evening and I dare say your sermon will not be unduly long."

The Colonial Bishop said ten minutes at the outside.

"Good, good," said Dr. Dale approvingly. "Tell me, Joram, in what sense exactly do you read the words in the ninth verse of the first chapter, 'And when ye brought it home, I did blow upon it?' I have my own theory, but it would greatly interest me to hear yours."

The Colonial Bishop made no answer. Dr. Dale, looking at his guest, was seriously alarmed to see him staring fixedly at the old coach house with every appearance of insanity.

"Is anything wrong, my dear friend?" said Dr. Dale, touching the Colonial Bishop on the arm.

The Colonial Bishop started and apologized, saying that he had been quite carried away.

"I caught sight of something that reminded me so vividly of Mngangaland that I quite forgot where I was. How on earth did it come here, Dr. Dale?"

He approached the battered form of Aunt Sally, leaning up against the mounting block, and looked at her with affectionate reverence.

"That's our old Aunt Sally," said Robin. "We tried to get rid of her in a raffle, but no one would have her."

"The absolute likeness of the Mnganga deity of cattle disease," said the Colonial Bishop in a low reverent voice. "The trouble I have had with her! You will hardly believe how difficult it was to stop the natives sacrificing every eighth child to her—very large families they have, you know; you must keep up at least fifty wives to have any position at all. But I did it in the end. I painted her with luminous paint just before the new moon and told them she was Queen Victoria. The light shining from her on a dark night frightened them nearly to death and ever since then they have only brought cigarette cards and empty gin bottles as offerings. I hope I did rightly. One never knows."

Dr. Dale said one could but do what lay to one's hand.

There was another and rather embarrassing silence. Robin, looking at his watch, said it was twenty minutes past six.

"Joram," said the Rector, touching the Colonial Bishop on the shoulder, who started.

"I say, Father," said Robin. "Do you think Bishop Joram would like to take Aunt Sally? It seems a shame for her to stay here doing nothing."

The Colonial Bishop, a man of action, the terror of all backsliders in his sub Equatorial diocese, closed with the offer at once.

"If you can really part with her, Dr. Dale," said he, "I shall be more grateful than I can say. I miss my black flock very much at times, and she will make me feel that we are not entirely separated. I will wrap her in my raincoat and put her in my little car if I may, just for the night, and she will be in my lodgings—with a very respectable French lady, a Madame Tomkins, a dressmaker, in Barley Street—to greet me when I come back from my work. Thank you, thank you."

Robin then hurried the Colonial Bishop and his father toward the church and came back to Jane.

"I do admire you, Robin," she said. "You don't think he'll worship it, do you? Aren't you going to church?"

Robin said he thought the Colonial Bishop could quite well look after himself and would not let Aunt Sally get the upper hand. And as his father had a real bishop, if a colonial one, to talk to, he thought he would take a holiday himself, and the Fieldings had asked him to supper to say good-bye before they left Hallbury.

"I'll see you some time soon then," said Jane. "I think—no, nothing. Good night, Robin."

She walked slowly home. No, she would not tell Robin yet. She would not tell Frank. Her father would not speak if she asked him not to. Mr. Adams she had already almost forgotten, and in any case he could hold his tongue. She knew now, at last, quite certainly, what she wanted, hoped for, waited for; and until the day of meeting came, not so far ahead, she could be patient. Others should share her relief, her joy, very soon; but for a little while it should be her private treasure.

So Robin went down Little Gidding and across the High Street to Hall's End. In the drawing room he found Anne alone with a good fire and Poe's poems.

"You know about Miss Bunting," she said.

Robin said he did.

"Poor Miss Bunting," said Anne.

Robin said he was very sorry indeed, but Lady Fielding, whom he had talked to after church that morning, had told him that she died very quietly in her sleep.

> "'I lie so composedly here in my bed
>   That you almost might, seeing me, fancy me dead,'"

said Anne thoughtfully. "I think Edgar Allan Poe is marvelous, Robin, don't you?"

Robin said he did, though some of his poems were better than others.

"Poor Gradka cried dreadfully," said Anne, who seemed to Robin somehow much more grown-up since the previous day. "She is going back to Mixo-Lydia quite soon and she is going to have a school and call it Bunting College; in Mixo-Lydian of course, but I can't properly pronounce the College part. And she will tell all her pupils that Miss Bunting was an English lady who always hated Slavo-Lydia."

At this Robin began to laugh and Anne, amused by her own quite good imitation of Gradka's speech, began to laugh too.

"Oh dear, Robin," she said, suddenly serious. "I shan't see you when I'm in Barchester."

"Never mind," said Robin. "I'll come to Barchester at the weekend sometimes. And when I'm at Southbridge I'll ask you all to tea in my bed sitting room on Speech Days and Sports Days. All the masters have tea parties then."

Anne, the fire shining on her face, said she would love that.

"And don't forget that when I'm a housemaster I shall need a wife," said Robin, half mocking. "But that won't be for quite some time of course."

Anne, pensively playing with Dr. Dale's ring on her left hand, slowly drew it off and put it on her right hand.

"Your father said I could be engaged to him until I wanted to be engaged to someone else," she said. "And I don't think I'm old enough to be engaged to anyone really, so I am going to wear his ring on my unengagement hand."

"If anyone asks you to put a real engagement ring on your proper engagement hand," said Robin, "will you consult me first? I think I ought to know, in case you need some good advice."

"Of course I will," said Anne. "But I don't think I'd like to be really engaged, unless it was somebody I liked *very* much, like you."

Robin took her ringless hand, put the lightest of kisses on it and laid it on her lap again.

Then Lady Fielding came in and summoned them to supper.

COLOPHON

This book is being reissued as part of Moyer Bell's Angela Thirkell Series. Readers may join the Thirkell Circle for free to receive notices of new titles in the series and to recieve a newsletter, bookmarks, posters and more. Simply send in the enclosed card or write to the address below.

The text of this book was set in Caslon, a typeface designed by William Caslon I (1692-1766). This face designed in 1725 has gone through many incarnations. It was the mainstay of British printers for over one hundred years and remains very popular today. The version used here is Adobe Caslon. The display faces are Adobe Caslon Outline, Calligraphic 421, and Adobe Caslon.

Composed by Alabama Book Composition, Deatsville, Alabama.

The book was printed by Thomson-Shore, Inc., Dexter, Michigan on acid free paper.

Moyer Bell
Kymbolde Way
Wakefield, RI 02879